WEDDING NIGHT

WEDDING NIGHT

Sophie Kinsella

WINDSOR
PARAGON

First published 2013
by Transworld Publishers
This Large Print edition published 2013
by AudioGO Ltd
by arrangement with
Transworld Publishers

Hardcover ISBN: 978 1 4713 5250 8
Softcover ISBN: 978 1 4713 5251 5

British Library Cataloguing in Publication Data available

Printed and bound in Great Britain by
T J International Limited

For Sybella

PROLOGUE:
ARTHUR

Young people! With their hurrying and their worrying and their wanting all the answers *now.* They wear me out, the poor, harried things.

Don't come back, I always tell them. *Don't come back.*

Youth is still where you left it, and that's where it should stay. Anything that was worth taking on life's journey, you'll already have taken with you.

Twenty years I've been saying this, but do they listen? Do they, hell. Here comes another of them now. Panting and puffing as he reaches the top of the cliff. Late thirties, I'd guess. Attractive enough, against the blue sky. Looks a bit like a politician. Do I mean that? Maybe a movie star.

I don't remember his face from the old days. Not that that means anything. These days I barely even recall my own face when I glimpse it in the mirror. I can see this chap's gaze raking the surroundings, taking in me sitting in my chair under my favorite olive tree.

"Are you Arthur?" he says abruptly.

"Guilty."

I scan him adroitly. Looks well off. Wearing one of those expensive-logo polo shirts. Probably good for a few double Scotches.

"You must want a drink," I say pleasantly. Always useful to steer the conversation in the direction of the bar early on.

"I don't want a drink," he says. "I want to know what happened."

I can't help stifling a yawn. So predictable. He wants to know what happened. Another merchant banker having a midlife crisis, returning to the scene of his youth. The scene of the crime. Leave it where it *was,* I want to answer. Turn round. Return to your adult, problematic life, because you won't solve it here.

But he wouldn't believe me. They never do.

"Dear boy," I say gently. "You grew up. That's what happened."

"No," he says impatiently, and rubs his sweaty brow. "You don't understand. I'm here for a reason. Listen to me." He comes forward a few paces, an impressive height and figure against the sun, intentness of purpose on his handsome face. "I'm here for a reason," he repeats. "I wasn't going to get involved — but I can't help it. I have to do this. I want to know *what exactly happened. . . .*"

1
LOTTIE

Twenty Days Earlier

I've bought him an engagement ring. Was that a mistake?

I mean, it's not a *girly* ring. It's a plain band with a tiny diamond in it, which the guy in the shop talked me into. If Richard doesn't like the diamond, he can always turn it round.

Or not wear it at all. Keep it on his night-stand or in a box or whatever.

Or I could take it back and never mention it. Actually, I'm losing confidence in this ring by the minute, but I just felt bad that he wouldn't have anything. Men don't get the greatest deal out of a proposal. They have to set up the occasion, they have to get down on one knee, they have to ask the question, *and* they have to buy a ring. And what do we have to do? Say "yes."

Or "no," obviously.

I wonder what proportion of marriage

proposals end in a "yes" and what proportion end in a "no"? I open my mouth automatically to share this thought with Richard — then hastily close it again. *Idiot.*

"Sorry?" Richard glances up.

"Nothing!" I beam. "Just . . . great menu!"

I wonder if he's bought a ring already. I don't mind, either way. On the one hand, it's fabulously romantic if he has. On the other hand, it's fabulously romantic to choose one together.

It's a win-win.

I sip my water and smile lovingly at Richard. We're sitting at a corner table overlooking the river. It's a new restaurant on the Strand, just up from the Savoy. All black-and-white marble and vintage chandeliers and button-back chairs in pale gray. It's elegant but not showy. The perfect place for a lunchtime proposal. I'm wearing an understated bride-to-be white shirt, a print skirt, and have splashed out on stay-up stockings, just in case we decide to cement the engagement later on. I've never worn stay-up stockings before. But, then, I've never been proposed to before.

Ooh, maybe he's booked a room at the Savoy.

No. Richard's not flash like that. He'd never make a ridiculous, out-of-proportion gesture. Nice lunch, yes; overpriced hotel room, no. Which I respect.

He's looking nervous. He's fiddling with his cuffs and checking his phone and swirling the water round in his glass. As he sees me watching him, he smiles too.

"So."

"So."

It's as though we're speaking in code, skirting around the real issue. I fiddle with my napkin and adjust my chair. This waiting is unbearable. Why doesn't he get it over with?

No, I don't mean "get it over with." Of course I don't. It's not a vaccination. It's . . . Well, what is it? It's a beginning. A first step. The pair of us embarking on a great adventure together. Because we want to take on life as a team. Because we can't think of anyone else we'd rather share that journey with. Because I love him and he loves me.

I'm getting misty-eyed already. This is hopeless. I've been like this for days, ever since I realized what he was driving at.

He's quite heavy-handed, Richard. I mean, in a good, lovable way. He's direct and to the point and doesn't play games. (Thank *God*.) Nor does he land massive surprises on you out of the blue. On my last birthday, he hinted for ages that his present

13

was going to be a surprise trip, which was ideal because I knew to get down my overnight bag and pack a few things.

Although, in the end, he *did* catch me out, because it wasn't a weekend away, as I'd predicted. It was a train ticket to Stroud, which he had biked to my desk with no warning, on my midweek birthday. It turned out he'd secretly arranged with my boss for me to have two days off, and when I finally arrived at Stroud, a car whisked me to the most adorable Cotswold cottage, where he was waiting with a fire burning and a sheepskin rug laid out in front of the flames. (Mmm. Let's just say that sex in front of a roaring fire is *the best thing ever.* Except when that stupid spark flew out and burned my thigh. But never mind. Tiny detail.)

So this time, when he began dropping hints, again they weren't exactly subtle indications. They were more like massive signposts plonked in the road: *I will be proposing to you soon.* First he set up this date and called it a "special lunch." Then he referred to a "big question" he had to ask me and half-winked (to which I feigned ignorance, of course). Then he started teasing me by asking if I like his surname, Finch. (As it happens, I do like it. I don't mean I won't miss being Lottie Graveney,

14

but I'll be very happy to be Mrs. Lottie Finch.)

I almost wish he'd been more roundabout and this was going to be more of a surprise. But, there again, at least I knew to get a manicure.

"So, Lottie, have you decided yet?" Richard looks up at me with that warm smile of his, and my stomach swoops. Just for an instant I thought he was being super-clever and that *was* his proposal.

"Um . . ." I look down to hide my confusion.

Of course the answer will be "yes." A big, joyful "yes." I can still hardly believe we've arrived at this place. Marriage. I mean, marriage! In the three years Richard and I have been together, I've deliberately avoided the question of marriage, commitment, and all associated subjects (children, houses, sofas, herbs in pots). We sort of live together at his place, but I still have my own flat. We're a couple, but at Christmas we go home to our own families. We're in *that* place.

After about a year, I knew we were good together. I knew I loved him. I'd seen him at his best (the surprise birthday trip, tied with the time I drove over his foot by mistake and he didn't shout at me) and his worst (obstinately refusing to ask for directions, all the way to Norfolk, with broken sat nav. It took six hours). And I still wanted to be with him. I *got* him. He's not the show-offy kind, Richard. He's measured and deliberate. Sometimes you think he's not even listening — but then he'll come to life so suddenly, you realize he was alert the whole time. Like a lion, half asleep under the tree but ready for the kill. Whereas I'm a bit more of a gazelle, leaping around. We complement each other. It's Nature.

(Not in a food-chain sense, obviously. In a *metaphorical* sense.)

So I knew, after a year, he was The One. But I also knew what would happen if I put a foot wrong. In my experience, the word "marriage" is like an enzyme. It causes all kinds of reactions in a relationship, mostly of the breaking-down kind.

Look at what happened with Jamie, my first long-term boyfriend. We'd been happily together for four years and I just happened to mention that my parents got married at the same age we were (twenty-six and twenty-three). That was it. One mention. Whereupon he freaked out and said we had to take "a break." A break from what? Until that moment we'd been fine. So clearly what he needed a break from was *the risk of hearing the word "marriage" again.*

16

Clearly this was such a major worry that he couldn't even face seeing me, for fear that my mouth might start to form the word again.

Before the "break" was over, he was with that red-haired girl. I didn't mind, because by then I'd met Seamus. Seamus, with his sexy Irish lilting voice. And I don't even *know* what went wrong with him. We were besotted for about a year — crazy all-night-sex nothing-else-in-life-matters besotted — until all of a sudden we were arguing every night instead. We went from exhilarating to exhausting in about twenty-four hours. It was toxic. Too many state-of-the-nation summits about "Where are we heading?" and "What do we want from this relation-ship?" and it wore us both out. We limped on for another year, and when I look back, it's as though that second year is a big black miserable blot in my life.

Then there was Julian. That lasted two years too, but it never really *took*. It was like a skeleton of a relationship. I suppose both of us were working far too hard. I'd recently moved to Blay Pharmaceuticals and was traveling all over the country. He was trying to get partnership at his accountancy firm. I'm not sure we ever even broke up properly

— we just drifted apart. We meet up occasionally, as friends, and it's the same for both of us — we're not quite sure where it all went wrong. He even asked me out on a date a year or so ago, but I had to tell him I was with someone now and really happy. And that was Richard. The guy I really do love. The guy sitting opposite me with a ring in his pocket (maybe).

Richard is definitely better-looking than any of my other boyfriends. (Maybe I'm biased, but I think he's gorgeous.) He works hard as a media analyst, but he's not obsessed. He's not as rich as Julian, but who cares? He's energetic and funny and has an uproarious laugh that makes my spirits lift, whatever mood I'm in. He calls me "Daisy," ever since we went on a picnic where I made him a daisy chain. He can lose his temper with people — but that's OK. No one's perfect. When I look back over our relationship, I don't see a black blot, like with Seamus, or a blank space, like with Julian. I see a cheesy music video. A montage, with blue skies and smiles. Happy times. Closeness. Laughter.

And now we're getting to the climax of the montage. The bit where he kneels down, takes a deep breath . . .

I'm feeling so nervous for him. I want this

to go beautifully. I want to be able to tell our children that I fell in love with their father all over again, the day he proposed.

Our children. Our home. Our life.

As I let my mind roll around the images, I feel a release inside me. I'm ready for this. I'm thirty-three years old and I'm ready. All my grown-up life, I've steered away from the subject of marriage. My friends are the same. It's as though there's been a crime-scene cordon around the whole area: NO ENTRY. You just don't go there, because if you do, you've jinxed it and your boyfriend chucks you.

But now there's nothing to jinx. I can *feel* the love flowing between us, over the table. I want to grab Richard's hands. I want to envelop him in my arms. He is such a wonderful, wonderful man. I'm so lucky. In forty years when we're both wrinkled and gray, perhaps we'll walk up the Strand hand in hand and remember today and thank God we found each other. I mean, what were the chances, in this teeming world of strangers? Love is so random. *So* random. It's a miracle, really. . . .

Oh God, I'm blinking. . . .

"Lottie?" Richard has noticed my damp eyes. "Hey, Daisydoo. Are you OK? What's up?"

19

Even though I've been more honest with Richard than I have with any other boy-friend, it's probably not a good idea to reveal my *entire* thought process to him. Fliss, my big sister, says I think in Holly-wood Technicolor and I have to remember that other people can't hear the swooping violins.

"Sorry!" I dab at my eyes. "Nothing. I just wish you didn't have to go."

Richard is flying off tonight to an assign-ment in San Francisco. It's three months — could be worse — but I'll miss him terribly. In fact, it's only the thought that I'll have a wedding to plan which is distracting me.

"Sweetheart, don't cry. I can't bear it." He reaches out to take my hands. "We'll Skype every day."

"I know." I squeeze his hands back. "I'll be ready."

"Although you *might* want to remember that, if I'm in my office, everyone can hear what you're saying. Including my boss."

Only a tiny flicker of his eyes gives away the fact that he's teasing me. The last time he was away and we Skyped, I started giv-ing him advice on how to manage his nightmare boss, forgetting that Richard was in an open-plan office and the nightmare boss was liable to walk past at any minute.

(Luckily, he didn't.)

"Thanks for that tip." I shrug, equally deadpan.

"Also, they can see you. So you might not want to be *totally* naked."

"Not *totally*," I agree. "Maybe just a transparent bra and panties. Keep it simple."

Richard grins and grasps my hands more tightly. "I love you." His voice is low and warm and melting. I will never, ever get sick of him saying that.

"Me too."

"In fact, Lottie . . ." He clears his throat. "I have something to ask you. . . ."

My insides feel as if they're going to explode. My face is a rictus of anticipation while my thoughts are spinning wildly. *Oh God . . . he's doing it. . . . My whole life changes here. . . . Concentrate, Lottie . . . savor the moment. . . . Shit! What's wrong with my leg?*

I stare down at it in horror.

Whoever made these "stay-up stockings" is a liar and will go to hell, because one of them *hasn't* bloody well stayed up. It's collapsed around my knee and there's a really gross plastic "adhesive" strip flapping around my calf. This is hideous.

I can't be proposed to like this. I can't

21

spend the rest of my life looking back and thinking, *It was such a romantic moment; shame about the stocking.*

"Sorry, Richard." I cut him off. "Just wait a sec. . . ."

Surreptitiously, I reach down and yank the stocking up — but the flimsy fabric tears in my hand. Great. Now I have both flapping plastic *and* shreds of nylon decorating my leg. I cannot believe my marriage proposal is being wrecked by hosiery. I should have gone for bare legs.

"Everything OK?" Richard looks a little baffled as I emerge from under the table.

"I have to go to the Ladies'," I mutter. "I'm sorry. Sorry. Can we put things on pause? Just for a nanosecond?"

"Are you OK?"

"I'm fine." I'm red with embarrassment. "I've had a . . . a garment mishap. I don't want you to see. Will you look away?"

Obediently, Richard averts his head. I push my chair back and walk swiftly across the room, ignoring the looks of other lunchtime diners. There's no point trying to mask it. It's a flappy stocking.

I bang through the door of the Ladies', wrench off my shoe and the stupid stocking, then stare at myself in the mirror, my heart pounding. I can't believe I've just put my proposal on pause.

I feel as though time is on hold. As though we're in a sci-fi movie and Richard is in suspended animation and I've got all the time in the world to think about whether I want to marry him.

Which, obviously, I don't need, because the answer is: I do.

A blond girl with a beaded headband turns to peer at me, lip liner in hand. I guess I do look a bit odd, standing motionless with a shoe and stocking in my hand.

"There's a bin over there." She nods. "Do you feel OK?"

"Fine. Thanks." I suddenly have the urge to share the momentousness of this occasion. "My boyfriend's in the middle of proposing to me!"

"No *way*." All the women at the mirrors turn to stare at me.

"What do you mean, 'in the middle of'?" demands a thin redheaded girl in pink, her eyebrows narrowed. "What's he said, 'Will you . . .'?"

"He started, but I had a stocking catastrophe." I wave the holdup. "So he's on pause."

"On *pause*?" says someone incredulously.

"Well, I'd get back out there quick," says the redhead. "You don't want to give him a chance to change his mind."

"How exciting!" says the blond girl. "Can we watch? Can I film you?"

"We could put it on YouTube!" says her friend. "Has he hired a flash mob or anything?"

"I don't *think* so —"

"How does this work?" An old woman with metal-gray hair cuts across our discussion imperiously. She's waving her hands angrily underneath the automatic hand-wash dispenser. "Why do they invent these machines? What's wrong with a bar of soap?"

"Look, like this, Aunt Dee," says the redheaded girl soothingly. "Your hands are too high."

I pull off my other shoe and stocking, and, since I'm here, reach for the hand lotion to slather on my bare legs. I don't want to look back and think, *It was such a romantic moment; shame about the scaly shins.* Then I get out my phone. I *have* to text Fliss. I quickly type:

He's doing it!!!

A moment later, her reply appears on my screen:

Don't tell me u r texting me in the

24

middle of a proposal!!!

In Ladies'. Taking a moment.

V exciting!!! You make a great couple.
Give him a kiss from me. xxx

Will do! Talk later xxx

"Which one is he?" says the blond girl as
I put away my phone. "I'm going to have a
look!" She darts out of the Ladies', then
returns a few seconds later. "Ooh, I saw
him. The dark guy in the corner? He's fab.
Hey, your mascara's smudged." She passes
me a makeup eraser pen. "Want to do a
quick fix?"

"Thanks." I smile companionably at her
and start to erase the tiny black marks below
my eyes. My wavy chestnut hair is swept up
in a chignon, and I suddenly wonder
whether to let it down so it tumbles over
my shoulders for the big moment.

No. Too cheesy. Instead, I pull some
tendrils out and twist them around my face
while I assess everything else. Lipstick: nice
coral color. Eye shadow: shimmery gray to
bring out my blue eyes. Blusher: hopefully
will not need touch-up as will be flushed
with excitement.

"I wish *my* boyfriend would propose," says a long-haired girl in black, watching me wistfully. "What's the trick?"

"Dunno," I reply, wishing I could be more helpful. "I suppose we've been together awhile, we know we're compatible, we love each other —"

"But so do my boyfriend and I! We've been living together, the sex is great, it's all great. . . ."

"Don't pressure him," says the blond girl wisely.

"I mention it, like, once a *year.*" The long-haired girl looks thoroughly miserable. "And he gets twitchy and we drop it. What am I supposed to do? Move out? It's been six years now —"

"Six years?" The old woman looks up from drying her hands. "What's wrong with you?"

The girl with the long hair flushes. "Nothing's *wrong* with me," she says. "I was having a private conversation."

"Private, pfft." The old woman gestures briskly around the Ladies' room. "Everyone's listening."

"Aunt Dee!" The redhead looks embarrassed. *"Shush!"*

"Don't you shush me, Amy!" The old woman regards the long-haired girl beadily. "Men are like jungle creatures. The minute

26

they've found their kill, they eat it and fall asleep. Well, you've handed him his kill on a plate, haven't you?"

"It's not as simple as that," says the long-haired girl resentfully.

"In my day, the men got married because they wanted sex. That was motivation all right!" The old woman gives a brisk laugh. "All you girls with your sleeping together and living together and *then* you want an engagement ring. It's all back to front." She picks up her bag. "Come along, Amy! What are you waiting for?"

Amy shoots us desperate looks of apology, then disappears out of the Ladies' with her aunt. We all exchange raised eyebrows. What a nutter.

"Don't worry," I say reassuringly, and squeeze the girl's arm. "I'm sure things will work out for you." I want to spread the joy. I want *everyone* to have the good luck that Richard and I have had: finding the perfect person and knowing it.

"Yes." She makes an obvious effort to gather herself. "Let's hope. Well, I wish you a very happy life together."

"Thanks!" I hand the eraser pen back to the blond girl. "Here I go! Wish me luck!"

I push my way out of the Ladies' and survey the bustling restaurant, feeling as

27

though I've just pressed *play*. There's Richard, sitting in exactly the same position as when I left him. He's not even checking his phone. He must be as focused on this moment as I am. The most special moment of our lives.

"Sorry about that." I slide into my chair and give him my most loving, receptive smile. "Shall we pick up where we left off?"

Richard smiles back, but I can tell he's lost a bit of momentum. We might need to work back into things gradually.

"It's such a special day," I say encouragingly. "Don't you feel that?"

"Absolutely." He nods.

"This place is so lovely." I gesture around. "The perfect place for a . . . a big talk."

I've left my hands casually on the table, and, as I intended, Richard takes them between his. He takes a deep breath and frowns.

"Speaking of that, Lottie, there's something I wanted to ask." As we meet eyes, his crinkle a little. "I don't think this will come as a *massive* surprise. . . ."

Oh God, oh God, here it comes.

"Yes?" My voice is a nervous squawk.

"Bread for the table?"

Richard starts in shock and my head jerks up. A waiter has approached so quietly, neither of us noticed him. Almost before I know it, Richard has dropped my hand and is talking about brown soda bread. I want to whack the whole basket away in frustration. Couldn't the waiter *tell*? Don't they train them in imminent-proposal spotting?

I can tell Richard's been thrown off track too. Stupid, *stupid* waiter. How dare he spoil my boyfriend's big moment?

"So," I say encouragingly, as soon as the waiter's gone. "You had a question?"

"Well. Yes." He focuses on me and takes a deep breath — then his face changes shape again. I turn round in surprise, to see that *another* bloody waiter has loomed up. Well, to be fair, I suppose it's what you expect in a restaurant.

We both order some food — I'm barely aware of what I'm choosing — and the waiter melts away. But another one will be back, any minute. I feel more sorry for Richard than ever. How's he supposed to propose in these circumstances? How do men *do* it?

I can't help grinning at him wryly. "Not your day."

"Not really."

"The wine waiter will be along in a minute," I point out.

"It's like Piccadilly Circus here." He rolls

his eyes ruefully, and I feel a warm sense of collusion. We're in this together. Who cares when he proposes? Who cares if it's not some perfect, staged moment? "Shall we get some champagne?" he adds.

I can't help giving him a knowing smile. "Would that be a little . . . *premature,* do you think?"

"Well, that depends." He raises his eyebrows. "You tell me."

The subtext is so obvious, I don't know whether I want to laugh or hug him.

"Well, in that case . . ." I pause a delicious length of time, eking it out for both of us. "Yes. My answer would be yes."

His brow relaxes and I can see the tension flood out of him. Did he really think I might say no? He's so unassuming. He's such a darling man. Oh God. We're getting married!

"With all my heart, Richard, yes," I add for emphasis, my voice suddenly wobbling. "You have to know how much this means to me. It's . . . I don't know what to say."

His fingers squeeze mine, and it's as though we have our own private code. I almost feel sorry for other couples, who have to spell things out. They don't have the connection we do.

For a moment we're just silent. I can feel

a cloud of happiness surrounding us. I want that cloud to stay there forever. I can see us now in the future, painting a house, wheeling a pram, decorating a Christmas tree with our little toddlers. . . . His parents might want to come and stay for Christmas, and that's fine, because I *love* his parents. In fact, the first thing I'll do when this is all announced is go and see his mother in Sussex. She'll adore helping with the wedding, and it's not as though I've got a mother of my own to do it.

So many possibilities. So many plans. So much glorious life to live together.

"So," I say at last, gently rubbing his fingers. "Pleased? Happy?"

"Couldn't be more happy." He caresses my hand.

"I've thought about this for ages." I sigh contentedly. "But I never thought . . . You just don't, do you? It's like . . . what will it *be* like? What will it *feel* like?"

"I know what you mean." He nods.

"I'll always remember this room. I'll always remember the way you're looking right now." I squeeze his hand even harder.

"Me too," he says simply.

What I love about Richard is, he can convey so much with simply a sidelong look or a tilt of his head. He doesn't need to say much, because I can read him so easily.

I can see the long-haired girl watching us from across the room, and I can't help smiling at her. (Not a triumphant smile, because that would be insensitive. A humble, grateful smile.)

"Some wine for the table, sir? Mademoiselle?" The sommelier approaches and I beam up at him.

"I think we need some champagne."

"Absolument." He smiles back at me. "The house champagne? Or we have a very nice Ruinart for a special occasion."

"I think the Ruinart." I can't resist sharing our joy. "It's a very special day! We've just got engaged!"

"Mademoiselle!" The sommelier's face creases into a smile. "*Félicitations!* Sir! Many congratulations!" We both turn to Richard — but to my surprise he's not entering into the spirit of the moment. He's staring at me as though I'm some sort of specter. Why does he look so spooked? What's wrong?

"What —" His voice is strangled. "What do you mean?"

I suddenly realize why he's upset. Of course. Trust me to spoil everything by jumping in.

"Richard, I'm so sorry. Did you want to tell your parents first?" I squeeze his hand.

"I completely understand. We won't tell anyone else, promise."

"Tell them what?" He's wide-eyed and starey. "Lottie, we're not engaged."

"But . . ." I look at him uncertainly. "You just proposed to me. And I said yes."

"No, I didn't!" He yanks his hand out of mine.

OK, one of us is going mad here. The sommelier has retreated tactfully, and I can see him shooing away the waiter with the bread basket, who was approaching again.

"Lottie, I'm sorry, but I have no idea what you're talking about." Richard thrusts his hands through his hair. "I haven't mentioned marriage or engagement, or anything."

"But . . . but that's what you meant! When you ordered the champagne, and you said, 'You tell me,' and I said, 'With all my heart, yes.' It was subtle! It was beautiful!"

I'm gazing at him, longing for him to agree, longing for him to feel what I feel. But he just looks baffled, and I feel a sudden pang of dread.

"That's . . . *not* what you meant?" My throat is so tight I can barely speak. I can't believe this is happening. "You didn't mean to propose?"

"Lottie, I *didn't* propose!" he says force-

33

fully. "Full stop!"

Does he have to exclaim so loudly? Heads are popping up with interest everywhere.

"OK! I get it!" I rub my nose with my napkin. "You don't need to tell the whole restaurant."

Waves of humiliation are washing over me. I'm rigid with misery. How can I have got this so wrong?

And if he wasn't proposing, then *why* wasn't he proposing?

"I don't understand." Richard is talking almost to himself. "I've never said anything, we've never discussed it —"

"You've said plenty!" Hurt and indignation are erupting out of me. "You said you were organizing a 'special lunch.'"

"It is special!" he says defensively. "I'm going to San Francisco tomorrow."

"And you asked me if I liked your surname! Your *surname*, Richard!"

"We were doing a jokey straw poll at the office!" Richard looks bewildered. "It was chitchat!"

"And you said you had to ask me a 'big question.'"

"Not a big question." He shakes his head. "A question."

"I heard 'big question.'"

There's a wretched silence between us.

The cloud of happiness has gone. The Hollywood Technicolor and swooping violins have gone. The sommelier tactfully slides a wine list onto the corner of the table and retreats quickly.

"What is it, then?" I say at last. "This really important, medium-size question?"

Richard looks trapped. "It's not important. Forget it."

"Come on, tell me!"

"Well, OK," he says finally. "I was going to ask you what I should do with my air miles. I thought maybe we could plan a trip."

"Air miles?" I can't help lashing out. "You booked a special table and ordered champagne to talk about *air miles*?"

"No! I mean . . ." Richard winces. "Lottie, I feel terrible about all this. I had absolutely zero idea —"

"But we just had a whole bloody conversation about being engaged!" I can feel tears rising. "I was stroking your hand and saying how happy I was and how I'd thought about this moment for ages. And you were agreeing with me! What did you *think* I was talking about?"

Richard's eyes are swiveling as though searching for an escape. "I thought you were . . . you know. Going on about stuff."

" 'Going on about stuff'?" I stare at him. "What do you mean, 'Going on about stuff'?"

Richard looks even more desperate. "The truth is, I don't always know what you're on about," he says in a sudden confessional rush. "So sometimes I just . . . nod along."

Nod along?

I stare back at him, stricken. I thought we had a special, unique silent bond of understanding. I thought we had a private code. And all the time he was just nodding along.

Two waiters put our salads in front of us and quickly move away, as though sensing we're not in any mood to talk. I pick up my fork and put it down again. Richard doesn't even seem to have noticed his plate.

"I bought you an engagement ring," I say, breaking the silence.

"Oh God." He buries his head in his hands.

"It's fine. I'll take it back."

"Lottie . . ." He looks tortured. "Do we have to . . . I'm going away tomorrow. Couldn't we just move away from the whole subject?"

"So, do you *ever* want to get married?" As I ask the question, I feel a deep anguish inside. A minute ago I thought I was engaged. I'd run the marathon. I was bursting through the finishing tape, arms up in elation. Now I'm back at the starting line, lacing up my shoes, wondering if the race is even on.

"I . . . God, Lottie . . . I dunno." He sounds beleaguered. "I mean, yes. I suppose so." His eyes are swiveling more and more wildly. "Maybe. You know. Eventually."

Well. You couldn't get a much clearer signal. Maybe he wants to get married to someone else, one day. But not to me.

And suddenly a bleak despair comes over me. I believed with all my heart that he was The One. How could I have got it so wrong? I feel as though I can't trust myself on anything anymore.

"Right." I stare down at my salad for a few moments, running my eyes over leaves and slices of avocado and pomegranate seeds, trying to get my thoughts together. "The thing is, Richard, I *do* want to get married. I want marriage, kids, a house — the whole bit. And I wanted them with you. But marriage is kind of a two-way thing." I pause, breathing hard but determined to keep my composure. "So I guess it's good that I know the truth sooner rather than later. Thanks for that, anyway."

"Lottie!" says Richard in alarm. "Wait! This doesn't change anything —"

"It changes everything. I'm too old to be on a waiting list. If it's not going to happen with us, then I'd rather know now and move on. You know?" I try to smile, but my happy muscles have stopped working. "Have fun in San Francisco. I think I'd better go." Tears are edging past my lashes. I need to leave, quickly. I'll go back to work and check on my presentation for tomorrow. I'd taken the afternoon off, but what's the point? I won't be phoning all my friends with the joyful news after all.

As I'm making my way out, I feel a hand grabbing my arm. I turn in shock to see the blond girl with the beaded headband looking up at me.

"What happened?" she demands excitedly. "Did he give you a ring?"

Her question is like a knife stabbing in my heart. He didn't give me a ring and he isn't even my boyfriend anymore. But I'd rather die than admit it.

"Actually . . ." I lift my chin proudly. "Actually, he proposed but I said 'No.' "

"Oh." Her hand shoots to her mouth.

"That's right." I catch the eye of the long-haired girl, who's eavesdropping blatantly at the next table. "I said 'No.' "

"You said *'No'*?" She looks so incredulous that I feel a pang of indignation.

"Yes!" I glare at her defiantly. "I said 'No.' We weren't right for each other after all, so I made the decision to end it. Even though he really wanted to marry me and have kids and a dog and everything . . ."

I can feel curious eyes on my back, and I swivel round to face yet more people listening agog. Is the whole bloody *restaurant* in on this now?

"I said 'No'!" My voice is rising in distress. "I said 'No.' *No!*" I call over loudly to Richard, who is still sitting at the table, looking dumbfounded. "I'm sorry, Richard. I know you're in love with me and I know I'm breaking your heart right now. But the answer's no!"

And, feeling a tiny bit better, I stride out of the restaurant.

I get back to work to find my desk littered with new Post-its. The phone must have been busy while I was out. I slump down at my desk and heave a long, shuddering sigh. Then I hear a cough. Kayla, my intern, is hovering at the door of my tiny office. Kayla hovers round my door a lot. She's the keenest intern I've ever met. She wrote me a two-sided Christmas card about how inspiring I was as a role model and how she would never have come to intern at Blay Pharmaceuticals if it wasn't for the talk I gave at Bristol University. (It *was* a pretty good talk, I must admit. As recruitment speeches for pharmaceutical companies go.)

"How was lunch?" Her eyes are sparkling.

My heart plummets. *Why* did I tell her Richard was going to propose? I was just so confident. It gave me a kick, seeing her excitement. I felt like an all-round super-woman.

"It was fine. Fine. Nice restaurant." I start to riffle through the papers on my desk, as though searching for some vital piece of information.

"So, are you engaged?"

Her words are like lemon juice sprinkled on sore skin. Has she no finesse? You don't ask your boss straight out, "Are you en-gaged?" Especially if she's not wearing a huge, brand-new ring, which clearly I'm not. I might refer to this in my appraisal of her. *Kayla has some trouble working within appropriate boundaries.*

"Well." I brush down my jacket, playing for time, and swallowing the lump in my throat. "Actually, no. Actually, I decided against it."

"Really?" She sounds confused.

"Yes." I nod several times. "Absolutely. I concluded that for me at my time of life, at

40

my career point, this wasn't a smart move."

Kayla looks poleaxed. "But . . . you guys were so great together."

"Well, these things aren't as simple as they appear, Kayla." I riffle the papers more quickly.

"He must have been devastated."

"Pretty much," I say after a pause. "Yup. Pretty crushed. In fact . . . he cried."

I can say what I like. She'll never see Richard again. *I'll* probably never see him again. And like a bludgeon to the stomach, the enormity of the truth hits me again. It's all over. Gone. All of it. I'll never have sex with him again. I'll never wake up with him again. I'll never hug him again. Somehow that fact, above all others, makes me want to bawl.

"God, Lottie, you're so inspiring." Kayla's eyes are shining. "To know that something is wrong for your career, and to have the courage to make that stand, to say, 'No! I *won't* do what everyone expects.' "

"Exactly." I nod desperately. "I was making a stand for women everywhere."

My jaw is trembling. I have to conclude this conversation right now, before things go horribly wrong in the bursting-into-tears-in-front-of-your-intern department.

"So, any vital messages?" I scan the Post-

41

its without seeing them.

"One from Steve about the presentation tomorrow, and some guy named Ben called."

"Ben who?"

"Just Ben. He said you'd know."

No one calls himself "Just Ben." It'll be some cheeky student I met at a recruiting seminar, trying to get a foot in the door. I'm really not in the mood for it.

"OK. Well. I'm going to go over my presentation. So." I click busily and randomly at my mouse till she leaves. Deep breath. Firm jaw. Move on. Move on, move on, move on.

The phone rings and I pick it up with a sweeping, authoritative gesture.

"Charlotte Graveney."

"Lottie! It's me!"

I fight an instinct to put the receiver straight back down again.

"Oh, hi, Fliss." I swallow. "Hi."

"So . . . how *are* you?"

I can hear the teasing note in her voice and curse myself bitterly. I should never have texted her from the restaurant.

It's pressure. All hideous pressure. Why did I ever share my love life with my sister? Why did I ever even tell her I was dating Richard? Let alone introduce them. Let alone start talking about proposals.

Next time I meet a man, I'm saying *nothing to anybody.* Nada. Zip. Not until we've been blissfully married for a decade and have three kids and have just renewed our wedding vows. Then, and only then, will I send a text to Fliss saying: Guess what? I met someone! He seems nice!

"Oh, I'm fine." I muster a breezy, matter-of-fact tone. "How about you?"

"All good this end. So . . . ?"

She leaves the question dangling. I know exactly what she means. She means, *So, are you wearing a massive diamond ring and toasting yourself with Bollinger as Richard sucks your toes in some amazing hotel suite?*

I feel a fresh, raw pang. I can't bear to talk about it. I can't bear her sympathy gushing over me. Find another topic. Any topic. Quick.

"So. Anyway." I try to sound bright and nonchalant. "Anyway. Um. I was just thinking, actually. I really should get round to doing that master's on business theory. You know I've always meant to do it. I mean, what am I waiting for? I could apply to Birkbeck, do it in my spare time. . . . What do you think?"

2
FLISS

Oh God. I want to weep. It went wrong. I don't know how, but it went wrong.

Every time one of Lottie's relationships ends, she immediately talks about doing a master's degree. It's like a Pavlovian reaction.

"Maybe I could even go on to do a PhD, you know?" she's saying, with only the tiniest shake in her voice. "Maybe do some research abroad?"

She might fool the average person — but not me. Not her sister. She's in a bad way.

"Right," I say. "Yes. A PhD abroad. Good idea!"

There's no point in pressing her for details or asking bluntly what happened. Lottie has her own distinct process for dealing with breakups. You can't hurry her and you must *not* express any sympathy. I've learned this the hard way.

There was the time she split up from

Seamus. She arrived on my doorstep with a carton of Phish Food and bloodshot eyes and I made the elementary error of asking, "What happened?" Whereupon she exploded like a grenade: "Jesus, Fliss! Can't I just come and share ice cream with my sister without getting the third bloody degree? Maybe I just want to hang out with my own sister. Maybe life isn't just about boyfriends. Maybe I just want to . . . reassess my life. Do a master's degree."

Then there was the time Jamie dumped her and I made the mistake of saying, "Oh God, Lottie, poor you."

She eviscerated me. "Poor me? What do you mean, poor me? What, Fliss, you're pitying me because I don't have a man? I thought you were a *feminist*." She vented all her hurt on me in one long tirade, and by the end I practically needed an ear transplant.

So now I listen in silence as she talks about how she's been meaning to explore the more academic side of herself for *ages,* and a lot of people don't appreciate how cerebral she is, and her tutor entered her for a university prize, did I know that? (Yes, I did: she mentioned it straight after she broke up with Jamie.)

At last she tapers off into silence. I don't

breathe. I think we might be getting to the nub of things.

"So, by the way, Richard and I aren't together anymore," she says in a careless, dropping-something-from-the-tips-of-her-fingers manner.

"Oh, really?" I match her tone. We could be talking about a minor subplot in *East-Enders*.

"Yeah, we split up."

"I see."

"Wasn't right."

"Ah. Well. That's a real . . ." I'm running out of anodyne one-syllable words. "I mean, that's . . ."

"Yes. It's a shame." She pauses. "In one way."

"Right. So, was he . . ." I'm treading on eggshells here. "I mean, weren't you . . ."

What the fuck went wrong when an hour ago he was in the middle of a bloody proposal? is what I want to demand.

I don't always trust Lottie's version of events. She can be a little starry-eyed. She can see what she wants to see. But, hand on heart, I believed as firmly as she did that Richard was planning to propose to her.

And now not only are they not engaged but they're *over*? I can't help feeling pro-foundly shocked. I've got to know Richard pretty well, and he's a good'un. The best she's ever dated, if you ask me. (Which she has, many times, often at midnight when she's drunk and interrupts before I've finished to announce she loves him *whatever* I think.) He's sturdy, kind, successful. No chippiness, no baggage. Handsome but not vain. And in love with her. That's the main point. In fact, the only point. They've got that vibe of successful couples. They've got that connection. The way they talk, the way they joke, the way they sit together, always with his arm hooked gently around her shoulders, his fingers playing with her hair. The way they seem to be heading for the same things — whether it's take-out sushi or a holiday in Canada. They have togetherness. You can just see it. At least, I can.

Correction: I could. So why couldn't *he*?

Bastard, stupid man. What exactly is he hoping to find in a partner? What exactly is wrong with my sister? Does he think she's holding him back from some great romance with a six-foot supermodel?

I let off steam by chucking a balled-up piece of paper aggressively into my bin. A moment later I realize I actually need that paper. Bugger.

The phone is still silent. I can feel Lottie's misery emanating down the line. Oh God, I can't bear this. I don't care how prickly she is, I *have* to know a bit more. It's insane. One minute they're getting married, the next we're on Stage One of Lottie's Breakup Process, do not pass Go.

"I thought you said he had a 'big question'?" I say as tactfully as I can.

"Yes. Well. He changed his story," she says in a determinedly nonchalant voice. "He said it wasn't a 'big question.' It was a 'question.' "

I wince. That's bad. A "big question" isn't a variety of "question." It's not even a subset.

"So what was the question?"

"It was about air miles, as it happens," she says, her voice flat.

Air miles? Ouch. I can imagine how *that* went down. Ian Aylward is at my office window, I suddenly notice. He's gesticulating energetically. I know what he wants. It's the speech for the awards ceremony tonight.

"Done," I mouth, in a blatant lie, and point at my computer, trying to imply that mere technology is holding up its arrival. "I'll email it. *Email. It.*"

At last he walks away. I glance at my watch, and my heart ups its pace a little. I have precisely ten minutes to listen supportively to Lottie, write the rest of my speech, and touch up my makeup.

No, nine and a half minutes.

I feel yet another stab of resentment, directed straight at Richard. If he really had to break my sister's heart, could he have chosen a day which *wasn't* my most insanely busy of the whole year? I hurriedly pull up the speech document on my screen and start typing.

In conclusion, I would like to thank everyone here tonight. Both those who have won awards and those who are gnashing their teeth furiously. I can see you! (Pause for laughter.)

"Lottie, you know it's our big awards event tonight," I say guiltily. "I'm going to have to go in five. If I could come round, you know I would in a heartbeat. . . ."

Too late, I realize I've made a heinous error. I've expressed sympathy. Sure enough, she turns on me.

"Come round?" she spits scathingly. "You don't need to come round! What, you think I'm upset about Richard? You think my whole life revolves around one man? I wasn't even *thinking* about him. I only called to tell you about my plans for a master's degree. That was the only reason."

"I know," I backtrack. "Of course it was."

"Maybe I'll see if there's an exchange

49

program in the States. Maybe I'll look at Stanford. . . ."

She carries on talking, and I type faster and faster. I've given this speech six times before. It's just the same old words, every year, in a different order.

The hotel industry continues to innovate and inspire. I am awed at the accomplishments and innovations that we see in our industry.

No. Crap. I press *delete* and try again.

I am awed at the accomplishments and advances that my team of reviewers and I have witnessed around the world.

Yes. "Witnessed" adds a nice touch of gravitas to the occasion. One could almost think we've spent the year engaging with a series of holy prophets rather than with tanned PR girls in stilettos showing us the latest technology in poolside towel-chilling.

My thanks are due to Bradley Rose, as ever. . . .

Do I thank Brad first? Or Megan? Or Michael?

I'll leave someone out. I know it. This is the law of the thank-you speech. You miss some vital person, then grab the microphone again and call out their name in a shrill voice, but no one's listening. Then you have to find them and spend a hideous half hour thanking them personally while you both

50

smile but above their head in a thought bubble are floating the words: *You forgot I exist.*

My thanks are due to everyone who put this awards ceremony together, everyone who didn't put this awards ceremony together, my entire staff, all your staffs, all our families, all seven billion people on this planet, God/Allah/ Other. . . .

". . . I actually see this as a positive. I really do, Fliss. This is my chance to reconfigure my life, you know? I mean, I *needed* this."

I drag my attention back to the phone. Lottie's refusal to admit that anything is wrong is one of her most endearing qualities. Her resolute bravery is so heartbreaking, it makes me want to hug her.

But it also slightly makes me want to tear my hair out. It makes me want to yell, *Stop talking about bloody master's degrees! Just admit you're hurt!*

Because I know how this goes. I've been here before. Every breakup is the same. She starts off all brave and positive. She refuses to admit anything is wrong. She goes days, maybe weeks, without cracking, a smile lodged on her face, and people who don't know her say, "Wow, Lottie coped with the breakup really well."

Until the delayed reaction happens. Which it does, every time. In the form of some impulsive, outrageous, total fuckwit gesture which makes her feel euphoric for about five minutes. Each time, it's something different. A tattoo on her ankle; an extreme haircut; an overpriced flat in Borough that she then had to sell at a loss. Membership of a cult. An "intimate" piercing which went septic. That was the worst.

No, I take it back, the cult was the worst. They got six hundred pounds of her money and she was still talking about "enlightenment." Evil, preying bastards. I think they circle London, sniffing out the newly dumped.

It's only after the euphoric period that Lottie finally, properly cracks. And *then* it's into the weeping and the days off work and "Fliss, why didn't you stop me?" And "Fliss, I hate this tattoo!" And "Fliss, how can I go to my GP? I'm so embarrassed! What will I dooooo?"

I privately call these post-breakup fuckwit actions her Unfortunate Choices, which is a phrase our mother used a lot while she was alive. It covered anything from a dodgy pair of shoes worn by a dinner-party guest to my father's eventual decision to shack up with a South African beauty queen. "Unfortunate choice," she would murmur, with that glacial stare, and we children would shiver, thanking our lucky stars it wasn't *us* who had made Unfortunate Choices.

I don't often miss my mother. But sometimes I wish there was another family member I could call on to help pick up the pieces of Lottie's life. My dad doesn't count. First of all, he lives in Johannesburg. And, second, if it's not a horse, or offering him a glass of whiskey, he's not interested in it.

Now, listening to Lottie babble on about sabbatical programs, my heart is sinking. I can sense another Unfortunate Choice looming. It's out there somewhere. I feel as though I'm scanning the horizon, my hand shading my eyes, wondering where the shark will surface and grab her foot.

I wish she would just curse and rant and throw things. Then I could relax; the madness would be out of her system. When I broke up with Daniel, I swore obscenely for two solid weeks. It wasn't pretty. But at least I didn't join a cult.

"Lottie . . ." I rub my head. "You know I'm off on holiday tomorrow for two weeks?"

"Oh yes."

"You'll be OK?"

"Of course I'll be *OK.*" Her scathing tone returns. "I'm going to have a pizza and a nice bottle of wine tonight. I've been meaning to do that for ages, actually."

"Well, have a good one. Just don't drown the pain."

That's another of our mother's sayings. I have a sudden memory of her in her pencil-slim white trouser suit and green glittery eye shadow. "Drowning the pain, darlings." She'd be sitting at the bar in that house we had in Hong Kong, cradling a martini while Lottie and I watched, in our matching pink dressing gowns flown out from England.

After she'd gone out, we would intone the phrase to each other like some kind of religion. I thought it was a general toast like "Down the hatch," and shocked a school friend many years later, at a family lunch, by raising my glass and saying, "Well, drown the pain, everyone."

Now we use it as a shorthand for "getting totally trashed in an embarrassing manner."

"I will *not* be drowning the pain, thank you," retorts Lottie, sounding offended. "And, anyway, you should talk, Fliss."

I may have drunk a few too many vodkas after Daniel and I split up, and I may have made a long speech to an audience of curry-house diners. It's a fair point.

"Yes, well." I sigh. "Talk soon."

I put the phone down, close my eyes, and give my brain about ten seconds to reboot and focus. I have to forget Lottie's love life. I have to concentrate on the awards ceremony. I have to finish my speech. Now. Go.

I open my eyes and swiftly type a list of people to thank. It goes on for ten lines, but better safe than sorry. I email it to Ian, headlined *Speech! Urgent!* and leap up from my desk.

"Fliss!" As I leave my office, Celia pounces on me. She's one of our most prolific freelancers and has the trademark crow's feet of the professional spa reviewer. You'd think that the spa treatments would cancel out the sun damage, but I find it tends to be the other way around. They really should stop putting spas in Thailand. They should situate them in northern wintry countries with no daylight at all.

Hmm. Is there a piece in that?

I quickly type into my BlackBerry: *Zero-daylight spa?* then look up. "Everything OK?"

"The Gruffalo is here. He looks livid." She swallows. "Maybe I should leave."

The Gruffalo is the industry nickname for Gunter Bachmeier. He owns a chain of ten luxury hotels and lives in Switzerland and has a forty-inch waist. I knew he was invited tonight, but I assumed he wouldn't turn up. Not after our review of his new spa–hotel in Dubai, the Palm Stellar.

"It's fine. Don't worry."

"Don't tell him it was me." Celia's voice is actually trembling.

"Celia." I grip her by both shoulders. "You stand by your review, yes?"

"Yes."

"Well, then." I'm willing some strength into her, but she looks terrified. It's amazing how someone who writes such savage, excoriating, witty prose can be so gentle and sensitive in the flesh.

Hmm. Is there a piece in that?

I type: *Meet our reviewers in the flesh?? Profiles??*

Then I delete it. Our readers don't want to meet the reviewers. They don't want to know that "CBD" lives in Hackney and is an accomplished poet on the side. They simply want to know that their massive slice of cash is going to buy them all the sunshine/ snow, white beach/mountains, solitude/ beautiful people, Egyptian cotton/ hammocks, haute cuisine/ expensive club sandwiches that they require of a five-star holiday.

"No one knows who 'CBD' is. You're safe." I pat her arm. "I have to run." I'm already striding down the corridor again. I head into the central atrium and look around. It's a large, airy, double-height hall — the only impressive space at Pincher International — and every year our over-crowded sub-editors suggest that it's converted into office space. But it comes into its own for the awards party. I scan the space, ticking off items in my head. Massive iced cake in shape of magazine cover, which no one will eat: check. Caterers setting out glasses: check. Table of trophies: check. Ian from IT is crouching by the podium, fiddling with the auto reader.

"All OK?" I hurry over.

"Grand." He jumps up. "I've loaded the speech. Want a sound check?"

I step onto the stage, switch on the microphone, and peer at the reader.

"Good evening!" I raise my voice. "I'm Felicity Graveney, editor of *Pincher Travel Review,* and I would like to welcome you to our twenty-third annual awards ceremony. And *what* a year it's been."

I can see from Ian's sardonic eyebrow that I'm going to have to sound a bit more excited than that.

"Shut up," I say, and he grins. "I have

eighteen awards to present. . . ."

Which is far too many. Every year we have a stand-up battle over which ones to get rid of, and then we get rid of none.

"Blah, blah . . . OK, fine." I switch off the mike. "See you later."

As I hurry back down the corridor, I see Gavin, our publisher, at the far end. He's ushering an unmistakable forty-inch waist into the lift. As I'm watching, the Gruffalo turns and flashes a menacing anti-smile at me. He holds up four stubby fingers and is still doing so as the doors close.

I know what that means, and I'm not going to be intimidated. So his new hotel got four stars from us instead of five. He should have created a better hotel. He should have invested in slightly more sand to lay on the concrete base of his "award-winning, man-created beach" and tried hiring slightly less pretentious staff.

I head into the Ladies', survey my reflection, and wince. Sometimes I'm genuinely shocked at the version of me in the mirror. Do I look *so* unlike Angelina Jolie? When did those shadows appear under my eyes? Everything about me is too dark, I abruptly decide. My hair, my brows, my sallow skin. I need to get something bleached. Or maybe everything, all at once. There must surely be a spa somewhere that has an all-in-one bleaching tank. One quick dip; keep your mouth open for the teeth-whitening option.

Hmm. Is there a piece in that? I type *Bleach?* into my BlackBerry, then attack everything I can with brushes. Finally I apply a generous amount of Nars Red Lizard. One thing: I can damn well wear lipstick. Perhaps they'll put it on my grave. FELICITY GRAVENEY LIES HERE. SHE COULD DAMN WELL WEAR LIPSTICK.

I head out, glance at my watch, and press *Daniel* on speed dial as I walk. He'll know I'm phoning now, we discussed the timing, he'll pick up, he has to pick up. . . . Go on, Daniel, pick up. . . . Where are you . . . ?

Voicemail.

Bastard.

With Daniel, I am quite capable of going from calm to seething in 0–60.

The beep sounds and I draw breath.

"You're not there," I say with elaborate calmness, walking toward my office. "That's a shame, because I have to be at this event soon, which you knew, because we discussed it. Several times."

My voice is shaking. I cannot allow him to get to me. Let it go, Fliss. Divorce is a process and this is a process and we're all part of the Tao. Or the Zen. Whatever. The

59

thing in all those books I was given with the word "Divorce" on the cover above a circle or a picture of a tree.

"Anyway." I take a deep breath. "Maybe you can let Noah listen to this message? Thank you."

I close my eyes briefly and remind myself I'm not talking to Daniel anymore. I have to shift his repulsive face out of my mind. I'm talking to the little face that lights up my life. The face that — against pretty tall odds — keeps the world making sense. I picture his shaggy fringe, his huge gray eyes, his school socks wrinkled around his ankles. Curled up on the sofa at Daniel's place, with Monkey under his arm.

"Sweetheart, I hope you're having a lovely time with Daddy. I'll see you soon, OK? I'll try calling later, but if I don't manage it, then night night and I love you."

I'm nearly at my office door now. I have stuff to do. But I can't help talking for as long as possible, till the beep tells me to go and get a life.

"Night night, sweetheart." I press the phone up against my cheek. "Have lovely dreams, OK? Night night —"

"Night night," answers a familiar little voice, and I nearly trip over my party Manolos.

60

What was that? Am I hallucinating? Has he overridden the voicemail? I peer at my phone to make sure, give it a quick bash against my palm, and listen again.

"Hello?" I say cautiously.

"Hello! Hello-hello-hello . . ."

Oh my God. That voice isn't coming from the phone. It's coming from —

I hurry round the corner into my office and there he is. My seven-year-old son. Sitting on the armchair I give to visitors.

"Mummy!" he yells in delight.

"Wow." I'm almost speechless. "Noah. You're here. At my office. That's just . . . Daniel?" I turn to my ex-husband, who is standing by the window, flicking through a past issue of the magazine. "What's going on? I thought Noah would be having tea by now? At your place?" I add with bright emphasis. "As we planned?"

"But I'm not," puts in Noah triumphantly.

"Yes! I can see that, darling! So . . . Daniel?" My smile has spread right across my face. Generally the rule is: the more I smile at Daniel, the more I'm feeling like stabbing him.

I can't help surveying his features with a critical eye, even though he has nothing to do with me anymore. He's gained a couple of pounds. New fine-stripe shirt. No hair

61

product. That's a mistake; his hair looks too floppy and wispy now. Maybe Trudy likes it that way.

"Daniel?" I try again.

Daniel says nothing, just shrugs easily, as though everything is obvious and words are superfluous. That shrug of his is new. It's a post-me shrug. When we were together, his shoulders were permanently hunched. Now he shrugs. He wears a Kabbalah bracelet under his suit. He bounces confrontation back like he's made of rubber. His sense of humor has been replaced by a sense of righteousness. He doesn't joke anymore: he pronounces.

I can't believe we used to have sex. I can't believe we produced Noah together. Maybe I'm in *The Matrix* and I'll wake up to something which makes *far* more sense, like all this time I've been lying in a tank attached to electrodes.

"Daniel?" My smile is fixed.

"We agreed Noah would spend tonight with you." He shrugs again.

"What?" I stare at him, dumbfounded. "No, we didn't. It's your night."

"I have to go to Frankfurt tonight. I sent you an email."

"No, you didn't."

"I did."

"You didn't! You did *not* send me any email."

"We agreed I'd drop Noah here."

He's totally calm, as only Daniel can be. I, on the other hand, am about to have a nervous breakdown.

"Daniel." My voice is trembling with the effort of not smashing his head in. "Why would I have agreed to have Noah here tonight when I'm hosting an awards ceremony? Why would I have done that?"

Daniel shrugs again. "I'm about to go to the airport. He's had something to eat. Here's his overnight bag." He dumps Noah's rucksack on the floor. "All right, Noah? Mummy's going to have you tonight, lucky thing."

There is no way out of this.

"Great!" I smile at Noah, who is eyeing the two of us anxiously. It breaks my heart to see worry in his huge eyes. No child of his age should ever worry about anything. "What a treat for me!" I ruffle his hair reassuringly. "Excuse me, I'll just be a moment. . . ."

I walk along the corridor to the Ladies'. It's empty, which is a good thing, because I cannot contain myself any longer.

"HE DID NOT SEND ME A FUCK-ING EMAIL!" My voice rockets round the cubicles. I'm panting as I meet my own eyes in the mirror. I feel about ten percent better. Enough to get through the evening.

I walk calmly back to the office, to see Daniel shrugging on his coat.

"Well, have a good trip or whatever." I sit down, unscrew my fountain pen, and write *Congratulations!* on the card for the bouquet which will be presented to the overall winner (that new spa–resort in Marrakesh). *With best wishes from Felicity Graveney and all the team.*

Daniel is still in my office. I can sense him lurking. He has something to say.

"You still here?" I lift my eyes.

"Just one other thing." He surveys me with that righteous expression again. "I've got a couple more points to raise over the settlement."

For a moment I'm so stunned I can't react.

"Wha-at?" I manage to utter at last.

He cannot raise more points. We've finished raising points. We're about to sign off. It's done. After a court case and two appeals and a million lawyers' letters. It's finished.

"I was talking it over with Trudy." He does his hand-spreading again. "She raised some interesting issues."

64

No way. I want to thwack him. He does *not* get to talk about our divorce with Trudy. It's ours. If Trudy wants a divorce, she can marry him first. See how she likes that.

"Just a couple of points." He puts a wad of papers down on the desk. "Have a read."

Have a read. As though he's recommending a good whodunit.

"Daniel." I feel like a kettle coming to the boil. "You can't start laying new stuff on me now. The divorce is *done.* We've thrashed everything out already."

"Surely it's more important to get it right?"

He sounds reproving, as though I'm suggesting we go for a shoddy, ill-prepared divorce. One with no workmanship in it. Botched together with a glue gun instead of hand-sewn.

"I'm happy with what we've agreed," I say tightly, although "happy" is hardly the right word. "Happy" would have been *not* finding his draft love letters to another woman stuffed in his briefcase, where anyone searching for chewing gum might stumble on them.

Love letters. I mean, love letters! I still can't believe he wrote love letters to another woman and not to his own wife. I can't believe he wrote explicit sexual poetry, illustrated by cartoons. I was genuinely shocked. If he'd written those poems to me, maybe everything would have been different. Maybe I would have realized what a self-obsessed weirdo he was *before* we got married.

"Well." He shrugs again. "Perhaps I have more of a long-term view. Maybe you're too close."

Too close? How can I be too close to my own divorce? Who is this rubber-faced, emotionally stunted idiot, and how did he get into my life? I'm breathing so fast with frustration, I feel like if I rose from my desk now, I could give Usain Bolt a run for his money.

And then it happens. I don't exactly *mean* for it to happen. My wrist moves sharply and it's done, and there are six little ink spots in a trail on his shirt and a bubble of happiness inside my chest.

"What was that?" Daniel looks down at his shirt and then up, his face aghast. "Is that ink? Did you just *flick your pen at me*?"

I glance at Noah to see if he witnessed his mother's descent into infantile behavior. But he's lost in the far more mature world of *Captain Underpants*.

"It slipped," I say innocently.

"It slipped. Are you five years old?" His

face crumples into a scowl and he dabs at his shirt, smearing one of the ink spots. "I could call my lawyer about this."

"You could discuss parental responsibility, your favorite subject."

"Funny."

"It's not." My mood suddenly sobers. I'm tired of playing tit for tat. "It's really not." I look at our son, who is bent over his book, shaking with laughter at something. His shorts are rucked up, and on his knee is a face drawn in ballpoint pen with an arrow pointing to it and *I AM A SUPERHERO* printed in wobbly letters. How can Daniel bail out on him like this? He hasn't seen him for a fortnight; he never calls to chat with him. It's as if Noah is a hobby that he bought all the equipment for and reached an elementary level — but then decided he's just not that into after all and maybe he should have gone for wall-climbing instead.

"It's really not," I repeat. "I think you should go."

I don't even look up as he departs. I draw his stupid pile of papers to me, flick through them, too angry to read a word, then open a document on my computer and type furiously:

D arrives at office, leaving N with me

with no notice, contravening agreement. Unhelpful manner. Wishes to raise more points regarding divorce settlement. Refuses to discuss reasonably.

I unclip my memory stick from its place on a chain round my neck and save the updated file to it. My memory stick is my comfort blanket. The whole dossier is on there: the whole sorry Daniel story. I replace it round my neck, then speed-dial Barnaby, my lawyer.

"Barnaby, you won't believe it," I say as soon as his voicemail answers. "Daniel wants to revisit the settlement *again.* Can you call me back?"

Then I glance anxiously at Noah to see if he heard me. But he's chortling over something in his book. I'll have to hand him over to my PA; she's helped me out with emergency childcare before.

"Come on." I stand up and ruffle his hair. "Let's find Elise."

The thing about avoiding people at parties is, it's quite easy if you're hosting. You always have an excuse to move away from the conversation just as you see a forty-inch pink-striped shirt bearing down on you. (*So* sorry, I *must* greet the marketing manager of the Mandarin Oriental, back in a moment. . . .)

The party has been going for half an hour and I've managed to avoid the Gruffalo completely. It helps that he's so massive and the atrium is so crowded. I've made it appear totally natural that every time he gets within three feet I'm striding away in the opposite direction, or out of the room completely, or, in desperation, into the Ladies'. . . .

Damn. As I emerge from the Ladies', he's waiting for me. Gunter Bachmeier is actually standing in the corridor, staking out the door of the Ladies'.

"Oh, hello, Gunter," I say smoothly. "How delightful to see you. I've been meaning to catch up with you —"

"You hef been avoiding me," he says in severe guttural tones.

"Nonsense! Are you enjoying the party?" I force myself to put a hand on his meaty forearm.

"You hef traduced my new hotel."

He pronounces "traduced" with a rich, rolling sound. "Trrrraduced." I'm quite impressed that he knows the word. I certainly wouldn't know the equivalent for "traduced" in German. My German extends to "Taxi, *bitte*?"

"Gunter, you're overreacting." I smile pleasantly. "A four-star review is hardly . . . traducement." Traduction? Traducedom? "I'm sorry that my reviewer found herself unable to allot you five stars —"

"You hef not reviewed my hotel yourself." He's bristling with anger. "You hef sent an amateur. You hef treated me with disrrrre-spect!"

"No, I hef not!" I retort before I can stop myself. "I mean hev. Have." My face is flaming. "Have not."

I didn't mean to do that; I just have a terrible parrot habit. I mimic voices and accents without intending to. Now Gunter is glaring at me even more viciously.

"Everything all right, Felicity?" Gavin, our publisher, comes bustling up. I can see his radar twitching and I know why. Last year, the Gruffalo shelled out for twenty-four double-page spreads. The Gruffalo is keeping us in business. But I can't give his hotel a five-star review simply because he bought some ads. A five-star review in *Pincher Travel Review* is a very big deal.

"I was just explaining to Gunter that I sent one of our top freelancers to review his hotel," I say. "I'm sorry he wasn't happy, but —"

"You should hef gone yourrrself." Gunter

70

spits the words dismissively. "Wherrrre is your crrrredibility, Felicity? Wherrre is your rrrreputation?"

As he stalks off, I secretly feel a bit shaken. As I lift my eyes to Gavin, my heart is pumping.

"Well!" I try to sound lighthearted. "What an overreaction."

"Why didn't you cover the Palm Stellar?" Gavin is frowning. "You review all major launches. That's always been the deal."

"I decided to send Celia Davidson," I say brightly, avoiding the question. "She's a great writer."

"Why didn't you cover the Palm Stellar?" he repeats, as though he hasn't heard me.

"I had some stuff going on with . . . with . . ." I clear my throat, unwilling to say the word. "Some personal stuff."

I watch as Gavin suddenly comprehends. "Your divorce?"

I can't bring myself to answer. I twist my watch round my wrist, as though suddenly interested in the mechanism.

"Your divorce?" His voice sharpens ominously. *"Again?"*

My cheeks are burning with embarrassment. I know my divorce has taken on epic, *Lord of the Rings*–style proportions. I know it's taken up more of my working time than

71

it should have. I know I keep promising Gavin that it's all done and dusted.

But it's not like I have a choice. And it's not like it's *fun.*

"I was talking to a specialist barrister based in Edinburgh," I admit at last. "I had to fly up there; his schedule was really busy —"

"Felicity." Gavin beckons me to one side of the corridor, and at the sight of his tight-lipped smile, my stomach turns over. That's the smile he wears to cut salaries and budgets and tell people their magazine is unfortunately being axed, could they please leave the building? "Felicity, no one could be more sympathetic to your plight than me. You know that."

He's such a liar. What does he know about divorce? He has a wife and a mistress, and neither of them seems to mind about the other.

"Thank you, Gavin," I feel obliged to say.

"But you cannot let your divorce get in the way of your job or the reputation of Pincher International," he raps out. "Under-stand?"

Suddenly, for the first time, I feel genu-inely nervous. I know from experience that Gavin starts invoking the "reputation of Pincher International" when he's thinking of firing someone. It's a warning.

I also know from experience, the only way to deal with him is to refuse to admit anything.

"Gavin." I draw myself up as tall as possible and affect a dignified air. "Let me make one thing *quite* clear." I pause, as though I'm David Cameron at Prime Minister's Questions. "*Quite* clear. If there's one thing I never, *ever* do, it's let my personal life compromise my job. In fact —"

"Pow!" An earsplitting shriek interrupts me. "Laser attack!"

My blood freezes. That can't be —

Oh *no.*

A familiar *rat-a-tat* sound assaults my ears. Orange plastic bullets are shooting through the air, hitting people in the face and landing in glasses of champagne. Noah is running down the corridor toward the atrium, laughing uproariously and firing all around him with his automatic Nerf gun. Fuck. Why didn't I check his backpack?

"Stop!" I launch myself at Noah, grab him by the collar, and snatch the plastic gun out of his hands. "Stop that! Gavin, I'm *so* sorry," I add breathlessly. "Daniel was supposed to look after Noah tonight, but he left me in the lurch, and — Shit! Argh!"

In my agitation, I've pressed some button

73

on the Nerf gun, and it's spraying more bullets out, like something out of *Reservoir Dogs,* hitting Gavin in the chest. *I'm massacring my boss with an automatic weapon* flashes through my mind. *This won't look good in my appraisal.* The stream of bullets rises to his face and he splutters in horror.

"Sorry!" I drop the gun on the floor. "I didn't mean to shoot. . . ."

With a shudder, I notice Gunter, ten feet away. There are three orange Nerf bullets lodged in his tufty white hair and one in his drink.

"Gavin." I swallow. "Gavin. I don't know what to say —"

"It was my fault," Elise interrupts me hastily. "I was looking after Noah."

"But he shouldn't have been at the office," I point out. "So it's *my* fault."

We turn to Gavin as though waiting for his verdict. He's just staring at the scene, shaking his head.

"Personal life. Job." He meshes his hands together. "Fliss, you need to sort yourself out."

My face is hot with mortification as I frog-march a protesting Noah to my office.

"But I was *winning!*" he keeps complaining.

"I'm sorry." Elise is clutching her head.

"He said it was his favorite game."

"No problem." I shoot her a smile. "Noah, we don't play with Nerf guns at Mummy's office. *Ever.*"

"I'll go and find him something to eat," says Elise. "Fliss, you need to get back to the party, quick. Go. Now. It'll be fine. C'mon, Noah."

She hustles Noah out of the room and I feel every cell of my body sag.

She's right. I need to hurry back, sweep in, gather up the Nerf bullets, apologize, charm, and turn this evening back into the slick professional affair it always is.

But I'm so *tired.* I feel like I could go to sleep right now. The carpet under my desk looks like the perfect place for me to curl up.

I sink down on my chair, just as the phone rings. I'll take this one call. Maybe it will be some uplifting piece of news.

"Hello?"

"Felicity? Barnaby here."

"Oh, Barnaby." I sit up, feeling freshly galvanized. "Thanks for ringing back. You won't believe what Daniel just did. He'd agreed to have Noah tonight, but then he left me in the lurch. And now he says he wants to revisit the settlement! We might end up back in court!"

"Fliss, calm down. Chill out." Barnaby's unhurried Mancunian tones greet me. I do often wish Barnaby spoke a bit more quickly. Especially as I'm paying him by the hour. "We'll sort it. Don't worry."

"He's so *frustrating.*"

"I hear you. But you mustn't stress. Try to forget about it."

Is he kidding?

"I've written the incident up. I can email it to you." I finger my memory stick on its chain. "Shall I do that now?"

"Fliss, I've told you, you don't need to keep a dossier of every single incident."

"But I want to! I mean, talk about 'unreasonable behavior.' If we put all this into the case, if the judge *knew* what he was like —"

"The judge does know what he's like."

"But —"

"Fliss, you're having the Divorce Fantasy," says Barnaby tranquilly. "What have I told you about the Divorce Fantasy?"

There's silence. I hate the way Barnaby can read my mind. I've known him since college, and although he costs a bomb even on mates' rates, I never considered going to anyone else. Now he's waiting for me to answer, like a teacher in class.

"The Divorce Fantasy will never happen," I mumble finally, staring at my fingernails.

"The Divorce Fantasy will never happen," he repeats with emphasis. "The judge will never read a two-hundred-page dossier on Daniel's shortcomings aloud in court, while a crowd jeers at your ex-husband. He will never start his summing up, 'Ms. Graveney, you are a saint to have put up with such an evil scumbag and I thus award you everything you want.' "

I can't help coloring. That is pretty much my Divorce Fantasy. Except in my version, the crowd throws bottles at Daniel too.

"Daniel will never admit to being wrong," Barnaby presses on relentlessly. "He'll never stand in front of the judge, weeping and saying, 'Fliss, please forgive me.' The papers will never report your divorce with the headline: TOTAL SHIT ADMITS FULL SHITTINESS IN COURT."

I can't help half-snorting with laughter. "I do know that."

"Do you, Fliss?" Barnaby sounds skeptical. "Are you sure about that? Or are you still expecting him to wake up one day and realize all the bad things he's done? Because you have to understand, Daniel will never realize anything. He'll never confess to being a terrible human being. I could spend a thousand hours on this case, it would still never happen."

"But it's so unfair." I can feel a ball of frustration. "He *is* a terrible human being."

"I know. He's a shit. So don't dwell on him. Flush him out of your life. Gone."

"It's not as easy as that," I mutter after a pause. "He is the father of my child."

"I know," says Barnaby more gently. "I didn't say it was easy."

There's silence for a while. I stare at my office clock, watching the crappy plastic hand tick round. At last I slump right down, resting my head in the crook of my elbow.

"God, divorce."

"Divorce, eh," says Barnaby. "Man's greatest invention."

"I wish I could just . . . I dunno." I sigh heavily. "Wave a magic wand and our marriage never happened. Except Noah. I'd keep Noah and the rest would all be a bad dream."

"You want an annulment, that's what you want," says Barnaby cheerfully.

"An annulment?" I stare at the phone suspiciously. "Is that a real thing?"

"Real enough. It means the contract is null and void. The marriage never existed. You'd be amazed how many clients ask for one."

"Could I get one?"

I'm seized by this idea. Maybe there's

78

some cheap, easy way round this I haven't seen before. "Annulment." Null and void. I like the sound of that a *lot.* Why didn't Barnaby mention this before?

"Not unless Daniel was a bigamist," says Barnaby. "Or forced you into marriage. Or you never consummated it. Or one of you was mentally unfit at the time."

"Me!" I say at once. "I was crazy to even *think* of marrying him."

"That's what they all say." He laughs. "Won't wash, I'm afraid."

My spark of hope slowly dies away. Damn. I wish Daniel *had* been a bigamist now. I wish some original wife in a Mormon bonnet would pop up and say, *I got there first!* and save me all this trouble.

"I guess we'll have to stick with the divorce," I say at last. "Thanks, Barnaby. I'd better go before you charge me another thirty thousand pounds just for saying hi."

"Quite right." Barnaby never sounds remotely offended, whatever I say. "But before you do, you're still going to France, right?"

"Yes, tomorrow."

Noah and I are heading off for two weeks to the Côte d'Azur. As far as he's concerned, it's our Easter holiday. As far as I'm concerned, I'm reviewing three hotels, six restaurants, and a theme park. I'll be working on my laptop every night till late, but I can't complain.

"I contacted my old mate Nathan Forrester. The one I told you about? Based in Antibes? You two should meet up while you're there, have a drink."

"Oh." I feel my spirits lift. "OK. That sounds fun."

"I'll email you the details. He's a nice guy. Plays too much poker, but don't hold that against him."

A poker-playing resident of the South of France. Sounds intriguing. "I won't. Thanks, Barnaby."

"My pleasure. Bye, Fliss."

I put the phone down and it immediately rings again. Barnaby must have forgotten some point or other.

"Hi, Barnaby?"

There's silence, except for some rather fast, rather heavy breathing. Hmm. Has Barnaby inadvertently pressed *redial* while snogging his secretary? But even as I'm thinking this, I know who it is really. I recognize that breathing. And I can hear Macy Gray's "I Try" faintly in the background: a classic Lottie breakup soundtrack.

"Hello?" I try again. "Lottie? Is that you?"

There's more heavy breathing, this time raspy.

"Lottie? Lotts?"

"Oh, Fliss . . ." She erupts into a massive sob. "I really, really thought he was going to propooooooose. . . ."

"Oh God. Oh, Lottie." I cradle the phone, wishing it was her. "Lottie, sweetheart —"

"I spent three whole years with him and I thought he loved me and wanted babeeeeees. . . . But he didn't! He didn't!" She's crying as bitterly as Noah does when he scrapes his knee. "And what am I going to do now? I'm thirty-threeeee. . . ." Now she's hiccuping.

"Thirty-three is nothing," I say quickly. "Nothing! And you're beautiful and you're lovely —"

"I even bought him a riiiiiing."

She bought him a ring? I stare at the phone. Did I hear that right? *She* bought *him* a ring?

"What kind of ring?" I can't help asking. I imagine her presenting Richard with some sparkly sapphire in a box.

Please don't say she presented him with a sparkly sapphire in a box.

"Just, you know." She sniffs defensively. "A ring. A manly engagement ring."

A manly engagement ring? No. Uh-uh.

81

Doesn't exist.

"Lotts," I begin tactfully. "Are you sure Richard is the engagement-ring type? I mean, could *that* have put him off?"

"It was nothing to do with the ring!" She erupts into sobs again. "He never even saw the ring! I wish I'd never bought the bloody thing! But I thought it would be fair! Because I thought he'd bought one for meeeeeeee!"

"OK!" I say hastily. "Sorry!"

"It's fine." She calms down a little. "*I'm* sorry. I don't mean to have a meltdown. . . ."

"Don't be silly. What else am I here for?"

It's awful to hear her so upset. Of course it is. Ghastly. But secretly I can't help feeling a bit relieved too. The façade is down. Her denial has cracked. This is *good*. This is *progress*.

"Anyway, I've decided what to do, and I feel so much better. It's all fallen into place, Fliss." She blows her nose noisily. "I feel like I have a purpose. A plan. A goal."

My ears twitch. Uh-oh. A "goal." That's one of my post-breakup alarm-bell terms. Along with "project," "change of direction," and "amazing new friend."

"Right," I say cautiously. "Great! So . . . um . . . what's your goal?"

My mind is already scurrying around the

possibilities. Please not another piercing. Or another crazy property purchase. I've talked her out of quitting her job so many times, it *can't* be that again, surely?

Please not move to Australia.

Please not "lose a stone." Because 1) she's skinny already, and 2) last time she went on a diet, she made me be her "buddy" and instructed me to phone up every half hour and say, "Keep to the plan, you fat bitch," then complained when I refused.

"So, what is it?" I press her as lightly as I can, my entire body screwed up with dread.

"I'm going to fly to San Francisco on the first flight I can get and surprise Richard and propose!"

"What?" I nearly drop the phone. "No! Bad idea!"

What's she planning to do, burst into his office? Wait on his doorstep? Kneel down and present him with the so-called "manly" engagement ring? I can't let this happen. She'll be utterly humiliated and devastated and *I'll* have to pick up the pieces afterward.

"But I love him!" She sounds totally hyper. "I love him so much! And if he can't see that we're meant to be together, then surely I have to *show* him! Surely it has to be *me* who makes the move! I'm on the Virgin Atlantic website right now. Should I

83

get premium economy? Can you get me a discount?"

"No! Do *not* book a flight to San Francisco," I say in the firmest, most authoritative tones I can muster. "Close down your computer. Step away from the internet."

"But —"

"Lottie, face it," I say more gently. "Richard had his chance. If he'd wanted to get married, it would be happening."

I know what I'm saying sounds harsh. But it's true. Men who want to get married propose. You don't need to read the signs. They propose and that's the sign.

"But he just doesn't *realize* he wants to get married!" she says eagerly. "He just needs *persuading.* If I just gave him a little *nudge . . .*"

Little nudge? Bloody great elbow in the ribs, more like.

I have a sudden vision of Lottie dragging Richard up the aisle by his hair, and I wince. I know exactly where that story ends up. It ends up in the office of Barnaby Rees, Family Lawyer, at five hundred quid for the first consultation.

"Lottie, listen," I say severely. "And listen hard. You don't want to go into a marriage anything less than two hundred percent sure it's going to work out. No, make that *six*

84

hundred percent." I eye Daniel's latest divorce demands morosely. "Believe me. It's not worth it. I've been there and it's . . . Well, it's hideous."

There's silence at the other end of the phone. I know Lottie so well. I can practically *see* her hearts-and-flowers image of proposing to Richard on the Golden Gate Bridge melting away.

"Think about it first, at least," I say. "Don't jump in. A few weeks won't make any difference."

I'm holding my breath, crossing my fingers.

"OK," says Lottie at last, sounding forlorn. "I'll think about it."

I blink in astonishment. I've done it. I've actually done it! For the first time in my life, I've headed off one of Lottie's Unfortunate Choices before it even happened. I've stamped out the infection before it could take hold.

Maybe she's getting more rational in her old age.

"Let's go out to lunch," I suggest, to cheer her up. "My treat. As soon as I get back from holiday."

"Yes, that would be nice," says Lottie in a small voice. "Thanks, Fliss."

"Take care. Talk soon."

She rings off and I exhale my frustration in a groan — although I'm not sure who I'm most frustrated with. Richard? Daniel? Gavin? Gunter? All men? No, not *all* men. Maybe all men except various honorable exceptions, viz: Barnaby; my lovely milkman, Neville; the Dalai Lama, obviously —

My eyes suddenly focus on my reflection in my computer screen and I lean forward in horror. I have a Nerf bullet stuck in my hair.

Great.

3
LOTTIE

I didn't sleep all night.

People say that, and what they mean is: I woke up a few times, made a cup of tea, and went back to bed. But I *really* didn't sleep all night. I counted every hour going past.

By one A.M. I'd decided that Fliss is totally, utterly wrong. By one-thirty I'd found myself a flight to San Francisco. By two A.M. I'd written the perfect, loving, and passionate proposal speech, including lines by Shakespeare, Richard Curtis, and Take That. By three A.M. I'd filmed myself making it (eleven takes). By four A.M. I'd watched myself and realized the horrible truth: Fliss is right. Richard will never say yes. He'll just get freaked out. Especially if I make that speech. By five A.M. I'd eaten all the Pralines & Cream. By six A.M. I'd eaten all the Phish Food. And now I'm slumped on a plastic chair, feeling nauseous and regretting the lot of it.

A tiny part of me still wonders if by walking out on Richard I made the biggest mistake of my life. If I'd hung on, bitten my tongue and never mentioned marriage, might our relationship have worked out? Somehow?

But the rest of me is more rational. People say that women work on intuition and men on logic, but they're talking rubbish. I studied logic at university, thank you very much. I *know* how it goes. A=B, B=C, therefore A=C. And what could be more logical than the following detached and succinct argument?

Premise one: Richard has no intention of proposing to me; he made that fairly clear.

Premise two: I want marriage and commitment and, hopefully, one day, a baby.

Conclusion: Therefore I am not destined to be with Richard. Therefore I need to be with someone else.

Other conclusion: Therefore I did the right thing, breaking up with him.

Further conclusion: Therefore I need to find another man, who *does* want to make a life with me and *doesn't* get that wide-eyed, starey look at the very mention of marriage, like it's such a terrifying idea. Someone who realizes that if someone spends three years with you, maybe they *are* thinking of commitment and kids and a dog, and . . . and . . . decorating a Christmas tree together . . . and why is that such a bad thing? Why is it so totally and utterly off the agenda and unmentionable? When everyone says we're such a great couple and we've been so happy together, and even your own *mother* was hinting that we might end up living near them, Richard?

OK, so maybe not that succinct. Or detached.

I take a sip of coffee, trying to soothe my nerves. Let's say I'm being as calm and logical as one could expect in the circumstances, which are that I had to catch the 7:09 to Birmingham on no sleep and all the *Metro*s had already gone. And I'm about to give a recruitment talk to a hundred students in an auditorium that smells of cauliflower cheese.

I'm with my colleague Steve, in the "backstage" room to the side of the auditorium, and he's sitting hunched over his coffee, looking about as perky as I feel. We do a lot of these recruitment talks together, Steve and I, in fact we're quite the double act. He does the science side; I do the general stuff. The idea is, he blows away all the students with how cutting edge our research-and-development department is. And I reassure them that they'll get looked after and their career will be an exciting one and they're not selling out.

"Biscuit?" Steve offers me a chocolate bourbon.

"No, thanks." I shudder. I've already crammed enough trans fats and food additives into my body.

Maybe I should go to some hard-core boot camp. Everyone says running changes their life and gives them a new outlook. I should go to some retreat where all you do is run and drink isotonic drinks. In the mountains. Or the desert. Something really tough and challenging.

Or do Iron Woman. *Yes.*

I reach for my BlackBerry and am about to Google *hardcore running camp iron woman* when the careers officer appears round the door. We haven't been to this particular college before, so I hadn't met Deborah before today. Quite frankly, she's weird. I've never met anyone so tense and jumpy.

"All OK? We'll start in about ten minutes. Keep it quite brief, I would." She's nodding nervously. "Quite brief. Nice and brief."

"We're happy to chat to the students afterward," I say, hefting a pile of "Why Work at Blay Pharmaceuticals?" brochures out of my canvas bag.

"Right." Her eyes are darting about. "Well . . . as I say, I'd keep it nice and brief."

I feel tempted to snap at her, *We've come all the way from London for this!* For God's sake. Most careers officers are *delighted* we'll take questions.

"So, normal pattern?" I say to Steve. "Me, you, clip one, me, you, clip two, questions?" He nods, and I hand the DVD to Deborah. "I'll cue you. It'll be pretty obvious."

The recruitment DVD is the worst bit about our presentation. It was shot like a 1980s music video, with bad lighting and bad electronic music and people with bad haircuts looking awkward as they pretend to have a meeting. But it cost a hundred grand, so we have to use it.

Deborah disappears to set up the DVD and I lean back in my chair, trying to relax. But my hands keep twisting together. I don't know what's wrong with me. Everything feels so crap. Where am I going in life? Where am I heading? What am I doing?

And this is *not* about Richard, by the way. It's absolutely unrelated. It's simply my life. I need . . . I don't know. A new direction. A different energy.

There's a book lying on a nearby chair and I reach for it. It's called *The Reverse*

Principle: Change Your Business Strategy Forever, and *10 million copies sold!!* is stamped across the cover.

I feel a stab of frustration at myself. Why don't I read more business books? *This* is where my life has gone wrong. I haven't put enough effort into my career. I flip through, trying to absorb the information as quickly as I can. There are lots of diagrams with arrows traveling one way, then flipping over and going the opposite way. Clearly the message is: reverse the arrow. Well, I got that in about two seconds. I must be a natural.

Maybe I should read all these books and become an expert. Maybe I should go to Harvard Business School. I have a sudden image of myself in a library, cramming my brain full of business principles. Coming back to England to run a FTSE 100 company. My world would be one of ideas and strategy. Cerebral, high-level thought.

I'm just Googling *Harvard overseas students* when Deborah reappears.

"So, the students should be assembled by now," she gulps, sounding desperate.

"Oh, OK." I drag my attention back to her. What on earth is her *problem*? Maybe she's new. Maybe this is her first-ever recruitment presentation and that's why she's so twitchy.

I refresh my lip gloss, trying to avoid the sight of my bloodshot eyes. Looking suicidal, Deborah disappears through the double doors onto the stage. I can hear her indistinct voice rising above the hubbub. After a few moments there's a round of applause, and I nudge Steve, who's just bitten into a croissant. Typical.

"Come on! We're on!"

As I stride onto the little stage and see our audience, I can't help doing a double take.

Recruiting for a science company, you get used to students who shamble in, hair unwashed, unshaved, with bags under their eyes. But this lot are stunning. There's a whole cluster of immaculate girls at the front, with long shiny hair, manicured nails, and full makeup. Behind them is a group of super-fit guys, their T-shirts bulging with muscles. I can't speak for astonishment. What kind of labs do they have here? Ones with treadmills incorporated?

"They look great!" I murmur encouragingly to Deborah. "Top marks for presentation."

"Well . . . we do advise them to make an effort," she says, reddening before she hurries off. I glance over at Steve, who is peering at the beautiful girls as if he can hardly believe his luck.

"Welcome, everyone!" I head to the front of the stage. "Thanks for coming today. My name is Lottie Graveney, and I'm here to talk to you about choosing a career at Blay Pharmaceuticals. You'll know us best for the range of global brands we sell at the pharmacy, from our Placidus range of painkillers to our bestselling Sincero baby cream. But a career with us is so much more than that —"

"It's an *exciting* career." Steve practically elbows me out of the way. "Yes, it'll challenge you, but it'll *thrill* you. We're working right at the edge of pioneering research and we want to take you on that roller coaster with us."

I glare at him. He's *tragic*. First of all, that's not the script. Second, where has that fake "sexy" voice come from? Third, he's now rolling up his sleeves, as though he's some sort of rugged, pharmaceutical-research version of Indiana Jones. He really shouldn't. His forearms are all white and veiny.

"If you want an adventure in life . . ." He pauses for effect and practically growls, "Then this is the place to start."

He's homed in on a girl in the front row,

94

whose white shirt is unbuttoned to reveal a deep, tanned cleavage. She has long blond hair and big blue eyes and seems to be scribbling down every word he's saying.

"Let's show the DVD, Steve," I say brightly, dragging him away before he actually drools over her. The lights dim and our first DVD clip starts rolling on the screen behind us.

"Bright lot," whispers Steve as he sits down beside me. "I'm impressed."

Impressed by what? Her bra size?

"You can't know if they're bright yet," I point out. "We haven't talked to them."

"You can see it in the eyes," Steve says airily. "I've been at this game long enough to know potential when I see it. That fair-haired girl in the front row looks very promising. *Very* promising. We should talk to her about the scholarship program. Scoop her up before any of the other pharmaceutical companies get to her."

For God's sake. He'll be offering her a six-figure contract next.

"We'll give them *all* information about the scholarship program," I say severely. "And maybe you could try not to address every remark to her boobs?"

The lights come up and Steve strides center stage, pushing his sleeves up still farther, as though he's about to split some lumber and single-handedly construct a cabin with it.

"Let me share with you a few of the newest advances we've made and those we hope to make in the future. Maybe with your help." He twinkles at the blond girl, and she smiles back politely.

Onto the screen comes a picture of a complicated molecule.

"You'll all be familiar with onium-poly hydrogen fluorides. . . ." Steve gestures at the screen with a pointer, then stops. "Before I continue, it would be useful to know what you're studying." He looks around. "There'll be biochemists here, obviously —"

"It doesn't matter what they study!" Deborah cuts him off sharply before anyone can answer. To my surprise, she's leapt up out of her seat and is heading toward the stage. "It doesn't matter what they study, surely?"

She's as tense as a spring. What's going on?

"It's just a useful guide," explains Steve. "If all the biochemists could raise their hands —"

"But you take students from all subjects." She cuts him off. "You say so in your materials. So it's irrelevant, surely?"

96

She looks panicky. I *knew* something was wrong.

"Any biochemists at all?" Steve is looking at the silent room, baffled. Normally, at least half our audience is biochemists.

Deborah is ashen. "Could we have a word?" she says at last, and beckons us desperately to one side. "I'm afraid . . ." Her voice trembles. "There was an error. I sent the email to the wrong set of students."

So that's it. She's left out the biochemists. What an idiot. But she looks so upset, I decide to be kind.

"We're very open-minded," I say reassuringly. "We're not only interested in biochemists. We also recruit graduates in physics, biology, business studies. . . . What are these students studying?"

There's silence. Deborah is furiously chewing her lips.

"Beauty," she mutters at last. "Most are trainee makeup artists. And some are dancers."

Makeup artists and dancers?

I'm so flummoxed I can't reply. No wonder they're all so stunning and fit. I catch a glimpse of Steve — and he looks so gutted I suddenly want to giggle.

"That's a shame," I say innocently. "Steve thought this seemed a very promising bunch. He wanted to offer them all scientific research scholarships. Didn't you, Steve?"

Steve scowls evilly at me and rounds on Deborah. "What the *fuck* is going on? Why are we giving a lecture on a career in pharmaceutical research to a room full of bloody makeup artists and dancers?"

"I'm sorry!" Deborah looks like she wants to weep. "By the time I realized what I'd done, it was too late. I've been set a target of attracting more blue-chip companies, and you're such a prestigious firm, I couldn't bear to cancel —"

"Does *anyone* here want to work in pharmaceutical research?" Steve addresses the room.

No one raises their hand. I don't know if I want to laugh or cry. I got up at six A.M. to be here. Not that I'd been asleep, but still.

"So what are you *doing* here?" Steve sounds like he's going to explode.

"We have to go to ten career seminars to get our career-search credit," says a girl with a bobbing ponytail.

"Jesus Christ." Steve picks up his jacket from his chair. "I do *not* have time for this." As he stalks out of the auditorium, I feel like doing the same thing myself. I've never met anyone as incompetent as Deborah in my life.

But, on the other hand, there's still a roomful of students watching me. They all still need a career, even if it's not in pharmaceutical research. And I've come all the way from London. I'm not just turning round and going home.

"OK." I take the remote from Deborah, flip off the DVD, and walk center stage. "Let's start again. I don't work in the beauty industry or the dance industry. So there's not much point me advising you on that. But I *do* employ people. So, how about I try to give some general advice? Do you have any questions for me?"

There's silence. Then a girl in a leather jacket hesitantly lifts her hand.

"Could you look at my CV and tell me if it's any good?"

"Of course. Good idea. Anyone else want me to look at theirs?"

A forest of arms shoots up. I've never seen such a well-manicured selection of hands in my life.

"OK. Form a line. That's what we'll do."

Two hours later, I've scanned the CVs of about thirty students. (If Deborah is their CV adviser, then Deborah should be fired. That's all I'm saying.) I've done a Q and A session on pensions and tax returns and self-employment law. I've shared all the advice I think might help these guys. And in return I've learned a lot about many areas I was totally ignorant of, such as: 1) How you make someone look wounded in a movie; 2) which actress currently filming in London seems really sweet but is actually a total bitch to her makeup artist; and 3) how you do a *grand jeté* (I failed on that one).

Now I've opened the floor to any subject at all, and a pale girl with pink streaky hair is speaking about the cost of shellac and how difficult it is to make the margins work if you want to open your own salon. I'm listening and trying to make helpful comments, but my attention keeps being drawn to another girl, sitting in the second row. Her eyes are red-rimmed and she hasn't said a word, but she keeps fingering her phone and blowing her nose and dabbing her tissue to her eyes.

There was one moment during the Q and A when I could have done with a tissue myself. I was talking about vacation benefits, and it brought all my anguish back in a whoosh. I'd been saving up vacation myself. Three weeks' worth. I thought I'd be needing it for a honeymoon. I'd even found this amazing place in St. Lucia —

No, Lottie. *Don't* go there. Move on. Move

on, move on. I blink hard and refocus on the girl with pink hair.

". . . do you think I should focus on brows?" she's saying, looking anxious.

Oh God, I wasn't listening properly. How did we get on to brows? I'm about to ask her to recap her main points for the benefit of the room (always a good way out) when the girl in the second row gives a massive sob. I can't ignore her anymore.

"Hi," I say gently, waving to attract her attention. "Excuse me. Are you OK?"

"Cindy's had a breakup." Her friend puts a protective arm round her. "Can she be excused?"

"Of course!" I say. "Absolutely!"

"But will she still get the credit?" chimes in another friend anxiously. "Because she's already failed one module."

"It's all *his* fault," says the first friend viciously, and about ten girls nod in agreement, murmuring things like "It *so* is" and "Tosser" and "He can't do a smoky eye."

"We were together for two years." The pale girl gives another sob. "Two whole years. I did half his coursework for him. And now he's all like, 'I need to focus on my career.' I thought he wanted to be with meeee. . . ." She dissolves into prolonged weeping and I stare at her, tears starting to my eyes. I know her pain. I *know* it.

"Of course you'll get the credit," I say warmly. "In fact, I'll give you a special mention for turning up when you're clearly in mental distress."

"Will you?" Cindy gives me a watery smile. "Will you really?"

"But you have to listen to me, OK? You have to listen to me."

I'm feeling a gathering urge to speak off-topic. To convey a universal truth, not about pensions, not about tax breaks, but about love. Or not-love. Or whatever limbo place we're both in. I know it's not in my remit, but this girl needs to know. She *needs* to know. My heart is beating strongly. I feel noble and inspirational, like Helen Mirren or Michelle Obama.

"Let me say one thing to you," I begin. "Woman to woman. Professional to professional. Human being to human being." My eyes fix on hers intently. "Don't let a breakup ruin your life." I feel so galvanized. I feel so sure of myself. I'm burning with my message. "You're strong." I tick off on my fingers. "You're independent. You have your own life, and you *don't need him.* OK?"

I wait until she whispers, "OK."

"We've all had breakups." I raise my voice to take in the whole room. "The answer isn't to cry. The answer isn't to eat chocolate or plot revenge. You need to move on. Every time I've had a breakup, do you know what I've done? I've taken my life in a new direction. I've found myself an exciting new project. I've changed my look. I've moved house. Because *I'm* in charge of my life, thank you." I pound my fist in my palm. "Not some guy who can't even do a smoky eye."

A couple of girls break into applause, and Cindy's friend whoops supportively. "That's what I said! He's a waste of space!"

"*No* more crying," I say for emphasis. "*No* more tissues. *No* more checking your phone to see if he's called. *No* more stuffing your face with chocolate. Move your life on. Fresh horizons. If I can do it, you can."

Cindy is gawping at me as though I'm a mind reader.

"But you're strong," she gulps at last. "You're amazing. I'm not like you. I never will be, even when I'm your age."

She's looking at me with such wonder, I can't help feeling touched, even though she doesn't have to behave as though I'm such a dinosaur. I mean, I'm only thirty-three, not a hundred.

"Of *course* you will," I say confidently. "You know, I was like you once. I was quite timid. I had no idea what I would do in life or what my potential was. I was an eighteen-year-old kid, floundering around." I can feel my All-Purpose Motivational Speech coming on. Do I have time to give it? I glance at my watch. Just about. The short version. "I was lost. Exactly like you feel now. But then I went on my gap year."

I've told this story many, many times. At student events, at team-building seminars, at preparation sessions for personnel going on sabbaticals. I never get bored of telling it, and it always gives me a tingle.

"I went on my gap year," I repeat, "and my whole life changed. I changed as a person. One pivotal night transformed me." I take a few steps forward and look directly at Cindy. "You know my theory of life? We all have special defining moments which set us on a path. I had my biggest defining moment on my gap year. You just need to have your own big moment. And you will."

"What happened?" She's agog, and so are all the others. I can even see someone switching off their iPod.

"I was staying at a guest house on Ikonos," I explain. "It's a Greek island. It was packed full of gap-year travelers, and I was there all summer. It was a magical place."

Every time I tell this story, it brings back

the same memories. Waking every morning to the Greek sun dazzling my eyelids. The feel of seawater on sunburned skin. Bikinis hung over peeling wooden shutters to dry. Sand in my trodden-down espadrilles. Fresh sardines grilled on the beach. Music and dancing every night.

"Anyway. One night there was a fire." I force myself back to the present. "It was terrible. The guest house was packed with people. I mean, it was a death trap. Everyone came out onto the upstairs veranda, but no one could get down; everyone was screaming; there weren't even any fire extinguishers. . . ."

Every time I remember that night, it's the same flashback: the moment the roof fell in. I can hear the thunderous sound and the screams. I can smell the smoke.

The room is utterly silent as I carry on.

"I had a vantage point. I was up in the tree house. I could see where people should be heading. You could jump off the side of the veranda onto the top of a nearby goat shed, only no one had realized. Everyone was panicking. So I took charge. I started directing people. I had to yell to be heard, and wave my arms, and jump up and down like a mad thing, but finally someone noticed me, and then they all listened. They

105

followed my instructions. They all jumped off the veranda onto the shed one by one, and they were all OK. It was the first time in my life that I realized I could be a leader. I could make a difference."

The room is absolutely still.

"Oh my God." Cindy exhales at last. "How many people?"

"Ten?" I shrug. "Twelve?"

"You saved twelve lives?" She sounds awe-struck.

"Well, who knows?" I try to lighten the atmosphere. "I'm sure they would have been saved anyway. The point is, I *realized* something about myself." I clasp my hands to my chest. "From that moment on, I had the confidence to go for what I wanted. I changed course, changed all my ideas. I can honestly say, it all dates from that point. That was my big defining moment. That was when I became the person I am. And you'll all have your defining moments. I know you will."

I always relive the moment and feel a little overcome when I tell that story. It was so terrifying. That's the bit I never put in: how scared and panicky I was, shrieking through the breeze, desperate to be heard, knowing it was all down to me. I blow my nose and smile around at the silent faces. *I made a*

106

difference. That mantra has stayed with me all these years. *I made a difference.* Whatever else I do that's crap and stupid, *I made a difference.*

There's silence in the room. Then the blond girl in the front row stands up.

"You're the best careers adviser we've ever had. Isn't she?" To my astonishment, she leads a round of applause. A couple of girls even cheer.

"I'm sure I'm not," I say hastily.

"Yes, you are," she insists. "You're ace. Can we say thank you properly?"

"You're absolutely welcome." I smile politely. "It's been a pleasure to be here, and good luck with your careers —"

"That's not what I mean." She approaches the platform, brandishing a massive black roll of brushes at me. "I'm Jo. Fancy a makeover?"

"Oh." I hesitate and glance at my watch. "I couldn't. I mean, that's very kind of you —"

"Don't take this personally," says Jo kindly. "But you need it. Your eyes are dead puffy. Did you get enough sleep last night?"

"Oh." I stiffen. "Yes. Yes, I did, thanks. Plenty of sleep. Loads."

"Well, you need some different eye cream, then. Whatever you're using really isn't working." She's peering closely at my face now. "And your nose is red. You haven't been . . . crying?"

"Crying?" I try not to sound too defensive. "Of course not!"

Jo has ushered me into a plastic chair and is gently patting the skin round my eyes. She sucks in breath, like a builder assessing someone else's dodgy plastering job.

"I'm sorry, but your skin's in a terrible state." She beckons over a couple of friends, who pull equally dismayed faces at the sight of my eyes.

"Ooh, that's painful."

"Your eyes are all pink!"

"Well, I've no idea why that is." I aim for an easy smile. "None. None at all."

"You must have an allergy to something!" says Jo in sudden inspiration.

"Yes." I seize on this idea. "That'll be it. An allergy."

"What makeup do you use? Can you show me?"

I reach for my bag and pull the zip open, but it's stuck.

"Let me," says Jo, and reaches for it before I can stop her. *Shit.* I don't particularly want anyone seeing the massive Galaxy bar I bought in WHSmith this morning and half consumed while waiting for Steve (moment of weakness).

"I'll do it," I say, grabbing it back. But her hand is already wrenching open the zip, and somehow the whole thing gets jostled and jerked, and before I know it the half-Galaxy has been tossed out of the bag, together with a mostly drunk miniature bottle of white wine (further moment of weakness). And the shreds of a ripped-up photo of Richard (even further moment of weakness).

"Sorry!" Jo says in horror, gathering the shreds. "I'm so sorry! What's —" She looks more closely. "Is that a photo? What *happened* to it?"

"Here's your chocolate," volunteers another girl, holding out the Galaxy.

"And I think this might be an old Valentine?" says her friend, gingerly picking up a charred piece of glittery card. "But it looks like it's been . . . burned?"

I did it with a match in a coffee cup in Costa before they told me to stop. (Ultimate moment of weakness.)

Richard's eye is staring at me out of a fragment of photo, and I feel my insides heave with sudden grief. I can detect a few meaningful looks passing between the girls, but I don't have any words. I can't find a noble and inspirational way out of this one. Jo

109

turns and surveys my bloodshot eyes again. Then she springs into life and starts stuffing all the things back into my bag.

"Anyway," she says briskly, "the *most* important thing is making you look totally fabulous. That'll show . . . whoever." She winks at me. "Or whatever. It might take a bit of time. Are you up for it?"

This is the answer. I don't know what the question is, but *this* is the answer. I'm sitting in a chair with my eyes closed, in a state of near bliss as my face is brushed and penciled by my new best friend Jo and her fellow students. They've sprayed my face with foundation and put rollers in my hair and they keep changing their mind about which eye look to give me, but I'm barely listening. I'm in a trance. I don't care if I'll be late back to the office. I'm zoned out. I keep drifting off to sleep and half waking up and my mind is a swirl of dream and color and thought.

Every time I find myself thinking of Richard, I wrench my mind away. Move on. Move on, move on. I'm going to be OK, I'm going to be fine. I just need to take my own advice. Find a new mission. A new track. Something to *focus* on.

Maybe I'll redecorate my flat. Or maybe I

should take up martial arts. I could start a course of intensive training and get superfit. Cut all my hair off and get amazing biceps like Hilary Swank.

Or pierce my belly button. Richard hates pierced belly buttons. That's what I should do.

Or maybe I should travel. Why have I not traveled more?

My thoughts keep drifting back to Ikonos. It *was* an amazing summer, until the fire happened and the police arrived and everything disbanded in chaos. I was so young. I was so *thin.* I lived in cutoff shorts and a string-bikini top. I had beads in my hair. And of course there was Ben, my first proper boyfriend. My first relationship. Dark hair and crinkly blue eyes and the smell of sweat and salt and Aramis. God, how much sex did we have? Three times a day, at least. And when we weren't having sex we were thinking about sex. It was insane. It was like a drug. He was the first guy I ever felt so hot for that I wanted to . . .

Wait. Wait a minute.

Ben?

My eyes pop open and Jo cries out in dismay. "Keep still!"

It couldn't be. Surely.

"Sorry." I blink, trying to stay composed.

111

"Actually . . . can we pause a moment? I need to make a call."

I turn away, rummage for my phone, and press Kayla's speed dial, telling myself not to be stupid. It can't be him. It's not him.

Obviously it's not him.

"Lottie, hi," comes Kayla's voice. "Everything OK?"

Why would he be phoning me after all this time? It's been fifteen years, for God's sake. We haven't been in touch since . . . Well. Since then.

"Hey, Kayla. I just wanted the number of that guy Ben." I try to sound relaxed. "The one who called yesterday while I was out, remember?"

Why am I clenching my fingers together?

"Oh yes. Hold on . . . Here we are." She dictates a mobile number. "Who is he?"

"I'm . . . not sure. You're positive he didn't give a surname?"

"No, just Ben."

I ring off and stare at the number. Just Ben. *Just Ben.*

It's a cheeky student candidate, I tell myself firmly. It's a careers officer who thinks we're on first-name terms. It's Ben Jones, my neighbor, ringing me at work for some reason. How many people are there in the world called Ben? About five zillion.

Precisely.

Just Ben.

But that's the thing. That's why my breath is coming just a little short and I'm instinctively sitting up straight in a more attractive manner. Who would call himself that *except* my old boyfriend?

I punch in the number, close my eyes tight, and wait. The ringing tone sounds. And again. And again.

"Benedict Parr." There's a pause. "Hello? It's Benedict Parr here. Is anyone there?"

I can't talk. My stomach is doing a little dance.

It's him.

4
LOTTIE

The first thing to say is that I look fabulous.

The second thing is, I am not going to sleep with him.

No. No, sirree. No, I am not.

Even though I've been thinking about it all day. Even though I've been gently fizzing just at the memory. Him. How it was. How we were. I feel surreal and a bit light-headed. I can't believe I'm going to see him. After all this time. Ben. I mean, *Ben.*

Hearing his voice was like some sort of time-travel trigger. At once I was sitting opposite him at that rickety little table we used to commandeer in the evening. Olive trees all around. My bare feet resting in his lap. A can of ice-cold Sprite. I'd forgotten about my Sprite addiction till that very instant.

Since then, memories and images have been resurfacing all day, some vague and some fully composed. His eyes. His scent. He was always so *intense.* That's what I remember most. His intensity. He made me feel as though we were starring in our own movie, as though nothing mattered except him and me and now. It was all about *sensation*. The sensation of him. Of sun and sweat. Sea and sand. Skin and skin. Everything was hot and heightened and . . . incredible.

And this, fifteen years later, this is — well. Bizarre. I glance at my watch and feel a little shiver of anticipation. Enough loitering in shop entrances. Time to go.

We're meeting at a new fish restaurant in Clerkenwell which has had good reviews. Apparently Ben works nearby, doing something or other — I didn't ask, which was stupid, so I had to resort to a hasty Google when I finally got back to the office. I couldn't track him down on Facebook, but there was some website about a paper company, which apparently he's a director of. I'm kind of surprised — he wanted to be an actor when we were together, but I guess it didn't work out. Or maybe he changed his mind. We didn't talk too much about careers or jobs back then. We were pretty much just interested in sex and how we were going to change the world.

I *do* remember lots of late-night discussions on Brecht, who he was reading, and

Chekhov, who I was reading. And global warming. And philanthropy. And politics. And euthanasia. We were a bit sixth-form debate-y, now that I look back. A bit earnest. But, then, fair enough. We'd only just left the sixth form.

I approach the restaurant, teetering a bit on my new high heels, feeling my hair bounce around my shoulders and admiring my immaculate manicure. As soon as Jo and her friends heard I was going on a date with an ex-boyfriend, they launched into a whole new level of activity. They did my nails. They dyed my brows. They even offered me a bikini wax.

Of course, I didn't need that. I'd already been to the salon three days ago, to get prepared for hot, joyous, post-proposal sex with Richard, much good it did me. *Total* waste of money.

I feel a painful, humiliated pang. I should invoice him for the salon bill. I should send it to him in San Francisco, together with a dignified letter saying simply, *Dear Richard. When you get this letter —*

No. Stop, Lottie. Do *not* think about Richard. Do *not* compose a dignified letter. Move on. Move on, move on.

I grip my clutch bag more tightly, willing strength into myself. Everything is meant. It all has a pattern. One minute I'm at my lowest ebb — the next, Ben is contacting me. It's kismet. It's fate.

Although I am *not* going to sleep with him. No. I'm not.

As I reach the entrance to the restaurant, I whip out my handbag mirror and check my reflection one last time. Bloody hell. I keep forgetting how amazing I look. My skin looks radiant. I have stunning new cheekbones, which Jo somehow invented with blusher and highlighter. My lips look fresh and luscious. To sum up: I'm gorgeous.

It's the opposite of that nightmare scenario where you bump into your ex-boyfriend, wearing only pajamas and a hangover. It's the dream scenario. I've never looked better in my life, and I'm fairly sure I never will again, not unless I hire ten makeup artists. This is my pinnacle, looks-wise.

With a sudden little burst of confidence, I push open the restaurant door, to be greeted by a warm, inviting smell of garlic and seafood. There are leather booths and a massive chandelier and the right kind of hubbub. Not show-offy and obnoxious but civilized and friendly. A mixologist is shaking a cocktail at the bar and I have an instant, Pavlovian desire for a mojito.

I'm not going to get drunk, I hastily

resolve. I'm not going to sleep with him *and* I'm not going to get drunk.

The maître d' is approaching me. Here goes.

"I'm here to meet a . . . a friend. He reserved a table. Benedict Parr?"

"Of course." The maître d' leads me a winding route through the restaurant, past about ten tables at which possible men are sitting with their faces averted. Each time, my stomach heaves with apprehension. Is that him? Is that him? Please not *that* one —

Oh God! I almost squeak. Here he is, rising from his chair. Stay cool. Smile. This is so, so, *so* surreal.

My eyes are running over him, registering details at top speed, as though I'm in the Assess Your Ex Olympics. Slightly odd patterned shirt; what's that about? He's taller than I remember. Thinner. His face is definitely thinner, and his dark wavy hair is short now. You'd never know that he once had Greek-god locks. There's a hole in his ear where his earring used to be.

"Well . . . hi there," I greet him.

I'm satisfied at the way I sound so understated. Especially since a bubble of excitement is growing inside me now that I've had a proper view. Look at him! He's gorgeous! Just like he always was, but better.

More grown-up. Less gawky.

He leans in for a kiss. A grown-up, civilized double kiss. Then he draws back and surveys me.

"Lottie. You look . . . incredible."

"You look pretty good yourself."

"You haven't aged a day!"

"Same goes!"

We're beaming at each other in a kind of amazed joy, like someone who's won a raffle and come up to collect a dodgy box of chocolates as a prize and found it's actually a thousand pounds in cash. We can't believe our luck.

I mean, let's face it, a lot can change in a man's twenties. Ben could have turned up looking like anything. He could have been bald. He could have been paunchy and stooped. He could have developed some kind of irritating tic.

And he's probably looking at me, thinking, *Thank* God *she hasn't had a trout pout put in/gone gray/gained sixty pounds.*

"So." He gestures charmingly at my chair and I sit down. "How have the last fifteen years been?"

"Fine, thanks." I laugh. "You?"

"Can't complain." He meets my eye with the same mischievous grin he always had. "OK, that's the catch-up done. You want a drink? *Don't* tell me you're teetotal now."

"Are you kidding?" I open the cocktail menu, feeling a sizzle of anticipation. This is going to be a great evening. I already know it. "Let's see what they've got."

Two hours later I'm buzzing all over. I'm exhilarated. I feel like a sportsman in the zone. I feel like a convert who's found religion. This is it. *This is it.* Ben and I are *amazing* together.

OK, so I haven't stuck to my resolution regarding alcohol. But that was a ridiculous, shortsighted, stupid resolution. Dinner with an ex-boyfriend is potentially quite a tense, sticky situation. This could have been awkward. As it is, with a few cocktails down me, I'm having the best evening of my life.

What's amazing is how *connected* Ben and I are. It's as though we've picked up exactly where we left off, as if the last decade and a half never happened. We're eighteen again. We're young and big-eyed. Sharing wild ideas and silly jokes and wanting to explore everything the world has to offer. Ben immediately started telling me about a play he'd seen the week before, and I countered with an art exhibition in Paris (I didn't mention that Richard took me), and our conversation has been flying since

120

then. There's so much to say. There are so many memories.

We haven't done the tedious list of who-what-when. We haven't exchanged job details, previous relationships, any of that boring crap. It's so refreshing not to hear the words "So, what do you do?" or "Is your flat a conversion or purpose built?" or "Do you get a pension?" It's so *liberating*.

I know he's single. He knows I'm single. That's the only update we needed.

Ben has drunk quite a lot more than I have. He also remembers much more than I do about our time in Greece. He keeps sparking old memories which I'd buried. I'd forgotten about the poker tournament. I'd forgotten about that fishing boat sinking. I'd forgotten about the night we played table tennis with those two Australian guys. But the moment Ben reminds me, there it all is in my head again, in a vivid flash.

"Guy and . . ." I'm crinkling up my nose, trying to remember. "Guy and . . . what was his name . . . oh yes, *Bill*!"

"Bill!" Ben chuckles and high-fives me. "Of course. Big Bill."

I can't believe I haven't given Big Bill a thought, all these years. He was like a bear. He used to sit in the corner of the terrace, drinking beers and sunning himself. He had

121

more piercings than I'd ever seen in my life. Apparently he'd done them all himself, with a needle. He had a really cool girlfriend called Pinky, and we all watched and cheered while he pierced her navel.

"The calamari." I close my eyes briefly. "I've never had calamari like that in my life."

"And the sunsets," chimes in Ben. "Remember the sunsets?"

"I'll never forget."

"And Arthur." He grins reminiscently. "What a character."

Arthur was the guest house owner. We all worshipped him and hung on his every word. He was the most mellow guy I've ever met, fiftyish or maybe older, who'd done everything from attending Harvard to founding his own company and going bust to sailing round the world and ending up on Ikonos, where he married a local girl. He would sit every night in the olive grove, getting gently stoned and telling people about the time he had lunch with Bill Clinton and turned down his job offer. He'd had so many adventures. He was so *wise.* I can remember getting drunk one night and weeping on his shoulder and him stroking me and saying some really amazing stuff. (I can't remember exactly what now — but it was amazing.)

"Remember the steps?"

"The steps!" I groan. "How did we *do* it?"

The guest house was set on top of a cliff. To get down to or up from the beach, it was 113 steps, set into the cliff. We used to spring up and down them several times a day. No wonder I was so thin.

"Remember Sarah? Whatever happened to her?"

"Sarah? What did she look like?"

"Stunning. Amazing body. Silky skin." He seems to inhale the memory. "She was Arthur's daughter. You *must* remember her."

"Oh right." I'm not wild about hearing descriptions of other girls' silky skin. "Not sure."

"Maybe she went off traveling before you came." He shrugs, moving on. "D'you remember those old videos of *Dirk and Sally*? How many times did we watch those?"

"Dirk and Sally!" I exclaim. "Oh my God!"

"Partners at the altar, partners on the block," begins Ben, in that corny voice-over voice.

"Partners to the death!" I join in, doing the *Dirk and Sally* arm salute.

Ben and I watched every single *Dirk and Sally* episode about five thousand times, mostly because it was the only box set of videos at the guest house, and you had to have *something* on apart from Greek news while you were eating your breakfast in the mornings. It's a 1970s detective show about a couple who meet while they're at police school and decide to keep their marriage secret while fighting crime as partners. Nobody knows except one serial killer, who keeps threatening to expose them. It's *genius.*

I have a sudden memory of sitting with Ben on that ancient sofa in the dining room, our tanned legs tangled up, both wearing espadrilles, eating toast, and watching *Dirk and Sally* while everyone else was out on the terrace.

"The episode where Sally is kidnapped by the neighbor," I say. "That was the best."

"No, when Dirk's brother comes to live with them, and he's become a chef for the Mafia, and Dirk keeps asking him where he learned to cook, and then the drugs are in the peach cobbler —"

"Oh my *God,* yes!"

We both pause a moment, lost in memories.

"No one I've ever met has seen *Dirk and Sally,*" says Ben. "Or even heard of it."

"Me neither," I agree, though the truth is, I'd pretty much forgotten about *Dirk and Sally* till he mentioned it just now.

"The cove." His thoughts have moved restlessly on again.

"The cove. Oh my God." I meet his eyes and it all comes flooding back. I'm almost transfixed again with hot, teenage-level desire. The secret cove was where we first got it together. And then again. Every day. It was a little tiny sheltered stretch of sand round the bay. You had to get there by boat, and no one else could be bothered. Ben would sail us there, saying nothing but occasionally flicking me a meaningful look. And I would sit there, my feet up on the side of the boat, almost panting with anticipation.

I look at him now, across the table. Ben's thinking exactly the same as me, I can tell. He's back there. He looks as intoxicated as I feel.

"The way you nursed me through the flu," he says slowly. "I've never forgotten that."

The *flu*? I don't remember nursing him through the flu. But, then, my memories are so fuzzy. I'm sure I did, if he says I did. And I don't want to interrupt or contradict him, because it would ruin the mood. So I just nod gently.

"You cradled my head. You sang me to sleep. I was delirious, but I could hear your voice, getting me through the night." He takes another swig of wine. "You were my guardian angel, Lottie. Maybe I went off the rails because I didn't have you in my life."

His guardian angel. That's so romantic. I'm quite interested to know how he went off the rails — but to ask him would spoil the moment. And who cares? Everyone goes off the rails. Then they come back on the rails. It doesn't matter what they were doing meanwhile.

Now he glances at my left hand. "How come you haven't been snapped up, anyway?"

"Haven't met the right guy," I say casually.

"A gorgeous girl like you? Should be fighting them off."

"Well, maybe I have been." I laugh, but for the first time this evening my composure slips a little. And all of a sudden — I can't help it — I have a flashback to the first time I met Richard. It was at the opera, which is weird, because I never go to the opera normally, and nor does he. We were both there as a favor to friends. It was a charity gala of *Tosca* and he was in black tie, looking tall and distinguished, and the moment I saw him with some blond woman on his arm I felt a pang of jealousy. I hadn't even met him and I was thinking, *Lucky her.* He was laughing and handing out champagne, and then he turned to me and said, "I'm sorry, we haven't been introduced," and I nearly fell into his gorgeous dark eyes.

And that was it. It felt magical. He wasn't with the blond woman after all, and after the intermission he switched seats to be next to me. We went back to the opera on our first anniversary, and I thought we'd do it every year for the rest of our lives.

So much for that. So much for telling the story at the wedding reception and everybody saying, *Ahh . . .*

"Oh God." Ben is peering at me. "I'm sorry. I've said something. What's wrong?"

"Nothing!" I smile hastily and blink. "Just . . . everything. You know. Life."

"Exactly. *Exactly.*" He nods fervently as though I've solved some massive problem he was wrestling with. "Lotts, do you feel as fucked up by life as I do?"

"Yes." I take a deep slug of wine. "Yes, I do. Even more so."

"When I was eighteen, when we were out there, I knew what I was about." Ben is staring moodily into space. "I had *clarity.* But you start out in life and somehow it all gets . . . corroded. Corrupted. Everything closes in on you, you know what I mean?

There's no escape. There's no way to say, 'Just stop a fucking moment. Let me work out what *I* want.' "

"Totally." I nod earnestly.

"That was the highest point of my life. Greece. You. The whole deal." He looks gripped by the memory. "Just the two of us, together. Everything was *simple.* There was no *shit.* Is it the same for you? Was that the best time of your life?"

My mind does a hazy rewind over the last fifteen years. OK, there have been a few high points here and there, but in general I have to agree. We were eighteen. We were hot. We could drink all night with no hang-over. When has life ever been that good?

I nod slowly. "Best time ever."

"*Why* didn't we stay together, Lottie? *Why* didn't we keep in touch?"

"Edinburgh–Bath." I shrug. "Bath–Edinburgh. Impossible geography."

"I know. But that was a crap reason." He looks angry. "We were idiots."

We had the "impossible geography" conversation many, many times on the island. He was going to Edinburgh University. I was going to Bath. It was only a matter of time before it ended. There was no point trying to keep things going beyond the summer.

The days after the fire were weird, anyway. Everything started to fall apart. We were all billeted in different guest houses, all over the island. People's parents swooped in. Some actually arrived on the next boat, with money and clothes and replacement passports. I remember seeing Pinky sitting disconsolately at the taverna with two very smart-looking parents. It felt like the party was over.

"Weren't we planning to meet once in London?" It comes back to me in a flash. "But then you had to go to Normandy with your family."

"That's right." He exhales sharply. "I should have bailed out on them. I should have switched to Bath." His eyes suddenly focus on me. "I've never met anyone like you, Lottie. Sometimes I think, what an idiot I was to let you go. What a fucking stupid idiot."

My stomach turns an almighty somersault and I almost choke on my wine. At the back of my mind, I was kind of hoping he might say something along these lines. But not so soon. His blue eyes are boring into me expectantly.

"Me too," I say at last, and take a forkful of halibut.

"Don't tell me you've ever had a relationship better than ours. Because *I* sure as hell haven't." Ben bangs the table with his fist. "Maybe we got our priorities screwed up. Maybe we should have said, *Fuck university, we're staying together.* Who knows what might have happened? We were good together, Lottie. Maybe we've wasted the last fifteen years *not* being together. Don't you ever think that?"

His speed is taking my breath away. I don't quite know how to react, so I stuff some more halibut into my mouth.

"We might be married by now. We might have kids. My life might make *sense.*" He's almost talking to himself, popping with a kind of suppressed emotion I can't read.

"Do you want kids?" I say before I can stop myself.

I can't believe I just *asked a guy on a first date if he wants kids.* I should be struck off. Except . . . it's not a first date. If it's anything, it's a zillionth date. And he mentioned them first. And, anyway, it's not a date at all. So.

"Yes, I want kids." His intent gaze lands on me again. "I'm ready for a family, prams, going to the park, all that shit."

"Me too." I feel tears spring to my eyes. "I'm ready for a family too."

Oh God. Richard has popped into my

130

head yet *again.* I didn't want him to, but he has. I'm remembering that fantasy I used to have of Richard and me making a tree house for our twins called Arthur and Edie. Almost savagely, I open my evening bag and reach for a tissue. Crying was *not* the plan. Thinking about Richard was *not* the plan.

Thankfully, Ben doesn't seem to have noticed. He refills my glass, then his own, with wine. We've already finished the bottle, I notice with a slight shock. How did we manage that?

"Remember the pact?" His voice takes me by surprise.

No *way.*

Adrenaline has flooded my body. My lungs are squeezed so tight, I can't breathe. I didn't think he'd remember the pact. I wasn't going to bring it up. It was a teeny, tiny, jokey promise we made once. It was nothing. It was *ridiculous.*

"Should we exercise it?" He's looking at me frankly. I think he might be half serious. Or serious. No. He *can't* be serious —

"Bit late," I manage, my throat tight. "We said if we were unmarried at thirty. I'm thirty-three."

"Better late than never." I feel a fresh jolt. His foot has found mine under the table and he's edging off my shoe. "My flat's

131

nearby," he murmurs. Now his hand is taking mine. My skin starts tingling all over. It's like muscle memory. Sex memory. I know where we're heading.

But . . . but . . . is that where I want to head? What's going on here? *Think,* Lottie.

"Would you care to see the dessert menu?" The waiter's voice snaps me out of my trance. My head jerks up and I take the chance to whip my hand away from Ben.

"Er . . . thanks."

I scan the dessert menu, my cheeks beating with blood, my mind circling furiously. What do I do now? What? What?

A little voice is telling me to rein in. I'm playing this wrong. I'm making a mistake. I have a terrible sense of déjà vu, of things following the same old pattern.

All my long-term relationships have started like this. Hand-holding over a table. Pulses racing all over my body. Nice underwear, and everything waxed, and hot, inventive, fabulous sex. (Or terrible sex, that one time with the doctor bloke. Yikes. You'd think a medic would be a bit more up on the way a body works. But I ditched him fairly swiftly.)

The point is: the beginning is *never* the problem. It's afterward.

I'm feeling a strange conviction I've never

felt before. I need to change everything I'm doing. Break the pattern. But how? What?

Ben has taken my hand again and is kissing the inside of my wrist, but I ignore him. I want to marshal my thoughts.

"What's wrong?" He looks up, his mouth against my skin. "You're tense. Lottie, don't fight it. This is meant to happen. You and me. You know it is."

His eyes have that languorous, drunken sexy look I remember. I'm already feeling turned on. I could surrender and have a sizzling, delicious night to cheer myself up. I deserve it, after all.

But what if there's a chance of more than a great night? How should I play this? What do I *do*?

It would really help if my head wasn't spinning.

"Ben, you have to understand." I pull my arm away again. "It's not like when we were eighteen, OK? I don't just want a shag. I want . . . other things. I want marriage. I want commitment. I want to plan a life together with someone. Kids, the whole lot."

"So do I!" he says impatiently. "Weren't you listening? It should have been you all along." His eyes are burning into mine. "Lottie. I never stopped loving you."

Oh my God, he loves me. I feel a rush of

tears again. And, looking at him, it comes to me that I never stopped loving him either. Maybe I just didn't realize it, because it was a kind of low-level, steady love. Like a background hum. And now it's swelling back up into full-blown passion.

"Nor did I," I say, my voice trembling with sudden conviction. "I've loved you for fifteen years."

"Fifteen years." He's clinging to my hand. "We were insane to let each other go."

The romance of it all is overwhelming me. Talk about a story to tell at a wedding reception. Talk about oohs and aahs. *We were apart for fifteen years, but then we found each other again.*

"We have to make up for lost time." He crushes my fingers to his mouth. "Darling Lottie. My love." His words are like balm. The feel of his lips on my skin is almost unbearably delicious. For an instant I close my eyes. But, no. Alarm bells are ringing. I can't bear this one to go wrong like all the others.

"Stop!" I whip my hand away. "Don't! Ben, I know how this will play out, and I can't bear it. Not again."

"What are you talking about?" He stares at me, baffled. "All I did was kiss your fingers."

134

His voice is a bit slurred. *Kish your fing-ersh.* But, then, so probably is mine.

I wait until the waiter has brushed away the crumbs from our table, then launch in again, my voice lowered and trembling.

"I've been here before. I know what happens. You kiss my fingers. I kiss your fingers. We have sex. It's great. We have more sex. We're besotted. We go on a mini-break to the Cotswolds. Maybe we buy a sofa together, or a bookshelf from Ikea. And then suddenly it's two years later and we should be getting married . . . but somehow we don't. We've gone off the boil. We argue and we break up. And it's horrible."

My throat is tight with misery at our fate. It's so inevitable and it's so sad.

Ben looks bewildered by the scenario I've painted.

"OK," he says at last, eyeing me warily. "Well . . . what if we don't go off the boil?"

"We do! It's the law! It always happens!" I gaze at him, my eyes full of tears. "I've gone off the boil with too many guys. I *know.*"

"Even if we don't buy a bookshelf from Ikea?"

I know he's trying to be funny, but I'm serious. I've spent fifteen years of my life dating, I suddenly realize. Dating is not the solution to anything. Dating gave me Rich-

135

ard. Dating is the *problem*.

"There's a good reason you went off the boil with those other guys." Ben tries again. "They weren't the right guys. But I am!"

"Who says you're the right guy?"

"Because . . . because . . . *Jesus*! What will it take?" He thrusts his fingers through his hair, looking exasperated. "OK! You win. We'll do it the old-fashioned way. Lottie, will you marry me?"

"Shut up." I scowl. "You don't have to make fun of me."

"I mean it. Will you marry me?"

"Funny." I take a slug of wine.

"I mean it. Will you marry me?"

"Stop it."

"Will you marry me?" Now he's speaking more loudly. A couple at the next table look over and smile.

"Shh!" I say irritably. "It's not funny."

To my utter shock, he gets out of his seat, kneels down, and clasps his hands. I can see other diners turning to watch.

My heart is pounding. No way. No *way.*

"Charlotte Graveney," he begins, swaying slightly. "I've spent fifteen years chasing pale imitations of you, and now I'm back here with the original I should never have let go. My life has been darkness without you and now I want to switch on the light. Will you do me the honor of marrying me? Please?"

A weird sensation is stealing over me. I feel as if I'm turning into cotton wool. He's proposing. He's actually proposing. For real.

"You're drunk," I parry.

"Not that drunk. Will you marry me?" he repeats.

"But I don't *know* you anymore!" I give a half laugh. "I don't know what you do for a living, I don't know where you live, I don't know what you want in life —"

"Paper supply. Shoreditch. To be as happy as I was when I was with you. To wake up every morning and shag your brains out. To make babies who have your eyes. Lottie, I know it's been years, but it's still me. It's still Ben." His eyes crinkle in the way they always did. "Will you marry me?"

I stare at him, breathing hard, my head ringing. But I can't quite tell if it's bells of joy or an alarm siren.

I mean, I did think there was a chance he was still interested in me. But this is beyond all my fantasies. He's held a torch for me, all these years! He wants to get married! He wants kids! A noise is playing at the back of my mind. I think it could be violin music. *Maybe this is it. MAYBE THIS IS IT! Richard wasn't it; Ben is it!*

I take a swig of water and try to fight a

137

way through my swirling thoughts. Let's be sensible. Let's just think this through carefully. Did we ever argue? No. Was he good company? Yes. Do I fancy him? Hell, yeah. Is there anything else I need to know about a potential husband?

"Do you have any nipples pierced?" I ask with sudden foreboding. Pierced nipples really aren't my thing.

"Not one." He rips open his shirt in a theatrical gesture, scattering buttons, and I can't help staring. Mmm. Brown. Taut. He's as tasty as he ever was.

"All you need to do is say 'Yes'." Ben spreads his arms with a drunken emphasis. *"All you need to do, Lottie, is say 'Yes'.* We spend most of our lives messing things up because we think too much. Let's not over-think this one. Fuck it, we've wasted enough time. We love each other. Let's just jump."

He's right. We do love each other. And he wants to make babies who have my eyes. No one's ever said anything so beautiful to me. Not even Richard.

My head is whirling. I'm trying to stay rational, but I'm losing my footing. Is this real? Is he just talking me into bed? Is this the most romantic moment of my life or am I an idiot?

"I . . . I think so," I say at last.

"You *think* so?"

"Just . . . give me a moment."

I grab my bag and head to the Ladies'; I have to think. Clearly. Or at least as clearly as I can, bearing in mind that the room is spinning and my face in the mirror looks like it has three eyes.

It could work. I'm sure it could work. But how can I *make* it work? How can I not fall into the same predictable pattern as all my other dead-end, fizzle-out relationships?

As I comb my hair, my mind starts ranging over other first dates with other boyfriends. Other beginnings. I've stood in so many Ladies' rooms over the years, refreshing my lipstick, thinking, *Is this The One?* Each time I've felt equally hopeful, equally fizzy. So where did I go wrong? What can I do differently? What can I *not* do that I normally do?

Suddenly I recall that book I was looking at this morning. *The Reverse Principle.* Flip the arrow. Change direction. That sounds good. Yes. But how do I change direction? And now the words of that mad old woman in the Ladies' yesterday are ringing in my head. What did she say again? *Men are like jungle creatures. The minute they've found their kill, they eat it and fall asleep.* Maybe she wasn't so mad after all. Maybe she had something.

Abruptly, I stop combing my hair. In a flash of inspiration, it has come to me. The answer. The left-field solution. I, Lottie Graveney, am going to reverse the pattern. I'm going to do the *opposite* of what I've done with all previous boyfriends.

I meet my eyes in the mirror. I look a little wild, but, then, is that any surprise? If I was exhilarated before, I'm euphoric now. I feel like a scientist who's discovered a new, game-changing subatomic particle. I'm right. I know I'm right. *I'm right!*

I stride back into the restaurant, staggering a little in my heels, and approach the table.

"No sex," I say firmly.

"What?"

"Till we're married. No sex." I sit down. "Take it or leave it."

"What?" Ben looks flabbergasted, but I just smile serenely back. I'm brilliant. If he really loves me, he'll wait. And there'll be no chance of anyone going off the boil. None. And the best part is, we'll have the hottest honeymoon *ever.* We'll be connected and united and blissed out. Exactly like honeymooners should be.

His shirt is still hanging open. I picture him naked, in some gorgeous hotel bed, surrounded by rose petals. Just the idea makes me quiver.

"You're kidding." His face has completely dropped. *"Why?"*

"Because I want things to be *different*. I want to break the mold. I love you, yes? You love me? We want to make a life together?"

"For fifteen years I've loved you." He shakes his head. "Fifteen fucking *years,* we wasted, Lottie —"

I can tell he's going to start another drunken speech.

"So." I cut him off. "We wait a bit longer. And then we can have a wedding night. A *proper* wedding night. Think about it. We'll both be gagging for it by then. Absolutely . . . gagging." I reach under the table with my bare foot and slowly walk it up the inside of his leg. His face is transfixed. Never fails, this one.

For a moment, neither of us talks. Let's say we're communicating in a different way.

"Actually . . . ," he says at last, his voice thick, "that could be fun."

"A lot of fun." Casually, I unbutton my top a couple of notches and lean forward, giving him maximum view of my uplift bra. My other foot is moving up to his crotch now. Ben seems unable to speak. "Remember the night of your birthday?" I say huskily. "On the beach? We could reprise that."

If we reprise that, I am wearing protective knee guards. I had scabs for a week. As if he's reading my mind, Ben closes his eyes and moans faintly. "You're killing me."

"It'll be amazing." I have a sudden memory of us as teenagers, lying entwined in my room at the guest house, lit only by the flickering of all my scented candles.

"Do you know how hot you are? Do you realize how badly I want to get under this table *now*?" He grabs my hand and starts nibbling at the tip of my thumb. But this time I don't move it away. My entire body seems wired to the feel of his lips and teeth on my skin. I want them everywhere. I remember this. I remember him. How could I have forgotten?

"Wedding night, huh?" he says at last. My toes are still doing their stuff, and there's pretty firm evidence that he's enjoying it. All still in working order, then.

"Wedding night." I nod.

"You realize I'll die of frustration meanwhile?"

"Me too. And then I'll explode." He takes my thumb right inside his mouth, and I gasp inwardly as the sensation rockets through my body. We need to leave soon or the waiter will be telling us to get a room.

And when Richard hears about this —

No. Don't go there. This has nothing to do with Richard. It's *fate.* It's part of a bigger picture. A huge, sweeping romantic story starring Ben and me, with Richard only a bit part along the way.

I know I'm drunk. I know this is rushed. But it feels so right. And if there's still a soreness deep in my heart, then this is like some magical soothing lotion. I was *meant* to break up with Richard. I was *meant* to be miserable. The karma for my suffering is that now I get a wedding ring and the hottest sex of my life.

I feel like my raffle prize wasn't a thousand pounds. It was a million pounds.

Ben's eyes are glazed. I'm breathing more and more heavily. I'm not sure I can stand this.

"When shall we get married?" I murmur.

"Soon." He sounds desperate. "Really, really soon."

5
FLISS

I hope Lottie's OK, I really do. I've been
away for two weeks and I haven't heard one
word from her. She hasn't answered any of
my friendly texts, and the last phone call we
had was when she was planning to fly to
San Francisco and surprise Richard. As
Unfortunate Choices go, that one took the
biscuit. Thank God I headed it off.

But since then: nothing. I've tried leaving
voicemails as well as texting, but no response. I did manage to get through to her
intern, who assured me that she was coming in to work every day — so at least I
know she's alive and well. But it's not like
Lottie to be incommunicado. It troubles me.
I'll go round and see her tonight, make sure
she's OK.

I pull out my phone and send her yet
another text: Hi, how's it going??? Then I
put it away and survey the school playground. It's thronging with parents, chil-

dren, nannies, dogs, and toddlers on scooters. It's the first day of term, so there are lots of tanned faces and shiny shoes and new haircuts. And that's just the mothers.

"Fliss!" A voice greets me as we get out of the car. It's Anna, another mother. She's clutching a Tupperware container in one hand and a dog lead in the other, at the end of which her Labrador is itching to get away. "How are you? Hi, Noah! Been meaning to have that coffee . . ."

"Love to." I nod.

Anna and I talk about having coffee every time we see each other — which would be getting on for two years now — and it hasn't yet happened. But somehow that doesn't matter. Somehow that's not the point.

"That bloody travel project," Anna is saying as we walk toward the school entrance. "I was up at five A.M. finishing that off. Up your street, I suppose, travel!" She gives a cheerful laugh.

"What travel project?"

"You know, the art thing?" She gestures to her container. "We did a plane. *Utterly* lame. We covered a toy with silver foil. Hardly homemade, but I said to Charlie, 'Sweetie, Mrs. Hocking won't *know* there's a toy underneath.' "

"What travel project?" I say again.

145

"*You* know. Make a vehicle or whatever. They're showing them all off at assembly. . . . Charlie, come on! The bell's rung!"

What bloody travel project?

As I approach Mrs. Hocking, I can see another mother, Jane Langridge, standing in front of her, holding out a model of a cruise ship. It's made out of balsa wood and paper. It has three funnels and rows of little portholes cut out perfectly and teeny clay figures on top, sunbathing round the blue-painted swimming pool. I stare at it, speechless in awe.

"I'm so sorry, Mrs. Hocking," Jane is saying. "Some of the paint is still wet. We've had *such* fun making it, haven't we, Joshua?"

"Hello, Mrs. Phipps," calls out Mrs. Hocking cheerfully. "Nice holiday?"

Mrs. Phipps. It sets my teeth on edge every time I'm addressed this way. I haven't got round to becoming "Ms. Graveney" for school purposes. Truth is, I'm unsure what to do. I don't want to unsettle Noah. I don't want to make a big deal of rejecting his surname. I *like* having the same name as Noah. It feels homey and right.

I should have chosen a brand-new surname when he was born. Just for us. Divorce-proof.

146

"Mummy, did you bring the hot-air balloon?" Noah is peering up at me anxiously. "Have we got the hot-air balloon?"

I stare at him blankly. I have no idea what he's talking about.

"Noah told us he was making a hot-air balloon. Super idea." Mrs. Hocking descends on us, beaming. She's a woman in her sixties who lives in tapered trousers. She's so cool and unhurried, I inevitably feel like a gabbling lunatic next to her. Now her eyes rest on my empty hands. "Do you have it?"

Do I *look* like I have a hot-air balloon about my person?

"Not on me," I hear myself saying. "Not exactly *on* me."

"Ah." Her smile fades. "Well, if there's *any* chance you could get it to us this morning, Mrs. Phipps, we're setting up the display for assembly."

"Right! Of course!" I flash her a confident smile. "I just need to — One tiny detail — Let me just talk to Noah a moment." I draw him away and bend down. "Which hot-air balloon, darling?"

"My hot-air balloon for the travel project," says Noah, as though it's obvious. "We have to bring them in today."

"Right." It's nearly killing me, staying

147

bright and breezy. "I didn't know you had a project. You never mentioned it."

"I forgot." He nods. "But remember we had a letter?"

"What happened to the letter?"

"Daddy put it in his fruit bowl."

I feel a volcanic surge of fury. I knew it. I bloody *knew* it.

"Right. I see." I grind my fingernails into my palms. "Daddy didn't tell me there was a project. What a pity."

"And we talked about what to make, and Daddy said, 'What about a hot-air balloon?' " Noah's eyes start to gleam. "Daddy said we would get a balloon and cover it with papiermâché and make a basket and people. And ropes. And paint it. And the people could be Batman." His little cheeks are glowing with excitement. "Has he made it?" He looks at me expectantly. "Have you got it?"

"I'll just . . . check." My smile feels glued into place. "Play on the climbing frame a moment."

I step away and speed-dial Daniel.

"Daniel Phi—"

"It's Fliss." I cut him off evenly. "Are you by any chance speeding toward the school holding a papier-mâché hot-air balloon with Batman in the basket?"

There's quite a long pause.

"Oh," Daniel says at last. "Shit. Sorry."

He doesn't sound remotely concerned. I want to kill him.

"No! Not 'Oh. Shit. Sorry.' You can't *do* this, Daniel! It's not fair on Noah and it's not fair on me and —"

"Fliss, relax. It's just some little school project."

"It's not little! To Noah, it's huge! It's — You're —" I break off, breathing fast. He'll never get it. There's no point wasting breath. I'm on my own. "Fine, Daniel. Whatever. I'll sort it."

I switch off before he can answer. I'm feeling a red heat of determination. I am not going to let Noah down. He's going to have his hot-air balloon. I can do this. Come on.

I bleep open the car and snap up the lid of my briefcase. I've got a tiny cardboard gift bag in there, from some fancy lunch. That can be the basket. Shoelaces out of my gym cross-trainers will be the ropes. I grab a sheet of paper and pen from my briefcase and beckon Noah over.

"I'm just going to finish off our hot-air balloon," I say brightly. "Why don't you draw Batman to put in the basket?"

As Noah starts drawing, leaning on the car seat, I swiftly take out my shoelaces.

149

They're brown and speckled. They'll make perfect ropes. I've got some Scotch tape in the glove compartment. And for the balloon itself . . .

Bloody hell. What can I use? It's not like I travel around with packets of balloons, on the off chance that —

A ridiculous, unspeakable idea grabs me. I could always —

No. No way. I *can't.* . . .

Five minutes later, I approach Mrs. Hocking, nonchalantly holding Noah's project. The mothers standing around gradually fall silent. In fact, it feels as though the whole playground has fallen silent.

"That's Batman!" Noah is pointing to the basket proudly. "I drew him."

All the children are looking at Batman. All the mothers are looking at the balloon. It's a blown-up Durex Fetherlite Ultra. It inflated to quite an impressive size, and the teat on the end is bobbing in the breeze.

I hear a sudden snort from Anna, but when I look around sharply, all I can see are innocent expressions.

"Goodness, Noah," says Mrs. Hocking faintly. "What a . . . big balloon!"

"That's obscene," snaps Jane, clutching her boat to her as though for protection.

"This is a *school,* in case you'd forgotten. There are *children* here."

"And as far as they're concerned, this is a perfectly innocent balloon," I retort. "My husband let me down." I turn apologetically to Mrs. Hocking. "I didn't have much time."

"It's very good, Mrs. Phipps!" Mrs. Hocking rallies herself. "What a creative use of . . ."

"What if it bursts?" says Jane.

"I've got spares," I shoot back triumphantly, and proffer the rest of my Durex variety pack, splayed out like a pack of cards.

A moment too late, I realize how this looks. My cheeks flaming, I surreptitiously adjust my hand to cover up the words *Ribbed for extra pleasure.* And *lube.* And *stimulation.* My fingers are doing a starfish impression, trying to censor the condom packets.

"I think we'll be able to find a balloon for Noah in the classroom, Mrs. Phipps," Mrs. Hocking says at last. "I'd keep those yourself, for . . ." She hesitates, clearly searching for a way to finish her sentence.

"Absolutely." I hastily head her off. "Good idea. I'll use them for . . . exactly. That. I mean, *not.*" I laugh shrilly. "Actually, I probably won't use them at all. Or at least . . . I am *responsible,* obviously. . . ."

I trail away into silence. I've just shared details of my condom use with my son's teacher. I'm not sure how that happened.

"Anyway!" I add in bright desperation. "So. I'll take those away now. And use them. For . . . some purpose or other."

Hastily, I stuff the condoms back in my bag, dropping a Pleasuremax and diving for it before any of the seven-year-olds can reach it. All the other mothers are staring, jaw-dropped, as though they've witnessed a car crash.

"I hope the assembly goes well. Have a lovely day, Noah." I hand him the hot-air balloon with a kiss, then swivel on my heel and march away, breathing hard. I wait until I'm on the road, then dial Barnaby from the car phone.

"Barnaby." I launch in. "You will not *believe* what Daniel just did. Noah had a school project which Daniel didn't say a *single word* about —"

"Fliss," says Barnaby patiently. "Calm down."

"I had to hand a blown-up condom to Noah's teacher! It was supposed to be a hot-air balloon!" I can hear Barnaby bursting into laughter down the line. "It wasn't funny! He's a shit! He pretends to care, but he's totally selfish; he lets Noah down —"

152

"Fliss." Barnaby's voice is suddenly harder and stops me in my tracks. "This has to stop."

"What has to stop?" I stare at the speakerphone.

"The daily rant. I'm going to say something to you now, as an old friend. If you keep going on like this, you'll drive everyone insane, including yourself. Shit happens, OK?"

"But —"

"It *happens,* Fliss." He pauses. "And it doesn't help to stir it up again and again. You need to move on. Get a life. Go on a date *without* mentioning your ex-husband's underpants."

"What are you talking about?" I say evasively.

"It was a *date. A date.*" I can hear Barnaby's frustration bursting through the phone. "You were supposed to *flirt* with Nathan. Not open up your laptop and read out your entire divorce dossier."

"I didn't read out the entire thing!" I finger my memory stick defensively. "We were just talking, and I happened to mention it, and he seemed interested —"

"He wasn't interested! He was being *polite.* Apparently you ranted for five solid minutes about Daniel's underwear."

153

"That's a total exaggeration," I retort hotly.

But my face has flamed. Maybe it *was* five minutes. I'd had a bit to drink by that stage. And there's a lot to say about Daniel's underwear, none of it good.

"Do you remember our first appointment, Fliss?" Barnaby continues relentlessly. "You said whatever you did, you wouldn't end up bitter."

I gasp at his use of the B-word. "I'm *not*. I'm . . . angry. Regretful." I search my mind for further acceptable emotions. "I'm rueful. Sad. Philosophical."

"The word Nathan used was 'bitter.' "

"I'm not bitter!" I almost yell at him. "I think I would know if I was bitter or not!"

There's silence at the other end. I'm breathing fast. My hands feel sweaty around the steering wheel. I'm flashing back to my date with Nathan. I thought I was talking about Daniel in an amusing, detached, ironic way. Nathan never said a word to indicate he wasn't having a good time. Is that what everyone's been doing? Humoring me?

"OK," I say at last. "Well, now I know. Thanks for the heads-up."

"Anytime." Barnaby's cheerful voice resounds through the car. "Before you say it,

154

I *am* your friend. And I *do* love you lots. But this is what you need. Tough love, Fliss. I'll talk to you soon."

He rings off, and I signal left, chewing my bottom lip and glaring darkly at the road. It's all very well. *It's all very well.*

When I get to work, I can see my in-box is full, but I sit at my desk, staring blindly at my computer. Barnaby's words have stung me more than I want to admit to myself. I'm turning into a bitter, twisted hag. I'm going to end up a gnarled old crone in a black hood who scowls at the world and battles her way along the street, hitting people with her stick and refusing to smile at the neighborhood children, who run away, terrified.

Worst-case scenario.

After a bit, I reach for the phone and call Lottie's office number. Maybe we can buoy each other up.

The girl who answers is Dolly, Lottie's junior.

"Oh, hi, Dolly," I say. "Is Lottie about?"

"She's out. Shopping. Don't know when she'll be back."

Shopping? I blink at the phone in surprise. I know Lottie sometimes gets frustrated with her job, but to go out shopping and blatantly tell your junior is really not the way to go in this economic climate.

"Any idea when she'll be back?"

"Dunno. She's buying stuff for her honey-moon."

I stiffen. Did I hear that right? Honey-moon? As in . . . *honeymoon*?

"Did you just say . . ." I swallow. "Dolly, is Lottie getting *married*?"

"Didn't you know?"

"I've been away! This is . . . I've been . . ." I can hardly speak. "Oh my God! Please say I rang and congratulations!"

I put down the phone and beam elatedly around the empty office. My gloomy mood has vanished. I want to dance. Lottie's engaged! It goes to show, some things in the world *do* go right in the end.

But, how?

How, how, how, how, how?

What *happened*? Did she fly out to San Francisco after all? Or did he fly back? Or did they call each other? What? I text her:

You're engaged???????

I'm expecting radio silence again, but a moment later she replies.

Yes!!!! Was waiting to tell u all about it!

156

OMG! What happened???

All very fast. Still can't believe it. He came back into my life out of nowhere, asked me in a restaurant, had no idea he would, absolute whirlwind!!!!

I *have* to talk to her. I call her mobile number, but it's engaged. Damn. I'll get myself a coffee, then try again. As I head to our in-house Costa outlet, I can't stop beaming. In fact, I'm so happy I really want to cry, but editors at Pincher International don't cry at work, so I'll settle for hugging myself.

Richard is perfect. He's everything I could ever have wanted for Lottie. Which sounds motherly — but, then, I *do* feel motherly toward her. Always have. Our own parents both kind of gave up on the job, what with the divorce and the alcohol and the affairs with loaded businessmen and South African beauty queens. . . . Put it this way: we were left alone a lot. Lottie is five years younger than me, and, well before our mother died, she started turning to me when things went wrong.

And as mother figure/sister/possible chief bridesmaid (?), I could not be more thrilled that Richard's joining our strange little family unit. For a start, he's good-looking but not to-die-for. This is important, I think. You want your sister to land a sex god *in her own eyes,* but you don't want to be lusting after him yourself. I mean, how would I feel if Lottie brought Johnny Depp home?

I try to examine my thoughts honestly, in the privacy of my own head. Yes, I would be unable to stay sisterly. I would probably try to steal him. I would feel like all bets were off.

But Richard isn't Johnny Depp. He's handsome, don't get me wrong, but not *overly* handsome. Not *gay* handsome, which that awful Jamie was, always preening and competing over carbs. Richard's a man. To my eye, he sometimes looks like a younger Pierce Brosnan and sometimes like a younger Gordon Brown. (Although I think I'm the only one who can see the Gordon Brown thing. I mentioned the resemblance to Lottie once, and she got quite offended.)

I know he's good at his job. (Obviously, when he first started dating Lottie I asked around all my City contacts for the low-down on him.) I also know he can have a short fuse and once bawled out his team so hugely, he had to take them all out to lunch to apologize. But he's also good-natured. The first time I ever saw him, he was holding an armchair, which Lottie wanted moved in her flat. She was wandering round the sitting room, saying, "There . . . no, there! Ooh, what about there?" And he just held that big heavy chair patiently while she dithered around, and I caught his eye and he grinned and I knew. *This* is the right guy for Lottie.

I want to jump up and down, I'm so happy. After all the shit of my divorce, we needed something good to come our way. So, how did it happen? What did he say? I want to know *everything.* As I head back to my desk, I impatiently dial her number again — and this time she answers.

"Hi, Fliss?"

"Lottie!" I erupt with excitement. "Congratulations! Amazing news! I can't believe it!"

"I know! I know!" She sounds even more euphoric than I was expecting. Richard must have swept her off her feet.

"So . . . when?" I sit down at my desk and sip my coffee.

"Two weeks ago. It still hasn't really sunk in!"

"Details!"

"Well, he just contacted me out of the blue." Lottie gives an exhilarated laugh. "I couldn't believe it. I thought I'd never see him again. Let alone *this*!"

If he proposed two weeks ago, that means he'd been gone for a day, max. He must have landed at San Francisco and turned right around. Good work, Richard!

"And what did he say? Did he get down on one knee?"

"Yes! He said he'd always loved me and he wanted to be with me and then he asked me to marry him about ten times, and at last . . . I said yes!" Her elation bubbles over again. "Can you *believe* it?"

I sigh happily and take another sip of coffee. It's so romantic. It's so dreamy. I wonder if I could skive my British Airways press conference and take Lottie out for a celebratory lunch.

"So . . . what else?" I probe for more details. "Did you give him the ring?"

"Well, no." Lottie sounds drawn up short. "Of course not."

Thank God for that. I was never into the ring idea.

"You just decided not to in the end?"

"It didn't even *occur* to me!" To my surprise, she sounds pained. "I mean, the ring was for Richard."

"What do you mean?" I blink at the phone, not following.

"Well, I bought the ring for Richard." She

sounds quite put out. "It would be weird, giving it to someone else. Don't you think?"

I try to answer, but my thoughts have jammed, as though a pencil's fallen into a smoothly whirring machine. What's this "someone else"? I open my mouth to reply — then close it again. Did I hear wrong? Is she using some figure of speech?

"So . . ." I proceed warily, feeling as though I'm speaking a foreign language. "You bought the ring for Richard . . . but you didn't give it to him?"

I'm only trying to work out what she meant. I'm not expecting her to flip out on me as though I've single-handedly ruined her day.

"Fliss, you *know* I didn't! God, you could be a bit more *sensitive*!" Her voice rises shrilly. "I'm trying to start afresh here! I'm trying to embark on a whole new life with Ben! You don't have to bring up Richard!"

Ben?

I'm completely confused. I think I'm going mad. Who's Ben and what does he have to do with this?

"Look, Lottie. Don't get upset, but I *really* don't understand. . . ."

"I told you just now in my text! Can't you read?"

"You said you were engaged!" A terrible

161

feeling grips me. Is this all some massive misunderstanding? "Are you *not* engaged?"

"Yes! Of course I'm engaged! To Ben!"

"Who the fuck is Ben?" I yell, more loudly than I meant to. Elise looks in at the door curiously, and I shoot her an apologetic smile, mouthing, "It's OK."

There's silence at the end of the phone.

"Oh," says Lottie at last. "Sorry. I just looked back at my text. I thought I'd told you. I'm not marrying Richard; I'm marrying Ben. Remember Ben?"

"No, I do not remember Ben!" I say, feeling increasingly frazzled.

"That's right, you never met him. Well, he was my gap-year boyfriend in Greece, and he's come back into my life and we're getting married."

I feel as though the ceiling has caved in. She was marrying Richard. It all made sense. Now she's running off with some guy called Ben? I don't even know where to start.

"Lotts . . . But, Lotts, I mean . . . How can you be getting married to him?" A thought suddenly comes to me. "Is this a visa thing?"

"No, it's not a visa thing!" She sounds indignant. "It's love!"

"You love this guy Ben enough to marry

162

him?" I can't believe I'm having this conversation.

"Yes."

"When exactly did he come back into your life?"

"Two weeks ago."

"Two weeks ago," I repeat calmly, although I want to burst into hysterical laughter. "After how long?"

"Fifteen years." She sounds defiant. "And before you ask me, yes, I *have* thought it through."

"OK! Well, congratulations. I'm sure Ben's wonderful."

"He's amazing. You'll love him. He's good-looking, and he's fun, and we're *totally* connected —"

"Great! Look, let's meet up for lunch, OK? And we can talk about it."

I'm overreacting, I tell myself. I simply have to adjust to this new situation. Maybe this guy Ben is perfect for Lottie and it will all work out brilliantly. As long as they have a nice long engagement and don't rush into anything —

"Shall we meet at Selfridges?" Lottie says. "I'm there now, actually. I'm buying honeymoon underwear!"

"Yes, I heard. So, when were you planning to get married?"

"Tomorrow," she says happily. "We wanted to do it as soon as possible. Can you take the day off?"

Tomorrow?

She's gone mad.

"Lotts, stay there." I can hardly get the words out. "I'll come and meet you. I think we should have a talk."

I should *never* have relaxed. I should *never* have gone on holiday. I should have realized Lottie wouldn't rest till she'd found something to channel all her hurt energy into. And it's this. A marriage.

By the time I get to Selfridges, my heart is thumping and I have a head full of questions. Lottie, on the other hand, has a basket full of underwear. No, not underwear, *sex kit.* She's standing looking at a transparent basque as I hurtle toward her, almost knocking over a rail of Princesse Tam Tam teddies. As she sees me, she holds it up.

"What do you think?"

I eye the stuff in her basket. She's clearly been at the Agent Provocateur concession. There's lots of black see-through lace. And is that an eye mask?

"What do you think?" she says impatiently, and jiggles the basque at me. "It's quite expensive. Shall I try it on?"

Isn't there a slightly bigger question we should be discussing? I want to yell. *Like: who is this Ben and why are you marrying him?* But if I know one thing about Lottie, it's that I need to play things carefully. I need to talk her down.

"So!" I say as brightly as I can. "You're getting married. To someone I've never met."

"You'll meet him at the wedding. You'll love him, Fliss." Her eyes are shiny as she tosses the transparent basque into her basket and adds a teeny thong. "I can't believe everything's worked out so perfectly. I'm so happy."

"Right. Wonderful! Me too!" I leave a tiny pause before adding, "Although — just a thought — do you *need* to get married so soon? Couldn't you have a long engagement and plan everything properly?"

"There's nothing to plan! It's all going to be so easy. Chelsea Register Office. Lunch at some lovely place. Simple and romantic. You're going to be bridesmaid, I hope." She squeezes my arm, then reaches for another basque.

There's something extra-weird about her. I survey her, trying to work out what's different. She's got that post-breakup manic air about her — but even more than usual.

165

Her eyes are overbright. She's hyper. Is Ben a dealer? Is she *on* something?

"So, Ben just contacted you out of the blue?"

"He got in touch and we had dinner. And it was as though we'd never been apart. We were so in tune with each other." She sighs blissfully. "He'd been in love with me for fifteen years. *Fifteen years.* And I'd been in love with him too. That's why we want to get married quickly. We've wasted enough time already, Fliss." Her voice throbs dramatically, as though she's in a TV true-life movie. "We want to get on with the rest of our life."

What?

OK, this is bollocks. Lottie has not been in love with someone called Ben for the last fifteen years. I think I might know if she had.

"You've been in love with him the last fifteen years?" I can't help challenging her. "Funny that you never mentioned him. At all."

"I loved him *inside.*" She clasps a hand to her side. "*Here.* Maybe I didn't tell you about it. Maybe I don't tell you everything." She defiantly throws a garter belt into her basket.

"Have you got a photo of him?"

166

"Not on me. But he's gorgeous. I want you to give a speech, by the way," she adds blithely. "You're chief-bridesmaid-slash-best-woman. And Ben's best man is his friend Lorcan. It'll just be the four of us at the ceremony."

I stare at her in exasperation. I was planning to be tactful and go softly, softly, but I can't. This is all too crazy.

"Lottie." I plant a hand on the packet of stockings she was about to pick up. "*Stop.* And listen a moment. I know you don't want to hear this, but you have to." I wait until she reluctantly turns her eyes toward me. "You split up from Richard about five minutes ago. You were about to commit to *him.* You'd bought him an engagement ring. You said you loved him. Now you're rushing off with some guy you barely know? Is this really a good idea?"

"Well, it's a good thing I did split up from Richard! A very good thing!" Lottie is suddenly bristling like a cat. "I've done a lot of thinking, Fliss. And I've realized Richard was all wrong for me. *All* wrong! I need someone romantic. Someone who can *feel.* Someone who'll put himself out there for me, you know? Richard's a nice guy and I thought I loved him. But now I realize the truth: he's limited."

She spits out "limited" as though it's the worst insult she can come up with.

"What do you mean, 'limited'?" I can't help feeling a bit defensive on Richard's behalf.

"He's narrow. He has no style. He'd never make some huge, reckless, wonderful gesture. He'd never come and find a girl after fifteen years and tell her that life was darkness without her and now he wants to turn on the switch." Her chin juts defiantly and I give an inward grimace. Was that Ben's line? He wanted to turn on the switch?

I mean, I do sympathize. I had a couple of terrible, misjudged rebound flings after Daniel and I separated. But I didn't *marry* one of them.

"Look, Lottie." I try a different tack. "I do understand. I know what it's like. You're hurt. You're confused. An old boyfriend comes along out of the blue — of course you're going to fall into bed with him. It's natural. But why do you have to get married?"

"You're wrong," she retorts with a triumphant look. "You are so, so wrong, Fliss. I didn't fall into bed with him. And I'm not going to. I'm saving myself for the honeymoon."

She . . .

What?

Of all the things I was expecting to hear, it wasn't this. I stare at Lottie blankly, unable to find an answer. Where is my sister and what has this man done with her?

"You're *saving* yourself?" I echo at last. "But. . . . why? Is he Amish?" I suddenly fear the worst. "Is he from some kind of cult? Did he promise you enlightenment?"

Please don't tell me she's handed over all her money. Not again.

"Of course not!"

"So . . . why?"

"So I'll have the hottest sex ever on my honeymoon night." She grabs the stockings. "We know we're good together, so why not save up for the moment? It's our wedding night. It should be special. As special as it can possibly be." She gives a sudden wriggle, as though she can't contain herself. "And believe me, it will be. God, Fliss, he's so hot. We can hardly keep our hands off each other. It's like we're eighteen again."

I stare at her, all the pieces falling into place. Her shiny eyes make sense. The basket of underwear makes sense. She's raring to go. This engagement is one great big session of fore-play. Why didn't I realize this straightaway? She *is* drugged up — on lust. And not only lust, *teenage* lust. She has the same look about her as teenagers snogging at the bus stop, as though the rest of the world doesn't exist. For a moment I feel a stab of envy. I wouldn't mind disappearing into a bubble of teenage lust, quite frankly. But I have to stay rational here. I have to be the voice of reason.

"Lottie, listen." I'm trying to speak slowly and clearly, to penetrate her trance. "You don't have to get married. You could just take a hotel suite somewhere."

"I *want* to get married!" Humming to herself, she chucks another expensive negligee into her basket, and I suppress a desire to scream. It's all very well. But if she took off the lust goggles for one bloody moment, maybe she'd see how much this escapade is potentially going to end up costing her. A shed-load of underwear. A marriage. A honeymoon. A divorce. All for one epic night of shagging? Which she could have for free?

"I know what you're thinking." She looks up at me resentfully. "You could be happy for me."

"I'm trying to be, I really am." I rub my head. "But it makes no sense. You're doing everything the wrong way round."

"Am I?" She turns on me. "Who says so? Isn't this the traditional way?"

"Lottie, you're being ludicrous." I'm starting to feel angry. "This is no way to start a marriage, OK? A marriage is a serious, legal thing —"

"I know!" She cuts me off. "And I want to make it work, and this is the way. I'm not *stupid,* Fliss." She folds her arms. "I have thought about this, you know. My love life has been a disaster. It's followed the same old pattern, with man after man. Sex. Love. No marriage. Over and over. Well, now I have a chance to do it differently! I'm reversing the strategy! Love. Marriage. Sex!"

"But it's nuts!" I can't help erupting. "The whole thing's nuts! You must see that!"

"No, I don't!" she retorts hotly. "I see a brilliant answer to the whole problem. It's retro! It's tried and tested! Did Queen Victoria have sex before she married Albert? And was their marriage a huge success? Did she love him desperately and build a great big memorial to him in Hyde Park? *Exactly.* Did Romeo and Juliet have sex before they got married?"

"But —"

"Did Elizabeth Bennet and Mr. Darcy have sex before they got married?" Her eyes flash at me as though this proves everything.

Oh, please. If she's going to use Mr. Darcy to prop up her arguments, I give up.

171

"Fair enough," I say at last. "You got me there. Mr. Darcy."

I need to back off for now and come up with a different angle.

"So, who's this Lorcan?" A new idea has come to me. "Who's this best man of Ben's you mentioned?"

Presumably Ben's best friend won't be any wilder than I am about this sudden, out-of-the-blue marriage. Maybe we can join forces.

"Dunno." She waves vaguely. "Some old friend. Works with him."

"Where?"

"The company's called something like . . . Decree."

"And what does Ben do, exactly?"

"Dunno." She holds up a pair of knickers that untie at the back. "Something or other."

I resist an urge to yell, *You're getting married to him and you don't even know what he does?*

I get out my BlackBerry and type in *Ben — Lorcan — Decree?*

"What's Ben's surname?"

"Parr. I'll be Lottie Parr. Isn't that lovely?" *Ben Parr.*

I tap at my BlackBerry, peer at the screen, and do a fake gasp. "Oh goodness. I forgot all about *that.* Actually, Lottie, I'm not sure

I've got time for lunch, after all. I'd better go. Have fun shopping." I give her a hug. "Talk to you later. And . . . congratulations!"

My bright smile lasts all the way out of the underwear department. Before I've even got to the lifts, I'm on Google, typing *Ben Parr*. Ben Parr, my potential new brother-in-law. Who the hell is he?

By the time I get back to my office, I've Googled *Ben Parr* as extensively as I can manage on my phone, but I haven't found any company called Decree, only a bunch of entries about a Ben Parr who does stand-up comedy. Badly, according to the reviews. Is that him?

Great. A failed stand-up. My favorite kind of brother-in-law.

At last I find an entry which mentions a Ben Parr in a news item about a paper company called Dupree Sanders. He has some made-up title like Strategic Overview Consultant. I type in *Ben Parr Dupree Sanders,* and a million new entries appear. Dupree Sanders is clearly a thing. A big company. Here's the home page . . . and sure enough, a page pops up with his picture and a little bio, which I scan. *Having worked with his father as a young man, Ben*

173

Parr was delighted to rejoin Dupree Sanders in 2011, in a strategic role . . . genuine passion for the business . . . Since his father's death, he is even more dedicated to the future of the company.

I lean toward the screen and scan the photo intently, trying to get a sense of this man who is zooming like a torpedo toward being related to me. He's good-looking, I'll have to agree. Boyish-looking. Slim. Affable. Not sure about his mouth. It looks kind of weak.

After a bit, the pixels start to dance in front of my eyes, so I sit back and type in *Lorcan Dupree Sanders.*

A moment later another page pops up, with a photo of a very different-looking man. Dark, thrusting hair, black eyebrows, and a frown. Strong, slightly beaky nose. He looks fairly forbidding. Underneath the picture it says, *Lorcan Adamson. Extension 310. Lorcan Adamson practiced law in London before joining Dupree Sanders in 2008 . . . responsible for many initiatives . . . developed the luxury stationery brand Papermaker . . . worked with the National Trust to expand the visitor center . . . committed to sustainable, responsible industry . . .*

A lawyer. Let's hope he's the rational, reasonable type, not the arrogant asshole type. I dial the number, simultaneously clicking on my emails.

"Lorcan Adamson." The voice that answers is so deep and gravelly, I drop my mouse in surprise. Surely that's not a real voice. It sounds made up.

"Hello?" he says again, and I stifle a giggle. This guy has a film-trailer voice. It's that deep-down rumbly, subwoofer voice you hear as you're scarfing down popcorn, waiting for your movie to begin.

We thought the world was safe. We thought the universe was ours. Till THEY came.

"Hello?" The gravelly voice comes again.

In a desperate fight against time, one girl must break the code —

"Hi. Er . . . hi." I try to assemble my thoughts. "Is this Lorcan Adamson?"

"It's he."

From Academy Award–winning director —

No. Stop, Fliss. Concentrate.

"Right. Right. Yes." I hastily compose myself. "Well, I think we need to speak. My name is Felicity Graveney. My sister is called Lottie."

"Ah." There's a sudden animation to his voice. "Well, excuse my French, but what the fuck is going on here? Ben just called me. Apparently he and your sister are getting *married?"*

175

Two things I pick up straightaway. First: he has a faint Scottish accent. Second: he's not keen on the whole marriage idea either. Thank God. Another voice of reason.

"Exactly!" I say. "And you're best man? I have no idea how this came about, but I was thinking maybe we could get together and —"

"And what? Plan the table decorations?" He talks right over me. "I have no idea how your sister talked Ben into this ridiculous plan, but I'm afraid I'm going to do everything I can to stop it, whether you and your sister like it or not."

I stare at the phone. *What* did he say?

"I work with Ben, and this is a crucial time for him," Lorcan presses on. "He can't just zoom off on some ludicrous, spur-of-the-moment honeymoon. He has responsibilities. He has commitments. Now, I don't know your sister's motivation —"

"What?" I'm so outraged, I don't know where to start.

"Excuse me?" He sounds puzzled that I've dared to interrupt. Oh, he's one of *those*.

"OK, *mister*." Instantly I feel stupid for saying "mister." But too late now. Better plow on. "First of all, my sister didn't talk anybody into anything. I think you'll find *your* friend arrived out of the blue and

176

bamboozled *her* into getting married. And, second, if you think I phoned you up to 'plan the table decorations,' you're very much mistaken. *I'm* intending to put a stop to this marriage myself. With or without your help."

"I see." He sounds skeptical.

"Is Ben saying that Lottie talked him into it?" I demand. "Because if so, he's lying."

"Not as such," says Lorcan after a pause. "But Ben can be . . . what shall we say? Easily swayed."

"Easily swayed?" I retort furiously. "If anyone was doing any swaying, *he* was. My sister is at a low point, she's very vulnerable, and she doesn't need some chancer coming along." I'm still half-expecting this Ben character to belong to some weirdo cult or time-share pyramid scheme. "I mean, what's his job? I don't know anything about him."

"You don't know his background." Again he sounds skeptical. God, this guy is pissing me off.

"I know nothing except he met my sister on her gap year and they had a teenage shag-fest and now he says he's always loved her and they're planning to get married tomorrow and resume the teenage shag-fest. And he works for Dupree Sanders."

177

"He *owns* Dupree Sanders," Lorcan corrects me.

"What?" I say stupidly.

I don't even know what Dupree Sanders is, exactly. I didn't stop to check it out.

"As of his father's death a year ago, Ben is the major shareholder in Dupree Sanders, a paper-manufacturing company worth thirty million pounds. And, for what it's worth, his life has been complicated and he's also pretty vulnerable."

As I digest his words, a boiling hot fury starts to rise within me.

"You think my sister's a *gold digger*?" I erupt. "*That's* what you think?"

I have never been so insulted in all my life. The arrogant . . . conceited . . . *shit.* I'm breathing faster and faster, staring daggers at his screen face.

"I didn't say that," he counters calmly.

"Just listen to me, Mr. Adamson," I say in my iciest tones. "Let's look at the facts, shall we? *Your* precious friend talked *my* sister into a ridiculous, rushed marriage. *Not* the other way round. How do you know she isn't an heiress worth even more? How do you know we're not related to the . . . the Gettys?"

"Touché," says Lorcan after a pause. "Are you?"

178

"Of course we're not," I say impatiently. "The point is, you jumped to conclusions. Surprising, for a lawyer."

There's another silence. I get the feeling I've needled him. Well, good.

"OK," he says finally. "I apologize. I didn't mean to imply anything about your sister. Maybe she and Ben are a match made in heaven. But that doesn't change the fact that we have some very big stuff happening at the company. Ben needs to be available in the UK now. If he wants to go on honeymoon, he'll have to do it later."

"Or never," I put in.

"Or never. Indeed." Lorcan sounds amused. "You're not a fan of Ben, then?"

"I've never even met him. But this has been a useful chat. It's all I needed to know. Leave it with me. I'll deal with it."

"*I'll* deal with it," he contradicts me. "I'll talk to Ben."

God, this guy is winding me up. Who says he should be in charge?

"I'll talk to Lottie," I counter as authoritatively as I can. "I'll fix it."

"I'm sure that won't be necessary." He talks straight across me. "I'll speak to Ben. The whole thing will be forgotten."

"I'll talk to Lottie," I repeat, ignoring him. "And I'll let you know when I've sorted everything out."

There's silence. Neither of us is going to concede, I can tell.

"Right," says Lorcan at last. "Well, good-bye."

"Goodbye."

I put down the receiver, then grab my mobile and dial Lottie's mobile. No more Ms. Nice Sister. I am stopping this marriage. Right here, right now.

6
FLISS

I can't *believe* she's ignored me for a full twenty-four hours. She's got some nerve.

It's the following afternoon, the wedding is due to start in an hour, and I still haven't spoken to Lottie. She's sidestepped my every call (approximately one hundred of them). But at the same time she's managed to leave a whole series of messages on *my* phone, about the registry office and the restaurant and meeting for pre-wedding drinks at Bluebird. A purple satin brides-maid's dress arrived at my office at lunch-time by bike. A poem arrived by email, along with a request for me to read it aloud during the ceremony: *It will make our day so special!*

She doesn't fool me. There's a reason she's not been taking my calls: she feels defensive. Which means I'm in with a chance. I know I can talk her out of this nonsense. I just need to work out exactly

181

where her vulnerability is and exploit it.

As I arrive at Bluebird, I can see her already sitting at the bar in a cream lace minidress, with roses in her hair and adorable vintage-style shoes with button straps. She looks radiantly beautiful, and for a moment I feel bad, coming in to derail her.

But, no. Someone has to stay sane around here. She won't be looking so radiant when she's being billed for her *decree nisi.*

Noah's not with me. He's having a sleepover with his friend Sebastian. I fibbed to Lottie, saying it was really special and he would be "so sorry to miss the wedding." The real reason is that I'm not intending for there to be any wedding.

Lottie has spotted me and waves to get my attention. I wave back and approach with an innocent smile. I'm walking into the paddock quietly, unthreateningly, the halter hidden behind my back. I'm the Bride Whisperer.

"You look gorgeous!" As I reach Lottie, I give her a huge hug. "How exciting. What a happy day!"

Lottie scans my face without replying, which proves I'm right: she's on the defensive. But I keep my smile steady, as though I haven't noticed a thing.

"I thought you weren't keen on the idea,"

she says at last.

"What?" I act shocked. "Of *course* I'm keen on the idea! I was just surprised. But I'm sure Ben is absolutely wonderful and you'll be happy for many, many years."

I hold my breath. She's visibly relaxing. Her guard is coming down.

"Yes," she says. "Yes, we will. Well, sit down. Have some champagne! Here's your bouquet." She hands me a little cluster of roses.

"Wow! Fabulous."

She pours me a glass and I raise it in a toast. Then I glance at my watch. Fifty-five minutes to go. I need to get cracking on the derailment strategy.

"So, any honeymoon plans?" I say casually. "You probably didn't manage to book anywhere at such short notice. What a shame. A honeymoon is such a special time, you want it to be perfect. If you'd held on a few weeks, I could have helped you arrange something amazing. In fact . . . shall we do that?" I put down my glass as though seized by a brilliant new idea. "Lottie, let's put off the wedding just a *teeny* bit and have fun planning the perfect honeymoon for you!"

"Don't worry," says Lottie happily. "We already have the perfect honeymoon arranged! One night at the Savoy and then off tomorrow!"

"Really?" I get ready to trump it. "Where are you going, then?"

"We're going back to Ikonos. Back to where we met. Isn't it perfect?"

"To a backpackers' guest house?" I stare at her.

"No, silly! To that amazing hotel! The Amba. The one with the waterfall. Didn't you review it?"

Damn. The Amba is pretty untrumpable. It opened three years ago and we've reviewed it twice since then — five stars each time. It's the most spectacular place in the Cyclades and was voted Top Honeymoon Destination two years running.

Since then, it's already become *just* a touch tacky, truth be told. It's been flooded with celebrity couples and *Hello!* magazine photo shoots, and it plays to the "honeymoon" market too strongly if you ask me. Still, it remains an amazing, world-class hotel. I'll need to work hard to talk her out of it.

"The only thing about the Amba is, you have to be on the best side." I shake my head gloomily. "At such short notice, they've probably shoved you in that awful side wing. There's no sun, and it smells. You'll be miserable." I suddenly brighten. "I know!

184

Wait a few weeks, and let me call in a favor. I can get you the Oyster Suite, I'm sure. Honestly, Lotts, the bed alone is worth waiting for. It's massive, with a glass dome above so you can see the stars. You *have* to have it." I proffer my phone. "Why don't you call Ben and say you want to put things off, only for a few weeks —"

"But we've *got* the Oyster Suite!" Lottie interrupts me joyfully. "It's all booked! We're having a bespoke honeymoon, with our own private butler and treatments every day and a day on the hotel yacht!"

"What?" I stare at her, my phone dangling limply in my hand. "How?"

"There was a cancelation!" She beams. "Ben uses some special concierge service and they fixed it up. Isn't it great?"

"Marvelous," I say after a pause. "Super."

"Ikonos is so special to us." She's bubbling over. "I mean, it's been totally ruined, I'm sure. When we were there, they didn't even have an *airport,* let alone any big hotels. We had to get there by boat. But, still, it'll be like going back in time. I can't wait."

There's no point pushing this one any further. I sip my champagne, thinking hard.

"Have you got a vintage Rolls-Royce today?" I try a different tack. "You always wanted a vintage Rolls-Royce for your wedding."

"No." She shrugs. "I can walk."

"But what a shame!" I put on a stricken expression. "It was your dream to have a vintage Rolls-Royce. If you just waited a bit, you could have one."

"Fliss." Lottie gives me a gently chiding smile. "Aren't you being rather shallow? The important thing is love. Finding a life partner. Not some random car. Don't you think?"

"Of course." I smile back tightly. OK, leave the car. Try another approach.

Dress? No. She's wearing a lovely dress.

Wedding-gifts list? No. She's not that materialistic.

"So . . . will there be any hymns at the wedding?" I ask at last. There's silence. Quite a long silence. I stare at Lottie in sudden hope. Her face has tightened.

"We're not allowed hymns," she says at last, and looks down into her drink. "You can't have them at a registry-office wedding."

Yes! Bingo!

"No hymns?" I raise a hand to my mouth in horror, as though I hadn't known this all along. "But how can you have a wedding without hymns? What about 'I Vow to Thee,

My Country'? You were always going to have that at your wedding."

Lottie was in the choir at our boarding school. She used to sing solos. Music was a big deal to her. I should have started with this tack first.

"Well. It's not important." She smiles briefly — but her whole demeanor has changed.

"What does Ben think?"

"Ben's not really into hymns," she says after a pause.

Ben's not really into hymns.

I want to whoop. This is it. Her Achilles' heel. I have her like putty in my hands.

"I vow to thee, my country," I start singing very quietly. "All earthly things above."

"Stop," she says, almost snapping.

"Sorry." I raise an apologetic hand. "Just . . . thinking aloud. For me, a wedding is all about the music. The beautiful, wonderful music."

This is untrue. I couldn't care less about music, and if Lottie were sharper, she'd instantly realize I'm winding her up. But she's looking away, lost in her own world. Are her eyes a little glassy?

"I always imagined you kneeling at the altar in a country church with the organ playing," I muse, rubbing it in. "Not at a

187

registry office. Funny, that."

"Yes." She doesn't even turn her head.

"Da-da-*daah*-da-da-da-*da-ah*-da . . ." I'm still humming the tune of "I Vow to Thee, My Country." Obviously I don't know all the words, but the tune is enough. That's what'll get her.

Her eyes *are* glassy. OK, time to go in for the kill.

"Anyway!" I break off from singing. "The important thing is that this is your special day. And it's going to be perfect. Nice and quick. No stupid fussing about with music, or choirboys, or bells pealing from a country steeple . . . Just in and out. Sign a paper, say a couple of words, and you're done. For life," I add. *"Finito."*

I feel almost cruel. I can see her bottom lip quivering very slightly.

"Do you remember the bridal scene in *The Sound of Music*?" I add casually. "When Maria walks up the aisle to the nuns' singing and her big long veil floating everywhere . . ."

Don't overdo it, Fliss.

I lapse into silence and sip my champagne, waiting. I can see Lottie's eyes flickering with thoughts. I can sense her inner battle between romance and lust. I think romance is just getting the edge. I think the violins are playing louder than the jungle drums. She looks as if she's coming to a decision. *Please* go the right way, go on. . . .

"Fliss . . ." She looks up. "Fliss . . ."

Just call me the World Champion Bride Whisperer.

There was no argument. No confrontation. Lottie thinks it was *her* idea to postpone. I was the one saying, "Are you sure, Lottie? Are you positive you want to call things off? Really?"

I've totally sold her on the idea of a country wedding with music and a choir and bells. She's already looked up the name of the chaplain at our old school. She's off on a new dream of satin and posies and "I Vow to Thee, My Country."

Which is fine. A wedding is lovely. Marriage is lovely. Maybe Ben is destined to be her life partner and I'll kick myself as she has her tenth grandchild and think, *What was my problem?* But at least this way gives her some breathing space. At least it gives her time to look at Ben and think, *Hmm. Sixty more years with you. Is this a good idea?*

Lottie's gone off to the registry office, to tell Ben the news. My work is done. The only task remaining is to buy her *Brides* magazine. We're going to meet up for coffee tomorrow and have a cozy chat about veils, and then, in the evening, *finally* I'll get to meet Ben.

I'm waiting to cross the King's Road, mentally congratulating myself for being so brilliant, when I see a face I recognize. Beaky nose. Windswept dark hair. Rose in his buttonhole. He's about ten feet tall and is striding along the pavement on the other side, with the kind of thunderous frown that you wear when your rich best friend has been grabbed by an evil gold digger and you've got to be best man. As he's walking, his rose suddenly falls out, and he stops to pick it up. He's looking at it with such a murderous expression, I almost want to laugh.

Ha. Well, wait till I tell *him.* What's his name again? Oh yes, Lorcan.

"Hi!" I wave frantically as he moves off. "Lorcan! Stop!"

His stride is so fast, I'll never catch up with him. He pauses and swivels round suspiciously, and I wave again to get his attention.

"Over here! Me! I need to speak to you!" I wait for him to cross, then approach him, brandishing my bouquet. "I'm Fliss Graveney. We spoke yesterday? Lottie's sister?"

"Ah." His face clears briefly, then it's back to the cheery, wedding-day scowl. "I suppose you're heading there now?"

I'd forgotten about the ridiculous movie-trailer voice. Although somehow it sounds less ridiculous when it's not a disembodied voice coming down a phone line. It matches his face. Dark and kind of intense.

"Well, *actually* . . ." I can't help sounding complacent. "I'm not heading there, because it's off."

He stares at me in shock. "What do you mean?"

"It's off. For now," I add. "Lottie's gone to postpone the wedding."

"Why?" he demands. He's so bloody *suspicious.*

"So she can make sure Ben's fortune is invested in a way that makes it easy to plunder," I say with a shrug. "Obviously."

Lorcan's face flickers with amusement. "OK. I deserved that. What's going on? Why is she postponing?"

"I talked her out of it," I say proudly. "I know my sister, and I know the power of suggestion. After our little chat, she wants a romantic wedding in a small stone church in the country. That's why she's postponing. My reasoning is: if they delay, at least it gives them a chance to see if they're right for each other."

"Well, thank God for that." Lorcan breathes out and runs a hand through his hair. Finally his hackles are coming down; finally his brow is starting to relax. "Ben is in no place to be getting married right now. It was nuts."

"Ridiculous," I agree.

"Insane."

"Stupidest idea ever. No, I take that back." I glance down at myself. "Putting me in a purple bridesmaid's dress was the stupidest idea ever."

"I think you look very nice." Another flicker of amusement passes across his face. He glances at his watch. "What should I do? I'm supposed to be meeting Ben at the registry office by now."

"I think we should stay away."

"Agreed."

There's a pause. This is weird, standing on a street corner, all dressed up with no wedding to go to. I finger my bouquet awkwardly and wonder if I should throw it in the bin. It seems wrong somehow.

"Do you feel like a drink?" says Lorcan abruptly. "I feel like a drink."

"I feel like about six drinks," I counter. "It takes it out of you, talking someone out of a wedding."

"OK. Let's do it."

A man of swift decisions. I like that. He's already ushering me down a side street, toward a bar with a striped canopy and French-looking tables and chairs.

"Hey, I assume your sister *did* call it off?" Lorcan stops dead in the doorway. "We're not going to get an irate text saying, *Where the hell are you?*"

"Nothing from Lottie." I check my phone. "She was pretty determined to cancel. I'm sure she did."

"Nothing from Ben either." Lorcan's looking at his BlackBerry. "I think we're in the clear." He ushers me to a corner table and opens the drinks menu. "You want a glass of wine?"

"I want a large gin and tonic."

"You earned it." He gives that flicker of a smile again. "I'll join you."

He orders the drinks, switches off his phone, and slips it into his pocket. A man who puts away his phone. I like that too.

"So, why is it a bad time for Ben to be getting married?" I ask. "In fact, who *is* this Ben? Fill me in."

"Ben." Lorcan's face twists wryly as though he doesn't know where to start. "Ben, Ben, Ben." There's a long pause. Has he forgotten what his best friend is like?

193

"He's . . . bright. Inventive. He has a lot going for him."

He sounds so strained and unconvincing, I stare at him. "Do you realize you sounded as if you were saying, 'He's an ax murderer.'"

"I did not." Lorcan looks caught out.

"You did. I've never seen anyone look so negative while they're trying to big up their friend." I put on a funereal voice. " 'He's bright. He's inventive. He kills people in their sleep. In inventive ways.' "

"Jesus! Are you always this —" Lorcan breaks off and sighs. "OK. I suppose I'm trying to protect him. He's in a difficult place, Ben. His father died. The company has an uncertain future, and he needs to decide which direction it's going in. He's a natural gambler but he lacks judgment. It's difficult for him. He's having a bit of an early midlife crisis, I guess."

An *early midlife crisis*? Oh, perfect. Just what Lottie needs.

"Not husband material, then?" I say, and Lorcan snorts.

"Maybe one day. When he's got his shit together. Last month he was buying a cabin in Montana. Then he was going to buy a boat, sail in races. Before that, he was all about investing in vintage motorbikes. Next

194

week it'll be some other craze. My guess is he won't stay married five minutes. I'm afraid your sister will be the casualty."

My heart is sinking, fast. "Well, thank God it's off."

"You did a good thing." He nods. "Not least because we need Ben around. He can't go AWOL again."

I screw up my eyes. "What do you mean, 'AWOL again'?"

Lorcan sighs. "He did it once before. When his father became ill. Disappeared for ten days. There was a hell of a fuss. We got the police involved, everything. Then he re-appeared. No apologies, no explanations. To this day I don't know where he got to."

The drinks arrive and Lorcan raises his glass. "Cheers. To canceled weddings."

"Canceled weddings." I lift my own glass and take a delicious gulp of gin and tonic, then return to the subject of Ben. "So, why is he having a midlife crisis?"

Lorcan hesitates, as though he doesn't want to break his friend's confidence.

"Come on," I prod. "I'm nearly related to him, after all."

"I suppose so." He shrugs. "I've known Ben since I was thirteen. We were at school together. My own parents are expats in Singapore and I don't have any other family. I

195

went to stay with Ben a couple of times in the holidays and I became close to the whole family. Ben's dad and I share a love of hiking. *Shared,* I should say." He pauses, fingers clasped gently round his glass. "Ben never came hiking with us. Not interested. And he never wanted to know about the family firm either. He saw it as this massive pressure. Everyone expected he'd join his father as soon as he left school, but it was the last thing he wanted to do."

"So how come *you* work for them?"

"I joined a few years ago." Lorcan gives an odd little half smile. "I was going through some . . . personal stuff. I wanted to get out of London, so I went to stay with Ben's dad, up in Staffordshire. At first I was just planning to spend a few days there, go on some hikes, clear my head. But I started getting involved with the company. Never left."

"Staffordshire?" I say in surprise. "But don't you live in London?"

"We have offices in London, of course." He shrugs. "I commute between the two, but I prefer being up there. It's a beautiful setting. The paper mills are set in a country estate. The offices are in the main house, the family home. It's Grade One listed. Did you see that BBC series *Highton Hall*?" he adds. "Well, that's us. They shot there for eight weeks. Little money-spinner for us."

"Highton Hall?" I stare at him. "Wow. That place is beautiful. And massive!"

Lorcan nods. "Lots of workers live in cottages on the estate. We do guided tours of the house, the mills, the woodland, we have local conservation projects. . . . It's kind of special." His eyes have lit up.

"Right." I'm digesting all this. "So you started working for the company — but Ben wasn't interested?"

"Not until his dad became ill and he had to face the fact he was going to inherit this thing," says Lorcan bluntly. "Before that, he did everything he could to avoid it. He trained as an actor, he tried out stand-up comedy —"

"It *was* him!" I put my gin and tonic glass down with a tiny crash. "I Googled him and all I could find were stand-up comedy reviews. Terrible ones. Was he that bad?"

Lorcan stirs his glass, his attention fixed on the remaining ice cubes.

"You can tell me." I lower my voice. "Between us. Was he embarrassing?"

Lorcan isn't answering. Well, of course he isn't. He doesn't want to dis his best friend. I respect that.

"All right," I say after a moment's thought. "Just answer me one thing. When I meet

197

him, is he going to tell me jokes and I have to pretend they're funny?"

"Watch out if he starts a riff on jeans." At last Lorcan looks up, his mouth twitching. "And laugh. He'll be upset if you don't."

"Jeans." I make a mental note. "OK. Thanks for the warning. Is there *anything* positive to say about this guy?"

"Oh." Lorcan seems shocked. "Of course! When Ben's on form, believe me, there's no one you'd rather spend the evening with. He's charming. He's funny. I can understand why your sister would have fallen for him. When you meet him, you'll understand too."

I take another gulp of my drink. I'm slowly starting to relax. "Well, maybe he'll become my brother-in-law. But at least it won't happen today. Job done."

"I'll talk to Ben later." Lorcan nods. "Make sure he doesn't get any stupid ideas."

At once I feel a tweak of irritation. I just said "Job done," didn't I?

"You don't have to talk to Ben," I say politely. "I've already sorted it. There's no way Lottie will get married in a hurry now. I'd leave it."

"It can't hurt." He looks unmoved. "Just to hammer the point home."

"Yes, it can!" I plonk my drink down.

"Don't do any hammering! I've spent half an hour making Lottie think that pulling out of the wedding was *her* idea. I was subtle. I was careful. I didn't go rushing in like a . . . a hammerer."

His face doesn't shift a millimeter. He's clearly a control freak. But so am I. And this is my sister.

"*Don't* talk to Ben," I command him. "Leave it. Less is more."

There's a pause — then Lorcan shrugs and drains his drink, without answering. I'm guessing he knows I'm right but doesn't want to admit it. I finish my gin and tonic too, then wait a beat, almost holding my breath. I'm hoping he suggests another drink, I realize. I only have an empty house to go to. No work. No plans. And the truth is, I *like* sitting here, sparring with this slightly too intense, slightly bad-tempered man.

"Another?" He looks up and meets my eye, and I feel things shift between us a little. The first drink was like a coda to the whole affair. It was resolution. It was just being polite.

This is more than polite.

"Yes, let's."

"Same again?"

I nod and watch as he summons the waiter

and orders. Nice hands. Good strong jaw. Unhurried, laconic mannerisms. He's a lot more appealing than his webpage gives away.

"Your website photo is terrible," I say abruptly, as the waiter disappears. "Really bad. Did you know that?"

"Wow." Lorcan raises his eyebrows, looking taken aback. "You're direct. Lucky I'm not vain."

"It's not about vanity." I shake my head. "It's not that you're better-looking in the flesh. It's that your *personality* is better. I'm looking at you and I'm seeing a guy who makes time for people. A guy who puts away his phone. Who listens. You're charming. In a way."

"In a *way*?" He gives an incredulous laugh.

"But your photo doesn't say that." I ignore him. "In your photo, you're scowling. You're giving out the message: *Who the hell are you? What are you looking at? I haven't got time for this.*"

"You got all that from one website photo?"

"I'm guessing you gave the photographer about five minutes and grumbled the whole time and checked your BlackBerry between every shot. Bad move."

Lorcan seems a bit speechless, and I

wonder if I've gone too far.

OK, of *course* I've gone too far. I don't even know the guy and I'm critiquing his photo.

"Sorry," I backpedal. "I can be . . . blunt."

"No kidding."

"Feel free to be blunt back." I meet his eyes. "I won't be offended."

"Fair enough," says Lorcan without missing a beat. "That bridesmaid's dress is terrible on you."

In spite of myself, I feel a flicker of hurt. I didn't think it was *that* bad.

"Earlier on, you said it looked very nice," I retaliate.

"I was lying. You look like a fruit pastille."

I guess I asked for it.

"Well, OK. Maybe I do look like a fruit pastille." I can't resist making a little extra dig. "But at least I don't have a picture of myself looking like a fruit pastille on my website."

The waiter puts down two more gin and tonics, and I pick mine up, feeling a bit fired up after our exchange. I'm also wondering how we've got so far off topic. Maybe we should get back to the subject in hand.

"Did you hear about Lottie and Ben's no-sex policy, by the way?" I say. "How ridiculous is that?"

"Ben mentioned something. I thought he was joking."

"It's no joke. They're waiting till the wedding night." I shake my head. "If you want my opinion, it's *irresponsible* to get married to someone without sleeping with them. It's asking for trouble!"

"Interesting idea." Lorcan shrugs. "Old-fashioned."

I take a deep gulp. I'm feeling a need to off-load my thoughts on the subject, and I can't exactly sound off to Noah.

"If you want my theory" — I lean forward — "it's skewed their judgment. The whole thing is about sex. Lottie's lost in a cloud of lust. The longer she waits, the less she can think straight. I mean, I get it. I'm sure he's very hot and she's longing to roll around with him. But does she have to *marry* him?"

"It's cockeyed." Lorcan nods.

"That's what I said! They should just go to bed. Spend a week in bed. A month if they want to! Have a good time. *Then* see if they still want to marry each other." I take another massive gulp of my drink. "I mean, you don't need to sign your life away just to have sex —" I break off as a thought suddenly occurs to me. "Are you married?"

"Divorced."

"Me too. Divorced. So. We know."

202

"About what?"

"Sex." I realize that came out wrong. "Marriage," I amend.

Lorcan thinks for a moment, sipping his drink. "The more I think back over the last few years," he says slowly, "the less I feel I know about marriage. Sex, on the other hand, I would hope I've nailed."

The gin has gone straight to my head. I can feel it buzzing around, loosening my tongue.

"I'm sure you have," I hear myself saying.

The air seems to thicken in the silence. A little too late, I realize I've just told a total stranger that I'm sure he's good in bed. Do I backtrack? Qualify in some way?

No. Move on. I cast around for something anodyne, but it's Lorcan who speaks next.

"Since we're speaking frankly — how've you found it? Your divorce? Total nightmare?"

Have I found my divorce a total nightmare?

I open my mouth and draw in a deep, long breath, automatically reaching for the memory stick round my neck. Then I stop.

Not bitter, Fliss. *Not* bitter. Sweet. I need to think spun sugar, candy, flowers, fluffy lambs, Julie Andrews. . . .

"Oh, you know." I give him a saccharine smile. "These things happen."

"How long ago was it?"

"Still happening." My smile broadens. "Should be sorted soon."

"And you're *smiling*?" He sounds incredulous.

"I like to be Zen about it." I nod several times. "Stay calm, move on. Look on the bright side. Don't dwell."

"Wow." Lorcan's eyes have widened. "I'm impressed. Mine was four years ago. Still hurts."

"That's a real pity," I manage. "Poor you."

My fake smile is nearly killing me. I want to ask him how it still hurts and what happened and shall we compare ways in which our exes are total louses? I'm desperate to spill out all the details and talk incessantly about it until I hear from him what I need to hear, i.e., that I'm in the right about everything and Daniel is in the wrong.

Which, no doubt, is why Barnaby gave me a talking-to.

He's always right. Bastard.

"So. Um. Shall I get some more drinks?" I reach for my bag and hurriedly pull out my purse.

Argh. *No.*

The purse flipped up as I tugged it out and with it came the contents of my Durex variety pack. Ribbed for Extra Pleasure falls on the table, and a Pleasuremax lands in Lorcan's drink, splashing him in the face. A Fetherlite has fallen on top of our bowl of peanuts.

"Oh!" I quickly start grabbing them. "Those aren't — They were for my son's school project."

"Ah." Lorcan nods, politely retrieving the Pleasuremax from his drink and handing it to me. "How old's your son?"

"Seven."

"Seven?" He looks scandalized.

"It's . . . Long story." I wince as he hands me the dripping condom. "Let me get you another drink. I'm so sorry." Automatically I've started drying the Pleasuremax with a paper napkin.

"I'd probably chuck that one," says Lorcan. "Unless you're desperate."

I glance up sharply. He looks deadpan but there's something about his voice that makes me want to laugh.

"It's fine," I counter. "Waste not, want not." I stuff it back into my bag. "Another gin? Without the contraceptive garnish?"

"I'll get them." He leans back, tilting his chair to signal at the waiter, and I find my eyes running over his long, lean body. I don't know if it's the gin or the frisson of having told him he's good in bed or this whole weird situation, but I'm becoming a little fixated. I'm mapping myself onto him in my head. Bit by bit. What would those hands feel like on my skin? What would his hair feel like between my fingers? His jaw is faintly stubbled, which is good. I like friction. I like spark. That's what I'm feeling between us. The right kind of spark.

I predict he's slow and determined in bed. Focused. Takes sex as seriously as he takes fixing his friend's love life.

Did I just say *predict*? What exactly am I thinking myself into here?

As Lorcan lets the chair rest back on the ground, he looks at me and his eyelids flicker. He's thinking something too. His eyes keep skimming over my legs and I casually shift in my seat so that my skirt rucks a little higher.

I bet he leaves teeth marks. No idea why. I just feel it instinctively.

I don't know what to say. I can't find any breezy conversational gambits in my head. I want to drink two more gins, I decide. Two gins should do it. And then . . .

"So." I break the silence.

"So." Lorcan nods, then adds casually, "Do you have to get back for your son?"

"Not tonight. He's sleeping over at a friend's."

"Ah."

And now he looks directly at me and my throat is suddenly tight with longing. It's been too long. Far too long. Not that I'll admit that to him. If he asks, I'll say casually, *Oh, I had a recent short-term relationship that didn't work out.* Easy. Normal. Not: *I've been so alone, so stressed, I'm totally gagging for it, not just the sex but the touching and the intimacy and the feeling of another human being beside me, holding me, even if it's only for a night or half a night or some portion of a night.*

That's what I *won't* say.

A waitress comes up with our fresh drinks. She sets them down and then eyes my bouquet, followed by Lorcan's buttonhole. "Oh! Are you two getting married?"

I can't help bursting into laughter. Of all the questions.

"No. No. Not at all."

"Definitely not," Lorcan affirms.

"Only we have a special champagne deal for wedding parties," she persists. "We get so many, what with the registry office down the road. Are you being joined by the bride and groom?"

"Actually, we're anti-marriage," I say. "Our motto is: make love, not vows."

"Here's to that." Lorcan lifts his glass, his

eyes glinting.

The waitress looks from Lorcan to me, laughs uncertainly, then retreats. I down about half my glass. My head is gently spinning and I feel another surge of longing. I'm imagining his lips on mine, his hands ripping off my dress. . . .

Oh God. Get a grip, Fliss. He's probably imagining his bus home.

I look away again and stir my drink, playing for time. I can never stand this uncertain stage of meeting a man, when you have no idea how things are going. You're chugging up the slow-climb roller coaster of a date. You know how far up you are, but you don't know how far he is, or even if he's really with you. Maybe he's mentally heading in the other direction. Here I am, already midway through sexual fantasy number 53, but he could be about to wrap up politely and head home.

"Would you like to go somewhere else?" Lorcan says abruptly, and my stomach lurches in anticipation. *Somewhere else.* Where?

"That would be great, yes." I force myself to sound low key and chilled. "What kind of place?"

He frowns deeply, attacking his ice cubes with his stirrer, as though he has no idea where to start tackling this profound and complex question.

"We could eat," he says finally, with no enthusiasm. "Sushi, maybe. Or . . ."

"Or we could not eat."

He looks up, his guard finally down, and I feel a delicious shiver. He's like a mirror image of me. He has a hungry look in his eye. A desperate longing. He wants to devour something, and I don't think it's sushi.

"That could work," he says, his eyes flicking to my legs again. Leg man, clearly.

"So . . . where do you live?" I ask lightly, as though it's a totally unrelated question.

"Not too far."

His eyes are now locked on mine. OK, we've reached the top. Together. I can see the view stretching ahead. I can't help an exhilarated little smile. I think we're in for a good time.

7
FLISS

I'm half awake. I think. Oh God. My head hurts.

So many thoughts. Where do I start? Remembered sensations are crowding out my brain in a blur. And sudden flashes: intense, astonishing memories like squeezes of lemon. Him. Me. Under. Over . . . Suddenly I realize I'm mentally intoning Noah's old picture book, *Opposites Are Fun!* Inside. Outside. This way. That way.

But now the fun's over. It must be morning, if the light dazzling my eyelids is a clue. I'm lying, one leg thrown over the duvet, not quite daring to open my eyes. You. Me. Then. Now. Oh God, *now.*

I open one eye a chink and get an eyeful of beige duvet. Ah yes. I remember the beige duvet from last night. Clearly the ex-wife took all the White Company Egyptian cotton and he went to the nearest Linen for Divorced Men store. My head is throbbing, and after a moment the beige starts to shimmer in front of my eyes. So I close them and roll onto my back. I haven't had a one-night stand in a long time. A looooong time. I've forgotten how they go. Awkward kiss? Exchange numbers? Coffee?

Coffee. I could do with the coffee.

"Morning." The sound of his rumbly voice finally brings me into reality. He's here. In the room.

"Oh. Um." I raise myself onto an elbow, playing for time, hastily rubbing sleep from my eyes. "Hello."

Hello. Goodbye.

Pulling the duvet around me, I sit up, trying to smile, although my face feels creaky. Lorcan is fully dressed in a suit and tie, holding out a mug. I blink at him for a moment, trying to reconcile the today-him with the last-night-him. Did I *dream* some of that stuff?

"Cup of tea?" The mug he's proffering is cheap and striped. From Crockery for Divorced Men, I'm guessing.

"Oh." I grimace. "Sorry. Don't do tea. Water's fine."

"Coffee?"

"I'd *love* a coffee. And a shower?"

And a change of clothes. And those documents I left at home and the Molton Brown gift set for Elise's birthday . . . My brain is slowly starting to crank into gear. This was really not a sensible move. I'll have to whiz back home, postpone my nine A.M. phone interview. . . . I'm already searching around for my phone. I need to call Sebastian's house, too, and say good morning to Noah.

My eye falls on the purple bridesmaid's dress. Double shit.

"Bathroom's this way." Lorcan gestures out the door.

"Thanks." I gather up the duvet and try to wrap it around myself elegantly, like an actress in a sitcom bedroom scene, but it's so heavy it's like trying to wear a polar bear. With an almighty effort I drag it off the bed, take one step, and immediately trip over, bumping into a bureau and hitting my elbow.

"Ow!"

"Dressing gown?" He holds out a rather swanky paisley number. I guess the wife couldn't swipe that.

I hesitate a moment. Wearing his dressing gown seems a bit cutesy. A bit *Let me put on your great big manly shirt and allow the sleeves to flap endearingly around my fingers.* But I have no choice.

"Thanks."

He averts his eyes politely, like a massage

212

therapist in a spa — i.e., completely point-lessly, since he's seen it all — and I slip into the gown.

"I'm sensing you're a coffee snob." He raises his eyebrows. "Would I be right?"

I open my mouth to say, "Oh no, any-thing's fine!" Then I stop. I *am* a coffee snob. And I'm a tad hungover. And, truth is, I'd rather have no coffee than some depressing cup of dishwater.

"Kind of. But don't worry. I'll have a two-second shower and get out of here —"

"I'll go out for it."

"No!"

"It'll take two seconds. Same as your shower."

He disappears, and I start to look around for my handbag. I've got a hairbrush in there. And some hand cream, which could double up as moisturizer. As my gaze rakes around the room, I find myself wondering if I like him. Whether I might see him again. Whether this might even become . . . a thing?

Not a *serious* thing. I'm mid-divorce; it would be nuts to leap into a relationship. But it was good last night. Even if I'm only remembering half of it accurately, that half was enough to want to reprise it. Maybe we could have some kind of regular arrangement, I find myself thinking. Every month, like a book club.

Where *is* my bag? I wander farther into the room and see a fencing mask hanging on a hook. There's a sword too, or whatever they call them. I've always liked the idea of fencing. Oh, I can't resist. Gingerly, I take the thing off its hook and put it on. There's a mirror hung on the wall, and I head over to it, brandishing the sword.

"Arise, Sir Thingummy," I say to my reflection. "Haaa-yah!" I do a kung fu action at myself, and the paisley dressing gown flaps round my ankles.

Now I've got the giggles. And suddenly I want to share this ridiculous moment with Lottie. I pull out my phone and speed-dial her.

"Hi, Fliss!" she answers at once. "OK, I'm on the *Brides* website. Veil or no veil? I think veil. What about a train?"

I blink at the phone, wanting to laugh. She's become a bridezilla. Naturally. The great thing about Lottie is she doesn't bear grudges or dwell when she's thwarted in life. She just changes direction and charges off, eyes on the horizon.

"Veil."

"What?"

"Veil." I realize my voice is muffled in the

214

helmet and shove it up to the top of my head. "*Veil.* So, you called the wedding off OK? Ben didn't mind?"

"I had to talk him into it, but he was OK in the end. He said he only wanted what I wanted."

"Did you take your honeymoon night at the Savoy anyway?"

"No!" She sounds shocked. "I told you, we're waiting till we're married!"

Damn. She's still on that crazy plan. I was hoping the lust goggles might have slipped a little.

"And Ben's happy with that?" I can't help sounding skeptical.

"Ben wants *me* to be happy." Lottie's voice takes on a familiar, syrupy tone. "You know what? I'm so glad we talked, Fliss. The wedding's going to be *so* much nicer. And the plus is: you and Ben can meet each other first!"

"Gosh, introduce him to your family *before* you walk up the aisle and commit your life to him forever? Are you sure about that?"

I don't think she gets my tone. I think the bridal happy haze is acting as a protective atmosphere. Sarcasm gets burned up before it even reaches her ears.

"Actually, I met his friend Lorcan last

night," I add. "He's already filled me in a little."

"Really?" She sounds excited. "You've met Lorcan? Wow! What did he say about Ben?"

What did he say about Ben? Let's think, now. *Ben is in no place to be getting married right now. . . . He's having a bit of an early midlife crisis . . . your sister will be the casualty. . . .*

"Just the basics," I prevaricate. "Anyway, I can't wait to meet Ben. Let's do it very soon. Tonight?"

"Yes! Let's all have drinks or something. Fliss, you'll love him. He's so funny. He used to be a comedian!"

"A *comedian.*" I adopt an amazed and delighted tone. "Wow. I can't wait. So . . . uh . . . anyway. Guess where I am right now? In Lorcan's flat."

"Huh?"

"We . . . we hooked up. We ran into each other near the registry office and we had a few drinks and one thing led to another."

She's going to hear about it anyway, and I'd rather be the one who told her.

"No *way*!" Lottie's voice fizzes over. "Oh, that's perfect! We can have a double wedding!"

Only Lottie. Only she would say this.

"Snap!" I say. "That's just what I was

216

thinking, too. Can we ride up the aisle on matching ponies?"

This time the sarcasm does reach her ears.

"Don't be like that!" she says reprovingly. "You never know. Keep an open mind. I met up with Ben on spec and look! Here we are."

Yes! Here we are. A girl on the rebound and a guy having a midlife crisis, hurtling into ill-considered matrimony. I'm sure there's a Disney song about that. It rhymes "kiss" with "bitter legal battle."

"It was a shag," I say patiently. "That's it. End of."

"It might lead to more," retorts Lottie. "He might turn out to be the love of your life. Did you have a good time? Did you like him? Is he hot?"

"Yes, yes, and yes."

"Well, then! Don't rule it out. Hey, I'm looking at this wedding website. Shall we have a profiterole cake? Or what about a pyramid of cupcakes?"

I shut my eyes. She's like a steamroller.

"That's what they had at Aunt Diana's wedding, remember," Lottie's saying. "How big was that?"

"Small."

"Are you sure? I remember it as quite a big occasion."

She was five at the time. Of course she

remembers it as big.

"Seriously, tiny. The whole night was such an ordeal. I had to pretend I was having a good time, and all along . . ." I pull a revolted face. I still remember the too-tight bridesmaid's dress they made me wear. And dancing with Aunt Diana's beery grown-up friends.

"Really?" She sounds puzzled. "But the ceremony was nice, wasn't it?"

"No. Terrible. And afterward wasn't much better."

"Ooh! You can get profiteroles with sparkly icing." She's not even listening. "Shall I send you the link?"

"I feel ill at the very thought," I say firmly. "In fact, I might throw up. And then Lorcan will *never* love me, and we'll *never* get married in a double wedding on matching ponies —"

A sound makes me turn. The blood rushes to my head. Shit. *Shit.*

He's there. Lorcan's standing there, about ten foot high in the doorway. How long has he been there? What did he hear me say?

"Gotta go, Lotts." I quickly turn off my phone. "Just talking to my sister," I add, as casually as I can. "Just . . . joking. Joking about things. Like you do."

Suddenly I remember I'm wearing his

218

fencing helmet. My stomach clenches with fresh embarrassment. Let's see this through his eyes: I'm standing in his house in his dressing gown, wearing his helmet, and talking about a double wedding. Hastily, I grab the helmet and lift it off my head.

"This is . . . nice," I say inanely.

"I didn't know if you wanted it black or not," he says after what seems like an eternity.

"Oh. The coffee."

There's some other vibe going on here. What? My own voice runs through my head: *I had to pretend I was having a good time. . . .*

He didn't hear that, surely? He didn't think I was talking about —

Seriously, tiny. The whole night was such an ordeal.

He couldn't have thought I meant —

My stomach drops in horror and I clap a hand over my mouth, quelling a shocked laugh. No. *No.*

Should I say — Should I apologize —

NO.

But shouldn't I at least explain —

I raise my eyes warily to his. His face is blank. He might not have heard anything. Or he might have.

There is simply no way to bring up this subject that will not backfire horrendously and make us both want to die. What I need to do is go. Move my feet. Now. Go.

"So . . . Thanks for the . . . um." I replace the helmet on the hook. Exit, Fliss. Now.

All morning, I feel aftershocks of embarrassment.

At least I managed to streak from the taxi to my front door with no neighbors seeing me. I ripped off the purple dress, had the quickest shower known to mankind, then called Noah on speakerphone while I was trying to do speedy makeup. (There is no point in rushing mascara application. I know this. So *why* do I always fall into the same trap and end up wiping blobs of it off my cheeks and forehead and mirror?) Evidently Noah's sleepover was a 100 percent rip-roaring, triumphant success. Wish I could say the same about mine.

I couldn't bring myself to call Lottie back, and anyway I didn't have time. Instead, I texted her, suggesting drinks at seven P.M.

Now I'm back at the office, speed-reading a review of a new luxury safari lodge in Kenya, which has just come in, about two thousand words over the limit. Clearly this journalist thinks he's writing the next *Out of Africa.* He hasn't mentioned the pool or the room service or the spa, only the hazy gathering light over the savannah, and the noble bearing of the zebras drinking at dawn, and the shimmering grasslands whose ancient stories beat on in the sound of the Masai drum.

I scribble *Room Service*??? in the margin and make a note to email him. Then I look at my phone. It's surprising that Lottie hasn't confirmed. I would have thought she'd be dying to tell me how many bridal magazines she's consumed today.

I glance at my watch. I've got some time now. I can make a little sisterly call. I lean back in my chair and speed-dial her, making a "Cup of coffee?" request to Elise through my office window. Elise and I have a pretty good sign-language system going on. I can communicate, "Cup of coffee?" "Tell them I'm out!!" and "Go home, it's late!" She can communicate, "Cup of coffee?" "I think this one's important," and "I'm off for a sandwich."

"Fliss?"

"Hi, Lottie." I kick off my shoes and take a swig from my Evian bottle. "So, are you on for drinks later? Do I get to meet Ben?"

There's silence at the other end. Why is there silence? Lottie doesn't do silence.

"Lottie? Are you there?"

"Guess what!" Her voice throbs impor-

221

tantly. "Guess what!"

She sounds so pleased with herself, I can tell she's pulled off something special.

"You're getting married in the school chapel and the choir is singing 'I Vow to Thee, My Country' while bells peal throughout the land?"

"No!" She laughs.

"You've found a wedding cake made of profiteroles *and* cupcakes, all covered in sparkly icing?"

"No, silly! We're married!"

"What?" I stare at the phone blankly.

"Yes! We've done it! Ben and I are married! Just now! Chelsea Register Office!"

I clench the Evian bottle so hard, a stream of water soars into the air and lands in splotches all over my desk.

"Aren't you going to say 'congratulations'?" she adds, a bit petulantly.

I can't say "congratulations," because I can't say anything. My mouth has seized up. I'm hot. No, I'm cold. I'm panicking. How did this happen?

"Wow," I manage at last, trying to keep calm. "That's . . . How come? You were going to delay. I thought you were going to delay. That's what we agreed. That you would delay."

You were meant to DELAY.

As Elise comes in with a cup of coffee, she looks at me in alarm and makes the "Is everything OK?" sign. But I don't have a sign for "My bloody sister has gone and wrecked her life," so I just nod with a rictus smile and take the cup of coffee.

"We couldn't wait," Lottie's saying happily. "*Ben* couldn't wait."

"But I thought you persuaded him?" I close my eyes and massage my brow, trying to get my head round this. "What happened to *Brides*? What happened to a little country church?"

What happened to Bridezilla? I want to moan faintly, *Bring back Bridezilla.*

"Ben was totally on for the church and everything," says Lottie. "He's actually got this sweet, traditional side to him —"

"So what happened?" I try to control my impatience. "Why did he change his mind?"

"It was Lorcan."

"What?" My eyes open sharply. "What do you mean, it was Lorcan?"

"Lorcan came to see him first thing this morning. He told Ben he mustn't marry me and it was all a huge mistake. Well, Ben went nuts! He came storming round to my office and said he wanted to be married to me *now* and everyone else could fuck off,

223

including Lorcan." Lottie sighs blissfully. "It was really romantic. Everyone in the office was staring. And then he picked me up and carried me out, just like *An Officer and a Gentleman,* and everyone cheered. It was amazing, Fliss."

I'm breathing hard, trying to keep control of myself. That idiot. That stupid, arrogant, fucking . . . *idiot.* I'd solved the problem. It was all sorted. I'd played the diplomatic card to perfection. And now what's Lorcan done? Blundered in. Stirred up this Ben into the most ludicrous, overblown gesture. No wonder Lottie fell for it.

"Luckily there was a cancelation at the registry office, so they could squeeze us in. And we can have a church blessing down the line," she's saying blithely. "So I get the best of both worlds!"

I want to throw my cup of coffee across the room. Or maybe I want to tip it over my own head. There's a nasty heaving feeling in my stomach. This is my fault too. I could have stopped this. If I'd told her everything Lorcan said.

He's having a bit of an early midlife crisis. . . . Your sister will be the casualty. . . .

"Where are you now?"

"Packing! We're off to Ikonos! It's *so* exciting."

"I'll bet it is," I say feebly.

What do I do? There's nothing I can do. They're married. It's done.

"Maybe we'll have a honeymoon baby," she adds coyly. "How do you feel about being an aunt?"

"What?" I sit bolt upright. "Lottie —"

"Fliss, I've got to go, the taxi's here, love you lots. . . ."

She rings off. Frantically, I speed-dial her again, but it goes to voicemail.

Baby? *Baby?*

I want to whimper. Is she insane? Does she have any idea what strain a baby will bring to the party?

My love life has been such a clusterfuck. I can't bear it if Lottie's is too. I wanted her to crack it the way I didn't. I wanted her fantasy to come true. Happy ever after. Picket fence. Strong, lasting happiness. Not a honeymoon baby with some flake-head who's on a brief domesticity craze before taking up motorbikes. Not sitting in Barnaby Rees's office with red eyes and hair that needs washing and a toddler trying to eat all the law books.

On impulse, I Google the Amba Hotel. At once, a series of holiday-porn images greets my eyes. Blue skies and sunsets. The famous grotto swimming pool, with its thirty-foot

225

tumbling waterfall. Beautiful couples strolling by the sea. Massive beds, scattered with rose petals. Let's face it, they'll have made a honeymoon baby before the wedding night is over. Lottie's ovaries will twang into action and she'll be vomiting all the way home.

Then if he *does* turn out to be a flake . . . if he *does* let her down . . . I close my eyes and bury my face in my hands. I can't bear it. I need to talk to Lottie. Face-to-face. Properly. With her brain engaged, not in fantasyland. At least make sure she's thought through all the consequences of what she's doing.

I'm sitting utterly still, my mind skittering back and forth like a mouse trapped in a maze. I'm trying to find a solution, I'm trying to find a way out, I keep coming up against dead ends. . . .

Until suddenly I lift my head and take a deep breath. I've come to a decision. It's huge and extreme, but I have no choice. I'm going to gate-crash her honeymoon.

I don't care if it's a heinous thing to do. I don't care if she never forgives me: I'll never forgive myself if I *don't*. Marriage was one thing. Unprotected sex is another. I need to get out there. I need to save my sister from herself.

Abruptly, I pick up the phone and dial

Travel.

"Hi," I say as Clarissa, our travel booker, answers. "Bit of an emergency, Clarissa. I need to get out to Ikonos asap. The Greek island. First available flight. And I need to stay in the Amba. They know me there."

"Right." I can hear her tapping at the computer. "There's only one flight direct to Ikonos a day, you know. Otherwise it's a change at Athens, which ends up taking forever."

"I know. Get me on the next direct flight you can. Thanks, Clarissa."

"Haven't you just reviewed the Amba?" She sounds surprised. "A few months ago?"

"I'm doing a follow-up," I lie smoothly. "Sudden decision. It's a new feature idea we've had," I add, to cement my story. "Spot checks on hotels."

This is the plus of being editor. No one questions me. Also: that *is* a good idea. I open my BlackBerry and type in: *Spot checks??*

"OK! Well, I'll let you know. Hopefully we can get you on the flight tomorrow."

"Thanks."

I ring off and drum my fingers, still tense. Even at my quickest, I won't get out there for a good twenty-four hours. Lottie is already on her way to the airport. She'll be

227

on today's afternoon flight. She'll get to the hotel by this evening. The Oyster Suite will be there, waiting, with its super-king bed and sunken Jacuzzi and champagne.

How many people conceive a baby on their wedding night? Could I find this out from Google? I type in *conceive baby first night honeymoon,* then restlessly cancel it. Google isn't the point. Lottie's the point. If only I could stop them. If only I could get in there before they . . . What's the word? Consummate it.

"Consummate." The word provokes a vague memory. What was it again? I blink, trying to recall. Oh yes, Barnaby telling me about annulments. I can hear his voice again: *It means the contract is null and void. The marriage never existed.*

The marriage never existed!

This is it. *This* is the answer. Annulment! The loveliest word in the English language. The solution to everything. No divorce. No legal tussle. Just blink and it's over. It never happened.

I need to do this for Lottie. I need to get her an opt-out. But how on earth can I achieve it? What can I — How can I — How does one —

And then a new idea zings across my brain.

I feel almost breathless as I consider it. I can't believe I'm thinking this. It's even more heinous and extreme than gate-crashing a honeymoon, but it would solve everything.

No. I can't. I mean, I *can't.* On every level. It's impossible. And wrong. Anyone who did this to her own sister would be some kind of monster.

OK. So I'm a monster.

My fingers are actually trembling as I pick up the phone. I'm not sure if it's with trepidation or determination.

"Amba Hotel, VIP Services, how may I help you?"

"Hi," I say, my voice a bit jumpy. "Could I please speak to Nico Demetriou? Tell him it's Fliss Graveney from *Pincher Travel Review.* Tell him . . . it's important."

As I'm put on hold, I picture Nico, all five foot three of him, his suit straining against his stomach. I knew Nico at the Mandarin Oriental in Athens and before that at Sandals in Barbados. He's been in hotels all his life, working his way up from bellboy, and he's now VIP concierge at the Amba. I can see him now, bustling across the marble floor of the lobby in his patent shoes, his eyes always sharply darting around.

His specialty is "Guest Experience."

Whether it's a personalized cocktail, a helicopter trip, swimming with dolphins, or a troupe of belly dancers in your room, he'll fix it. If I could have any partner in crime, it would be Nico.

"Fliss!" His voice booms happily down the phone. "I have heard this very minute that you are planning to pay us a visit?"

"Yes. I'll arrive tomorrow night, I hope."

"We are honored to see you again so soon! Can I assist you with anything in particular? Or perhaps this is a personal visit?"

I can hear the question in his voice. A hint of suspicion. Why am I coming back? What's up?

"It's kind of personal." I pause, marshaling my words. "Nico, I have a favor to ask. My sister is heading out to the Amba today. She's just got married. She's on honeymoon."

"Wonderful!" His voice almost blasts me away. "Your sister will have the holiday of her lifetime. I will appoint my most trusted butler for her benefit. We will meet her on arrival, and over a glass of champagne we will tailor-make her experience. Perhaps an upgrade, perhaps a special dinner —"

"Nico, no. You don't understand. I mean, that sounds wonderful. But I have a different favor to ask you." I twist my fingers together. "It's . . . unusual."

"I have been in this job for many years," says Nico kindly. "Nothing is unusual for me, Nico. You wish to surprise her? You would like me to place a present in her room? You would like me to arrange a couples' massage on the beach in a private cabana?"

"Not exactly."

Oh God. How do I put this?

Come on, Fliss. Just say it.

"I want you to stop them from having sex," I say in a rush.

There's absolute silence down the line. I've confounded even Nico.

"Fliss, repeat to me your request again," he says at last. "I fear I have not understood."

I fear he has.

"I want you to stop them from having sex," I repeat, enunciating as clearly as I can. "No sex. No wedding night. At least, not till I get out there. Do whatever you can. Put them in separate rooms. Distract them. Kidnap one of them. Whatever it takes."

"But they are on their honeymoon." He sounds utterly flummoxed.

"I know. And that's why."

"You are trying to disrupt your own

231

sister's wedding night?" His voice rises in shock. "You are trying to come between a man and his new wife? Who have been joined before God?"

I should have explained this better.

"Nico, she's rushed into this marriage. And it wasn't before God! It's a big, stupid mistake. I need to talk to her. I'm flying out as soon as I can, but in the meantime, if we can just keep them apart . . ."

"Does she not like the fellow?"

"She likes him very much." I wince. "In fact, she's kind of desperate to leap into bed with him. So it's going to be a challenge to stop them."

There's another silence. I can only imagine Nico's perplexed expression.

"Fliss, I'm afraid I cannot agree to this strange request," he says finally. "I can, however, offer your sister a complimentary dinner at the chef's table at our five-star seafood restaurant —"

"Nico, please. *Please* listen," I cut across him desperately. "This is my little sister, OK? She was dumped by the man she loves and she rushed into marriage like a kind of revenge. She barely knows this guy. Now she's talking about getting pregnant. I've never even met him, but apparently he's a flake. Imagine if your daughter was letting

232

her life be ruined by the wrong guy. You'd do everything you could to stop it, wouldn't you?"

I've met Nico's daughter, Maya. She's an adorable ten-year-old with ribbons in her hair. Surely that will get to him?

"If they don't have sex, the marriage can be annulled." I spell it out for him. "It won't be legally consummated. But if they *do* —"

"If they do, it is their business!" Nico sounds at the end of his tether. "This is a hotel, Fliss, not a prison! I cannot constantly supervise my guests' whereabouts! I cannot monitor their . . . activity."

"You're telling me you *couldn't* do it?" I throw down the challenge. "You couldn't stop them from getting it on for twenty-four hours?"

The thing about Nico is, he prides himself on being able to solve any problem. *Any* problem. I bet he's already imagining how he'd do it.

"If you can do this for me, I'll be *eternally* grateful." I lower my voice. "And of course I'll express my gratitude by reviewing the hotel again. Five stars. Guaranteed."

"We have already had the privilege of a five-star review in your magazine," he bats me back.

"Six stars, then," I improvise. "I'll invent a

233

new category, just for you. 'The new world-class super-luxe.' And I'll flag the hotel on the front cover. Do you know how much that's worth? Do you know how pleased your directors would be?"

"Fliss, I understand your dilemma," Nico shoots back. "However, you must realize that I cannot possibly interfere with guests' private lives, especially when they are here to enjoy their honeymoon!"

He sounds fairly resolute. I'm going to have to pull something pretty massive out of the bag.

"OK!" I drop my voice still lower. "*Listen.* If you help me out with this, I'll publish a profile of you in the magazine. You personally, Nico Demetriou. I'll call you . . . the secret of the Amba's success. The most prized asset of the hotel. The go-to VIP manager. Everyone in the industry will see it. *Everyone.*"

I don't need to spell out the rest. The magazine is distributed in sixty-five countries. Every CEO of every hotel at least glances through it. A profile like that would be his ticket to any job he wanted in the world.

"I know you've always dreamed about the Four Seasons, New York," I add softly.

My heart is pounding a little. I've never

abused my power before, and it's giving me a rush. Partly good, partly bad. This is how corruption starts, I reflect. Next thing, I'll be exchanging reviews for suitcases of cash and Trident missiles.

It's a one-off, I tell myself firmly. A one-off with extenuating circumstances.

Nico is quiet. I can feel his conscience rubbing against professional ambition, and I feel bad for putting him in this position. But it's not me who began this whole charade, is it?

"You're a master, Nico." I add some flattery. "You're a genius at making things happen. If anyone in the world can do this, you can."

Is he persuaded? Am I nuts? Is he even now sending an email to Gavin?

I'm on the point of giving up, when his voice suddenly comes low down the phone: "Fliss, I do not promise anything."

I feel a sudden bubble of hope.

"I understand completely," I reply, matching his tone. "But . . . you'll try?"

"I will try. Just for twenty-four hours. What is your sister's name?"

Yes!

"Charlotte Graveney." I'm almost gabbling with relief. "Although I guess she'll be under Mrs. Parr. Her husband's Ben Parr.

They're booked into the Oyster Suite. And I don't mind what they do, as long as they don't have sex. With each other," I add as an afterthought.

There's a long silence, then Nico says simply:

"This will be a very strange honeymoon."

8
LOTTIE

I'm married! My mouth is fixed in a permanent, gleeful smile. I'm so euphoric, I feel like I might float away. Today has been the best, most magical, most extraordinary day of my life. I'm married!! *I'm married!!!*

I still keep replaying the moment when I looked up from my desk to see Ben marching into the office, holding a bouquet of roses. His jaw was set and his eyes were flashing, and you could see he meant business. Even my boss, Martin, came out of his office to watch. The whole place was hushed as Ben stood at my office door and proclaimed, "I'm going to marry you, Lottie Graveney, and I'm going to do it today."

Then he lifted me up — *lifted me up* — and everyone cheered, and Kayla came running after me with my bag and phone, and Ben handed me the bouquet and that was it. I was a bride.

I barely remember the marriage ceremony.

I was in a state of shock. Ben practically jumped on each answer; I do remember that. He didn't pause for a moment — in fact he sounded almost aggressive as he said, "I do." He'd brought along some environmental confetti, which we sprinkled on ourselves, and he opened a bottle of champagne and then it was time to pack and leave for the airport. I haven't even got changed; I'm still in my work suit. I got married in my work suit and I don't care!

I catch sight of myself in the mirror above the drinks bar and want to giggle. I look as flushed and giddy as I feel. We're in the business-class lounge at Heathrow, waiting for the Ikonos flight. I haven't eaten anything since breakfast, but I'm not hungry. I'm hyped up. My hands won't stop trembling.

I take a few slices of fruit and a sliver of Emmental, just for the sake of it, then jump as I feel a hand on my leg.

"Fueling up?" comes Ben's voice in my ear, and I feel a delicious shiver. I turn to face him and he nuzzles my neck, his hand traveling up discreetly under my skirt. That's good. Oh, that's good.

"I can't wait," he murmurs in my ear.

"Me neither," I murmur back.

"You're so hot." His breath is warm

against my neck.

"You're hotter."

Yet again I work out how long we have to wait. Our flight to Ikonos is three and a half hours. It can't take more than two hours to go through customs and get to the hotel. Ten minutes for them to take our luggage up . . . five minutes to show us how the light switches work . . . thirty seconds to put up the DO NOT DISTURB sign . . .

Nearly six hours. I'm not sure I can wait nearly six hours. Ben seems the same way too. He's actually panting. Both his hands are roaming between my thighs. I can hardly concentrate on the fig compote.

"Excuse *me.*" An elderly man pushes his way between us and starts forking Emmental slices onto his plate. He eyes Ben and me with disfavor. "As they say," he adds ponderously, "get a room."

I feel myself flush. We *weren't* that obvious.

"We're on our honeymoon," I shoot back.

"Congratulations." The old man looks unimpressed. "I hope your young man will wash his hands before serving himself any food."

Spoilsport.

I glance at Ben and we both move away, to a set of plushy chairs. I'm pulsating all

239

over. I want his hands back where they were, doing what they were doing.

"So. Um. Cheese?" I proffer the plate to Ben.

"No, thanks." He frowns moodily.

This is torture. I look at my watch. Only two minutes have passed. We're going to have to fill the time somehow. Conversation. That's what we need. Conversation.

"I love Emmental," I begin. "Don't you?"

"I hate it."

"Really?" I log this new fact about him. "Wow. I had no idea you hated Emmental."

"I went totally off it the year I lived in Prague."

"You lived in Prague?" I say with interest.

I'm intrigued. I had no idea Ben had lived abroad. Or hated Emmental. This is the great advantage of marrying someone *without* spending years living together first. You still have stuff to find out. We're on an adventure of discovery together. We'll spend our whole lives exploring one another. Unwrapping each other's secrets. We'll never be that couple sitting in dead silence because they know everything and have said everything and are just waiting for the bill.

"So . . . Prague! Why?"

"I don't remember now." Ben shrugs. "That was the year I learned circus skills."

Circus skills? I wasn't expecting that one. I'm about to ask what else he's done, when his phone bleeps with a text and he pulls it out of his pocket. As he reads it, his brow creases angrily and I look at him in concern.

"Everything OK?"

"It's from Lorcan. He can fuck off."

Lorcan again. I'm dying to meet this Lorcan. I'm actually feeling quite grateful to him. If he hadn't said whatever he did to Ben, Ben would never have rushed to my office and I would never have had the most romantic experience of my life.

I rub Ben's arm sympathetically. "Isn't he, like, your oldest friend? Shouldn't you make up?"

"Maybe he was once." Ben scowls.

I glance over his shoulder at the screen and catch a bit of the text.

You can't run away from these decisions, Ben. You know how hard everyone has worked, and to go AWOL now is simply

Ben moves the phone out of sight and I don't like to ask if I can read the rest.

"What decisions?" I venture.

"It's just some tedious, boring piece of crap." Ben glowers at the phone. "And I'm not *running away*. Jesus. The thing with Lorcan is, he wants me to do everything his way. He got used to running the show with my dad. Well, things have changed."

He types something short, his thumbs stabbing at the phone. Almost at once a reply arrives, and he curses under his breath.

"Priorities. He's talking to me about *priorities*. I'm having a *life*. I'm doing what I should have done fifteen years ago. I should have married you then. We'd have ten kids."

I feel a swell of love for him. He wants a big family! We've never talked about it before, but I was really hoping he wanted lots of kids too. Maybe four. Maybe six!

"We can make up for that now." I lean in and nuzzle his neck. After a few seconds, Ben lets his phone drop onto the seat.

"You know what?" he says. "Nothing matters except us."

"Exactly," I breathe.

"I remember the moment I fell for you. It was that day you did cartwheels on the beach. You were sunbathing on that rock in the middle of the sea. You dived off the rock and swam to the beach, and then, instead of walking back, you did cartwheels all the way along. I don't think you knew anyone was watching you."

I remember that too. I remember the feel of the flat sand beneath my palms. My hair swinging. I was lithe and athletic. I had abs like a washboard.

And of *course* I knew he was watching me.

"You drive me wild, Lottie." His hands are edging up my skirt again. "You always did."

"Ben, we *can't*." I glance over at the elderly gentleman, who catches my eye over the top of his newspaper. "Not here."

"I can't wait."

"Neither can I." My body is pulsating all over again. "But we have to." I check my watch yet again. Barely ten minutes have passed now. How are we going to last?

"Hey." Ben meets my eyes, lowering his voice. "Have you been to the loos here? They're big." He pauses. "And unisex."

I stifle a giggle. "You don't mean —"

"Why not?" His eyes glint. "You up for it?"

"Now?"

"Why not? Still twenty minutes till boarding."

"I . . . I don't know." I hesitate, feeling torn. It's not exactly the way I pictured my honeymoon night — a quick encounter in a Heathrow loo. On the other hand, I didn't realize I'd be so desperate. "What about our wedding night?" I can't help clinging to my plan. "What about making it special and romantic?"

"Still will be." His fingers are gently playing with my earlobe, sending starbursts of sensation down my neck. "This isn't the main event. This is the preview." His fingers have found my bra strap. "And, quite frankly, if we don't soon, I'll burst."

"I'll burst too." I quell a gasp. "OK, you go first. Find us somewhere."

"I'll text."

He gets up and walks swiftly toward the unisex washrooms. I lean back on my seat and try not to giggle. This place is so quiet and stuffy, I don't know how we'll pull it off.

I get out my phone to wait for his text and, on impulse, pull up Fliss's number. She and I have always joked about the Mile-High Club. I can't resist telling her. I send a quick text:

Have u ever wondered what it's like doing it in an airport lounge loo? I'll let you know.☺

I'm not really expecting her to reply. It's only a silly, jokey text. So I'm gobsmacked when a moment later my phone pings with a reply:

244

Stop STOP!!!!!!!! Don't! Stupid idea. Wait till hotel!!!!!!!!

I peer at the phone, baffled. What is her problem? I fire off another text:

Don't worry, we're married.☺

I take a sip of water, then hear another ping. This time it's a text from Ben.

3rd cubicle on left. Knock twice.

I feel a delicious shiver and text back:

Coming.

As I pick up my bag, I see that Fliss has texted again:

Really, really think you should wait!!!! Save till hotel!!!!

This is getting annoying. I only texted her for fun, not to get some stupid lecture. What's she worried about, that we'll get caught and somehow people will link her to me and her precious magazine will be brought into disrepute? I send a cross reply:

None of your business.

245

As I cross the lounge toward the washrooms, I'm actually trembling with anticipation. I knock twice on the third cubicle door, and as Ben sweeps me in, he's already half undressed.

"Oh God. Oh God . . ."

His mouth is immediately on mine, his hand is in my hair, now he's unhooking my bra and I'm wriggling out of my knickers. I've never moved so fast. I've never wanted it so fast. I've never needed it so badly in my life.

"Shh!" we keep whispering to each other as we bump against the cubicle walls. Thank God they're sturdy. We're maneuvering into position as quickly as we can, Ben's braced against the wall, we're both breathing like steam engines, I can tell this is going to take about ten seconds. . . .

"Condom?" I whisper.

"No." He meets my eye. "Right?"

"Right." I feel an extra spurt of excitement. We might make a baby!

"Hey." He suddenly pauses. "Have you got into any kinky stuff since we last did it? Anything I should know?"

"A bit," I say breathlessly, hoicking my skirt up farther. "Tell you later. Come *on*."

"OK! Give me a chance —"

Rap-rap-rap-rap!

The knocking at the cubicle door nearly gives me a heart attack, and I bash my knee on the cistern. What? *What?*

"Excuse me?" a female voice is calling from the other side of the door. "This is the lounge manager speaking. Is there someone in there?"

Fuck.

I can't answer. I can't move. Ben and I eye each other in panic.

"Could you please open the door?"

My leg is still wrapped round Ben's back. The other foot is on the loo seat. I have no idea where my underwear is. Worst of all, my entire body is still throbbing with need.

Could we just ignore this lounge manager? Keep going? I mean, what can they do?

"Carry on?" I mouth at Ben. "Really quietly?" I gesture to make myself clear, and the loo seat creaks. Shit.

"If you don't come out, I'm afraid I will have to use a passkey to gain access," the voice is saying.

They have a passkey to the loos? What is this, a fascist state?

I'm still breathing as hard as ever. But now it's with miserable frustration. I can't do this. I can't consummate my marriage with a lounge manager listening six inches away, the other side of the door, poised with a passkey.

There's more knocking at the door. In fact, it's becoming more like a pounding.

"Can you hear me?" the woman is demanding. "Can anyone hear me in there?"

I meet Ben's eyes ruefully. We're going to have to answer, before she bursts in with a SWAT team.

"Oh, hi there!" I call back, hastily hooking my bra up. "Sorry! I was just . . . fixing my . . . head."

My *head*? Where did that come from?

"My husband was helping me," I add, searching around for my knickers. Ben is pulling up his trousers. It's over.

Dammit. I can't find my knickers. I'll have to leave them. I quickly brush back my hair, glance at Ben, pick up my handbag, then unlock the door and smile at the gray-haired woman standing outside the door, together with a younger brunette sidekick.

"So sorry," I say smoothly. "I have a medical complaint. My husband has to help me administer a serum. We prefer privacy for the application."

The woman's eyes run over me suspiciously. "Do you need me to call a doctor?"

"No, thank you. I'm fine now. Thank you, darling," I add to Ben, for good measure.

Her eyes drop to the floor. "Are those

yours?" I follow her gaze and curse inwardly. My knickers. That's where they were.

"Of *course* they're not mine," I say with cutting dignity.

"I see." She turns to the sidekick. "Lesley, please tell a cleaner to come and refresh this cubicle."

Oh God. Those knickers are by Aubade. They cost forty pounds. And they match the bra I'm wearing. I can't bear for them to disappear into the bin.

"Actually . . ." I peer at the knickers as though suddenly noticing something about them. "On second thought . . . perhaps they *are* mine." I scoop them up as nonchalantly as I can and examine a small rosebud. "Ah yes." I stuff them in my pocket, avoiding the lounge manager's steely gaze. "Thank you so much for your help. Keep up the good work. Lovely lounge."

"May we compliment you on the buffet," adds Ben. He holds out an arm and escorts me away before I can explode. I don't know if I want to laugh or scream. How did that happen? How the fuck did they *know*?

"We were silent," I mutter to Ben as we walk. "We were totally silent."

"I bet it was the old man," he mutters back. "He must have shopped us. He guessed what we were doing."

"Bastard."

I slump into one of the plushy chairs and look around disconsolately. Why don't they provide facilities for sex, anyway? Why is it all about surfing the Net and eating grapes?

"Let's have some champagne," says Ben, and squeezes my shoulder. "Never mind. Bring on tonight."

"Bring on tonight," I agree fervently.

I check my watch again. Five hours, thirty minutes to go until we can put up that DO NOT DISTURB sign. I'll be counting down every millisecond. As Ben heads to the bar, I pull out my phone and text Fliss.

We were found out. Someone shopped us. Bastards.

There's quite a long pause — then her reply arrives.

Poor you! Safe flight. Xxx

9
FLISS

Educational. It's an *educational* trip. Yes.

I haven't asked permission. I haven't given warning. I haven't sat in the headmistress's study and been lectured. I feel that in this instance the element of surprise is crucial.

"Mrs. Phipps?" Mrs. Hocking puts her head round the door of the classroom. "You wanted to see me?"

"Ah, hello." I smile as confidently as I can. "Yes. Just a small matter. I'm going to have to take Noah out of school for a few days. To a Greek island. It will be very educational."

"Ah." She frowns off-puttingly. "I'm afraid you'll have to ask permission from the headmistress —"

"I understand." I nod. "Unfortunately, I don't have time to ask the headmistress, as I understand she's away today."

"Really? When were you planning to go?"

"Tomorrow."

"Tomorrow?" Mrs. Hocking looks aghast. "But we only started term two days ago!"

"Ah yes." I act surprised, as though this hadn't occurred to me. "Well, I'm afraid it's an emergency."

"What sort of emergency?"

A honeymoon-connected, sex-related emergency. You know the kind.

"A . . . family crisis," I improvise. "But, as I say, it'll be a very educational trip. Incredibly educational." I spread my arms, as though to indicate just how educational this trip will be. "Highly, highly educational."

"Hmm." Mrs. Hocking clearly doesn't want to give way. "Is this the fourth time Noah's been taken out of school this year?"

"Is it?" I act dumb. "I'm not sure."

"I know things have been" — she clears her throat — "difficult for you. What with your job and . . . everything."

"Yes."

We're both staring at the ceiling, as though to expunge the memory of that time Daniel had just brought in his new set of big-gun lawyers and I burst into tears at pickup time and practically sobbed on her shoulder.

"Well." She sighs. "Very well. I'll tell the head."

"Thank you," I say humbly.

"Noah's having his extra lesson at the moment, but if you come in, I'll give you his bag."

I follow her into the empty classroom, which smells of wood and paint and Play-Doh. The assistant teacher, Ellen, is tidying away some plastic counters and she beams up at me. Ellen has a high-salaried husband in banking and is a great fan of five-star hotels. She reads the magazine every month and is always questioning me about the latest spa treatments and whether Dubai is over.

"Mrs. Phipps is taking Noah on an educational trip to a Greek island," says Mrs. Hocking, in deadpan tones that clearly mean, *This irresponsible parent is going on a drugs-and-booze mini-break and is dragging her poor son along to get high on the fumes; what can I do?*

"Lovely!" Ellen says. "But what about your new puppy?"

"My what?" I stare at her blankly.

"Noah was telling us about your new puppy. The cocker spaniel?"

"Cocker spaniel?" I laugh. "I don't know where he's got that idea from. We don't have a puppy, nor are we getting a puppy —" I break off. Mrs. Hocking and Ellen are exchanging looks. "What is it?"

There's silence — then Mrs. Hocking

sighs. "We did wonder. Tell me, has Noah's grandfather died recently?"

"No." I stare at her.

"And he didn't have an operation on his hand during the holidays?" chimes in Ellen. "At Great Ormond Street?"

"No!" I look from face to face. "Is that what he's been saying?"

"Please don't worry," says Mrs. Hocking hurriedly. "We noticed last term that Noah seemed to have . . . quite an imagination. He's been coming out with all sorts of stories, some of which are obviously untrue."

I stare at her in dismay. "What other stories?"

"It's perfectly normal for children to live in a fantasyland at his age." She's deflecting me. "And, of course, he has had an unsettling time at home. He'll grow out of it, I'm sure."

"What other stories?" I persist.

"Well." Again Mrs. Hocking exchanges looks with Ellen. "He said he'd had a heart transplant. Obviously we knew that wasn't the case. He mentioned a surrogate baby sister, which again we thought probably wasn't true. . . ."

A heart transplant? A *surrogate baby sister*? How does Noah even know about

254

things like that?

"Right," I say at last. "Well, I'll have a word with him."

"Tread lightly." Mrs. Hocking smiles. "As I say, it's a perfectly normal phase. He may be attention-seeking or he may not even realize he's doing it. Either way, I'm sure he'll grow out of it."

"He even said you once threw all your husband's clothes onto the street and invited the neighbors to help themselves!" says Ellen with a bright laugh. "He's got such an imagination!"

My face flames. Damn. I thought he was asleep when I did that.

"What an imagination!" I try to sound natural. "Who on *earth* would do a thing like that?"

My face is still hot as I arrive at the special-educational-needs department. Noah has special after-school lessons every Wednesday, because his handwriting is terrible. (The official reason has "spatial coordination" in the title, and costs sixty pounds per session.)

There's a waiting area outside the door, and I sit down on the miniature sofa. Opposite me is a shelf full of pencils with special grips and odd-shaped scissors and beanbags. There's a rack of books with titles like *How Do I Feel Today?* On the wall, a TV is softly burbling away with some special kids' program.

They could do with a department like this at the office, I find myself thinking. I wouldn't mind escaping for half an hour a week to play with beanbags and point to the flash card reading *Today I'm Sad Because My Boss Is a Git.*

". . . I had an operation at Great Ormond Street." A voice from the TV attracts my attention. "My hand was sore afterward and I couldn't write anymore." I look up to see a small Asian-looking girl talking to the camera. "But Marie helped me learn to write again." Music starts playing, and there's a scene of the little girl struggling with a pencil while a woman guides her. The final shot is of the girl beaming proudly while holding up a picture she's drawn. The image fades and I blink at the TV, puzzled.

Great Ormond Street. Is that coincidence?

"My mummy is having a surrogate baby." A freckled boy appears on-screen as the music changes. "At first I felt left out. But now I'm really excited."

What?

I grab the remote and turn up the volume as Charlie introduces his surrogate baby sister. The piece ends with them all sitting in the garden together. Next up is Romy, who has had a cochlear implant, and then Sara, whose mummy has had plastic surgery and looks different now (but that's OK), and then David with his new heart.

The DVD doesn't have a point to it, I swiftly appreciate. It's a promotional freebie for *other* DVDs. And it's just running on a loop. One inspirational, heart-churning story after another.

I'm almost blinking with tears as each kid tells his or her poignant tale. But I'm seething with frustration too. Did no one think to watch this DVD? Has no one linked Noah's stories to what he's been watching?

"Now I can run and play," David is saying joyfully to the camera. "I can play with Lucy, my new puppy."

Lucy is a cocker spaniel. Of course.

The door suddenly opens, and Noah is ushered out by the SEN teacher, Mrs. Gregory.

"Ah, Mrs. Phipps," she says as she does every week. "Noah's making very good progress."

"Great." I smile pleasantly back. "Noah, sweetheart, put on your coat." As he heads to the pegs, I turn back to Mrs. Gregory and lower my voice. "Mrs. Gregory, I was just watching your interesting DVD. Noah has quite an imagination, and I think he may be identifying with the kids shown in it a little too much. Could you possibly turn it off when he's sitting there?"

"Identifying?" She looks puzzled. "In what way?"

"He told Mrs. Hocking he'd had a heart transplant," I say bluntly. "And an operation on his hand in Great Ormond Street. It all came from that DVD." I gesture at the TV.

"Ah." Her face falls. "Oh goodness."

"No harm done, but maybe you could put on a different DVD? Or just turn it off?" I smile sweetly. "Thank you so much."

Some children think they're Harry Potter. Trust mine to think he's the star of a self-help DVD. As I walk out with Noah, I squeeze his hand.

"So, darling, I was watching your teacher's DVD. It's fun to watch stories, isn't it? Stories about *other people*," I add for emphasis.

Noah considers this for a long, thoughtful moment.

"If your mummy has plastic surgery," he says at last, "it doesn't matter. Even if she looks different. Because she's probably happier now."

My smile freezes. *Please* don't say he's

told the teachers I've had plastic surgery and am happier now.

"Absolutely." I try to sound relaxed. "Um, Noah. You do know that Mummy hasn't had plastic surgery, don't you?"

Noah's avoiding my gaze. Oh God. What's he said?

I'm about to reiterate to him my complete lack of plastic surgery (one Botox session doesn't count) when my phone bleeps. It's a text from Lottie. Oh God. Please don't say they've somehow managed it.

We're boarding. What do u think of the Mile-High Club? Could call baby Miles ☺ Or Miley ☺ xxx

Swiftly I text back:

Don't be gross! Have a good one xxx

I stare at my phone for a few seconds after I've pressed *send.* They won't try to do it on the plane. Surely not. Anyway, the airport staff will have put in a discreet call to the cabin crew, warning them about the frisky couple in business. They'll be on the case; I can relax.

Still, my heart's thudding. I glance at my watch and feel a renewed frustration at the totally crap travel options. One direct flight to Ikonos a day? It's insane. I want to be there *now.*

But since I can't, I'm going to do a bit of research.

I find it exactly where I expected to: in the box under her bed, stacked with all the others. Lottie started keeping a diary when she was fifteen, and it was a pretty big deal. She used to read bits out to me and talk about getting them published one day. She would say portentously, "As I wrote in my *diary* yesterday . . ." as though somehow that made her thoughts far more significant than mine (unrecorded, lost to the mists of time. History will weep, obviously).

I've never read Lottie's diaries before. I'm a moral person. Also: I can't be bothered. But I have to know a little about this Ben guy, and this is the only source I can think of. No one will ever know what I did.

Noah's safely watching *Ben 10* in the kitchen. I sit down on her bed, and Lottie-scent wafts up from the duvet cover: floral, sweet, and clean. When she was eighteen she wore Eternity, and I can catch a whiff of that too, coming from the pages of the diary.

Right. Let's dive in, quick. I feel very tense

and guilty sitting here, even though I'm Lottie's key holder and have a perfect right to be in her flat and she's on a plane, miles away, and, anyway, if someone *did* walk in I would thrust the diary very quickly under a pillow and say, *Just here for security reasons.*

I open the diary at random.

Fliss is such a bitch.

What?

"Fuck off!" I automatically respond.

OK, that was needless and immature. I shouldn't jump to conclusions. There'll be some explanation. I look more closely at the entry. Apparently I wouldn't lend her my denim jacket to take on her gap-year trip.

Oh, really? I'm a bitch because I wouldn't just hand over *my* jacket which I paid for? I'm so outraged I feel like phoning her up right now and having this out. And, by the way, where has she written about how I *did* give her about six pairs of flip-flops and never saw them back *and* my Chanel sunglasses because she begged and begged?

I stare at the diary, seething gently, then force myself to turn over a few pages. I can't wallow in some fifteen-year-old argument. I need to skip ahead. I need to get to Ben. As I turn the pages, skimming the text, I almost feel like I'm on her gap-year journey with her: first to Paris and then to the South of France, then Italy, all in bite-size snippets. It's kind of addictive.

. . . think I might move to Paris when I'm older . . . ate too many croissants, urgh, God, I'm fat, I'm hideous . . . this guy called Ted who's at university and REALLY COOL . . . he's really into existential-ism . . . I should get into that, he said I was a natural . . .

. . . AMAZING sunset . . . drank too many rum-and-Cokes . . . really REALLY sun-burned . . . slept with this guy called Pete, shouldn't have . . . made this plan to move to the South of France when we're all like thirty . . .

. . . I WISH I spoke Italian better. This is where I want to live, forever. It's AMAZ-ING . . . ate too many gelati, urgh, my legs are hideous . . . leaving for Greece tomor-row . . .

. . . this place is INCREDIBLE . . . amaz-ing party atmosphere, like we all just GET each other . . . I could LIVE on feta . . . diving in these underwater caves . . . this guy called Ben . . . picnic with some of the guys and Ben . . . slept with Ben . . . AMAZING . . .

"Lottie?" A male voice interrupts my concentration, and I start so violently the diary flies up into the air. I make an instinctive grab for it, then realize that's incriminating, so I draw my hand away sharply and it falls on the floor, where I kick it away, then finally lift my head.

"Richard?"

He's standing in the doorway in a raincoat, his hair disheveled and a suitcase in his hand. His face is agitated, and he's definitely looking more young Gordon Brown than young Pierce Brosnan.

"Where's Lottie?" he demands.

"I'm here for security," I mumble hurriedly, my face blazing with shame and my eyes darting to the diary. "Security."

Richard looks at me as though I'm making no sense at all. Which, to be fair, I'm not.

"Where's Lottie?" he demands again, more forcefully. "What's wrong? I go to her work, no one will tell me where she is. I come here, you're sitting on her bed. Just tell me." He drops his suitcase. "Is she ill?"

"Ill?" I almost want to laugh hysterically. "No, not ill. Richard, what are you *doing* here?"

His case has an airline tag on it. He must have come straight from the airport in a dashing, romantic manner. I feel quite sad that Lottie isn't here to see it.

"I made a mistake. A bad mistake." He strides to the window and stares out a moment, then darts me a look. "I don't know how much she tells you."

"A fair amount," I say diplomatically.

I don't think he'll want to hear that she's told me absolutely *everything,* including his penchant for doing it blind-folded and her penchant for sexy toys, which she's terrified the cleaner will find.

"Well, we split up," he says heavily. "A few weeks ago."

No kidding.

"Yes, I heard that." I nod. "She was very upset."

"Well, so was I!" He wheels round, breathing hard. "It came out of nowhere! I thought we were happy together. I thought *she* was happy."

"She was happy! But she couldn't see where things were heading."

"You mean . . ." He hesitates for a long time. "Marriage."

I feel a flick of irritation. I'm not such a huge fan of marriage myself, but he doesn't need to look *quite* so unenthusiastic.

"It's not such an outlandish idea," I point out. "It *is* what people do when they love

264

each other."

"Well, I know, but . . ." He makes a face, as though we're talking about some freaky hobby pursued by people on freaky reality shows. Now I'm starting to feel furious. If he'd just manned up and bloody well proposed in the first place, none of this would have happened.

"What do you want, Richard?" I ask abruptly.

"I want Lottie. I want to talk to her. I want to get things back on track. She wouldn't return my calls or my emails. So I told my new boss I had to come back to England." There's a throb of pride in his voice. He clearly reckons he's made the supreme gesture.

"And what are you going to say to her?"

"That we belong together," he says steadily. "That I love her. That we can work things out. That maybe marriage *is* a possibility, down the line."

Maybe marriage is a possibility down the line. Wow. He really knows how to woo a girl.

"Well, I'm afraid you're too late." I feel a sweet, sadistic pleasure at saying the words. "She's married."

"What?" Richard frowns blankly, clearly unable to process my words.

"She's married."

"What do you mean, she's married?" He still looks baffled.

For God's sake, what does he bloody think I mean?

"She's married! She's taken! In fact, she's just flown off on her honeymoon to Ikonos." I check my watch. "She's in the air right now."

"What?" A thunderous scowl buries itself in his forehead. Definitely Gordon. He'll throw his laptop at me in a minute. "How can she be *married*? What the fuck are you *talking* about?"

"She split up with you, practically had a nervous breakdown, met up with an old flame, who proposed on the spot, and said yes because she was in shock and desperately miserable and fancies him rotten. *That's* what I'm talking about." I glare at him. "Get it?"

"But . . . but who is he?"

"Her gap-year boyfriend. She hadn't seen him for fifteen years. First love, all that."

He's gazing at me suspiciously. I can see the cogs of his brain working, the realization dawning: this isn't a windup. I'm telling the truth. She's married.

"Fucking . . . *fuck.*" He bangs both fists to his forehead.

"Yup. That's how I feel about it too."

There's a dejected silence. A light flurry of rain patters against the window, and I wrap my arms around myself. Now that the exhilaration of punishing Richard has ebbed away, all I can feel is sore and miserable. What a mess.

"Well." He exhales. "I guess that's it."

"I guess so." I shrug. I'm not going to share my plans with him. The last thing I need is him interfering or offering stupid suggestions. My priority is to get Lottie off the hook with Ben, for her own sake. If Richard wants to make some fresh salvo afterward, that's up to him.

"So . . . what do you know about this guy?" Richard suddenly emerges from his trance. "What's he called?"

"Ben."

"Ben." He repeats the word suspiciously. "I've never heard her talk about a Ben."

"Well." I shrug again.

"I mean, I know about her other old boyfriends. Jamie. And Seamus. And what's-his-name. The accountant."

"Julian," I can't help supplying.

"Exactly. But she's never even *mentioned* a Ben." Richard's eyes rake the room, as though he's trying to find clues, then they fall on her diary, which is lying half open on the ground. He lifts his gaze to me incredulously.

"Were you reading her diary?"

Damn. I should have known Richard would pick up on that. He always notices more than you think he will. Lottie used to say he's like a lion half asleep under a tree, but I think he's more like a bull: one minute peacefully grazing; the next charging, head down.

"I wasn't exactly *reading* it." I try to stay poised. "I was just doing a little research about this Ben."

Richard's eyes focus on me alertly. "What did you find out?"

"Nothing much. I've only just got to the bit where they met on Ikonos —" He makes a sudden grab for the diary. With a lightning reaction, I reach for it too and seize a corner. We're both gripping it, trying to pull it out of the other's grasp. He's far stronger than I am, but I'm *not* letting him have her diary. There are limits.

"I can't *believe* you'd read your sister's diary," says Richard, trying to wrench it out of my fingers.

"I can't believe you'd read your girlfriend's diary," I retort breathlessly. "Give. *Give.*"

At last I manage to yank it away from him

and cradle it protectively in my arms.

"I deserve to know." Richard is glowering at me. "If Lottie's chosen this guy over me, I deserve to know who he is."

"OK," I snap. "I'll read you out a bit. Be patient."

I flip through the pages again, fast-forwarding through France and Italy to Ikonos. OK. Here we are. Pages and pages full of the word "Ben." Ben this. Ben that. Ben, Ben, Ben.

"She met him at this guest house they were all staying in."

"The guest house on Ikonos?" Richard's face jerks in recognition. "But she's told me about that place a million times. The place with the steps? Where they had the fire and she saved everyone? I mean, that place changed her life. She always says it's the place where she became the person she is today. She has a photo of it somewhere. . . ." He looks around the room, then jabs a finger. "Here."

We both survey the framed picture of Lottie in a swing seat, dressed in a tiny frilly white skirt and a bikini top, with a flower behind her ear. She looks thin and young and radiant.

"She's never said anything about a guy

called Ben," says Richard slowly. "Not once."

"Ah." I bite my lip. "Well, perhaps she was being selective."

"I see." He falls into her desk chair, his face moody. "Go on, then."

I survey Lottie's handwriting again. "Basically, they checked each other out on the beach . . . then there was a party and they got it together —"

"Read it," he interrupts. "Don't summarize."

"Are you sure?" I raise my eyebrows at Richard. "You're sure you want to hear this?"

"Read it."

"OK. Here goes." I draw a breath and choose a paragraph at random.

Watched Ben waterskiing this morning. God, he's cool. He plays the harmonica and he's so brown. Had sex all afternoon on the boat, no tan lines, ha-ha. Bought more scented candles and massage oil for tonight. All I want is to be with Ben and have sex with Ben forever. I will never love anyone else like this. NEVER.

I fall into silence, feeling uncomfortable.

"She'd kill me if she knew I'd read you that."

Richard doesn't reply. He looks stricken.

"It was fifteen years ago," I say awkwardly. "She was eighteen. That's what you write in your diary when you're eighteen."

"D'you think . . ." He pauses. "D'you think she's ever written anything like that about me?"

Alarm bells start clanging in my head. Uh-oh. No way. Not going there.

"I have no idea!" I clap the book shut briskly. "It's different. Everything's different when you grow up. Sex is different, love is different, cellulite is *very* different." I'm trying to lighten the atmosphere, but Richard doesn't even seem to hear. He's staring at the photo of Lottie, his brow furrowed so deeply I think it might cave in. The sudden sound of the doorbell makes us both start, and as we meet eyes I can tell we've both had the same crazy thought: *Lottie?*

Richard strides into the narrow hall, and I follow, my heart pounding. He throws open the door and I peer in disappointment at a thin, elderly man.

"Ah, Mr. Finch," he says in querulous tones. "Is Charlotte at home? Because, despite her promises, she has done no work on the roof terrace at all. It's still an absolute mess."

The roof terrace. Even I know about the roof terrace. Lottie rang me up to tell me she was totally getting into gardening and had ordered loads of cute gardening accessories, and she was going to design an urban potager.

"Now, I'm a reasonable man," the man is saying, "but a promise is a promise, and we *have* all contributed to the plant fund, and I really feel this is —"

"She'll do it, OK?" Richard pushes forward, his voice thundering so loudly that the light fittings practically tremble. "She's planning a great project. She's creative. These things take time. So *back off*!"

The elderly man recoils in alarm, and I raise my eyebrows at Richard. Wow. I wouldn't mind someone fighting in my corner like that once in a while.

Also: I was right. He's definitely a bull, not a lion. If he were a lion, he would even now be stalking Ben with stealthy patience through the undergrowth. Richard's too straightforward to do that. He'd rather charge furiously at the nearest target, even if it means a thousand teacups broken in the process. So to speak.

The door closes and we look at each other

uncertainly, as though the interruption has changed the air.

"I should go," says Richard abruptly, and buttons up his raincoat.

"You're going back to San Francisco?" I say in dismay. "Just like that?"

"Of course."

"But what about Lottie?"

"What about her? She's married and I wish her every happiness."

"Richard . . ." I wince, not knowing what to say.

"They were Romeo and Juliet and now they've found each other again. Makes total sense. Good luck to them."

He's upset, I realize. Really upset. His jaw is taut and his gaze is distant. Oh God, I feel terrible now. I shouldn't have read her diary out. I simply wanted to shock him out of his complacency.

"They *aren't* Romeo and Juliet," I say firmly. "Look, Richard, if you really want to know, they're both having complete fuckwit meltdowns. Lottie hasn't been thinking straight since you and she split up, and apparently this Ben is having his own midlife crisis. . . . Richard, listen. Please." I put a hand on his arm and wait till he gives me his attention. "The marriage won't last. I'm pretty sure of that."

"How can you be pretty sure?" He scowls as though he hates me for even raising his hopes.

"I just have a feeling," I say mysteriously. "Call it sisterly intuition."

"Well, whatever." He shrugs. "That'll be a way down the line." He heads back into the bedroom and picks up his suitcase.

"No, it won't!" I hurry after him and grab his shoulder to make him stop. "I mean . . . it might be sooner than you think. Much sooner. The point is, if I were you, I wouldn't give up. I'd hang fire and see."

Richard is silent a few moments, clearly fighting his own hopes. "When exactly did they get married?" he asks suddenly.

"This morning." I wince inwardly as I realize how crap his timing was. If only he'd arrived one day earlier . . .

"So tonight's their —" He breaks off as though he can't bear to say it.

"Wedding night. Yes. Yes, I suppose it is." I pause and examine my nails, my face carefully blank, my demeanor innocent. "Well. Who knows how that will go?"

10
LOTTIE

I can't stand it. I can't *stand* it any longer. I'm going to be the first person who ever died from sexual frustration.

I can remember long, unbearable waits as a child. Waiting for pocket money. Waiting for my birthday. Waiting for Christmas. But I've never had a wait as nightmarish as this. It's been absolute torture. Five hours, four hours, three hours to go . . . All through the plane journey and the car ride from the airport, I've been silently chanting, *Soon . . . soon . . . soon . . .* It's the only way to keep sane. Ben keeps fondling my leg. He's staring straight ahead, breathing evenly. I can tell he's as pent up as I am.

And now it's just minutes to go. The hotel is half a kilometer away. The driver is turning off the main road. The closer we get, the less I can bear it. These last moments of delay are killing me. All I want is Ben.

I'm trying to look around and show an

interest in our surroundings, but it's only road and scrubby hills and garish billboards for Greek drinks with unfamiliar names. The airport is on the other side of the island from the guest house we stayed at all those years ago. I probably never even came here. So I'm not having any reminiscences or recognizing anything. I'm just feeling desperate.

Soon . . . soon . . . soon . . . We'll be in our massive honeymoon suite bed, and our clothes will be lying on the floor, and we'll be facing each other, skin-to-skin, nothing to stop us, and finally, *finally . . .*

"The Amba Hotel," the driver announces with a proud flourish, and leaps out to open our doors.

As I get out of the car, the warm Greek air seems to bathe my shoulders. I look around, taking in a huge white-pillared entrance, four marble lions, and a series of fountains crashing into an ornamental pond. Bougainvillea is falling in vivid pink cascades from balconies to the left and right. Candles are flickering in massive hurricane lanterns. I can hear the chirp of evening crickets as well as the distant strains of a string quartet. This place is spectacular.

As we head up the shallow marble steps, I feel a sudden wave of euphoria. This is going to be perfect. The perfect, perfect honeymoon. I squeeze Ben's arm.

"Isn't this *amazing*?"

"Stunning." He slides a hand around my waist and up under my top to my bra catch.

"Don't! This is a posh hotel!" I jerk away, even though my whole body is longing for him to keep going. "We have to wait."

"I can't wait." His darkened eyes meet mine.

"Nor can I." I swallow. "I'm dying."

"I'm dying more." His fingers move down to the waistband of my skirt. "Don't tell me you're wearing anything under that."

"Not a stitch," I murmur.

"Jesus." He makes a low, growling noise. "OK, we're going to get our room key, and we're going to lock the door, and —"

"Mr. and Mrs. Parr?" A voice interrupts us and I look up to see a short, dark man in a suit approaching us swiftly down the steps. His shoes are very shiny, and as he gets nearer I see a badge that reads NICO DEMETRIOU, VIP MANAGER. In one hand is a massive bouquet of flowers, which he proffers to me. "Madame. Welcome to the Amba Hotel. We are delighted to welcome you. You are on honeymoon, I understand!"

He's ushering us through the large glass doors into a massive domed lobby. It has a

277

marble floor and a sunken pool in which are floating little candles. Low music is playing and there's a wonderful musky scent in the air.

"Many congratulations. Please. Sit." He gestures to a long linen sofa. "A glass of champagne for you both!"

A waiter has appeared from nowhere, bearing two glasses of champagne on a silver tray. I hesitate, then take one, glancing at Ben.

"That's very kind," Ben says, not moving toward the sofa. "But we'd like to get to our suite as quickly as possible."

"Of course. Of course." Nico twinkles understandingly. "Your luggage is being taken up. If you can simply fill in some details . . ." He offers a leather-bound book to Ben, along with a pen. "Please, sit. You will find it more comfortable."

Reluctantly, Ben sinks into the sofa and starts scrawling at top speed. Meanwhile, Nico hands me a printed sheet headed *Welcome Mr. and Mrs. Parr,* followed by a list of facilities and experiences. I run my eyes over the list, which is pretty awesome. *Guided snorkeling and champagne picnic . . . day trip on the hotel's sixty-foot yacht . . . dinner cooked by a private chef on your terrace . . . starlight aromatherapy couples' massage . . .*

"We are delighted to present our Superlative Honeymoon Experience." Nico beams at me. "You will be attended by a private twenty-four-hour butler. You will enjoy complimentary treatments within the private spa area in your suite. I, personally, will be at your service at all times. No request is too great or too small."

"Thanks." I can't help smiling back, he's so charming.

"Your honeymoon is a special, special time. I, Nico, will make it the experience of your lifetime." He clasps his hands together. "Never to be forgotten."

"OK, done." Ben stamps a final full stop and hands the forms back. "Can we get into our room? Where is it?"

"I will escort you personally!" exclaims Nico. "Come this way, to your private penthouse lift."

We have our own *lift*? I flash a look at Ben. I can tell that's given him ideas. Me too.

As we stand in the lift, I'm trying to appear composed, but I can see Ben eyeing up my skirt. He's not going to hang about. We're going to take all of thirty seconds, and then we'll have to do it again, and then maybe have dinner and then, *really* slowly, start all over again. . . .

"And here we are!" The lift doors ping

open and Nico leads us cheerfully into a lobby, with marble floor and dark-wood paneled walls. "The Oyster Suite. It was recently voted top honeymoon suite by *Condé Nast Traveler.* After you."

"Wow," I breathe as he swings open the door. Fliss was right: this is incredible. The whole place is designed like a grotto, with Greek pillars and low daybeds and statues of Greek gods on pedestals. The only immediate downside is that the TV is blaring out *Teletubbies.* I've loathed *Teletubbies,* ever since I had to watch about twenty episodes while babysitting Noah. Who on earth put that on?

"Can we turn that off, please?" I say.

"Of course, madame. Let me first show you the amenities. As well as the lift entrance, there is a dedicated front door." Nico strides briskly through the marble-floored rooms. "Here we have the bathroom, with a walk-in rain shower. Here is your private spa room, kitchen with staff entrance, small library, sitting room with cinema screen. . . ."

I'm trying to look interested as he demonstrates how to use the DVD player. But my head is fuzzy with desire. We're here. We're actually *here.* In our honeymoon suite. On our wedding night. And as soon

as this guy finishes his spiel and leaves . . .
in a matter of seconds, maybe . . . Ben will
be ripping off my skirt and I'll be ripping
off his shirt, and . . . Oh God, I can't wait a
moment longer. . . .

"The minibar is situated within this cabi-
net and works by electronic sensor —"

"Uh-huh." I manage a polite nod, but my
whole body is pulsing with lust. I don't care
how the bloody minibar works. *Just stop
talking and leave us alone to have sex.*

"And through here is the bedroom." Nico
swings open a door. I take an expectant step
forward — then stop in dismay.

"Whaaat?" I hear Ben exclaim beside me.

The room is large and grand, with a
domed glass ceiling. And under the dome
are two single beds.

"I . . . wh—" I'm so wrong-footed I can
barely get out a word. "Beds." I turn to Ben
and point. "The beds."

"Yes, these are the beds, madame." Nico
gestures at the singles with a proud beam.
"This is the bedroom."

"I *know* those are beds!" I'm gulping for
air. "But why are they singles?"

"On the website, it shows a super-king
bed," Ben takes over. "I saw a picture of it.
Where's that gone?"

Nico looks baffled at the question. "We

offer many different sleeping options for the suite. The previous occupants of the suite must have ordered two beds, such as you see. They are two very fine beds." He slaps one. "Finest quality. Is this not satisfactory?"

"No, it's not bloody satisfactory!" snaps Ben. "We need a double bed. *One* bed. Super-king. Best you've got."

"Ah." Nico pulls a regretful face. "A thousand apologies, sir. I am desolated. Since this was not ordered in advance —"

"We shouldn't have to order it in advance! It's our honeymoon! This is the honeymoon suite!" Ben's breathing hard. "What kind of honeymoon suite has two single beds in it?"

"Please, sir. Do not alarm yourself," says Nico soothingly. "I understand. I will order a double bed immediately." He takes out his phone and launches into a stream of Greek. At last he switches off and beams again. "The matter is in hand. Again, my apologies. While we are sorting out this problem, may I offer you a complimentary cocktail downstairs at the bar?"

I quell a snappy reply. I don't want a cocktail at the bar. I want my wedding night. *Now.*

"Well, how long is it going to take?" Ben scowls. "This is *ridiculous.*"

"Sir, we will complete the substitution as quickly as possible. The removers will be with us as soon as — Ah!" There's a knocking sound at the door, and Nico brightens. "Here we are!"

Six guys in white overalls troop into the room, and Nico addresses them in Greek. One guy lifts up the end of a bed and looks at it doubtfully. He says something in Greek to another guy, who shrugs and shakes his head.

"What?" says Ben in agitated tones, looking from one to the other. "What's the problem?"

"No problem," says Nico reassuringly. "Perhaps I could recommend that you take a seat in your sitting room while we address this small matter?"

He ushers us out and we find ourselves in the sitting room. The TV is still playing *Teletubbies* at full volume. I jab at it with the remote, but it doesn't switch off. Nor does the volume control work. Is the remote out of juice?

"Please," I say shortly. "I can't stand this. Could you turn it off?"

"And it's cold in here," adds Ben. "How do we adjust the air-conditioning?"

It *is* pretty freezing in here. I'd already noticed.

283

"I will summon your butler," says Nico with a beam. "He will attend to you."

He disappears out the door and I look at Ben in disbelief. We should have been having sex by now. We should have been having the hottest time of our life. Not sitting on a sofa with "Time for Tubby Bye-Bye" blaring at us, in a subzero room with six workmen next door.

"Come on," says Ben suddenly. "The library. That's got a sofa."

He hustles me in there and shuts the door. There are shelves of fake-looking books and a desk with hotel writing paper and a chaise longue upholstered in heavy brown linen. Ben shuts the door and faces me.

"Oh my *God,*" he exhales incredulously.

"Oh my God." I echo. "Insane." We both draw breath. And then it's as if the starting pistol has been fired for the Most Erogenous Zones in a Minute contest. He's all over me. I'm all over him. His hands are everywhere. My bra is unhooked, my top is ripped off, and I'm unbuttoning his shirt. . . . His skin is so warm, so delicious, I want to savor him for a bit, but Ben's already looking purposefully around the room.

"Sofa?" he pants. "Or desk?"

"Don't care," I manage.

284

"I can't wait any longer."

"What if they hear?"

"They won't hear." He's unhooking my skirt. I'm almost popping. *At last, at last, at last . . . yes . . . yes . . .*

"Sir? Madame?" There's a rapping at the door. "Sir, madame? Mr. Parr?"

What?

"Noooo," I whimper. "Noooooo . . ."

"What the *fuck* —" Ben looks livid. "Hello?" he raises his voice. "We're busy. Come back in ten."

"I have a gift from the management," comes a voice through the door. "Fresh cookies. Where would you like me to put it?"

"Anywhere," Ben calls back impatiently. "Don't care."

"Please, sir, could you kindly sign for the gift?"

I think Ben might explode. For a moment neither of us speaks.

"Sir?" The rapping comes again. "Can you hear me? I have here fresh cookies, courtesy of the management."

"Just sign quickly," I mutter. "Then we'll come back in here."

"Jesus *Christ* —"

"I know."

We're both trying to tidy ourselves up a

bit. Ben buttons up his shirt and takes a few deep breaths.

"Think about tax returns," I suggest helpfully. "OK, let's get these bloody cookies."

Ben swings open the library door to reveal an elderly man in a smart gray braided jacket, holding a silver salver with a dome on it.

"Welcome to the Amba Hotel, Mr. and Mrs. Parr," he says with grave dignity. "I am your personal butler, Georgios, at your service any time of day. I present some fresh cookies, courtesy of the management."

"Thank you," says Ben curtly. "Put them anywhere." He scribbles on the pad that the butler is holding out.

"Thank you, sir." Georgios places the silver salver on a coffee table. "My colleague will be here presently with the juice."

"Juice?" Ben stares at him. "What juice?"

"Fresh juice, courtesy of the management," Georgios says. "To accompany the cookies. My assistant butler, Hermes, will bring it directly. If you need more ice, you call for me." He hands Ben a card. "Here is my number. At your service."

Ben is breathing hard. "Listen," he says. "We don't want any juice. Cancel the juice. We want a little *privacy*. OK?"

"I understand," says Georgios at once.

"Privacy. Of course." He nods solemnly. "This is your honeymoon and you wish for privacy. This is a special time for a man and a woman."

"Precisely —"

Ben's voice is cut off as an almighty banging noise starts.

"What the *hell* . . ." We both hurry into the sitting room. A guy in white overalls is standing at the door to the bedroom, having an altercation with someone in the room. Nico comes hurrying over, wringing his hands anxiously.

"Mr. and Mrs. Parr, my apologies for this dreadful noise."

"What's going on?" Ben's eyes are wild and starey. "What's that hammering sound?"

"There is a small problem with the removal of the beds," Nico replies placatingly. "Very, very small."

Another man in white overalls appears round the side of the door, a massive hammer in his hand. He shakes his head ominously at Nico.

"What's that?" demands Ben. "What's he shaking his head for? Have you switched the beds yet?"

"And can you *please* do something about that TV?" I chime in with a wince. "It's unbearable." Every time there's a pause in the banging, the Teletubbies blare out. Is it my imagination, or are they even louder than before?

"Sir, madame, my humblest of apologies. We are working on the bed with all haste. And as for the TV . . ." Nico is holding a remote, which he jabs at the wall. Immediately the volume doubles.

"No!" I clap my hands to my ears. "Too loud! Wrong way!"

"Apologies!" shouts Nico over the racket. "I try again!"

He zaps the remote several times, but nothing happens. He bangs it against his head and shakes it. "It has jammed!" he says in tones of astonishment. "I call an engineer."

"Excuse me." Another man in a braided jacket has appeared out of nowhere. "The door was open. I have here some fresh juice courtesy of the management. Madame, where would you like me to place the juice?"

"I . . . I . . ." I'm almost gibbering. I want to scream. I want to erupt. This is supposed to be our wedding night. Our *wedding night.* And we're standing in a hotel suite, surrounded by hammering workmen, butlers with salvers, and the noise of *Teletubbies* drilling into my brain.

"Madame," says Nico gently. "I am mortified that we are inconveniencing you. Please may I offer you again a complimentary cocktail in the bar?"

11
FLISS

I almost can't look at the texts. It's like spy-
ing. It's like rubbernecking a car crash. But
I have to, even though they make me want
to clap my hands over my eyes.

Lottie and Ben are having the worst wedding night known to man. No other way to
put it. It's horrendous. It's ghastly. And it's
all my fault. My stomach is one big guilty,
acidy twinge. With every bulletin I feel
worse. But it's all in a good cause, I tell
myself sternly, already clicking on the new
text.

Another round of margaritas. This fellow can certainly hold his drink. N

Nico's been keeping me updated all
evening with every development. His latest
four texts have been reports on all the
complimentary cocktails that Lottie and
Ben have consumed. It's an eye-watering

amount. They started drinking at ten, local time. It's midnight there now. Lottie *has* to be blotto.

But what about Ben? I pause a moment, tapping my phone thoughtfully against my palm. Something Lorcan said about Ben is coming back to me: *He's a natural gambler but he lacks judgment.*

A natural gambler. Hmm. I fire a text back to Nico:

He likes to gamble. . . .

I'll leave it at that. Nico will know what to do with the information.

I press *send,* then briskly shut my suitcase, trying to calm my unsettled mind. But conflicting thoughts are shooting back and forth like arrows, each landing with a piercing little stab:

I'm sabotaging my sister's honeymoon. I'm a horrible person.

But it's only because I care about her happiness.

Exactly.

Exactly!

I mean, what if I decided not to interfere and she got pregnant and they split up and she regretted the whole thing? What then? Wouldn't I regret NOT doing something?

Would I be like the people who kept their heads down and pretended not to see when the Nazis invaded?

Not that Ben is a Nazi. As far as I know.

I feel bad about the whole Teletubbies *thing. That was cruel. Lottie's almost phobic about that program.*

I wheel my suitcase out to the hall and put it next to Noah's. He's asleep in his room, clasping Monkey and breathing peacefully, and I pop in for a moment to watch him. He took the news of our trip with utter calmness and went straight-away to pack his little case, asking only how many pairs of pants he needed. He's going to run the world one day, Noah.

I head into the bathroom and run a bath, sloshing in one of the many duty-free bath fragrances cluttering my bathroom. I shop almost exclusively at airports, I've realized. I try on clothes before boarding and pick them up on my return. I pick up Clarins sets on the plane. I have enough cured Spanish sausage and hunks of Parmesan to last me a year. And Toblerones.

I hesitate. I have Toblerone on my mind now. A Toblerone in the bath, with a glass of wine . . .

After only a millisecond's internal debate, I head to the treats cupboard in the kitchen.

Six outsize Toblerones are nestling next to a ridiculously large duty-free box of Ferrero Rocher chocolates, which I give to Noah three at a time, every Saturday. He thinks they come in threes. It has never occurred to him that they might be available in quantities larger than three.

I'm just cracking off a chunk of Toblerone when my phone rings and I pick it up, wondering if it might be Nico. But the display reads: *Lottie.*

Lottie? I'm so shocked, I drop the Toblerone on the floor. I'm staring at the phone, my heart suddenly thumping, my thumb hesitating over the *answer* button. I don't want to answer. Anyway, I've left it too late: it's gone to voicemail. I put my phone down on the counter in relief, but almost at once it starts ringing again. *Lottie.*

I swallow hard. I'm going to have to do this. Otherwise I'll only have to call her back, which might be worse. I close my eyes, take a deep breath, and press *answer.*

"Lottie! You're supposed to be on honeymoon!" I aim for a bright, innocent tone. "What are you doing, ringing me?"

"Fliiissss?"

I perform an instant analysis on her voice. She's drunk. Well, I knew that. But she's tearful too. Most important, she has no idea

I am involved in anything untoward, or it wouldn't be "Fliiissss?" with a question mark.

"What's up?" I say lightly.

"Fliss, I don't know what to do!" she wails. "Ben's *totally* drunk. Like, almost passed out. How do I sober him up? What do I do? Haven't you got some magic cure?"

I do in fact have a tried and tested formula, involving black coffee, ice cubes, and deodorant squirted in the nostrils. But I'm not sharing that with her right now.

"Gosh," I say sympathetically. "Poor you. I . . . I don't know what to suggest. Maybe some coffee?"

"He can't even sit up! He drank all these stupid cocktails, and I had to help him up to our room, and then he just crashed out on the bed and it's supposed to be our *wedding* night."

"Oh no!" I try to sound shocked. "So haven't you even —"

"No! We haven't!"

I can't help exhaling with relief. I was worried they might have slipped in a quick one without anyone knowing.

"We haven't done *anything*," Lottie wails in distress. "And I know you recommended this hotel, Fliss, but, quite frankly, it's awful! I'm going to complain! They've *ruined*

294

our honeymoon. We've got single beds! They say they can't move them! I'm sitting on a single bed right now!" Her voice shrills higher. "Single beds! In a honeymoon suite!"

"Goodness. I can't believe it!" I'm sounding more and more stagy, but Lottie is on such a roll, she doesn't notice.

"So then they give us all this free booze to apologize, and this concierge guy bets Ben that he can't drink some special Greek cocktail. Next thing, he's downed the whole thing and everyone in the bar is cheering and he's practically comatose! I mean, what was in it? Absinthe?"

I dread to think what was in it.

"We were snogging in the lift on the way back up to the room," Lottie carries on agitatedly. "And I thought, here we go, at last — and suddenly there was this dead weight on my shoulder and Ben had fallen asleep! Mid-snog! I had to man-handle him into the room and he weighs a ton and now he's snoring!" She sounds close to tears.

"Look, Lottie." I run a hand through my hair, trying desperately to think of the best way to play this. "It's not such a big deal. Just get a good night's sleep and . . . er . . . enjoy the hotel facilities."

"I'm suing this place." She doesn't even

seem to be listening. "I don't know how it won an award for Best Honeymoon Suite. It's the worst!"

"Have you eaten? Why don't you have something from room service? They do really good sushi, or there's an Italian pizza place. . . ."

"OK. Maybe I'll do that." Her fury seems to subside and she gives a gusty sigh. "Sorry to lay all this on you, Fliss. I mean, it's not *your* fault."

I can't bring myself to answer.

I'm doing the right thing, I remind myself furiously. *What's better, frustrated and upset for one night or married, pregnant, and regretting it your whole life?*

"Fliss? Are you still there?"

"Oh, hi." I swallow. "Yes. Look, try to get some sleep. I expect tomorrow will be better."

"Night, Fliss."

"Night, Lottie."

I switch off and stare ahead for a moment, trying to calm my guilt.

I expect tomorrow will be better.

Total lie. I've already talked to Nico. Tomorrow won't be better.

296

12
LOTTIE

I don't want to be negative. But if I could describe how I expected the morning after my wedding night to be, it would not be this.

It would not be this.

I always imagined my new husband and me nestled in a huge white cottony bed, like in a soap-powder ad. Birds singing outside. Sunlight gently passing over our faces as we turn to each other and kiss, remembering our fabulous time last night, and murmuring sweet nothings to each other before moving seamlessly into spectacular morning sex.

Not waking up on a single bed, with a cricked neck, un-brushed teeth, the smell of last night's room-service pizza, and the sound of Ben groaning on the opposite bed.

"Are you OK?" I try to sound sympathetic, even though I want to kick him.

"I think so." He lifts his head with what

appears to be a huge effort. He looks pretty green and he's still wearing his suit. "What *happened*?"

"You won a bet," I say shortly. "Well done, you."

Ben's gaze is distant and his eyes are moving back and forth. He's clearly trying to piece it all together.

"I fucked up, didn't I?" he says at last.

"Just a bit."

"I'm sorry."

"Yeah. Whatever."

"No, I'm sorry."

"Got it."

"No, I'm really, *really* sorry." He swings his legs round and gets to his feet, swaying theatrically for a moment. "Mrs. Parr, my greatest, humblest apologies. How will I make this up to you?" He bows low, nearly falling over, and I stifle a smile. I can't stay cross. Ben always was a charmer.

"I can't think." I pout at him.

"Any room in that bed?"

"Might be . . ."

I shuffle up, pulling open the duvet invitingly for him to snuggle in. It's luxury goose down. We also have the choice of a pillow menu, with twenty different varieties. I read them all last night, over my pizza. But right now I couldn't care less whether the pillow

298

is buckwheat, hypoallergenic, or silk-covered. My husband is in bed with me. Awake. This is what matters.

"Mmmm." He buries his face in my neck. "You're all cozy. Yum."

"You're all hangover-y." I wrinkle my nose. "Get your suit off."

"With pleasure." He pulls his jacket and shirt off together in one movement, over his head, then straddles me, bare-chested, and grins down. "Hello, wife."

"Hello, idiot."

"Like I said, I'll make it up to you." He runs a finger down my cheek, down my neck, and under the duvet, fingering the top of my incredibly expensive cami. "We have all morning."

"All day." I reach up to pull him down for a kiss.

"We've earned this," he murmurs. "Oh God. Oh Jesus." His hands are tugging off my cami-knickers. "Lottie. I remember you."

"I remember you," I manage, my voice heavy with lust. His clothes are all off now. He's as hot as I remember; he's as hard as I remember. This is just as good as I remember; it's going to be amazing. . . .

"Madame?" The grave voice of Georgios hits my ear. For a moment I think it's Ben, fooling around with an impression. Then I realize it's not Ben. Which means it's the butler. Which means —

I sit bolt upright, clasping the duvet round me, my heart pumping.

The butler's in the *suite*?

"Good morning!" I call in a strangled voice.

"Is madame ready for breakfast?"

What the *fuck*? I pull an agonized face at Ben, who looks as though he wants to hit someone.

"Didn't you put on the DO NOT DISTURB sign?" he whispers.

"I thought I did!"

"Then what —"

"I don't know!"

"Good morning." Georgios appears at the door to the bedroom. "Sir, madame, I have taken the liberty of ordering you a very special treat. Most highly recommended by all our VIP honeymoon guests. Our Champagne Breakfast with Music."

I stare back at him, speechless. Music? What does he mean? What on earth —

No *way*. I nearly convulse with shock as a girl appears at the door. She's got long blond hair and is wearing a white Grecian tunic, and she's wheeling along a massive harp.

300

I exchange looks wildly with Ben. How do we stop this? What do we do?

"Mr. and Mrs. Parr. Congratulations on your marriage! Today I will be playing for you a selection of love tunes, to accompany your breakfast," the girl says, and takes a seat on a fold-up stool. Next moment she's plucking away briskly at the harp and Georgios plus his assistant are bringing trays on stands to the bed and pouring out glasses of champagne and peeling fruit and offering us little finger bowls to refresh our hands in.

I haven't managed to utter a word. This is too surreal. I was about to have the hottest sex of my life. I was about to consummate my marriage. And instead I'm having a kiwi fruit peeled for me by a sixty-year-old man in a braided jacket while a harpist twangs "Love Changes Everything."

I've never really been one for the harp. But this one is making me want to hurl my basket of mini-croissants at it.

"Please. A loving-cup toast, to celebrate your marriage." Georgios gestures at our champagne flutes. Obediently, we link arms to sip our champagne, and with no warning Georgios throws a handful of pink confetti over us. I splutter in shock. Where did *that* come from? A moment later there's a flash in my face and I realize Georgios has taken a photo.

"A commemorative photograph," he says gravely. "We will present it in a leather-bound album. Compliments of the management."

What? I stare at him in horror. I don't want a commemorative photo of me looking hungover and disheveled with confetti stuck to my lip.

"Eat," Ben whispers in my ear. "Quick. Then they'll go."

That's a point. I reach for the teapot, and Georgios leaps forward reprovingly.

"Madame. Let me." He pours me a cup of tea and I take a couple of gulps. I swallow some kiwi fruit, then clutch my stomach.

"Mmm. Delicious! But I'm stuffed."

"Me too." Ben nods. "It's been a great breakfast, but maybe you could clear it away now?"

Georgios hesitates, seeming reluctant.

"Sir, madame, I have for you a special egg dish. They are the finest, double-yolk eggs, prepared with saffron —"

"No, thanks. No eggs. None." Ben stares Georgios down. "No. Eggs. Thank you."

"Of course, sir," says Georgios at last. He nods at the girl, who comes to a hasty final cadence, stands up, bows, then starts trundling her harp away. The two butlers pack the trays up and remove them to a trolley outside. Then Georgios appears back in the bedroom area.

"Mr. and Mrs. Parr, I hope you have enjoyed the Champagne Breakfast with Music. Now I will await your command. I am at your disposal entirely. No request is too large or too small." He waits expectantly.

"Great," says Ben off-puttingly. "Tell you what, we'll call you."

"I await your command," repeats Georgios, and withdraws, shutting the doors to the bedroom.

Ben and I just look at each other. I feel a bit hysterical.

"Oh my God."

"Fucking hell." Ben rolls his eyes. "That's a first."

"Didn't you want your eggs?" I say teasingly. "They've got saffron, you know."

"I know what I want." He pushes down the straps of my cami, and just the feel of him sends sparks of lust through me.

"Me too." I reach for him and he gives a little shudder.

"Where were we again?" His hands travel down under the covers, slow and purposeful. I'm so sensitive to his touch I can't help moaning.

His eyes are huge and urgent. His breathing is raspy. Now I'm pulling him toward me, and his lips are everywhere, and my mind is emptying as my body takes over. OK, here we go. *Here* we go. I'm making sounds and so is he, and it's going to happen, it's really going to happen. . . . I'm going to explode . . . come on, come *on*. . . .

And then I freeze. I can hear a sound. A rustling sound. Just outside the bedroom door.

In reflex, I shove Ben away and sit up, every sense on alert.

"Stop! Stop it. Listen." I can barely frame the words properly. "He's still here."

"What?" Ben's face is contorted with desire, and I'm not sure he's understanding anything I'm saying.

"He's still here!" I bat Ben's hand off my breast and gesture frantically at the door. "The butler! He hasn't left!"

"What?" A murderous scowl comes over Ben's face. He swings his legs round and gets out of bed, totally naked.

"You can't go out like that!" I squeak. "Put on a robe."

Ben's scowl becomes yet more murderous. He shrugs on a terry-cloth dressing

304

gown and throws open the door to the bedroom. Sure enough, there's Georgios, arranging glasses neatly on the cocktail bar.

"Ah, Georgios," says Ben. "I think you misunderstood. Thanks very much. That will be all for now. Thank you."

"I understand, sir." Georgios makes a little bow. "I await your command."

"Right." I can sense Ben's temper starting to fray. "Well, my command is for you to go. Leave the room. Go. *Adiós.*" He makes a shooing motion. "Leave us *alone.*"

"Ah." At last light dawns on Georgios's face. "I see. Very good, sir. You call me if you need anything." He gives another bow, then heads toward the kitchen. Ben hesitates a moment, then follows him to make sure he actually exits.

"That's right," I can hear him say firmly. "You go and put your feet up, Georgios. Don't worry about us. No, we can pour our own water, thank you. Bye, then. Bye . . ." His voice recedes as he enters the kitchen.

A few moments later, he appears at the door of the bedroom and pumps the air. "Gone! At last!"

"Well done!"

"Stubborn bastard."

"Just doing his job, I suppose." I shrug.

305

"He's obviously got a really strong sense of duty."

"He didn't want to leave," says Ben incredulously. "You'd think he'd leap at the chance for some time off. But he kept telling me we'd need him to pour our mineral water, and I kept telling him, no, we wouldn't, we're not total lazy gits. Makes you wonder what kind of people stay here —" Ben breaks off mid-sentence and his jaw drops. As I turn my head, I can feel mine dropping too.

No.

That *can't* be . . .

Both of us stare in disbelief as Hermes, the assistant butler, strides into the sitting room.

"Good morning, Mr. and Mrs. Parr," he says cheerfully. He approaches the cocktail bar and starts arranging exactly the same glasses that Georgios was tidying ten seconds ago. "May I offer you a drink? A small snack? May I help you with your entertainment for the day?"

"What . . . what . . ." Ben seems almost incapable of speech. "What the hell are you *doing* here?"

Hermes looks up, apparently perplexed by the question.

"I am your assistant butler," he says at

last. "I am on duty while Georgios is resting. I await your command."

I feel like I've gone mad.

We're trapped in butler hell.

Is this how rich people live? No wonder celebrities look so miserable the whole time. They're thinking, *If only the butler would let us have some bloody* sex.

"Please." Ben looks almost demented. "Please go. Now. Go." He's ushering Hermes toward the door.

"Sir," says Hermes in alarm. "I do not use the guest entrance, I use the kitchen entrance —"

"I don't care which bloody entrance you use!" Ben practically yells. "Just go! Get out! Vamoose! Scram!" He's batting Hermes toward the door as though he's a pest, and Hermes is backing away, looking terrified, and I'm watching from the doorway, the duvet wrapped around me, and all three of us jump violently as the doorbell rings. Ben stiffens and looks around as though suspecting a trick.

"Sir." Hermes is composing himself. "Please, sir. You permit I answer the door?"

Ben doesn't answer. He's breathing heavily through his nostrils. He glances at me and I give an agonized shrug. The doorbell rings again.

"Please, sir," repeats Hermes. "You permit I answer the door?"

"Go on, then," says Ben, glowering. "Answer it. But no cleaners. No turndown service, no turnup service, no champagne, no fruit, and no bloody harps."

"Very good, sir," says Hermes, eyeing him anxiously. "You permit me."

Hermes edges past Ben, into the lobby, and opens the door. In sweeps Nico, followed by the six workmen from last night.

"Good morning, Mr. Parr, Mrs. Parr!" he breezes. "I trust you slept well? A thousand apologies for last night. But I have good news! We have come to change your bed."

13
LOTTIE

This can't be happening. We've been turfed out of our own honeymoon suite.

What is *wrong* with them? I've never seen such an inept crew in my life. They unscrewed the legs of one bed, shuffled it round, and lifted it up and pronounced it too big, then Nico suggested they screw the legs back on and start again . . . and all the time Ben was simmering to a boil.

At last he started yelling so loudly, the workmen gathered protectively around Nico. To his credit, Nico kept his cool, even when Ben started brandishing the hair dryer. Nico asked if we would please leave the suite while the workmen were operational and perhaps we would enjoy a complimentary à la carte breakfast on the veranda?

That was two hours ago. There's only so much à la carte breakfast you can eat. We've been back to the room to get our beach stuff and there are *still* people in there, all peering at the beds and scratching their heads. The room is full of bed legs and headboards and a super-king mattress propped up against the wall. Apparently it's the "wrong kind of bed." What does that even mean?

"How hard can it be to swap a couple of beds?" says Ben with a furious scowl, as we head toward the beach. "Are they morons?"

"That's just what I was thinking."

"It's ridiculous."

"Ludicrous."

We pause by the entrance to the beach. It's quite something. Blue sea, golden sand, rows of the plushiest sun beds I've ever seen, white umbrellas billowing in the breeze, and waiters hurrying around with drinks on trays. Any other day, I'd be salivating at the sight.

But there's only one thing I want right now. And it's not a suntan.

"They should have given us another room," says Ben for the hundredth time. "We should be suing."

As soon as they asked us to leave, Ben requested a substitute room, and for one heavenly moment I thought everything was going to work out after all. We could disappear into a spare room, have a wonderful morning together, emerge in time for lunch. . . . But, no, Nico wrung his hands and said he was devastated and mortified but the hotel was fully booked, could he offer sir a complimentary hot-air-balloon ride instead?

A complimentary bloody hot-air-balloon ride. I thought Ben was going to throttle him.

As we're pausing by the towel stand, I become aware of a presence lurking. It's Georgios. Where did he appear from? Has he been following us? Is this all part of the service? I nudge Ben, and he raises his eyebrows.

"Madame," says Georgios gravely. "May I help you with your towels?"

"Oh. Um, thanks," I say awkwardly. I don't really need help, but it would be rude to tell him to go away.

Georgios collects two towels and we follow a beach attendant to a pair of sun beds facing the sea. Lots of guests are already ensconced, and there's a smell of sun cream in the air. Waves are washing gently onto the beach. This is fairly blissful, I have to admit.

Between them, the beach attendant and Georgios are laying out our towels with military precision.

"Bottled water." Georgios sets a chiller on

our table. "Should I open the cap for madame?"

"Don't worry. Maybe I'll have some later. Thanks so much, Georgios. That will be all for now. Thank you." I sit down on a bed, and Ben takes the other. I kick off my flip-flops, peel off my caftan top, lean back, and close my eyes, hoping this will give the message to Georgios. A moment later a shadow crosses my eyelids and I open them. To my disbelief, Georgios is neatly straightening my flip-flops and folding up my caftan.

Is he planning to hang around with us all bloody *day*? I glance at Ben, who is clearly thinking the same thing.

As he catches me sitting up, Georgios leaps to attention.

"Madame wishes to swim? Madame wishes to cross the hot sand?" He proffers the flip-flops.

What?

OK, this is just stupid. These five-star hotels have gone way, way too far. Yes, I'm on holiday; yes, it's nice to have some personal service. But that doesn't make me suddenly incapable of laying out a towel or unscrewing a bottle cap or putting on my own flip-flops.

"No, thanks. What I'd really like is . . ." I try to think of some time-consuming challenge. "I'd like a freshly squeezed orange juice with honey drizzled in it. And some M&M's. The brown ones only. Thank you so much, Georgios."

"Madame." To my relief, he bows and walks away.

"Brown M&M's?" says Ben incredulously. "You diva."

"I was trying to get rid of him!" I retort in an undertone. "Is he going to stalk us all day? Is that what a personal butler does?"

"God knows." Ben seems distracted. He keeps eyeing my bikini top. Or, rather, the contents of my bikini top.

"Let me rub your sun cream in," he says. "I'm not giving that job to the butler."

"OK. Thanks." I hand him the bottle and he squeezes a big dollop of cream onto his palm. As he starts to apply it, I hear him inhale sharply.

"Let me know if I'm too rough," he murmurs. "Or not rough enough."

"Er . . . Ben," I whisper. "I meant my back. I don't actually need help applying it to my cleavage."

I don't think Ben can hear, because he doesn't stop. A nearby woman is giving us an odd look. Now Ben takes another dollop of sun cream and starts rubbing it *under* my bikini top. With both hands. He's breathing very heavily. And now several people are looking.

"Ben!"

"Just being thorough," he mumbles.

"Ben! Stop!" I jerk away. "Do my *back.*"

"Right." He blinks a few times, his eyes unfocused.

"Maybe I should do it myself." I take the bottle from him and start slathering it on my legs. "Do you want some? Ben?" I wave to get his attention, but he seems in a trance. Then suddenly he comes to.

"I've had an idea."

"What kind of idea?" I say warily.

"A brilliant idea."

He gets up and approaches a couple lying on sun beds nearby. I noticed them earlier, at breakfast. They both have red hair and I'm already worried about them burning in the sun.

"Hi, there." Ben smiles charmingly down at the woman. "Enjoying your holiday? I'm Ben, by the way. We've just arrived."

"Oh. Hi, there." The woman has a slightly suspicious tone.

"Lovely hat." He gestures at her head.

Lovely hat? It's the most nondescript straw hat I've ever seen. What is he up to?

"Actually, I was wondering," Ben carries on. "I'm in a bit of a bind. I've got a very

314

important call to make and our room is out of action. Would you mind if I used yours? Just briefly. I'd pop up really briefly. With my wife," he adds carelessly. "We'd be quick."

The woman looks a bit flummoxed.

"A call?" she says.

"An important business call," Ben says. "As I say, we'd be super quick. In and out."

He glances at me and gives the tiniest of winks. I'd smile if I weren't so transfixed with longing. A room. Oh God, we *so* need a room. . . .

"Darling?" The woman leans over and nudges her husband. "These people want to borrow our room." The husband sits up and stares at Ben, shading his eyes against the sun. He's older than his wife and is doing *The Times*'s crossword.

"Why on earth would you need to do that?"

"For a call," says Ben. "A really quick business call."

"Why can't you use the conference center?"

"Not private enough," says Ben without missing a beat. "This is a very confidential, discreet kind of call. I'd very much appreciate a secluded space."

"But —"

"I'll tell you what . . ." Ben hesitates. "Why don't I give you a little gift for your trouble? Say, fifty quid?"

"What?" The husband sounds flabbergasted. "You want to pay us fifty quid just to use our room? Are you serious?"

"I'm sure the hotel would find you a room for nothing," puts in the wife helpfully.

"They wouldn't, OK?" Ben sounds a tad impatient. "We've tried. Which is why I'm asking you."

"Fifty quid." The husband puts down his crossword, frowning thoughtfully as though this is a new clue. "What — cash?"

"Cash, check, whatever you like. A credit on your room bill. Don't care."

"Wait a minute." The husband jabs his finger at Ben as if he's suddenly worked it all out. "Is this a scam? You run up hundreds of pounds on my phone bill and give me fifty quid for the pleasure?"

"No! I just want your room!"

"But there are so many other spaces." The wife looks puzzled. "Why do you want our room? Why not a corner of the lobby? Why not —"

"Because I want to have sex in it, OK?" Ben explodes. I can see heads popping up everywhere under umbrellas. "I want to have sex," he repeats more calmly. "With my

316

wife. On my honeymoon. Is that too much to ask?"

"You want to have *sex*?" The wife draws herself away from Ben as though she might catch a disease. "On *our* bed?"

"It's not your bed!" says Ben impatiently. "It's a hotel bed. We can have the sheets changed. Or use the floor." He turns to me as though for confirmation. "The floor would be OK, right?"

My entire face is prickling. I can't believe he's dragging me into this. I can't believe he's telling the whole beach we're going to do it on the floor.

"Andrew!" The wife turns to her husband. "Say something!"

Andrew is silent, frowning for a moment — then looks up.

"Five hundred and not a penny less."

"What?" Now it's the wife's turn to explode. "You have to be joking! Andrew, that's *our* room and this is *our* honeymoon and we're not having some strange couple going in it to do . . . anything." She grabs the room card, which is lying on Andrew's sun bed, and stuffs it down her swimsuit defiantly. "You're sick." She glowers at Ben. "You *and* your wife."

Heads have turned all over the beach. Great.

"Fine," says Ben at last. "Well, thank you for your time."

As Ben is heading back to me, a large, hairy guy in tight swimming trunks leaps up from a nearby sun bed and taps Ben on the shoulder. Even from here I can smell his after-shave.

"Hey," he says in a heavy Russian accent. "I have a room."

"Oh, really?" Ben turns, interested.

"You, me, your wife, my new wife, Natalya — you want to make some fun?"

There's a pause — then Ben swivels to meet my gaze, eyebrows raised. I stare back in slight shock. Is he actually *asking me*? I shake my head violently, mouthing, "No, no, no."

"Not today," says Ben, in what sound like genuinely regretful tones. "Another time."

"No worries." The Russian guy claps him on the shoulder, and Ben comes back over to his sun bed. He slides onto it and stares savagely out to sea.

"Well, so much for that bright idea. Bloody frigid cow."

I lean over and poke him hard in the chest. "Hey, what was that? Did you want to take him up on his offer? That Russian?"

"At least it would have been something."

Something? I stare at him incredulously,

till he looks up.

"What?" he says defensively. "It *would* have been something."

"Well, excuse me for not wanting to share my wedding night with a gorilla and a girl with rubber boobs," I say sarcastically. "Sorry to spoil your fun."

"Not rubber," says Ben.

"You've looked, have you?"

"Silicone."

I can't help snorting. Meanwhile, Ben is deftly flinging a couple of towels up over our parasol. What's he doing?

"Just creating a bit of privacy," he says with a wink, and squeezes next to me on my sun bed, his hands all over me like an octopus. "God, you're hot. You haven't got a crotchless bikini on, have you?"

Is he serious?

Actually, a crotchless bikini would have been handy.

"I don't think they even exist —" I suddenly notice two children watching us in curiosity. "Stop!" I hiss, and drag Ben's hand out of my bikini bottoms. "We're *not* doing it on a sun bed! We'll get arrested!"

"Shaved ice, madame? Lemon flavor?" We both jump about a million miles as Hermes ducks his head under the towels and proffers a tray bearing two cones. I am honestly going to have a heart attack before I leave this place.

For a while we sit in silence, slurping at our shaved ice and listening to the low hum of beach chatter and waves lapping the sand.

"Look," I say at last. "It's a shit situation, but there's nothing we can do about it. Either we sit here, boiling with frustration and getting ratty with each other, or we go and do something till the room's ready."

"Like what?"

"You know." I try to sound optimistic. "Fun holiday activities. Tennis, sailing, canoeing. Ping-Pong. Whatever they've got."

"Sounds riveting," says Ben moodily.

"Let's go for a walk, anyway, and see what we can find."

I want to get away from this beach. Everyone keeps turning to look at us while they whisper behind their paperbacks, and the Russian guy keeps winking at me.

Ben finishes his shaved ice and leans over to kiss me, his icy lips parting mine with a delicious lemony, salty taste.

"We *can't*," I say as his hand automatically finds my bikini top. "Look, stop." I wrench his hand away. "It makes it too hard. No touching. Not till our room's ready."

"No touching?" He stares at me incredulously.

"No touching." I nod resolutely. "Come on. Let's walk through the hotel and whatever activity we find first, we'll do. Yes? Deal?"

I wait for Ben to get to his feet and slip into his flip-flops. Georgios is heading toward us down the path from the hotel, and to my disbelief he's actually holding a salver bearing a glass of orange juice and a dish of brown M&M's.

"Madame."

"Wow!" I drain the orange juice in one gulp and crunch a couple of M&M's. "That's wonderful."

"Is our room ready yet?" demands Ben abruptly. "It must be."

"I believe not, sir." Georgios's gloomy expression descends yet further. "I believe a problem has arisen with the fire alarm."

"The fire alarm?" Ben echoes incredulously. "What do you mean, the fire alarm?"

"A sensor was knocked as the beds were moved. Unfortunately, this must be fixed before we can allow you back into the room. It is for your own safety. My deepest apologies, sir."

Ben has both his hands to his head. He looks so apoplectic, I'm almost scared.

"Well, how long will it be now?"

Georgios spreads his hands. "Sir, I only

wish —"

"You don't know," Ben interrupts tensely. "Of course you don't know. Why would you know?"

I have a horrible feeling he's going to flip out in a minute and hit Georgios.

"Anyway." I hastily join in the conversation. "Never mind. We'll go and amuse ourselves."

"Madame." Georgios nods. "How can I assist you with this?"

Ben scowls at him. "You can —"

"Get me some more juice, please!" I trill, before Ben says something *really* offensive. "Maybe some . . . some . . ." I hesitate. What's the most time-consuming juice there is? "Some beet juice?"

A flicker passes across Georgios's otherwise impassive face. I think perhaps he's cottoned onto my ruse.

"Of course, madame."

"Great! See you later." We head up a path lined with white walls and bougainvillea. The sun is beating down on our heads and it's very quiet. I know Georgios is following us, but I'm not making chitchat with him. Then he'll *never* go.

"The beach bar's this way," observes Ben as we pass a sign. "We could look in."

"The *beach bar*?" I give him a sardonic

look. "After last night?"

"Hair of the dog. Virgin Mary. Whatever."

"OK." I shrug. "We could have a quick one."

The beach bar is large and circular and shady, with Greek bouzouki music playing softly. Ben immediately slumps onto a bar stool.

"Welcome." The barman approaches us with a wide smile. "Many congratulations on your marriage." He gives us a laminated drinks menu and moves away.

"How did he know we were just married?" Ben regards him with narrowed eyes.

"Saw our shiny new wedding rings, I suppose? What shall we have?" I start looking down the menu, but Ben is lost in thought.

"That bloody woman," he mutters. "We'd be there now. In their bed."

"Well. I'm sure they'll fix the fire alarm soon," I say unconvincingly.

"This is our bloody *honeymoon.*"

"I know," I say soothingly. "Come on, let's have a drink. A proper drink." I feel like having one myself, to be honest.

"Did you say it was your honeymoon?" A blond girl heralds us across the bar. She's wearing an orange caftan with bobbles on the sleeves and has jeweled sandals with very high heels. "Of course it is! *Everyone* here is on honeymoon. When were you married?"

"Yesterday. We just arrived last night."

"We were Saturday! Holy Trinity Church in Manchester. My dress was Phillipa Lepley. We had a hundred and twenty to the reception. It was a buffet. Then in the evening we had dancing to a band, and fifty additional guests attended." She looks at us expectantly.

"Ours was . . . smaller," I say after a pause. "Quite a lot smaller. But lovely."

Lovelier than yours, I add silently. I turn to Ben to back me up, but he's swiveled away and is talking to the bartender instead.

This is the first time I've noticed a trait that Ben has in common with Richard — i.e., being totally antisocial and narrow-minded about new people. The number of times I've struck up a conversation with some really interesting, fun person, and Richard just wouldn't join in. Like that fascinating woman we met at Greenwich once, who he point-blank refused to be introduced to. And, OK, it turned out she was a bit of a weirdo and tried to get me to invest £10,000 in a houseboat, but he wasn't to *know* that, was he?

"Ring?" The girl shoves her hand forward. Her nails are orange to match her caftan, I notice. Does that mean all her caftans are orange or that she repaints her nails every night? "I'm Melissa, by the way."

"Lovely!" I thrust my left hand forward to match, and my platinum wedding band glints in the sunshine. It's studded with diamonds and is really quite fancy.

"Very nice!" Melissa raises her eyebrows, impressed. "It's an amazing feeling, isn't it, wearing a wedding ring?" She leans forward conspiratorially. "I catch my reflection and see the ring on my hand and I think, *Bloody hell! I'm married!*"

"Me too!" I suddenly realize I've missed this: girly chat about getting married. That's the downside of rushing off with no family or bridesmaids at your side. "And being called 'Mrs.' is weird too!" I add. "Mrs. Parr."

"I'm Mrs. Falkner." She beams. "I just love it. Falkner."

"I like Parr." I smile back.

"You know this place is *the* honeymoon resort? They've had celebs here and everything. Our suite is to *die* for. And we're renewing our vows tomorrow night, on the Love Island. That's what they call it, the Love Island."

She gestures down toward the sea, at a wooden jetty extending into the distance. At the end it broadens into a large platform which has been set up with a gauzy white canopy.

"We're having cocktails afterward," she adds. "You should come along! Maybe you could renew your vows too!"

"Already?"

I don't want to sound rude, but that's the weirdest thing I've ever heard. I got married yesterday. Why would I renew my vows?

"We've decided to renew ours every year," says Melissa complacently. "Next year we're going to do them in Mauritius, and I've already seen exactly the dress I want to wear. Last month's *Brides.* The Vera Wang on page fifty-four. Did you see it?" Melissa's phone trills before I can answer, and she frowns. "Excuse me a moment. . . . Matt? Matt, what on earth are you doing? I'm at the bar! As we arranged. The bar . . . No, not the spa, the *bar!*"

She exhales impatiently, then puts her phone away and beams at me again. "So, you two *must* go in for the Couples' Quiz this afternoon."

"Couples' Quiz?" I echo blankly.

"You know. Like the TV show. You answer questions about your partner and the winners are the couple who know each other best." She gestures at a nearby poster, which reads:

TODAY at 4 PM:
COUPLES' QUIZ on the BEACH.
BIG PRIZES!! FREE ENTRY!!

"Everyone's entered," she adds, sipping at her drink through a straw. "They put on loads of activities for honeymooners here. It's all marketing nonsense, of course." She casually brushes back her hair. "I mean, honestly, as if marriage were a competition."

I almost snort with laughter. Nice try. She wants to win so badly, it's practically etched on her skin.

"So, are you in?" She peers at me over her Gucci shades. "Go on! It's only a laugh!"

I suppose she's right. I mean, let's face it, what else are we doing with our time?

"OK. Sign us up."

"Yianni!" Melissa calls over to the bartender. "I've got you another couple for Couples' Quiz."

"What?" Ben turns to me with a frown.

"We're going in for a competition," I inform him. "We agreed to do the first activity we saw, didn't we? Well, this is it."

Yianni passes two paper flyers to Ben and me, along with a bottle of wine and two

327

glasses, which Ben must have ordered. Melissa has stood up from her bar stool. She's on the phone again and sounds even more irate than before.

"The beach bar, not the lobby bar. The beach bar! . . . OK, stay there, I'm coming. . . . See you later," she mouths, and totters off in a swirl of orange caftan.

When she's gone, Ben and I are silent for a moment, studying the Couples' Quiz flyers. *Demonstrate your love! Prove you have what it takes as a couple!*

Despite everything, I can feel my competitive spirit rising. Not that I need to prove anything at all. But I just *know* there isn't any couple at this resort more intimate and connected than Ben and me. I mean, look at them. And look at us.

"We're *so* going to lose this," says Ben, with a snort of amusement.

Lose?

"No, we're not!" I stare at him in dismay. "Why do you say that?"

"Because we need to know stuff about each other," replies Ben, as though it's obvious. "Which we don't."

"We know *heaps* about each other!" I say defensively. "We've known each other since we were eighteen! If you ask me, we're going to win."

Ben raises an eyebrow. "Maybe. What kind of questions do they ask?"

"I don't know. I never watched the show." I have a sudden idea. "But Fliss has got the board game. I'll call her."

14
FLISS

We're at the departure gate at Heathrow when my phone rings. Before I can move, Noah plucks it out of the side pocket of my bag and studies the display.

"It's Aunt Lottie phoning!" His face lights up in excitement. "Shall I tell her we're coming to surprise her on her special holiday?"

"No!" I grab the phone. "Just sit down a minute. Look at your sticker pack. Do the dinosaurs." I press *answer* and take a couple of steps away from Noah, trying to compose myself. "Lottie, hi!" I greet her.

"There you are! I've been trying to reach you! Where are you?"

"Oh . . . you know. Just around." I force myself to pause before I add, light as gossamer, "Any luck with your room yet? Or the bed? Or . . . anything?"

I know from Nico that she's still roomless. But I also know Ben tried to hire a room off another guest on the beach. Sneaky little sod.

"Oh, the room." Lottie sounds disconsolate. "It's been such a bloody saga. We've given up for now. We're just going to enjoy the day."

"Right. Sensible plan." I breathe a slight sigh of relief. "So, how is it out there? Sunny?"

"Boiling." Lottie sounds preoccupied. "Listen, Fliss, d'you remember that game Couples' Quiz?"

I wrinkle my brow. "You mean the TV show?"

"Exactly. You had the board game, didn't you? What kind of questions do they ask?"

"Why?" I say, puzzled.

"We're doing a Couples' Quiz contest. Are the questions hard?"

"*Hard?* No! They're just fun. Silly things. Basic stuff that couples know about each other."

"Ask me some." Lottie sounds a bit tense. "Give me some practice."

"Well, OK." I think for a moment. "What kind of toothpaste does Ben use?"

"Don't know," says Lottie after a pause.

"What's his mother called?"

"Don't know."

"What is his favorite meal that you cook

for him?"

There's a longer pause. "Don't know," she says at last. "I've never cooked for him."

"If he was going to the theater, would he choose Shakespeare, a modern play, or a musical?"

"I don't *know*!" wails Lottie. "I've never been to the theater with him. Ben's right! We're going to lose!"

Is she insane? Of course they're going to lose.

"Does Ben know any of those things about you, do you think?" I ask mildly.

"Of course not! Neither of us knows anything!"

"Right. Well . . ."

"I really don't want to lose," says Lottie, lowering her voice savagely. "There's this bridezilla girl here and she's been boasting about her wedding, and if I don't know anything about my husband and he doesn't know anything about me . . ."

Then maybe you shouldn't have married each other! I want to yell.

"Could you maybe . . . talk to each other?" I suggest at last.

"Yes! Yes, that's it," says Lottie, as though I've cracked some fiendish code. "We'll learn it all. Give me a list of the stuff I need to know." She sounds determined. "Tooth-

paste, name of mother, favorite meals . . .
Can you text all the questions to me?"

"No, I can't," I say firmly. "I'm busy.
Lottie, why on earth are you doing this?
Why aren't you lying on the beach?"

"I got talked into it. And now we can't
back out, or we'll look like we're not a
happy couple. Fliss, this place is mad. It's
Honeymoon Central."

I shrug. "You knew it would be, didn't
you?"

"I suppose. . . ." She hesitates. "But I
didn't realize it would be *this* honeymoon-y.
They have loved-up couples everywhere,
and you can't take a step without someone
saying 'Congratulations' or chucking confetti over you. That bridezilla girl is renewing her vows already, can you believe? She
was trying to talk me into doing it too."

For a moment I've forgotten where I am
and the whole situation. I'm just chatting
with Lottie.

"Sounds like it's become totally gim-
micky."

"It is a bit."

"So don't do the Couples' Quiz."

"I have to." She sounds resolute. "I'm not
backing out now. So, should I know where
Ben went to high school, all that kind of
stuff? What about hobbies?"

My frustration returns in a flash. This is *ridiculous.* She sounds like someone mugging up, trying to fool an immigration officer. For an instant I consider saying all this to her right now.

But, at the same time, my deeper instincts tell me not to try anything by phone. All that will happen is we'll have a steaming row and she'll ring off and get Ben to impregnate her right then and there, probably on the beach in full view of everyone, just to show me.

I need to get out there. Pretend that I simply wanted to surprise her. I'll assess the territory, let her relax. Then I'll draw her aside and we'll have a chat. A frank chat. A long, relentless chat, from which I will not let her escape till she's seen the whole picture. *Really* seen it.

This Couples' Quiz has played into my hands, I realize. She's going to fall flat on her face in quite a public way. And then she'll be ripe to hear the voice of reason.

A flight is being announced, and Lottie immediately demands, "What's that? Where are you?"

"Station," I lie smoothly. "Better go. Good luck!"

I switch off my phone and look around for Noah. I left him sitting on a plastic chair two feet away, but he's made his way to the desk and is deep in conversation with an air hostess, who is crouching down and listening intently to him.

"Noah!" I call, and both their heads turn. The air hostess raises a hand in acknowledgment, stands up, and leads him back to me. She's very curvy and tanned, with huge blue eyes and hair in a bun, and as she approaches I catch a waft of perfume.

"Sorry about that." I smile at her. "Noah, stay here. No wandering."

The air hostess is gazing at me, transfixed, and I put my hand to my mouth, wondering if I have a crumb on my lip.

"I just want to say," she says in a rush, "that I heard about your little boy's ordeal, and I think you're all really brave."

For a moment I can't find a reply. What the hell did Noah say?

"And I think that paramedic should get a medal," she adds, her voice trembling.

I look daggers at Noah, who returns my gaze, serene and untroubled. What do I do? If I explain that my son is a complete fantasist, we all look stupid. Maybe it's easier to go along with it. We'll be boarding in a minute; we'll never see her again.

"It wasn't that big a deal," I say at last. "Thank you so much —"

"Not a big deal?" she echoes incredulously. "But it was all so dramatic!"

"Er . . . yes." I swallow. "Noah, let's buy some water."

I hurry him off to a nearby drinks machine, before this conversation can go any further. "Noah," I say as soon as we're out of earshot, "*what* did you say to the lady?"

"I said I want to be in the Olympics when I grow up," he replies promptly. "I want to do the long jump. Like this." He breaks free of my grasp and leaps across the airport carpet. "Can I be in the Olympics?"

I give up. We'll have to have a big chat at some time — but not now.

"Of course you can." I ruffle his hair. "But, listen. No more chatting to strangers. You know that."

"That lady wasn't a stranger," he points out reasonably. "She had a badge, so I knew her name. It was Cheryl."

Sometimes the logic of a seven-year-old is undefeatable. We return to our seats and I sit him firmly down next to me.

"Look at your sticker book and *do not move.*" I take out my BlackBerry and polish off a few quick emails. I've just agreed to an entire supplement on Arctic holidays when I pause, frowning. Something has attracted my attention. The top of a head, behind a newspaper. A dark crest of hair. Long-fingered, bony hands turning a page.

No *way.*

I stare, riveted, until he turns another page and I catch a glimpse of cheekbone. It's him. Sitting five yards away, a small travel bag at his feet. What the fuck is he doing here?

Don't tell me he's had the same idea as me.

As he turns yet another page, looking calm and unruffled, I start to feel a burning anger. This is all his fault. I've had to disrupt my life, take my son out of school, and stress out all night, simply because he couldn't keep his mouth shut. *He* was the one who went blundering in. *He* caused all this. And now here he is, looking as cool and relaxed as though he's off on holiday.

His phone rings, and he puts down his paper to answer.

"Sure," I can hear him saying. "I'll do that. We'll discuss all those issues. Yes, I *know* there's a time factor." Strain appears in his face. "I *know* this is not ideal. I'm doing the best I can in tricky circumstances, OK?" There's a pause as he listens, then replies, "No, I'd say not. Need to know only. We don't want to start the rumor mill. . . . OK. Right. Talk to you when I get there."

He puts his phone away and resumes reading the paper, while I watch with growing resentment. That's right. Lean back. Smile at a joke. Have a good time. Why not?

I'm glaring at him so hard, I feel I might start burning holes in the paper. An elderly lady sitting next to him picks up on my glare and eyes me nervously. I smile at her quickly, to indicate that it's not *her* I'm livid with — but this seems to freak her out even more.

"I'm sorry," she says. "But . . . is something wrong?"

"Wrong?" says Lorcan, misunderstanding and turning to her. "No, nothing's wrong —" He catches sight of me and starts in surprise. "Oh. Hello."

I wait for him to add a fulsome, groveling apology, but he seems to feel this greeting is enough. His dark eyes meet mine, and with no warning I have a flashback: a blurred moment of skin and lips from the middle of that night. His hot breath on my neck. My hands clutching his hair. The color comes to my cheeks and I glare at him even more venomously.

"Hello?" I echo. "Is that all you can say? 'Hello'?"

"I guess we're headed to the same place?" He puts his newspaper down and leans forward, his face suddenly intent. "Are you in touch with them? Because I have to talk to Ben, urgently. I have documents for him to sign. I need him to be at the hotel when I arrive. But he won't pick up when I call. He's avoiding me. He's avoiding everything."

I stare at him in disbelief. All he's concerned with is some business deal. What about the fact that his best friend has married my sister in a totally stupid knee-jerk gesture *caused by him*?

"I'm in touch with Lottie. Not Ben."

"Huh." He frowns and turns back to the paper. How can he read the paper? I feel deeply, mortally offended that he can concentrate on the sports pages when he's created such a mess.

"Are you OK?" He peers up at me. "You seem a little . . . fixated."

I'm simmering all over with rage. I can feel my head prickling; I can feel my fists clenching. "Funnily enough, no," I manage. "I'm not OK."

"Oh." He glances at the paper yet again, and something inside me snaps.

"Stop looking at that!" I leap up and grab it from his hands before I'm fully aware of what I'm doing. "Stop it!" I crumple the paper furiously and throw it on the floor.

I'm panting and my cheeks are blazing.

Lorcan stares at the paper, apparently bemused.

"Mummy!" says Noah, in delighted shock. "Litterbug!"

All the other airline passengers have turned to stare at me. Great. And now Lorcan is gazing up at me too, dark brows drawn together, as though I'm some inscrutable mystery.

"What's the problem?" he says at last. "Are you pissed off?"

Is he joking?

"Yes!" I erupt. "I *am* a little pissed off that, after I had sorted out the whole situation with Ben and my sister, you had to go barging in and wreck it!"

I can see the truth slowly dawning on his face. "You're blaming *me*?"

"Of course I'm blaming you! If you'd said nothing, they wouldn't be married!"

"Uh-uh." He shakes his head adamantly. "Incorrect. Ben's mind was made up."

"Lottie said it was because of you."

"Lottie was wrong."

He's not going to back down, is he? Bastard.

"All I know is, I'd sorted the situation," I say stonily. "I'd managed it. And then this happened."

340

"You *thought* you'd sorted it," he corrects me. "You *thought* you'd managed it. When you know Ben as well as I do, you'll realize that his mind flips direction like a fish. Previous agreements count for nothing. Agreements to sign crucial, time-sensitive documents, for example." There's a sudden irritation in his voice. "You can pin him down all you like. He still slips away."

"That's why you're here?" I glance at his briefcase. "Just for these documents?"

"If Muhammad won't come to the mountain, the mountain has to cancel all his plans and get on a plane." His phone bleeps with a text and he reads it, then starts typing a reply. "It would *really* help me if I could talk to Ben," he adds as he types. "Do you know what they're doing?"

"Couples' Quiz," I reply.

Lorcan looks baffled, then types some more. Slowly, I sit down. Noah has descended onto the floor and is making a hat out of Lorcan's newspaper.

"Noah," I say, without conviction. "Don't do that. My son," I add to Lorcan.

"Hello," says Lorcan to Noah. "Nice hat. So, you never told me. What are you doing here, exactly? Joining the happy couple, I assume. Do they know?"

The question takes me off guard. I sip the

water, my mind working hard.

"Lottie asked me to go out there," I lie at last. "But I'm not sure if Ben knows yet, so don't mention that you've seen me, OK?"

"Sure." He shrugs. "A little odd, asking your sister to join you on honeymoon. Isn't she having a good time?"

"Actually, they're thinking of renewing their vows," I say in sudden inspiration. "Lottie wanted me there as a witness."

"Oh, please." Lorcan scowls. "What kind of shit idea is that?"

His tone is so dismissive, I find myself getting irritated.

"I think it's rather a nice idea," I contradict him. "Lottie's always wanted a ceremony by the sea. She's quite a romantic."

"I'm sure." Lorcan nods as though digesting this, then looks up, deadpan. "What about the ponies? Is she having those?"

Ponies? I peer at him blankly. What on earth —

Matching ponies. Great. So he *did* hear me yesterday morning. My face fills with blood, and just for an instant I feel myself losing my cool.

The way to deal with this, I swiftly decide, is to be direct. We're grown-ups. We can acknowledge an embarrassing situation and move on. Exactly.

"So. Um." I clear my throat. "Yesterday morning."

"Yes?" He leans forward, with mock interest. He's not going to make this easy for me, is he?

"I don't know exactly what you . . ." I try again. "Obviously I was talking on the phone to my sister when you came into the room. And what you heard was totally out of context. I mean, you've probably forgotten what I said. But *just* in case you haven't, I wouldn't want you to . . . misinterpret anything. . . ."

He's not paying me any attention. He's taken out a notepad and is writing on it. So rude. Still, at least that means I'm off the hook. I offer the water bottle to Noah, who sips absentmindedly, his attention fixed on his newspaper hat. Then I look up as Lorcan taps me on the shoulder. He hands me his notepad, on which are lines of writing.

"I believe I have a good memory for words," he says politely. "But please correct me if any of it is wrong."

As I read the lines, my jaw drops in dismay.

Small. Seriously, tiny. The whole night was such an ordeal. I had to pretend I was having a good time, and all along . . . No. Ter-

343

rible. And afterward wasn't much better. I feel ill at the very thought. In fact, I might throw up. And then Lorcan will never love me, and we'll never get married in a double wedding on matching ponies.

"Look," I manage at last, my face puce. "I didn't mean . . . that."

"Which bit?" He raises his eyebrows.

Bastard. Does he think this is funny?

"You know as well as I do," I begin icily, "that those words were taken out of context. They didn't refer to . . ." I trail off as a growing hubbub attracts my attention. It's coming from the desk. Two air hostesses are remonstrating with a man in a linen shirt and chinos, who's trying to squash a suitcase into the hand-baggage measuring stand. As he raises his voice angrily to answer, I realize it's familiar.

He turns, and I quell a gasp of shock. I thought so: it's Richard!

"Sir, I'm afraid the case is clearly too big for the cabin." A woman from the airline is addressing him. "And it's too late to check it in now. Might I suggest that you wait and catch a later flight?"

"A later flight?" Richard's voice erupts from him like the sound of a tormented animal. "There aren't any other flights to this godforsaken place! One a day! What kind of service is that?"

"Sir —"

"I need to get on this flight."

"But, sir —"

To my astonishment, Richard vaults up so that he's resting on the high desk, his eyes level with the airline woman's.

"The girl I love has tethered herself to another man," he says intensely. "I was too slow off the mark, and I'll never forgive myself for that. But if I can do nothing else, I can tell her how I really feel. Because I never showed her. Not properly. I'm not even sure I knew myself."

I gape at him, absolutely astonished. Is this Richard? Making declarations of love in public? If only Lottie could see this! She'd be bowled over! The airline woman, on the other hand, looks supremely unmoved. She has black dyed hair pulled into a harsh bun and a doughy face with mean little eyes.

"Be that as it may, sir," she says, "your case is too big for the cabin. Could you step aside from the desk?"

What a bitch. I've seen plenty of people take luggage that size onto planes. I know I should step forward and tell Richard I'm here, but something inside me needs to see what will happen next.

345

"Fine. I won't bring the bag." Glowering at her, Richard jumps back down to the floor and snaps open the clasps of his case. He grabs a couple of T-shirts, a wash bag, a pair of socks, and some boxer shorts, then kicks the case aside.

"There. This is my hand luggage." He brandishes it all at her. "Happy now?"

The airline woman regards him evenly. "You can't leave that case there, sir."

"Fine." He snaps the case shut and dumps it on top of a litter bin. "There."

"You can't leave it there either, sir. It's a security issue. We don't know what's in it."

"You do."

"No, we don't."

"You just saw me unpack it."

"Be that as it may, sir."

The entire place has turned to watch this exchange. Richard is breathing hard. His broad shoulders are raised. Again I'm reminded of a bull about to charge.

"Uncle Richard!" Noah has suddenly noticed him. "Are you coming on holiday with us?"

Richard's whole body jolts in astonishment as he registers first Noah, then me.

"Fliss?" He drops a pair of boxer shorts on the floor and stoops to pick them up, looking a little less bull-like. "What are you

346

doing here?"

"Hi, Richard." I try to sound nonchalant. "We're joining Lottie. What — er —" I spread my hands questioningly. "I mean, what exactly —"

Clearly I know the gist of what he's up to, as does everyone here, but I'm interested in the details. Does he have a plan?

"I couldn't just sit back," he says gruffly. "I couldn't just lose her and walk away and never even tell her what I —" He breaks off, his face working with emotion. "I should have proposed when I had the chance," he adds suddenly. "I should have cherished what I had! I should have proposed!"

His roar of grief rises through the silent air. The whole place is agog, and, quite frankly, I'm flabbergasted. I've never seen Richard moved to such passion. Has Lottie?

I *wish* I'd recorded his whole speech on my BlackBerry.

"Sir, please remove your case from that bin." The airline woman is addressing Richard. "As I say, it's causing a security alert."

"It's not mine anymore," he counters, brandishing his boxer shorts at her. "This is my hand luggage."

The woman's chin tightens. "Do you want me to call security and have your case destroyed, thus delaying the flight by six hours?"

I'm not the only person who gasps in horror. Around us, polite murmurs of protest start swelling into hostile, pointed comments. I'm sensing Richard is not the most popular passenger in the place. In fact, I'm sensing that the boos and slow hand-claps may begin any moment.

"Uncle Richard, are you coming on holiday with us?" Noah is consumed with joy. "Can we do wrestling? Can I sit next to you on the plane?" He throws himself at Richard's legs.

"Doesn't look like it, kiddo." Richard gives him a wry smile. "Unless you can persuade this lady."

"This is your *uncle*?" Noah's friend Cheryl springs into life at the other desk, where she's been watching proceedings with a vacant stare. "The uncle you were telling me about?"

"This is Uncle Richard," confirms Noah happily.

I should never have let him get into the habit of calling Richard "Uncle," I think to myself. It started one Christmas and we thought it was cute. We didn't predict a breakup. We thought Richard had become part of the family. We never thought —

Suddenly I'm aware that Cheryl is almost hyperventilating.

"Margot!" At last she manages to speak through her gasps. "You've got to let this man on the plane! He saved his nephew's life! He's a brilliant man!"

"What?" Margot scowls.

"Huh?" Richard gapes at Cheryl.

"Don't be modest! Your nephew told me the whole story!" Cheryl says tremulously. "Margot, you have no idea. This whole family. They've been through such a lot." She steps out from behind her desk. "Sir, let me take your boarding pass."

I can see Richard's mind whirring in disbelief. He glances suspiciously at Noah, then at me. I pull an agonized face, trying to convey the message, *Just go with it.*

"And you too." Cheryl turns gushingly to me. "You must have been deeply affected by your little boy's ordeal."

"We take each day as it comes," I murmur vaguely.

This seems to satisfy her, and she moves away. Richard is still clutching his underpants, looking gobsmacked. I'm not even going to *try* to explain.

"So, um, you want to sit down?" I say. "I could get us a coffee or something?"

"Why are you joining Lottie?" he demands

without moving. "Is there a problem?"

I'm not sure how to answer. On the one hand, I don't want to give him false hope. On the other, could I perhaps hint that all is not perfect in paradise?

"They're renewing their vows, aren't they?" says Lorcan over his newspaper.

"Who's this?" Richard reacts with instant suspicion. "Who are you?"

"Right," I say awkwardly. "Um, Richard, this is Lorcan. Ben's best man. Best friend. Whatever. He's flying out there too."

Immediately, Richard stiffens into his bull-like posture again.

"I see," he says, nodding. "I see."

I don't think he does see, but he's so tense I don't dare interrupt. He's instinctively squared up to Lorcan, his fists clenched.

"And you are?" says Lorcan politely.

"I'm the idiot who let her go!" says Richard with sudden passion. "I couldn't see the vision she wanted for us. I thought she was, I don't know, starry-eyed. But now I can see the stars too. I can see the vision. And I want it too."

All the women nearby are listening to him, rapt. Where did he learn to speak like that? Lottie would *love* that stuff about stars. I've been fumbling at my BlackBerry, trying to surreptitiously record him, but I'm too slow.

"What are you doing?"

"Nothing!" I quickly lower my phone.

"Oh God. Maybe this is a bad idea." Richard suddenly seems to come to and see himself standing in the middle of a departure lounge with underwear in his hands and an audience of passengers. "Maybe I should just bow out."

"No!" I say quickly. "Don't bow out!"

If only Lottie could see Richard right now. If only she could know his true feelings. She'd see sense, I know she would.

"Who am I kidding?" He sags in desolation. "It's too late. They're *married.*"

"They're not!" I retort before I can stop myself.

"What?" Richard and Lorcan both stare at me. I can see lots of other interested faces leaning in to listen too.

"I mean they haven't, you know, consummated it yet," I explain as quietly as I can. "So technically that means they could still get a legal annulment. The marriage would never have existed."

"Really?" I can see a glimmer of hope rising on Richard's face.

"Why haven't they consummated it?" says Lorcan incredulously. "And how do you know?"

"She's my sister. We tell each other every-

351

thing. And as for why . . ." I clear my throat evasively. "It's simply bad luck. The hotel messed up with the beds. Ben got drunk. That kind of thing."

"Too much information," says Lorcan, and starts putting his papers away in his briefcase.

Richard says nothing. His brow is furrowed and he appears to be taking this all in. At last he sinks down on the seat next to me and savagely screws his boxer shorts into a ball. I watch him, still feeling disbelief that he's here at all.

"Richard," I say at last. "You know the phrase 'Too little, too late'? Well, you're more like 'Too much, too late.' Flying halfway across the world. Rushing to the airport. Making romantic speeches all over the place. Why didn't you do any of this *before*?"

Richard doesn't answer the question but stares at me glumly. "You think I'm too late?"

That's a question *I* don't want to answer.

"It's just an expression," I say after a pause. "Come on." I pat him reassuringly on the shoulder. "We're boarding."

About half an hour into the flight, Richard comes up to the front, where Noah and I are sitting in a row of three in club class. I haul Noah onto my lap and Richard slides in next to me.

"How tall would you say this Ben is?" he says with no preamble.

"Don't know. I've never met him."

"But you've seen pictures. Would you say . . . five eight? Five nine?"

"I don't *know*."

"I'd say five nine. Definitely shorter than me," Richard adds, with a grim satisfaction.

"Well, that's not hard," I point out. Richard is at least six foot two.

"Never thought Lottie would go for a short-arse."

I have no reply to make to this, so I roll my eyes and carry on reading the airline magazine.

"I looked him up." Richard mashes an airsick bag between his fingers. "He's a multimillionaire. Owns a paper company."

"Mmm. I know."

"I tried to find out if he's got a private jet. It didn't say. Expect he has."

"Richard, stop torturing yourself." I finally turn to him. "It's not about private jets. Or height. There's no point comparing yourself to him."

Richard looks at me for a few silent seconds. Then, as though I hadn't even spoken, he says, "Have you seen his house? They used it for *Highton Hall.* He's a multi-millionaire *and* he's got a stately home." He scowls. "Bastard."

"Richard —"

"But he's pretty puny, don't you think?" He's tearing the airsick bag into strips. "Never thought Lottie would go for someone so puny."

"Richard, stop it!" I exclaim in exasperation. If he's going to go on like this the whole journey, I'll go mad.

"Is this our special guest?" A sugary voice interrupts us, and we look up to see an air hostess with a French plait, bearing down on us with a wide smile. She's holding a teddy bear, an airline wallet, some lollipops, and a huge box of Ferrero Rocher chocolates. "Cheryl told us *all* about you," she addresses Noah brightly. "I've got some special gifts for you here."

"Cool! Thank you!" Noah grabs the presents before I can stop him and gasps, "Mummy, look! A *big* box of Ferrero Rocher chocolates! You *can* get them!"

"Thanks," I say awkwardly. "That's really unnecessary."

"It's the least we can do!" the air hostess assures me. "And is this the famous uncle?" She bats her eyelashes at Richard, who

354

stares back with a blank frown.

"My uncle can speak three languages," says Noah proudly. "Uncle Richard, talk Japanese!"

"A surgeon *and* a linguist?" The air hostess opens her eyes wide, and I dig my fingers into Richard's hand before he can protest. I don't want Noah mortified in public.

"That's right!" I say quickly. "He's a very talented man. Thanks so much." I smile at the air hostess fixedly till she leaves, after a final pat on the head for Noah.

"Fliss, what the hell's going on?" expostulates Richard in an undertone as soon as she's walked away.

"Can I have a credit card to put in my wallet?" asks Noah, examining it. "Can I have an AmEx? Can I have points?"

Oh God. He knows about AmEx points at the age of seven? This is mortifying. Almost as bad as when we checked in to a hotel in Rome and, by the time I'd found change for a tip, Noah had already asked to see a different room.

I get out my iPod and hand it to Noah, who whoops with delight and slots the earphones into his ears. Then I lean toward Richard and lower my voice.

"Noah told some made-up story to the

ground staff." I bite my lip, feeling a sudden relief at sharing my worries. "Richard, he's turned into a complete fantasist. He does it at school. He told one teacher he'd had a heart transplant and another he had a surrogate baby sister."

"What?" Richard's face drops.

"I know."

"Where did he get those kind of ideas, anyway? A surrogate baby sister, for God's sake?"

"Off a DVD they were playing in the special-needs department," I say wryly.

"Right." Richard digests this. "So what story did he tell this lot?" He gestures at the air hostess.

"No idea. Apart from the fact that you play a starring role as a surgeon." I meet his eye and we suddenly both snort with laughter.

"It's not funny." Richard shakes his head, biting his lip.

"It's awful."

"Poor little guy." Richard ruffles Noah's head, and he looks up briefly from his iPod trance, a beatific smile on his face. "Do they think he's doing it because of the divorce?"

My residual laughter melts away. "Probably," I say lightly. "Or, you know, the evil career mother."

356

Richard winces. "Sorry." He pauses. "How's that all going, anyway? Have you signed the settlement yet?"

I open my mouth to answer honestly — then stop myself. I've bored Richard many times over dinner about Daniel. I can see he's bracing himself for the rant. Why did I never notice people bracing themselves before?

"Oh, fine." I give him my new saccharine smile. "All good! Let's not talk about it."

"Right." Richard looks taken aback. "Great! So . . . any new men on the horizon?" His voice suddenly seems to have doubled in volume, and I flinch. Before I can stop myself, I glance at Lorcan, who is sitting by the opposite window, engrossed in his laptop, and thankfully didn't seem to hear.

"No," I say. "Nothing. No one."

I'm telling myself furiously not to look at Lorcan, not to even think about Lorcan. But it's like telling yourself not to think about a rabbit. Before I can stop them, my eyes have darted to him again. This time, Richard follows my gaze.

"What?" He peers at me in astonishment. "Him?"

"Shhh."

"Him?"

"No! I mean . . . yes." I feel flustered. "Once."

"Him?" Richard sounds mortally offended. "But he's on the other side!"

"There aren't *sides.*"

Richard is surveying Lorcan with narrowed, suspicious eyes. After a moment, Lorcan looks up. He seems startled to see us both gazing at him. My whole body floods with heat and I abruptly turn away.

"Stop it!" I hiss. "Don't look at him!"

"You were looking at him too," points out Richard.

"Only because you were!"

"Fliss, you seem hassled."

"I'm not *hassled,*" I say with dignity. "I'm simply trying to be an adult in an adult situation — You're looking at him again!" I jab at his arm. "Stop!"

"Who is he, exactly?"

"Ben's oldest friend. A lawyer. Works at his company." I shrug.

"So . . . is it a thing?"

"No. It's not a *thing.* We just hooked up and then . . ."

"You unhooked."

"Exactly."

"He looks like a bundle of laughs," says Richard, still surveying Lorcan critically. "I'm being sarcastic," he adds after a pause.

"Yup." I nod. "Got that."

Lorcan looks up again and raises his eyebrows. The next minute he's unbuckling his seat belt and coming over to where we're sitting.

"Great," I murmur. "Thanks, Richard. Hello." I smile sweetly up at Lorcan. "Enjoying the flight?"

"It's tremendous. I need to talk to you." His dark eyes are opaque as they meet mine, and my heart jumps in trepidation.

"Right. OK. But maybe this isn't the place —"

"Both of you," he cuts across me, taking in Richard with his glance too. "I'm flying out to Ikonos for good reason. I have some important business to discuss with Ben. He needs to be focused. So if you're planning to yell at him or beat him up or steal his wife from him, or whatever you're going to do, I have a request. Please leave it till our meeting is over. Then he's all yours."

I feel an instant surge of resentment.

"That's all you have to say?" I jut out my chin.

"Yes."

"You're only interested in your business. Not in the fact that *you* caused this marriage?"

"I did *not* cause it," he retaliates. "And of

course the business is my priority."

" 'Of course'?" I echo sarcastically. "Business is more important than marriage? Interesting viewpoint."

"Right now, yes. And it needs to be Ben's priority too."

"Well, don't worry." I roll my eyes. "We're not going to beat him up."

"I might beat him up." Richard pounds his palm with his fist. "I might just do that."

The elderly lady sitting next to me looks appalled. "Excuse me," she says hurriedly to Lorcan. "Would you like to exchange seats so you can talk to your friends?"

"No, thank you," I begin, as Lorcan says, "Thank you so much."

Great. A minute later, Lorcan is buckling up his seat belt next to me while I stare studiously ahead. Just the sense of him so close to me is making my skin prickle. I can smell his aftershave. It's giving me Proustian flashbacks to that night, which are *really* not helpful.

"So," I say shortly. It's only one syllable, but I think it successfully conveys the message: *You're wrong on everything, from who's to blame for this marriage, to what exactly I meant that morning, to your priorities generally.*

"So," he replies with a curt nod. I have a

feeling he means much the same thing.

"So." I open my newspaper. I'm hereby going to ignore him for the whole flight.

The only trouble is, I can't help glancing over at his laptop every so often and seeing phrases that interest me. Richard and Noah are listening to the iPod together while Noah makes inroads into his lollipops. There's no one else to talk to, even if he is an arrogant bighead on the other team.

"So, what's going on?" I say at last, with a shrug to indicate I'm really not interested.

"We're rationalizing the company," says Lorcan after a pause. "Expanding one part of our business, refinancing another, jettisoning another. It all needs to be done. The paper industry these days —"

"Nightmare," I agree before I can stop myself. "The price of paper affects us too."

"Of course. The magazine." He nods. "Well, then, you'll know."

The two of us are making a connection again. I don't know if this is a mistake or not, but somehow I can't help it. It's such a relief to have someone to talk to who isn't my boss or my staff or my child or my ex-husband or my loopy little sister. He doesn't *need* anything from me. That's the difference. He's just sitting there, composed, as though he doesn't give a fuck.

"I read online you developed Paper-maker," I say. "That was you?"

"My brainchild." He shrugs. "Others more talented than me design the stuff."

"I like Papermaker," I allow. "Nice cards. Expensive."

"But you still buy them." He gives me a tiny grin.

"For now," I retaliate. "Till I find another brand."

"Touché." He winces and I give him a sidelong look. Maybe that was a bit harsh.

"Are you actually in trouble?" Even as I ask, I know it's an inane question. Everyone's in trouble right now. "I mean, *real* trouble?"

"We're at a junction." He exhales. "It's a tricky time. Ben's dad died with no warning, and we've been treading water ever since. We need to make a few brave decisions." He hesitates. "The right brave decisions."

"Ah." I consider this. "Do you mean Ben has to make the right brave decisions?"

"You catch on quickly."

"And is he likely to? You can tell me. I won't let on." I pause, wondering whether to be tactful or not. "Are you about to go bust?"

"No." He reacts so hotly, I know I've hit a nerve. "We are *not* about to go bust. We're profitable. We can be more profitable. We have the brand names, the resources, a very loyal workforce. . . ." He sounds as though he's trying to convince some imaginary audience. "But it's hard. We held off a bid for the company last year."

"Wouldn't that be a solution?"

"Ben's father would turn in his grave," says Lorcan shortly. "It was from Yuri Zhernakov."

I raise my eyebrows. "Wow." Yuri Zhernakov is one of those guys who appear in the paper every other day with words like "billionaire" and "oligarch" attached to their names.

"He saw the house on TV and his wife fell in love with it," Lorcan says drily. "They wanted to live there for a few weeks every year."

"Well, that could be good, couldn't it?" I say. "Sell up while there's some cash on offer?"

There's silence. Lorcan is glowering at the screen saver on his laptop, which I notice is a Papermaker design that I've bought myself.

"Maybe Ben will sell," he says at last. "But to *anyone* but Zhernakov."

363

"What's wrong with Zhernakov?" I challenge him, laughing. "Are you a snob?"

"No, I'm not a snob!" retorts Lorcan forcefully. "But I care about the company. A guy like Zhernakov isn't interested in some two-bit paper company spoiling his view. He'd close down half the company, relocate the rest, ruin the community. If Ben ever spent any time up there, he'd realize —" He stops himself and exhales. "Besides which, the offer's wrong."

"What does Ben think?"

"Ben . . ." Lorcan takes a gulp of his mineral water. "Unfortunately, Ben's pretty naïve. He doesn't have the business instinct of his father but he thinks he does. Which is dangerous."

I glance at his briefcase. "So you want to get out there and persuade Ben to sign all the restructuring contracts before he can change his mind."

Lorcan is silent for a while, drumming his fingers lightly together.

"I want him to start taking responsibility for his inheritance," he says at last. "He doesn't realize how lucky he is."

I take a few sips of champagne. Some of this makes sense to me and some of it really doesn't.

"Why does it matter so much to you?" I

say at last. "It's not *your* company."

Lorcan blinks, and I sense I've touched a nerve again, although he's careful to hide it.

"Ben's dad was an amazing guy," he says at length. "I just want to make things work out the way he would have wanted. And they can," he adds with sudden vigor. "Ben's creative. He's smart. He could be a great leader, but he needs to stop dicking around and offending people."

I'm tempted to ask exactly how Ben has offended people, but I can't quite bring myself to be that nosy.

"You were a lawyer in London, weren't you?" My thoughts head off in a new direction.

"Freshfields are still wondering where I am." Lorcan's face flashes with humor. "I was on gardening leave between law firms when I went up to stay with Ben's dad. That was four years ago. I still get calls from recruitment companies, but I'm happy."

"Do you do annulments?" The words are out of my mouth before I can stop them.

"Annulments?" Lorcan raises his eyebrows very high. "I see." As he meets my eyes, his expression is so quizzical, I nearly laugh. "You have a Machiavellian mind, Ms. Graveney."

"I have a practical mind," I correct him.

"So they really haven't —" Lorcan interrupts himself. "Hey. What's going on there?"

I follow his glance and see that the old woman who was sitting next to me is clutching her chest and fighting for breath. A teenage boy is looking around helplessly, and he calls out, "Is there a doctor? Is anyone here a doctor?"

"I'm a GP." A gray-haired man in a linen jacket hurries to the seat. "Is this your grandmother?"

"No! I've never seen her before!" The teenager sounds panicky, and I don't blame him. The old lady doesn't look very well. We're all watching the doctor talk to the old woman in a low voice and feel for her pulse, when suddenly the air hostess with the French plait appears.

"Sir," she says breathlessly to us. "Please could we ask for your help?"

Help? What on earth —

I realize the truth just as Richard does. They think he's a doctor. Oh shit. He glances at me wildly and I pull an agonized face back.

"We have an expert here!" the air hostess is saying to the man in the linen jacket, her eyes alive with excitement. "Don't worry, everyone! We have a very senior pioneering surgeon from Great Ormond Street on

366

board! He'll take charge!"

Richard's eyes are bulging in alarm. "No!" he manages. "No. Really. I'm . . . not . . ."

"Go on, Uncle Richard!" says Noah, his face bright. "Cure the lady!" Meanwhile, the GP looks affronted.

"It's a straightforward case of angina," he says testily, getting up. "My medical bag's on board if you'd like me to assist. But if you want to give a second opinion —"

"No." Richard looks desperate. "No, I don't!"

"I've given her sublingual nitroglycerin. Would you agree with that?"

Oh God. This is bad. Richard looks absolutely desperate.

"I . . . I . . ." He swallows. "I —"

"He never practices on board planes!" I come to his rescue. "He has a phobia!"

"Yes," gulps Richard, shooting me a grateful glance. "Exactly! A phobia."

"Ever since a flight which went dreadfully wrong." I shudder dramatically, as though from a painful memory. "Flight 406 to Bangladesh."

"Please don't ask me to talk about it." Richard plays along.

"He's still in therapy." I nod gravely.

The GP stares at us both as if we're crazy.

"Well, good thing I was here," he says

shortly. He turns back to the old woman, and both Richard and I subside. I feel weak. The air hostess shakes her head in disappointment and heads over to the other side of the plane.

"Fliss, you have to get Noah sorted out," says Richard in a low, urgent voice. "He can't go around just making up stories. He'll get someone in real trouble."

"I know." I wince. "I'm so sorry."

The old lady is being taken to some farther bit of the plane. The GP and the cabin crew are having what looks like a tense discussion. They all disappear behind a curtain, and for a little while there's no sign of life. Richard is staring ahead intently, his forehead creased in concern. He must be worried about the old woman, I find myself thinking benevolently. He has a kind heart, Richard.

"So, listen. Tell me." He turns to me at last, his brow still furrowed. "They really haven't done it yet?"

Oh, *honestly.* Silly me. He's a man. Naturally he's thinking about only one thing.

"Not as far as I know." I shrug.

"Hey, maybe this Ben can't get it up." Richard's face brightens in sudden animation.

"I don't think that's it." I shake my head.

"Why not? It's the only explanation! He can't get it up!"

"Can't get what up?" asks Noah with interest.

Great. I glare at Richard, but he's so triumphant, he doesn't notice. I'm sure there's some special long German word meaning "the joy you feel at your rival's sexual impotence," and right now Richard has it with bells on.

"Poor guy," he adds, as he finally notices my disapproving look. "I mean, I feel for him, obviously. Nasty affliction."

"You have no evidence for this," I point out.

"It's his honeymoon," retorts Richard. "Who doesn't do it on their honeymoon unless he can't get it up?"

"Can't get what up?" Noah's voice pipes louder.

"Nothing, darling," I say hastily to Noah. "Just something very grown-up and boring."

"Is it a grown-up thing that goes up?" asks Noah with piercing curiosity. "Does it ever go down?"

"He can't get it up!" Richard is exultant. "It all falls into place. Poor old Lottie."

"Who can't get it up?" says Lorcan, turning toward us.

"Ben," says Richard.

369

"Really?" Lorcan looks taken aback. "Shit." He frowns thoughtfully. "Well, that explains a *lot.*"

Oh God. This is how rumors start. This is how misunderstandings happen and arch-dukes get shot and world wars begin.

"Listen, both of you!" I say fiercely. "Lottie has said *nothing* whatsoever to me about anything being up . . . or down."

"Mine is up," volunteers Noah matter-of-factly, and I gasp in horror before I can stop myself.

OK, Fliss. Don't overreact. Be cool. Be an enlightened parent.

"Really, darling? Gosh. Well." My cheeks have flamed. Both men are waiting with expressions of glee. "That's . . . that's interesting, sweetheart. Maybe we'll have a little talk about it later. Our bodies do wonderful, mysterious things, but we don't always talk about them *in public.*" I give a meaningful look at Richard.

Noah seems perplexed. "But the lady talked about it. She told me to put it up."

"*What?*" I stare at him in equal confusion.

"For takeoff. 'Put your tray table up.'"

"Oh." I gulp. "Oh, I see. Your *tray table.*" I can feel a snort of mirth rising.

"Poor Uncle Ben's tray table doesn't go up," says Richard, deadpan.

"Stop!" I try to sound admonishing, but I'm in fits of laughter. "I'm sure it does —" I break off as the air hostess's voice comes over the sound system.

"Ladies and gentlemen, may I have your attention? I have a very important announcement."

Uh-oh. I hope the old lady's OK. I suddenly feel mortified that we've been laughing while a drama's going on.

"I regret to inform you that, due to a medical emergency on board, the plane will be unable to land at Ikonos as originally planned but will be landing at our nearest available airport with full medical facilities, which, at this moment, is Sofia."

I'm pinned to the seat with shock. My hilarity has melted away. We're being *diverted*?

"I do apologize for any inconvenience this may cause you and will of course give you any further information when I have it."

A ruckus of protest has broken out all around me, but I barely hear it. This cannot be happening. Lorcan turns to me incredulously.

"Sofia, *Bulgaria*? How many hours will that delay us?"

"I don't know."

"What's wrong?" Noah is looking from

371

face to face. "Mummy, what's wrong? Who's Sofia?"

"It's a place." I swallow hard. "Turns out we're going there first. Won't that be fun?" I glance again at Richard. He's lost all his ebullience too. He's sagged right down and is gazing at the seat back with a savage scowl.

"Well, that's it. We'll be too late. I thought we had a chance to get there before they . . . you know." He spreads his hands. "But now it's impossible."

"It's not impossible!" I retort, trying to reassure myself as much as him. "Richard, listen. The truth is, Lottie's so-called marriage is already falling to bits."

I wasn't going to say as much as that, but I think he needs a shot of confidence in the arm.

"You don't know that," he growls.

"I do! What you don't know is, there's a history here. Every time Lottie breaks up with someone, she does this."

"She gets *married*?" Richard looks scandalized. "Every time?"

"No!" I want to laugh at his expression. "I just mean she does something rash and idiotic. And then she comes to. I'll probably get off the plane and find a text waiting for me, saying, *Fliss, I made a huge mistake! Help!*"

I can see Richard digesting this idea. "You really think so?"

"Believe me, I've been here before. I call them her Unfortunate Choices. Sometimes she joins a cult, sometimes she gets a tattoo. . . . Think of this marriage as an extreme piercing. Right this minute, they're doing a Couples' Quiz," I add to encourage him. "I mean, what a joke! They haven't got a clue about each other. Lottie will see that, and she'll start to think straight, and then she'll realize."

"Couples' Quiz?" says Richard after a pause. "You mean like that TV game?"

"Exactly. Like, 'What is your partner's favorite meal that you cook for her?' That kind of thing."

"Spaghetti carbonara," says Richard, without missing a beat.

"There you go." I squeeze his hand. "If you guys did it, you'd win. Ben and Lottie are going to tank. Then she'll come to her senses. You wait and see."

15
LOTTIE

It's a game. Just a game. It doesn't mean *anything.*

Even so, I'm feeling more irritable by the second. Why can't I remember this stuff? And, more to the point, why can't Ben? Isn't he *interested* in the details of my life?

We're sitting in the hotel garden with ten minutes to go before Couples' Quiz starts, and I've never felt less prepared for a test in my life. Ben is lying in a hammock, drinking beer and playing some new rap song on his iPad, which really isn't improving my mood.

"Let's go again," I say. "And, this time, concentrate. What shampoo do I use?"

"L'Oréal."

"No!"

"Head and Shoulders, extra strong for monster dandruff." He smirks.

"No!" I kick him. "I *told* you. Kerastase. And you use Paul Mitchell."

"Do I?" he says blankly.

I feel instant rage boiling up inside me. "What do you mean, 'do I'? You told me you use Paul Mitchell! We have to be on the same page for this, Ben. If you say Paul Mitchell once, you have to *stick* to Paul Mitchell!"

"Jesus." Ben takes a sip of beer. "Lighten up." He turns up the volume on his iPad, and I flinch. Does he really like that music?

"Let's do another." I try to control my impatience. "What's my favorite alcoholic drink?"

"Smirnoff Ice." He grins.

"Funny," I say politely.

No wonder he didn't make it as a comedian. The bitchy thought comes from nowhere. Oops. I clench my lips together, praying my expression isn't readable. I didn't mean it, of course I didn't. . . .

Richard would have made an effort. The even bigger thought flashes through my head like a powerful bird in flight, leaving me breathless in its wake. I blink at my piece of paper, feeling hot about the face. I'm not going to think about Richard. No. Absolutely not.

Richard would have thought Couples' Quiz was ridiculous too, but, the difference is, he'd have made an effort, because if it mattered to

375

me it would matter to him —

Stop it.

Like the time he did charades at my office party and everyone loved him —

LISTEN UP, STUPID BRAIN. Richard is OUT of my life. Right now he's probably fast asleep on the other side of the world in some glossy San Francisco apartment block, having forgotten all about me, and I'm with my husband — repeat, husband —

"*The Jeweled Path*? Are you serious?"

I've been wrangling so hard with my thoughts, I didn't notice Ben pick up the crib sheet I prepared for him earlier. Now he's staring at it incredulously.

"What?"

"*The Jeweled Path* can't be your favorite book." He looks up from the paper. "Please tell me you're joking."

"I'm not joking," I say, nettled. "Have you read it? It's brilliant."

"I wasted thirty valuable seconds of my life downloading it and skimming the first chapter." He pulls a face. "I want those thirty seconds back."

"You obviously missed the point," I say, offended. "It's really insightful if you read it carefully."

"It's a pile of new-age shit."

"Not according to eighty million readers."

I'm glaring at him.

"Eighty million morons."

"Well, what's your favorite book, then?" I grab the piece of paper to see, but my gaze is halted. I clap a hand over my mouth in shock and raise my eyes to his. "That's *not* how you vote?"

"Don't you?"

"No!"

We're staring at each other as though we've discovered we're aliens. I swallow twice, then look at the sheet again.

"OK! Right." I'm trying not to give away how disconcerted I feel. "So . . . so obviously we need to recap on a few basics. Voting preference we've covered . . . favorite pasta?"

"Depends on the sauce," he says promptly. "Stupid question."

"Well, I like tagliatelle. You say tagliatelle too. Favorite TV show?"

"Dirk and Sally."

"*Dirk and Sally,* definitely." He grins, and the atmosphere lifts a shade.

"Favorite episode?" I can't help asking.

"Let me think." His face lights up. "The one with the lobsters. Classic."

"No, the wedding," I object. "It *has* to be the wedding. 'With this Smith and Wesson 59, I thee wed.' "

I watched that episode about ninety-five times. It was Dirk and Sally's second wedding (after they'd divorced and left the force and been recruited back in season four), and it was the best TV wedding *ever.*

"No, the kidnap double bill." Ben has sat up in his hammock and is hugging his knees. "That was epic. Hey, listen. *Listen.*" His face brightens. "We'll do it as Dirk and Sally."

"What?" I stare at him, puzzled. "Do what?"

"The quiz! I can't remember any of this shit." He waves my crib sheet at me. "But I know what Sally likes and you know what Dirk likes. We'll be them, not us."

He can't be serious. Is he serious? A giggle rises out of me before I can help myself.

"I mean, we can't do any *worse,* can we?" Ben adds. "I know everything about Sally. Test me."

"OK, what shampoo does she use?" I challenge him.

Ben screws up his face to think. "I know this. . . . It's Silvikrin. It's in the opening sequence. What's Dirk's favorite drink?"

"Bourbon straight up," I say without missing a beat. "Easy. When's Sally's birthday?"

"June twelfth, and Dirk always gets her white roses. When's yours?" he asks, looking alarmed. "It's not soon, is it?"

He's right. We know the marriage of a fictional TV detective couple better than we know our own. It's so ridiculous I can't help grinning at him.

"OK, Dirk, it's a deal." I look up to see Nico approaching, flanked by Georgios and Hermes. The Three Stooges, as Ben's started calling them. We're in the most secluded, hidden spot in the garden, but even so, they managed to track us down. They've been hovering round us endlessly all afternoon, offering drinks, snacks, and even appearing with the most unflattering IKONOS-branded sun hats in case we were getting overheated.

"Mr. and Mrs. Parr, I believe you are entered for the Couples' Quiz? It's beginning in a few minutes, down on the beach," Nico addresses us pleasantly. He's changed into a jacket with glittery braid, which makes me wonder if he's quizmaster.

"We were just coming."

"Excellent! Georgios will assist you."

We don't need bloody assistance, I want to retort, but I bite my lip and smile.

"Lead the way."

"Bring it on, Sally," mutters Ben in my ear, and I stifle a giggle. Maybe this will be fun after all.

379

■ ■ ■ ■

They've really gone to town. There's a wooden platform set up on the beach, decorated with a skirt of red foil strips. Clusters of red-heart helium balloons are anchored at each side. A massive banner reads COUPLES' QUIZ, and a three-piece band is playing "Love Is All Around." Melissa is pacing about on the sand in her orange caftan, followed two steps behind by a sandy-haired man in Vilebrequin trunks and an aqua polo shirt. I assume he's her husband, as they're both wearing prominent badges reading COUPLE ONE, along with their printed names.

"Stella McCartney," she's saying furiously as we approach. "You *know* it's Stella McCartney. Oh! Hi! You made it!"

"Ready to do battle?" says Ben, with a mischievous glint.

"It's just a bit of fun!" she replies, almost aggressively. "Isn't it, Matt?"

Matt is holding *The Couples' Quiz Official Question Book,* I suddenly notice in disbelief. Did they bring that with them?

"Oh, we happened to have that," says Melissa, flushing as she sees me register it. "Put it *away,* Matt. It's too late now, anyway," she adds to him in a savage under-tone. "I *really* think you could have made more effort. . . . Hello! You must be the other competitors! Just a bit of fun!" She greets an older-looking couple who are ap-proaching hand in hand, looking a bit perplexed by the whole thing. They have graying hair, coordinated beige slacks, and short-sleeved Hawaiian cotton shirts, and the man has socks on with sandals.

"Mr. and Mrs. Parr, your badge." Nico descends and gives us our COUPLE THREE badges. "Mr. and Mrs. Kenilworth, here are your name badges."

"Are you on honeymoon?" I can't help asking the woman, who it turns out, is called Carol.

"Bless you, no!" She's fiddling with her lapel. "We won this trip at our bridge-club auction. Not our kind of thing, really, but you have to show willing, and we do enjoy a quiz. . . ."

Nico ushers all six of us onto the platform, and we survey the audience, which is a middle-size crowd of guests in sarongs and T-shirts, with cocktails in their hands.

"Ladies and gentlemen!" Nico has switched on his radio mike, and his voice booms round the beach. "Welcome to the hotel's very own Couples' Quiz!"

Actually this *is* quite fun. It's just like it is on the telly. All of us women are led away to a nearby gazebo and given headphones which blast music into our ears, while the men answer questions onstage. Then we swap places and it's our turn. As I write down my answers, I feel suddenly nervous. Did Ben stick to the plan? Did he really answer as Dirk? What if he chickened out?

Well, too late now. I scribble my final answer and hand in the paper.

"And now!" Nico says to an accompanying drumroll from the band. "Let us reunite our couples! No conferring!" The audience applauds as the men come back onto the stage. The men are on one side of Nico and the women on the other, and I can see Melissa trying to attract Matt's attention while he resolutely ignores her.

"First question! What would your wife never go out without? Gentlemen, please answer clearly into the microphone. Couple One?"

"Handbag," says Matt promptly into the microphone.

"And your wife said . . ." Nico consults the paper. "Handbag. Ten points! Couple Two, same question?"

"Fresh breath mints," says Tim Kenilworth after some deliberation.

"And your wife said . . . Life Savers. Close enough." Nico nods. "Ten points! And Couple Three?"

"Easy," says Ben laconically. "She never leaves without her Smith and Wesson 59."

"Is that a gun?" says Melissa, looking astonished. "A *gun?*"

"And your wife said . . ." Nico consults my writing. "*My Smith and Wesson 59.* Congratulations, ten points!" He turns to me, his eyebrows raised. "You don't have it with you now, I hope?"

"I never go anywhere without it." I twinkle back at him.

"A *gun?*" persists Melissa. "Are you serious? Matt, did you hear that?"

"Next question!" announces Nico. "You have no food in the larder. Where do you head for a spontaneous meal out? Gentlemen, please answer again. First, Couple One."

"Er . . . fish and chips?" says Matt uncertainly.

"Fish and chips?" Melissa glares at him. "Fish and *chips?*"

"Well, it's quick, easy. . . ." Matt quails at her expression. "Why, what did you put?"

"I put Le Petit Bistro!" she says furiously. "We always go there when we want a quick bite. You know we do!"

"I sometimes go for fish and chips," mumbles Matt rebelliously, but I'm not sure anyone hears him except me.

"Zero points," says Nico sympathetically. "Couple Two?"

"The pub," says Tim, after about half an hour's thought. "I'd say we'd go to the pub."

"And your wife said . . ." Nico squints at the paper. "Madame, my apologies, I cannot read your writing."

"Well, I didn't know *what* to put." Carol looks perturbed. "We never do run out of food. We'd always have a soup in the freezer, wouldn't we, love?"

"True enough." Tim nods. "We make it up in batches, you see. Every Sunday during *Midsomer Murders.* Ham and pea."

"Or chickpea and chorizo," Carol reminds him.

"Or plain old tomato."

"And we freeze the rolls too," explains Tim, "so it only takes a few minutes in the microwave."

"Whole grain *and* crusty white," puts in Carol. "We do half and half, usually. . . ." She trails off into silence.

Everyone seems slightly stunned by this domestic catalog, including Nico, but at last he springs back to life.

"Thank you for your wonderfully thorough answer." He beams at Carol and Tim. "But, alas! Zero points. Couple Three?"

"We go to Dill's Diner *now*," I say. "Is that what he put?"

"Sorry," begins Nico, "but that is not the answer —"

"Wait!" I interrupt, as a relieved smile spreads across Melissa's face. "I haven't finished. We go to Dill's Diner now, but we used to go to Jerry and Jim's Steakhouse, until it was blown up by the mob." I glance over at Ben, who gives an imperceptible nod.

"Ah," says Nico, peering at the paper. "Yes. Your husband wrote, *We went to Jerry and Jim's till Carlo Dellalucci's lot blew it up; now we go to Dill's Diner.*"

"Where's that?" demands Melissa. "Where do you live?"

"Apartment Forty-three-D, West Eightieth Street," we say in unison. It's part of the opening titles.

"Oh, New York," she says, as though she's saying, *Oh, the rubbish dump.*

"Blew up, as in exploded?" chimes in Matt, looking impressed. "Was anyone killed?"

"Chief of police," I say, with a terse nod. "And the ten-year-old daughter he'd only just met, who died in his arms."

385

It was the finale to season one. Absolutely major telly. I almost want to recommend it to them all. Except that would slightly defeat the point.

"Question three!" Nico exclaims. "Now the competition heats up!"

By question eight we've covered season one, season two, and the Christmas special. Melissa and Matt are ten points behind, and Melissa's looking more and more tetchy.

"This *can't* be true," she says, as Ben finishes describing our "most memorable day together," which involved an armed siege, a police chase through the Central Park Zoo, and blowing out the candles on his birthday cake in a jail cell (long story). "I dispute these answers." She raps on the microphone as though it's a gavel and she's a judge. "Nobody has a life like this!"

"Dirk and Sally do!" I say, trying not to giggle as I meet Ben's eye.

"Who're Dirk and Sally?" she demands at once, looking from face to face as though we're tricking her in some new way.

"Our pet names for each other," says Ben blandly. "And may I ask what exactly you're suggesting? That we learned an entire set of fake answers especially for this competition? Do we look like tragic losers?"

"Come on!" Her eyes spark indignantly. "Are you telling me your first date was really at a *mortuary*?"

"Are you telling me yours was really at the *Ivy*?" he counters at once. "No one goes to the Ivy for a first date unless they already know they'll be so bored they'll need to do some people-watching. Sorry," he adds politely to Matt. "I'm sure you had a great time."

I can't stop laughing. Melissa's getting crosser and crosser, and I don't blame her. More and more people have joined the audience, and they're loving it too.

"Question nine!" Nico tries to get control of the situation. "Where is the most unusual place you have had . . . amorous relations? Couple Two, would you like to answer first?"

"Well!" Carol is growing pinker and pinker. "I wasn't sure about this question. Very *personal.*"

"Indeed," says Nico sympathetically.

"I believe the correct word is . . ." She pauses, wriggling awkwardly. "Fellatio."

There's an explosion of laughter from the audience, and I clamp my lips together so that I don't join in. Carol gave Tim a blow job? No way. I cannot imagine that in a million years.

"Your husband put *A cottage in Anglesey,*"

says Nico, grinning widely. "Zero points, I am afraid, dear lady. Although full marks for trying."

Carol looks as though she wants to spontaneously combust.

"By 'place,' " she begins, "I thought you meant . . . I thought . . ."

"Indeed." He nods sympathetically. "Couple One?"

"Hyde Park," says Melissa promptly, as though she's a child in class.

"Correct! Ten points! Couple Three?"

I had to think about this one. There are a few options. I just hope Ben remembered the episode.

"The boardwalk at Coney Island." As I look at Ben's face, I know I got it wrong.

"Alas! Your husband wrote, *On the district attorney's desk.*"

"The district attorney's desk?" Melissa looks livid. "Are you kidding me?"

"Zero points!" Nico chimes in hurriedly. "And now we reach the climax of our quiz. All rests on the final question. The most personal, intimate question of all." He pauses dramatically. "When did you first realize you were in love with your wife?"

An expectant hush comes over the audience, and there's a low drumroll from the band.

"Couple Three?" says Nico.

"It was when we were tied together to a railroad track with a train approaching," says Ben reminiscently. "She reached over, kissed me, and said, 'If it ends here, I'll be happy.' And then she freed us both with her nail file."

"Correct!"

"A *railroad track*?" Melissa looks from face to face. "Can I appeal that?"

I beam at Ben and raise my fist in a victory salute. But he doesn't respond; his eyes are out of focus as though he's still remembering.

"Couple Two?"

"Wait!" says Ben suddenly. "I haven't finished my answer. That time on the railroad track — that's when I realized I was in love with my wife. But the moment I realized I *loved* her . . ." He glances over at me with an unreadable look. "That was quite another time."

"What's the difference?" says Melissa petulantly. "Are you trying to wind us all up again?"

"You fall in and out of love," says Ben. "But when you really *love* someone . . . it's forever."

Is that a line from the show? I don't recognize it. I'm feeling a bit confused here.

What's he talking about?

"The day I realized I loved my wife was right here on the island of Ikonos, fifteen years ago." He leans toward the microphone and his voice rises, now resonant. "I'd had the flu. She nursed me all night. She was my guardian angel. I still remember that sweet voice telling me I'd be OK. Now I realize I've loved her since that day, though I didn't always know it."

He finishes to silence. Everyone seems thunderstruck. Then a girl from the audience whoops appreciatively, and it's as though the spell is broken, and applause breaks out, louder than ever.

I'm so gripped, I barely hear the others give their answers. He was talking about us. Not Dirk and Sally: *us*. Ben and Lottie. A warm glow has stolen over me, and I can't stop smiling. He's loved me for fifteen years. He's stood up and said it in public. Nothing so romantic has ever happened to me, *ever*.

The only tiny, minuscule niggle is . . .

Well. Just a teeny point, which is that I still don't remember it happening. My mind is blank. I don't remember Ben having the flu, nor do I remember nursing him. But, then, there's a lot about that time I don't remember, I reassure myself. I'd forgotten all about Big Bill. I'd forgotten about the poker tournament. It's probably buried somewhere deep inside me.

". . . you know it was on that picnic! You've always said so!"

Abruptly, I become aware that Melissa and Matt are still squabbling about his answer.

"It wasn't on the picnic," says Matt obstinately. "It was in the Cotswolds. But the way you're carrying on, maybe I wish I hadn't!"

Melissa takes a sharp breath, and I can practically see smoke puff from her ears.

"I think I know when we fell in love, Matt! And it wasn't in the bloody Cotswolds!"

"Which brings us to the end of our contest!" Nico puts in deftly. "And I am delighted to say that our winners are Couple Three! Ben and Lottie Parr! You win a special open-air couple's massage and will be awarded the Happy Couple of the Week trophy at our gala prize ceremony tomorrow evening. Congratulations!" He leads an uproarious round of applause, and Ben winks at me. We take a bow, and I feel Ben squeeze my hand tightly.

"I like the sound of this couple's massage," he says into my ear. "I read about it earlier. They do it on the beach in a special curtained arbor with essential oils. You get glasses of champagne, and after they've finished, they leave you alone for some 'private time.' "

Private time? I meet his eyes. At last! Ben and I alone on a beach in our own private space, with the waves crashing on the shore and glasses of champagne and our bodies slick with oil . . .

"Let's do it as soon as we can." My voice is thick with longing.

"Tonight." His hand lightly brushes against my breast, making me shiver with anticipation. I guess we've abandoned the no-touching rule. We bow again to the audience and then head down off the platform. "And now let's go for a drink," adds Ben. "I want to ply you with alcohol."

Turns out there *are* advantages to having a butler. The minute we say that we want a celebratory drink, Georgios swings into action, securing us a corner table at the posh beach restaurant, complete with champagne on ice and special lobster canapés brought down from the main restaurant. For once I don't mind the fuss and bother as the butlers dance around us. It feels right. We should be fussed over. We're the champions!

"So!" says Ben when at last we're left

alone. "Good day, as it turns out."

"Very good." I grin back.

"Two hours till our massage." He meets my eyes, and his mouth twitches with a smile.

Two delicious hours of savoring the spectacular beach sexathon which is to come. I can cope with that. I sip my champagne and lean back, feeling the sun on my face. Life is just about perfect right now. There's only the tiniest strain in my thoughts, which I'm trying to ignore. I can ignore it. Yes. I can.

No. I can't.

As I sip my champagne and crunch salted almonds, I'm aware of a glitch in my mood. A weak point I keep trying to skate over. But I can't fool myself. And I know it's only going to worry me more, the longer I leave it.

I don't know him. Not properly. He's my husband and I don't *know* him.

I mean, it's fine that he votes differently from me — but the point is, I had no idea. I thought we'd covered so much ground over the last few days — but now I realize there are some gaping holes. What other surprises am I going to come across?

In recruitment, we ask the same basic question whenever we want to get to know our candidates quickly: "Where do you want to be in one year, five years, and ten years?" I'd have no idea what to put for Ben, and that can't be right, surely?

"You're very distant." Ben touches my nose. "Earth to Lottie."

"Where do you want to be in five years' time?" I ask abruptly.

"Excellent question," he says promptly. "Where do you want to be?"

"Don't deflect." I smile at him. "I want to know the Ben Parr official game plan."

"Maybe I had an official game plan." His eyes soften as they meet mine. "But maybe it's changed now I've got you."

I'm so disarmed by his expression that I feel my doubts melting away. He's gazing at me with the most charming lop-sided smile and a distant look to his eyes, as though he's imagining our future together.

"I feel the same," I can't help blurting out. "I feel as though I've got a whole new future."

"A future with you. Anywhere we like." He spreads his hands. "What's the dream, Lottie? Sell it to me."

"France?" I say tentatively. "A farmhouse in France?" I've always fantasized about moving to France. "Maybe the Dordogne, or Provence? We could do up a house, find a real project. . . ."

"I *love* that idea." Ben's eyes are sparkling. "Find a wreck, turn it into something amazing, have friends to stay, long lazy meals —"

"Exactly!" My words tumble out, mingling with his. "We'd have a great big table and wonderful fresh food, and the children would help make the salad. . . ."

"They'd learn French too —"

"How many children do you want?"

My question halts the conversation for a moment. I'm holding my breath, I realize.

"As many as we can," says Ben easily. "If they all look like you, I'll have ten!"

"Maybe not *ten*." I'm laughing in relief. We chime perfectly! My worries were unfounded! We're totally on the same page when it comes to life choices. I almost want to get out my phone and start finding old French properties to drool over. "You really want to move to France?"

"If there's one thing I want to do in the next two years, it's settle myself down," he says seriously. "Find a lifestyle I can love. And France is a passion of mine."

"Do you speak French?"

He reaches for the paper dessert menu, produces a pencil, and scribbles a few lines on the back, then turns it to show me.

L'amour, c'est toi
La beaute, c'est toi
L'honneur, c'est toi
Lottie, c'est toi

I'm enchanted. No one's ever written me a poem before. And certainly not in French.

"Thank you so much! I love it!" I read it through again, bring the paper right up to my face as though trying to inhale the words, then put it down.

"But what about your work?" I'm so desperate for this plan to come true now, I can't help pressing him, just to make sure. "You couldn't leave that."

"I can dip in and out."

I don't even know quite what Ben's work consists of. I mean, it's a company which makes paper, obviously, but what does he *do*? I'm not sure he ever explained it properly, and it feels a bit late to ask.

"Have you got someone who could take the reins? What about Lorcan?" I remember Ben's best friend. "He works with you, doesn't he? Could he step in?"

"Oh, I'm sure he'd love to." There's a sudden bitter twist to Ben's voice, and I take a mental step back.

Yikes. I've obviously touched a nerve. Not that I know the details, but Ben's manner instantly evokes a background of tense meetings in boardrooms and slammed doors and emails regretted the following day.

"He's your best man," I say cautiously. "Aren't you best friends?"

Ben is silent for a few moments, pre-occupied with some thought or other.

"I don't even know why Lorcan's in my life," he says at last. "That's the truth. I turned round and there he was. Just *there.*"

"What do you mean?"

"His marriage broke up four years ago. He went up to Staffordshire to stay with my dad. Fair enough; they'd always been friendly, since we were at school together. But next thing, Lorcan's advising my dad and getting a job in the company and running the whole bloody show. You should have seen him and my dad, striding around the place together, making plans, leaving me out completely."

"That sounds awful," I say sympathetically.

"It all came to a head two years ago." He gulps his champagne. "I just upped and left. Went AWOL. I needed to sort myself out. It freaked them so much they contacted the police." He spreads his hands. "I never told them where I was. After that, they behaved as though I was some sort of fragile nut-case. My dad and Lorcan were thicker than ever. Then my dad goes and *dies*. . . .”

There's a rawness to his voice which makes my skin prickle.

“And Lorcan stayed at the company?” I venture.

“Where else would he go? He's got a cushy number. Nice salary, cottage on the estate — he's sorted.”

“Does he have kids?”

“No.” Ben shrugs. “I suppose they never got round to it. Or weren't into them.”

“Well, then, why don't you quietly get rid of him?” I'm about to suggest a legal firm I know which specializes in tactfully exiting staff, but Ben doesn't seem to be listening.

“Lorcan thinks he knows best about everything!” The words come shooting out in a resentful stream. “What I should do with my life. What I should do with my company. What advertising agency I should employ. What I should pay my cleaners. What grade of paper is best for which . . . I don't know, *desk diary.*” He exhales. “And I don't know the answer. So he wins.”

“It's not a question of winning,” I say, but I can tell Ben isn't paying attention.

“He once confiscated my phone in public, because he thought it ‘wasn't appropriate.’ ”

Ben is burning with resentment.

"That sounds like harassment!" I say, shocked. "Do you have an effective HR head?"

"Yes." Ben sounds sulky. "But she's leaving. She'd never say anything to Lorcan, anyway. They all love him."

Listening with my professional hat on, I'm aghast. This all sounds like a shambles. I want to get a piece of paper and start a five-point action plan for Ben to manage Lorcan more effectively, but that's not exactly sexy honeymoon talk.

"Tell me," I say instead, my voice gentle and coaxing. "Where *did* you go when you went AWOL?"

"You really want to know?" Ben gives me a curious, wry smile. "Not my finest moment."

"Tell me."

"I went to have lessons in comedy from Malcolm Robinson."

"Malcolm Robinson?" I stare at him. "For real?"

I *love* Malcolm Robinson. He's hilarious. He used to have this brilliant sketch show, and once I saw him live at Edinburgh.

"I bought them anonymously at a charity auction. It was originally a weekend, but I persuaded him to extend it to a week. Cost me a fortune. At the end of the week, I asked him to tell me, straight up, if I had any talent."

There's silence. I'm already cringing inside at his expression.

"What —" I say at last, and clear my throat. "What did he —"

"He said no." Ben cuts me off, almost tonelessly. "He was blunt. Told me to give it up. Did me a favor, really. I haven't cracked a joke since."

I wince. "That must have been devastating."

"It hurt my pride, yes."

"How long had you been . . . ?" I trail off awkwardly. I don't know quite how to phrase it. Luckily, Ben gets the gist.

"Seven years."

"And you just gave up?"

"Yup."

"And you didn't tell anybody? Your dad? Lorcan?"

"I thought they might notice I'd stopped doing gigs and ask why. They didn't." The hurt in his voice is unmistakable. "I didn't have anyone else to . . . you know. Tell stuff."

Spontaneously, I reach for his hand and squeeze it tight. "You've got me now," I say softly. "Tell me stuff."

He squeezes my hand back and our eyes

are locked. For a moment I feel totally connected to him. Then two waiters come to clear our canapé plates; we release hands and the spell is broken.

"Strange honeymoon, huh?" I say wryly.

"I don't know. I'm starting to enjoy it."

"Me too." I can't help laughing. "I'm almost *glad* it's been so weird. At least we won't forget it."

And I mean it. If we hadn't had all the bedroom disasters, maybe we wouldn't have had this drink and I might never have found out these things about Ben. It's funny how things work out. I entwine my leg around Ben's under the table and start working my toe up his thigh in my signature maneuver, but he shakes his head vigorously.

"No," he says shortly. "Uh-uh. Can't stand it. Too horny."

"How on earth will you survive the couple's massage, then?" I tease him.

"By telling them to keep it to ten minutes flat and then leave us alone in utter privacy," he replies seriously. "I'm prepared to tip heavily."

"An hour to go." I glance at my watch. "I wonder what kind of oil they use?"

"Change the subject from oil." He looks strained. "Give a man a break."

I can't help laughing. "OK, here's a new

subject. When shall we go and visit the guest house? Tomorrow?"

I'm half excited, half terrified about visiting the guest house. It's where we met. It's where the fire happened. It's where my life changed. It's where *everything* happened. All at one little guest house, fifteen years ago.

"Tomorrow." Ben nods. "You have to do cartwheels along the beach for me."

"I will." I smile at him. "And you have to dive off that rock."

"And then we'll find that cave we used to go in . . ."

We're both hazy-eyed and smiling, lost in memories.

"You used to wear those tiny tie-dyed shorts," says Ben. "They drove me wild."

"I brought them with me," I confess.

"You didn't!" His eyes light up.

"I've kept them, all this time."

"You *angel.*"

I grin wickedly back at him, feeling my desire rocket. Oh God. How am I going to wait an hour? How can I fill the time?

"I'm going to let Fliss know how we got on." I reach for my phone and type a quick text:

Guess what? WE WON!!!! All going brilliantly. Ben and I make a fab team. Totally happy.☺

I can't help smiling as I type. She won't believe her eyes! In fact, I hope the news cheers her up a bit. She sounded hassled before. I wonder what's going on. On impulse, I add to my text:

Hope u r having a lovely day too. Everything OK?? L xxx

16
FLISS

There's nothing wrong with Sofia, Bulgaria.
It's a great city. I've been here many times
before. It boasts beautiful churches and
interesting museums and an outdoor book
market. However, it is not where I want to
be standing at six in the evening, hot,
sweaty, and harassed, waiting for my baggage at the carousel, *when I should be on the
Greek island of Ikonos.*

The only plus point of the situation: I
can't blame Daniel. Not this time. This one
is firmly fate/act of God. (Thanks a lot,
God. Is this because of what I said in
religious studies class, age eleven? I was *joking.*) Although I'd actually like to blame
Daniel right now. More specifically, I'd like
to kick him. Failing that, I may well kick my
baggage trolley.

The crowd around the carousel is five
deep. There are people waiting for luggage
from several flights, and no one is in a good

mood, least of all my fellow passengers from Flight 637 to Ikonos. Not many smiles. Not a lot of jolly banter.

Sofia, bloody Bulgaria. I *mean.*

Years of traveling for work have made me fairly Zen about airlines and delays and cock-ups, but I must say, this cock-up is of epic proportions. We couldn't just land, wave the poor old lady off to hospital, and then efficiently resume our journey. Oh no. Her luggage needed to be found, and then there was a problem getting a takeoff slot, and then it turned out something had gone wrong with an engine. The upshot is an unscheduled overnight stay in Sofia. We're being put up at the City Heights Hotel. (Not bad, four stars, great rooftop bar, as I remember.)

"That's ours!" yells Noah for the fifty-first time. He's tried to claim nearly every black suitcase that has appeared on the carousel, despite the fact that ours has a distinctive red strap and is probably on its way to Belgrade right now.

"It's not, Noah," I say patiently. "Keep looking." A woman steps heavily on my toe, and I'm trying to remember any curse words I know in Bulgarian when my phone beeps with a text and I pull it out of my pocket.

Guess what? WE WON!!!! All going brilliantly. Ben and I make a fab team. Totally happy. ☺Hope u r having a lovely day too. Everything OK?? L xxx

I'm so shocked I can't move for a moment. They *won*? How the hell did they win?

"Who's that from?" Richard has seen me reading my phone. "Is that from Lottie?"

"Er, yes." I'm too slow off the mark to lie.

"What does she say? Has she realized she's made a mistake?" His face is so eager that I cringe inside. "Presumably they did terribly at the quiz?"

"Actually . . ." I hesitate. How do I break this to him? "Actually, they won."

His face drops and he stares at me, aghast. "They *won*?"

"Apparently."

"But I thought they didn't know anything about each other."

"They don't!"

"You said they would tank." Richard becomes accusing.

"I know!" I say, feeling rattled. "Look, I'm sure there's some explanation. I must have got my wires crossed. I'll give her a ring." I speed-dial Lottie's number and turn away.

"Fliss?" Even from that one syllable I can hear how ebullient she is.

"Congratulations!" I try to match her tone. "You . . . you *won*?"

"Isn't it *amazing*?" she says exultantly. "You should have been there, Fliss. We did it in character! We were Dirk and Sally, you know, from that TV show we always used to watch?"

"Right," I say in confusion. "Wow."

"Now we're celebrating and I've just had the most delicious lobster canapés and champagne. And we're going back to the guest house tomorrow. And Ben wrote me a love poem in French." She sighs blissfully. "This is the perfect honeymoon."

I stare at the phone in mounting horror. Champagne? French love poetry? The *perfect honeymoon*?

"Right." I'm trying to stay calm. "That's . . . really surprising."

What the fuck has Nico been *doing*? Has he gone to sleep?

"Yes, we were having a terrible time!" Lottie laughs happily. "You wouldn't believe it. We haven't even . . . you know. Done it yet. But somehow that doesn't matter." Her tone softens lovingly. "It's as if all the crazy disasters have brought Ben and me closer together."

The disasters have brought them closer together? *I've brought them closer together?*

407

"Wonderful!" My voice is shrill. "That's great! So you made the right decision to marry Ben?"

"A million times over," says Lottie ecstatically.

"Great! Marvelous!" I screw up my face, debating how best to proceed. "Only . . . I was just thinking about Richard. Wondering how he was doing. Are you in touch with him?"

"Richard?" Her vitriolic tone nearly takes my ear off. "Why would I be in touch with *Richard*? He's well out of my life, and I wish I'd never ever met him!"

"Ah." I rub my nose, trying not to look at Richard. I hope he can't hear.

"Can you believe I was prepared to fly across the Atlantic for him? He would never have made such an effort for me. *Never.*" Her bitterness makes me flinch. "He hasn't got a single romantic bone in his body!"

"I'm sure he has!" I retort before I can stop myself.

"He hasn't," she says resolutely. "You know what I think? He never loved me at all. He's probably forgotten all about me already."

I look at Richard — hot, sweaty, and resolute — and I want to scream. If only she *knew.*

408

"Anyway, Fliss, I think it's really tasteless of you to mention Richard," she adds crossly.

"Sorry," I backtrack hastily. "Just thinking aloud. I'm glad you're having a good time."

"I'm having a fantastic time," she says emphatically. "We've been talking and bonding and making plans — oh, by the way. That guy you hooked up with. Lorcan."

"Yes? What about him?"

"He sounds a nightmare. You should avoid him. You haven't seen him again, have you?"

Instinctively, I glance over at Lorcan, who is up near the carousel and has hoisted Noah onto his shoulders.

"Er . . . not a lot," I prevaricate. "Why?"

"He's the most dreadful, arrogant man. You know he works for Ben's company? Well, he basically talked Ben's dad into giving him a job there, and now he has a cushy number and he's taking over everything and trying to control Ben."

"Oh," I say, nonplussed. "I had no idea. I thought they were mates."

"Well, I thought so too. But Ben really hates him. Apparently he once confiscated Ben's phone in public!" Her voice rises indignantly. "Like some kind of schoolteacher. Isn't that atrocious? I told Ben he should charge him with harassment! And there's loads of other stuff too. So promise me you won't go and fall for him or anything."

I resist the desire to give a hollow, sardonic laugh. Some chance.

"I'll do my best," I say. "And you promise me you'll . . . er . . . carry on having a wonderful time." It's killing me to say the words. "What's up next?"

"Couple's massage on the beach," she says happily.

Every fiber in my body stiffens in alarm.

"Right." I swallow. "So, when's that? Exactly?"

I'm already planning the ear-bashing I'm going to give Nico. What's going on? How can he have been so negligent? Why are they drinking champagne and eating lobster? Why did he allow Ben to write a French love poem? He should have leapt in and grabbed the pencil.

"It's in half an hour," says Lottie. "They rub you with oil and then leave you alone for some private time. Honestly, Fliss." She lowers her voice. "Ben and I are just *gagging* for it."

I'm hopping with agitation. This was not the plan. I'm stuck in bloody Sofia and she and Ben are about to conceive a baby on the beach, whom no doubt they'll christen

"Beach" and then viciously fight over in the high court when it all falls apart. As soon as I've said goodbye, I speed-dial Nico.

"Well?" Richard instantly questions me. "What's the situation?"

"The situation is: I'm on top of the situation," I say curtly as I'm put through to voicemail. "Hello, Nico, it's Fliss. We need to talk, asap. Give me a call. Bye."

"So what did Lottie say?" demands Richard as I end the call. "Did they win?"

"Apparently so."

"Bastard." He's breathing heavily. "*Bastard.* What does he know about her that I don't? What's he got that I haven't? Apart from, obviously, the stately home —"

"Richard, stop!" I snap in exasperation. "It's not a competition!"

Richard stares at me as though I'm the thickest moron that ever existed. "Of course it's a competition," he says.

"No, it isn't!"

"Fliss, *everything* in a man's life is a competition!" He suddenly loses it. "Don't you realize that? From the moment you're a three-year-old boy, peeing up against the wall with your friends, all you really care about is: Am I bigger than him? Am I taller? Am I more successful? Is my wife hotter? So, the day that some smooth bastard with a private jet runs off with the girl you love: yes, it's a competition."

"You don't know he's got a private jet," I say after a pause.

"I'm guessing."

There's silence. In spite of myself, I'm rating Richard against Ben in my mind. Well, Richard would win in my book — but, then, I've never met Ben.

"Well, OK. Suppose you're right," I say at last. "What counts as winning? Where's the finish line? She's married to someone else. So doesn't that mean you've already lost?"

I don't mean to be harsh — but these are the facts.

"When I've told Lottie how I really feel . . . and she's still said no," says Richard resolutely, "*then* I'll have lost."

My stomach twinges with sympathy for him. He's putting himself on the line here. No one can say he's taking the easy way out.

"OK." I nod. "Well, you know which way I would vote." I squeeze his shoulder.

"What are they doing now?" He glances at my phone. "Tell me what they're doing. I know she'll have told you."

"They've just had champagne and lobster," I say reluctantly. "And Ben's written her a love poem in French."

412

"In French?" Richard looks as though someone has kneed him in the stomach. "Smarmy *bastard.*"

"And they're planning to go to the guest house tomorrow," I tell him, as Lorcan joins us. He and Noah are wheeling three cases between them. "Well done, you two! That's all the luggage."

"High five," says Noah solemnly to Lorcan, and smacks his proffered palm.

"The guest house?" Richard looks stricken by this piece of news. "The guest house where they met?"

"Exactly."

His scowl deepens. "She always goes on about that place. The calamari that was unlike any calamari in the world. And the secluded beach that was better than any other beach. I took her to Kos once, and all she could say was it wasn't as good as the guest house."

"Oh, jeez, the guest house." Lorcan nods in agreement. "I hate that place. If I have to hear Ben tell me one more time about how the sunset was like a mind-altering experience . . ."

"Lottie went on about the sunset too." Richard nods.

"And how they all used to get up at dawn and do fucking yoga —"

"— and the people —"

"— the atmosphere —"

"And the sea was the clearest, most turquoise, most perfect sea in existence," I chime in, rolling my eyes. "I mean, get over it."

"Bloody place," says Lorcan.

"I wish it *had* burned down," adds Richard.

We all look at each other, immensely cheered. There's nothing like having a common enemy.

"So, we should go," says Lorcan. He proffers the handle of my wheelie case and I'm about to take it when my phone rings. I check the ID: it's Nico. At *last*.

"Nico! Where have you been!"

"Fliss! I know what you are thinking, and I am mortified —" As he launches into some long, rambling apology, I cut him off.

"We haven't got time for all that. They're about to get it together on the beach. You need to move fast. Listen."

17
LOTTIE

This is the *perfect* setting for a wedding night. I mean, our own private beach! How cool is that?

We're in a secluded little cove that you reach from the main beach over stepping stones and there's a DO NOT DISTURB sign placed on a rock. Our two massage therapists led us here in a little procession, followed by Georgios and Hermes carrying champagne and oysters, which are waiting for us on ice. Now we're lying on a huge double massage bed, while the two massage therapists, Angelina and Carissa, rub oil into our bodies. Billowing all around us are white curtains, so we're totally private in our enclosure. The sky is that intense blue you only get at a certain point in the early evening, and scented candles planted in the sand are giving off a sweet aroma. Birds are swooping and calling. I can hear the tiny splash of waves on the sand, and the air has a salty tang. It's all so scenic, I feel as though I'm in some arty pop video.

Ben reaches out his hand to take mine, and I squeeze it back, wincing as Carissa tackles a particularly stubborn knot in my neck. Mmm. Ben and me and a canopied bed on the beach, which we'll have to ourselves for two hours afterward. The therapists have stressed that several times. "Two hours," Angelina kept saying. "Plenty of private time. You will be relaxed as a couple. . . . All the senses will be stimulated. . . . No one will disturb you, this is guaranteed. . . ."

She didn't quite wink, but she might as well have. Obviously this is the open-air shagging service, which they're too coy to spell out in the brochure.

Carissa has finished with my neck. She and Angelina move to the head end of the bed and in synchronization begin a head massage. I'm relaxing more and more — in fact, I'd probably fall asleep if it weren't that I'm also absolutely hopping with lust. Just the sight of Ben slick with oil and naked beside me was enough. We are going to use every minute of that two hours, I vow. We have *earned* this sex. He'll only have to touch me and I'll explode —

Ting!

I'm jolted out of my reverie. From no-where, Angelina and Carissa have produced matching little bells, which they've struck above our heads in a kind of ritual.

"Finish," whispers Carissa, and tucks my sheet around me. "Now relax. Take it easy."

Yes! It's over! Sexy private time, here we come. I watch through semi-closed eyes as Angelina and Carissa withdraw from our curtained enclosure. There's no sound at all except for the cotton curtains, flapping gently in the breeze. I stare up at the blue, unable to speak, I'm so overcome by torpor and lust. I think this is the most blissful state I've ever been in. Post-massage; pre-sex.

"So." Ben's hand squeezes mine again. "At last."

"At *last*." I'm about to lean over and kiss him, but he's too fast. Before I know it, he's straddling me, holding a small bottle of oil. He must have brought it along secretly. He thinks of everything!

"I don't like anyone massaging you but me." He pours oil onto my shoulders. It smells musky and sensual and gorgeous. I inhale pleasurably as he covers me all over with it, using firm, sweeping gestures which make me shiver.

"You know, you're very talented, Mr. Parr," I say, my voice jerky with lust. "You could set up a spa."

"I want only one client." He starts to rub the oil into my nipples, over my stomach, lower down. . . . At once I'm whimpering with desire. I have so, so wanted him. . . .

"You like this?" His eyes are intent.

"I'm tingling all over. It's unbearable."

"So am I." He leans in to kiss me, his hands moving down with purpose, between my thighs. . . .

"Oh God." I'm breathless. "I really am tingling."

"Me too."

"Ow!" I can't help wincing.

"I know you like it a bit rough." He chuckles, but I'm not sure I can join in. I'm tingling too much. Something's wrong.

"Can we stop a moment?" I push him away. My skin feels like it's crawling with insects. "I'm a little sore."

"Sore?" His eyes glint with amusement. "Babe, we haven't even started."

"It's not funny! It's painful!" I stare agitatedly at my arm. It's turned red. Why is it red? Ben moves in on me again, and I try my hardest to moan with appreciation as his lips nuzzle their way down my neck. But, truthfully, they're moans of pain.

"Stop!" I say at last, in desperation. "Time out! I feel like I'm on fire!"

"So do I," pants Ben.

"Really! I can't do this! *Look* at me!"

At last Ben moves back and surveys me, his eyes cloudy with desire. "You look great," he says briefly. "You look awesome."

"No, I don't! I'm all red." I survey my arms with mounting alarm. "And I'm swelling up! Look!"

"These are swelling up, all right." Ben cups one of my breasts appreciatively. Isn't he *listening*?

"Ow!" I wrench his arm away. "This is serious. I think I've had an allergic reaction. What's in that oil? Not peanut oil? You *know* I'm allergic to peanuts."

"It's just oil." Ben seems evasive. "I don't know what's in it."

"You must! You must have looked at the label when you bought it." There's a short silence. Ben looks a bit sulky, as though I've caught him out.

"I didn't buy it," he says at last. "Nico gave it to me, compliments of the hotel. It's their signature blend or something."

"Oh." I can't help feeling disappointed. "And you didn't check? Even though you know I'm allergic?"

"I'd forgotten, OK?" Ben sounds thrown. "I can't remember every tiny little thing!"

"I hardly think your wife's allergy is 'every

419

tiny little thing'!" I say furiously, feeling an uncharacteristic urge to hit him. It was all going so brilliantly. *Why* did he have to slather me with evil peanut oil?

"Look, maybe if we get the right angle it won't hurt you so much." Ben looks around desperately and pushes aside the curtains. "Try standing on those rocks."

"OK." I'm as eager as he is to make this work. If we minimize actual contact . . . I clamber onto the rocks, trying not to flinch too much. "Ow —"

"Not like that —"

"Ouch! Stop!"

"Try the other way. . . ."

"If you could rotate a bit . . . Oof!"

"Was that your *nostril*?"

"This isn't working," I say, after slipping off the rocks for the third time. "I could try kneeling on the rocks if we had some padding. . . ."

"Or on the edge of the bed . . ."

"I'll go on top. . . . No! Ow! Sorry," I wince, "but that's really painful."

"Can you put your leg behind your head?"

"No, I can't," I say resentfully. "Can you?"

The atmosphere has totally disintegrated, as we try one acrobatic position after another. I keep gasping, and not in a good way. By now my skin is seriously inflamed. I need some soothing aqueous cream, urgently. But I also need to have sex. It's unbearable. I want to weep with frustration.

"Come on!" I say to myself crossly. "I've had root-canal surgery. I can do this."

"Root-canal surgery?" Ben sounds mortally offended. "Sex with me is like *root-canal surgery*?"

"That's not what I meant!"

"You've been avoiding sex with me all holiday," he snarls, suddenly losing his temper. "I mean, what kind of a bloody honeymoon is this?"

This is such an unfair accusation that I recoil with shock.

"I haven't avoided sex!" I cry. "I want it as much as you do, but I . . . It's so painful. . . ." I cast around desperately. "Could we try tantric sex?"

"*Tantric* sex?" Ben sounds contemptuous.

"Well, it works for Sting." I feel near tears of disappointment.

"Is your mouth sore?" says Ben, a note of hope in his voice.

"Yes, I got oil on my lips. They're really smarting." I catch his drift. "Sorry."

Ben unhooks his leg from mine and slumps onto the bed, his shoulders hunched. Despite everything, I can't help feeling relieved that he's not chafing against me anymore. It was sheer torture.

For a while we just sit there in stony misery. My flesh is still swollen and vivid red. I must look like an overgrown glacé cherry. A tear rolls down my cheek, then another.

He hasn't even asked me if my allergy is dangerous. I mean, not that it is, but still. He isn't exactly concerned, is he? The first time Richard saw me react to peanuts, he wanted to drive me to the ER right then. And he's always scrupulous about checking menus and the boxes of ready meals. He's really thoughtful —

"Lottie." Ben's voice makes me jump a mile with guilt. How can I be thinking about my ex-boyfriend when I'm on my honeymoon?

"Yes?" I turn quickly, in case he guessed my thoughts. "Just thinking about . . . nothing in particular . . ."

"I'm sorry." Ben spreads his hands in a frank gesture. "I didn't mean it, but I'm so desperate for you."

"Me too."

"It's just bad luck."

"We seem to be having more than our fair share of bad luck," I say ruefully. "How can one couple have such a catalog of disasters?"

"Less 'honeymoon,' " he quips, "more

'horrormoon.' "

I smile at his feeble joke, feeling mollified. At least he's making an effort.

"Maybe it's fate," I say, not really meaning it, but Ben seizes on this idea.

"Maybe you're right. Think about it, Lottie. We're going back to the guest house tomorrow. We're returning to the place we first got it together. Maybe *that's* where we're meant to consummate our marriage."

"It would be pretty romantic." This idea is growing on me. "We could find the same spot in that little cave."

"You still remember?"

"I'll always remember that night," I say in heartfelt tones. "It's one of my all-time great memories."

"Well, maybe we can top it," says Ben, his good humor restored. "How long will you be out of action?"

"Dunno." I glance down at my lobster skin. "It's a pretty bad reaction. Probably till tomorrow."

"OK. So we press *pause*. Agreed?"

"Agreed," I say gratefully. "We are hereby pressing *pause.*"

"And tomorrow will be *play.*"

"And then *rewind* and *play* again." I grin wickedly at him. "And again. And again."

I can tell, we're both cheered by this plan.

We sit gazing out to sea, and I feel myself gradually soothed by the repetitive noise of the surf, punctuated by the cry of birds and, far away, the throb of music coming from the main beach. A band is playing there tonight. Maybe we'll wander over in a while, drink a cocktail, and have a listen.

It feels as if we've made our peace. As we're sitting there, Ben carefully extends his arm behind me, then bends it round as though to cradle my back, without actually touching. It's like a ghost embrace. My skin prickles mildly in response, but I don't mind. All my resentment has faded away; in fact, I can't think why it was there at all.

"Tomorrow," he says. "No peanut oil. No butlers. No harps. Just us."

"Just us." I nod. Maybe Ben's right: maybe we were supposed to do it at the guest house all along. "I love you," I add impulsively. "Even more because of this."

"I feel the same way." He gives me that lopsided smile and my heart swells. And suddenly I feel almost euphoric, despite my stinging skin and frustrated libido and a cricked ankle from climbing on the rocks. Because, after all, here we are, back on Ikonos, after all these years. And tomorrow we come full circle. Tomorrow we return to the most important place of our lives: the guest house. The place where we found love and experienced seismic events and changed our destinies forever.

Ben holds out his hand as though to take mine, and I curl my fingers underneath without quite touching (my hands are swollen too). I don't need to tell him how important this visit to the guest house is to me. He understands. He gets it like no one else does. And that's why we're meant to be together.

18
FLISS

No. Nooo! What is this drivel?

Ben understands me at a profound level. He thinks it's Destiny and I do too. We've made so many plans for our future. He wants to do all the same things that I do. We'll probably end up living in France in a *gîte*. . . .

I click briskly through the next three texts with mounting dismay.

. . . amazing atmosphere with white curtains next to the sea, and, OK, it didn't work out, but that's not important . . .

. . . We weren't touching but I could FEEL him, it's like a psychic connection, you know what I mean. . . .

. . . happiest I've ever been . . .

They haven't shagged, yet she's the happiest she's ever been. Well, if I was trying to drive them apart, I've squarely failed. I've driven them together instead. Good work, Fliss. Marvelous.

"Everything OK?" says Lorcan, observing my expression.

"Everything's dandy," I almost snarl back, and flip viciously through the leather-bound cocktail menu.

My spirits have not exactly been high since the touchdown in Sofia. Now they're plummeting to rock bottom. Everything has backfired and I'm bone weary and my minibar was lacking tonic water and now I'm surrounded by Bulgarian prostitutes.

OK, they may not *all* be Bulgarian prostitutes, I allow, as I do another sweep of the hotel rooftop bar. Some may be Bulgarian glamour models. Some may even be business types. The light in here is dim, but it's glinting off all the diamonds and teeth and Louis Vuitton buckles on show. Hardly the most understated place, the City Heights. Although, to their credit, they knew my name and I didn't even need to ask for an upgrade. I'm in the most bling suite I've stayed in for a while, complete with two massive bedrooms, a sitting room with cinema screen, and a vast mirrored art-deco-style bathroom. I may be compelled to show it off to Lorcan later on.

I feel an anticipatory squeeze inside. Not quite sure where things are with Lorcan and me. Maybe after a few drinks I'll find out.

This bar is fairly bling too, with glass floor-to-ceiling windows and a narrow wraparound swimming pool tiled in black, which all the beautiful people/glamour models/business types are regarding with disdain. Unlike Noah, who is hopping up and down, demanding to be allowed in.

"Your swimsuit is all packed away," I say for the fifth time.

"Let him swim in his underpants," says Lorcan. "Why not?"

"Yes!" crows Noah, enchanted by this idea. "Underpants! Underpants!" He's jumping up and down, totally hyper after the flight. Maybe a swim is a good idea after all.

"OK." I relent. "You can go in in your underpants. But *quietly*. Don't splash anyone."

Eagerly, Noah starts to strip off, discarding his clothes with abandon.

"Look after my wallet, please," he says with grown-up precision, and hands me the airline wallet he was given on the flight. "I want some credit cards to go in it," he adds.

"You're not quite old enough for credit cards," I say, folding up his trousers and putting them neatly on a velvet-upholstered banquette.

"Here's one," says Lorcan, and hands him a Starbucks card. "Expired," he adds to me.

"Cool!" says Noah in delight, and carefully slots it into his wallet. "I want it to be full like Daddy's."

I'm about to make a barbed comment about Daddy's bulging wallet — but rein myself back just in time. That would be bitter. And I'm not doing bitter. I'm doing sweetness and light.

"Daddy works hard for his money," I say in sugary tones. "We should be *proud* of him, Noah."

"Geronimo!" Noah is running up to the pool. A moment later he lands in a bomb with the most almighty splash. Water showers onto a nearby blonde in a minidress, who recoils in horror and brushes the drops off her legs.

"So sorry," I call over cheerfully. "Occupational hazard of drinking next to a swimming pool!"

Noah has begun his extremely splashy version of the front crawl and is drawing looks of consternation from beautiful people and beautiful waitstaff alike.

"What's the betting that Noah is the first person *ever* to swim in this pool?" says Lorcan in amusement.

As we're watching, Richard enters the bar, along with a group of travelers I recognize from the plane. He looks wearier than he did earlier on, and I feel a twinge of sympathy for him.

"Hi," he greets us, and sinks onto the banquette. "Heard from Lottie again?"

"Yes, and the good news is they still haven't got it together!" I say, to cheer him up.

"Still?" Lorcan sets down his glass with an incredulous crash. "What is *wrong* with them?"

"Allergic mishap." I shrug carelessly. "They used peanut oil or something on Lottie and she swelled up."

"Peanut oil?" Richard looks up suddenly, concerned. "Well, is she OK? Did they call a doctor?"

"I think she's fine. Really."

"Because those reactions can be dangerous. Why did they use peanut oil, for God's sake? Didn't she warn them?"

"I . . . don't know," I say evasively. "What's that?" I add, to change the subject, and nod

430

at the piece of paper Richard is holding.

"It's nothing," says Richard protectively, as Noah bounds up, wrapped in a chic black towel. "Nothing much."

"It must be something."

"Well . . . OK." Richard looks fiercely from Lorcan to me, as though daring us to laugh. "I've started a poem in French. For Lottie."

"Good for you!" I say encouragingly. "Can I have a look?"

"It's a work in progress." Grudgingly, he hands over the paper and I shake it out, clearing my throat.

"*Je t'aime, Lottie. Plus qu'un zloty.*" I hesitate, not sure what to say. "Well, it's a start. . . ."

" 'I love you, Lottie, More than a zloty'?" Lorcan translates incredulously. "Seriously?"

"Lottie's a difficult rhyme!" Richard says defensively. "You try!"

"You could have used 'potty,' " suggests Noah. " 'I love you, Lottie, Sitting on the potty.' "

"Thanks, Noah," says Richard grouchily. "Appreciate it."

"It's very good," I say hastily. "Anyway, it's the thought that counts."

Richard grabs the paper back from me

and reaches for the bar menu. On the front it reads *Delectable Bulgarian Specialties,* and inside are lists of bar snacks and light meals.

"That's a good idea. Have something to eat," I say soothingly. "You'll feel better."

Richard gives the menu a cursory glance, then flags down a waitress, who approaches with a smile.

"Sir? Can I help?"

"I have some questions about your 'delectable Bulgarian specialties,' " he says with an uncompromising stare. "The tricolore salad. Is that a Bulgarian specialty?"

"Sir." The girl's smile widens. "I will check."

"And the chicken korma. Is that a Bulgarian specialty?"

"Sir, I will check." The girl is scribbling on her notepad.

"Richard." I kick him. "Stop it."

"Club sandwich." Richard presses on. "Is *that* a Bulgarian specialty?"

"Sir —"

"Curly fries. Which area of Bulgaria do they come from?"

The girl has stopped writing now and is gazing at him, perplexed.

"Stop!" I hiss at Richard, then smile up at the girl. "Thanks so much. We'll need a couple more minutes."

"I was just asking," says Richard, as she walks away. "Clarifying. I'm allowed to clarify, aren't I?"

"Just because you can't write French love poetry, there's no need to take it out on an innocent waitress," I say sternly. "Anyway, look. Meze platter. That's a Bulgarian specialty."

"It's Greek."

"And Bulgarian."

"Like you know all about it." He looks at the menu broodingly, then closes it. "Actually, I think I'll turn in."

"Aren't you going to eat?"

"I'll get room service. See you in the morning."

"Sleep well!" I call after him, and he gives me a gloomy nod over his shoulder.

"Poor guy," says Lorcan, after Richard has disappeared from view. "He really loves her."

"I think so."

"No one writes a poem like that unless they're so in love that their faculties have become temporarily defective."

"More than a zloty," I quote, suddenly getting the giggles. *"Zloty?"*

" 'Sitting on the potty' was better." Lorcan raises his eyebrows. "Noah, you may have a future as Poet Laureate."

Noah bounds off to leap back into the swimming pool, and we both watch him splashing around for a moment.

"Nice kid," says Lorcan. "Bright. Well balanced."

"Thanks." I can't help smiling at the compliment. Noah *is* bright. Although "well balanced" I'm not so sure about. Do well-balanced kids boast about their fictitious heart transplants?

"He seems very happy." Lorcan takes a handful of peanuts. "Was custody amicable?"

At the word "custody," my internal radar springs into action and I feel my heart automatically start to pound, ready for battle. My body is flooding with adrenaline. I'm fingering my memory stick nervously. I have speeches lined up in my head. Long, erudite, scathing speeches. Also: I want to punch someone.

"Only, some of my friends have had fairly torrid times with custody battles," Lorcan adds.

"Right." I'm trying to achieve composure. "Right. I bet."

Torrid? I want to exclaim. *You want to hear about torrid?*

But at the same time Barnaby's voice is ringing in my ears like the chime of a warn-

434

ing bell. *You said whatever you did, you wouldn't end up bitter.*

"But you haven't suffered?" says Lorcan.

"Not at all." From nowhere, I've mustered the most relaxed, serene smile. "Actually, it's all been very easy and straightforward. And quick," I add for good measure. "Very quick."

"You're lucky."

"Very lucky." I nod. "So, so lucky!"

"And you and your ex get on?"

"We're like this." I cross my fingers.

"You're incredible!" says Lorcan in marveling tones. "Are you sure you want to be divorced from him?"

"I'm just super-glad he's found happiness with another woman." I smile yet more sweetly. My ability to lie is unnerving even to myself. Essentially, I'm saying the diametric opposite of the truth. It's almost a game.

"And do you get on with his new partner?"

"Love her!"

"And does Noah?"

"It's like one big happy family!"

"Would you like another drink?"

"No, I'd hate one!" Abruptly I remember that Lorcan doesn't know we're playing the game. "I mean, love one," I amend.

As Lorcan summons a waiter, I eat a couple of nuts and try to come up with more divorce-related lies. But even as I'm composing them — *We all play table tennis together! Daniel's naming his new baby after me!* — my head is buzzing. My fingers are fiddling at the memory stick with more and more agitation. I don't like this game anymore. My inner good fairy is losing her glow. The bad fairy is barging in and wants to have a say.

"So, your husband must be a great guy," says Lorcan, after he's given our order. "For you two to have such a special relationship."

"He's a star!" I nod, my teeth gritted.

"Must be."

"He's just so thoughtful and kind!" I'm clenching my fists by my sides. "He's such a charismatic, charming, unselfish, caring —" I break off. I'm panting. There are actual stars in front of my eyes. Complimenting Daniel is bad for my health; I can't do it anymore. "He's a . . . a . . . a . . ." It's like a sneeze. It has to come out. *"Bastard."*

There's a slight pause. I can see some men at a nearby table looking over with interest.

"A bastard in a good way?" hazards Lorcan. "Or . . . oh." He sees my face.

"I lied. Daniel is the biggest nightmare that any divorced wife has had to put up with, and I'm bitter, OK? I'm bitter!" Just saying it is a relief. "My bones are bitter,

my heart's bitter, my blood is bitter. . . ."
Something occurs to me. "Wait. You've had
sex with me. You know I'm bitter."

There's no way he couldn't have picked
that up from our night together. I was fairly
tense. I think I swore a lot.

"I wondered." Lorcan tilts his head af-
firmatively.

"Was it when I shouted, 'Screw you,
Daniel!' just as I came?" I can't help cracking, then lift a hand. "Sorry. Bad-taste joke."

"No apology needed." Lorcan doesn't
even blink. "The only way to survive a
divorce is to tell bad-taste jokes. What do
you do if you miss your ex-wife? Take better
aim next time."

"Why is divorce so expensive?" I automatically counter. "Because it's worth it."

"Why do divorced men get married again?
Bad memory."

He waits for me to laugh, but I'm lost in
thought. My adrenaline tidal wave has
ebbed away, leaving behind the detritus of
old familiar thoughts.

"The thing is . . ." I rub my nose hard.
"The thing is, I *haven't* survived my divorce.
Wouldn't 'survival' imply I'm the same
person I was before?"

"So who are you now?" says Lorcan.

"I don't know," I say after a long pause. "I

feel scalded inside. Like, third-degree burns. But no one can see them."

Lorcan winces but doesn't reply. He's one of those rare people who can wait it out and listen.

"I started to wonder if I was going mad," I say, staring into my glass. "Could Daniel *really* see the world that way? Could he *really* be saying those awful things and could people be believing him? And the worst thing is, no one else is in it with you. A divorce is like a controlled explosion. Everyone on the outside is OK."

"Everyone on the outside." Lorcan nods vigorously. "Don't you *hate* those people? Telling you not to think about it."

"Yes!" I nod in recognition. "And saying, 'Be positive! At least you haven't been horribly disfigured in an industrial accident!' "

Lorcan bursts into laughter. "You know the same people I know."

"I just wish beyond anything that he was out of my life." I exhale, resting my forehead briefly in my hands. "I wish they could do . . . I don't know. Keyhole surgery for ex-husband removal." Lorcan gives an appreciative smile and I gulp my wine. "What about you?"

"It was fairly grim." He nods. "There was some nastiness about money, but we didn't have kids, so that made it simpler."

"You're lucky you didn't have kids."

"Not really," he replies tonelessly.

"No, really, you are," I persist. "I mean, when you get into custody, it's a whole other —"

"No, really, I'm *not.*" There's an acerbic edge to his voice I haven't heard before, and I suddenly remember I know very little of his private life. "We couldn't," he adds shortly. "I couldn't. And I would say that that fact contributed about eighty percent to our breakup. Make that a hundred percent." He takes a deep gulp of whiskey.

I'm so shocked I don't know what to say. In those few words, he's conveyed a background story of such sadness that I feel instantly guilty for having complained about my own plight. Because at least I have Noah.

"I'm sorry," I falter at last.

"Yes. Me too." He gives me a wry, kind smile, and I realize that he can tell I'm feeling guilty. "Although, as you say, it would have complicated things more."

"I didn't mean —" I begin. "I didn't realize —"

"It's fine." He lifts a hand. "It's fine."

I recognize his tone; I use it myself. It isn't fine: it just is.

"I really am sorry." I repeat myself feebly.

"I know." He nods. "Thanks."

For a while we're silent. Thoughts are spinning around my head, but I don't quite dare to share any of them with him. I don't know him well enough. They might inadvertently hurt him.

At last I retreat to the safe, once-removed territory of Lottie and Ben.

"The thing is . . ." I exhale. "I just want to save my sister from the same kind of hurt that we've both experienced. That's all. That's why I'm here."

"Can I make a small point?" says Lorcan. His mouth twitches with humor, and I can tell he wants to lighten the mood. "You haven't even met Ben."

"I don't need to," I retort. "What you don't realize is there's a history to this. Every time Lottie breaks up with someone, she makes some stupid, rash, insane gesture that she then has to undo. I call them her Unfortunate Choices."

" 'Unfortunate Choices.' I like it." Lorcan raises an eyebrow. "So you think Ben is her Unfortunate Choice."

"Well, don't you? I mean, *really*. Getting hitched after five minutes, planning to live in a *gîte* —"

"A *gîte*?" Lorcan looks surprised. "Who said that?"

440

"Lottie! She's full of it. They're going to have goats and chickens and we all have to visit them and eat baguettes."

"This doesn't sound like Ben at all," says Lorcan. "Chickens? Are you sure?"

"Precisely! It sounds like some ridiculous pipe dream. And it'll crumble to bits and she'll end up divorced and bitter and just like me —" Too late, I realize I'm almost shouting. The men at the next table are looking at me again. "Just like me," I repeat more quietly. "And that would be a disaster."

"You do yourself a disservice," says Lorcan. I think he's trying to be nice. But I'm really not in the mood for flattery.

"You *know* what I mean." I lean forward. "Would you wish the sheer hell of divorce on someone you cared about? Or would you try to prevent it?"

"So you're going to arrive out of the blue, tell her to get an annulment and marry Richard. You think she'll listen?"

I shake my head. "It's not like that. I happen to think Richard's great and perfect for Lottie, but I'm not going out there under the banner of Team Richard. Richard will have to be his own team. I'm on Team Don't Mess Your Life Up."

"Providential for you that they've had

such a nightmare of a honeymoon," says Lorcan, raising an eyebrow.

There's a brief, charged pause in which I wonder whether to tell him about my secret operation — then decide against it.

"Yes," I say as nonchalantly as I can. "Lucky."

Noah comes pattering up again, his feet leaving wet marks in the deep-gray carpet. He snuggles onto my knee and at once I feel myself lighten. Noah carries hope round with him like an aura, and whenever I touch him a little bit of it filters into me.

"Here!" Suddenly he's waving at someone. "This table!"

"Here we are." A waitress appears, bearing a silver tray on which is an ice-cream sundae. "For the brave little soldier. You must be *so* proud," she adds to me.

Oh God. Not again. I smile back, my expression carefully vague, trying to hide my embarrassment. I have no idea where we're heading with this. It could be heart transplant. It could be bone marrow. It could be new puppy.

"Training for three hours a day!" She squeezes Noah's shoulder. "I admire your dedication! Your son was telling me about his gymnastics," she adds to me. "Thinking of the Olympics 2024, are you?"

My smile freezes. His *gymnastics*? OK, I can't put this off any longer. I'm having the Talk, right here, right now.

"Thank you," I manage. "Wonderful. Thank you so much." As soon as the waitress has disappeared, I turn to Noah. "Darling. Listen to me. This is important. You know the difference between truth and lies, don't you?"

"Yes." Noah nods confidently.

"And you know that we mustn't tell lies."

"Except to be polite," chimes in Noah. "Like, 'I do like your dress!' "

This comes from another Big Talk we had, about two months ago, after Noah was disastrously honest about his godmother's cooking.

"Yes. But generally speaking —"

"And 'What delicious apple pie!' " Noah warms to his theme. "And 'I'd love some more, but I'm just too full!' "

"Yes! OK. But the point is, *most* of the time we have to be truthful. And not — for example — say that we've had a heart transplant when we haven't." I'm watching Noah closely for a reaction, but he seems unmoved. "Darling, you haven't had a heart transplant, have you?" I say gently.

"No," he agrees.

"But you told the airline staff that you'd

443

had one. Why?"

Noah thinks for a bit. "Because it's interesting."

"Right. Well. Let's be interesting and *truthful,* OK? From now on, I want you to tell the *truth.*"

"OK." Noah shrugs as though it's neither here nor there. "Can I start my sundae now?" He picks up his spoon and digs in, sending chocolate flakes everywhere.

"Nicely done," says Lorcan quietly.

"I don't know." I sigh. "I just don't *get* it. Why does he say this stuff?"

"Big imagination." Lorcan shrugs. "I wouldn't worry. You're a good mother," he adds, so matter-of-factly that I wonder if I misheard.

"Oh." I don't quite know how to react. "Thanks."

"And you're like a mother to Lottie too, I'm guessing?" He's pretty perceptive, this Lorcan.

I nod. "Our own mother didn't do a great job. I've always had to watch out for her."

"Makes sense."

"Do you get it?" I look up, suddenly wanting to hear his true opinion. "Do you understand what I'm doing?"

"Which bit?"

"All of it." I spread my arms wide. "This.

Trying to save my sister from the biggest mistake of her life. Am I right, or am I insane?"

Lorcan is silent for a while. "I think you're very loyal and very protective and I respect you for that. And, yes, you're insane."

"Shut up." I shove him.

"You asked." He shoves me back and I feel a tiny electric dart, coupled with a flashback to our night together. It's so graphic that I gasp. Looking at the way Lorcan's mouth is tightening, I think he's remembering exactly the same bit.

My skin has started to prickle in a mixture of memory and anticipation. Here we are: the two of us, in a hotel. No-brainer. The thing about great sex is, it's a gift from God which should be enjoyed to the max. That's my theory, anyway.

"So, do you have a big suite?" Lorcan asks, as though reading my mind.

"Two bedrooms," I reply carelessly. "One for me, one for Noah."

"Ah."

"Lots of space."

"Ah." His eyes are locked onto mine with a promise of more, and I feel an involuntary shiver. Not that we can run upstairs and rip our clothes off straightaway. There is the small matter of my seven-year-old son sitting next to me.

"Shall we . . . eat?" I suggest.

"Yes!" Noah, finishing his ice-cream sundae, tunes in to the conversation with precision accuracy. "I want a burger and chips!"

An hour later, between the three of us, we've eaten one club sandwich, one burger, one bowl of normal fries, one bowl of sweet-potato fries, one platter of shrimp tempura, three chocolate brownies, and a basketful of bread. Beside me, Noah is half asleep on the banquette seat. He's had a riotous time, darting around the bar, making friends with all the Bulgarian prostitutes, scoring Cokes and packets of crisps and even some Bulgarian money, which, to his dismay, I made him give straight back.

Now a six-piece band is playing and everyone is listening, and the lights are even dimmer than before, and I'm feeling fairly blissful. I've mellowed after my three glasses of wine. Lorcan's hand keeps brushing against mine. We have an entire empty, delicious night ahead of us. I reach over to take the last sweet-potato chip from the bowl and glimpse Noah's precious airline wallet on the seat next to him. It's stuffed with what look like credit cards. Where on earth did he get those?

"Noah?" I nudge him awake. "Sweetheart, what have you got in your wallet?"

"Credit cards," he says sleepily. "I found them."

"You *found* credit cards?" My blood freezes. Oh God. Has he stolen someone's credit cards? I grab the wallet and pull out the cards in consternation. But they're not credit cards after all. They're — *"Room keys!"* says Lorcan, as I pull out about seven at once. The entire wallet is stuffed with electronic room keys. He must have about twenty of them.

"Noah!" I shake him awake again. "Darling, where did you get these from?"

"I told you, I *found* them," he says resentfully. "People put them down on tables and things. I wanted some credit cards for my wallet. . . ." His eyes are already closing again.

I look up at Lorcan, my hands full of room keys splayed out like playing cards.

"What do I do? I'll have to give them back."

"They all look the same," observes Lorcan, and gives a snort of laughter. "Good luck with that."

"Don't laugh! It's not funny! There'll be a riot when everyone finds out they're locked out of their rooms. . . ." I look again at the

447

electronic cards and suddenly snuffle with laughter myself.

"Just put them back," says Lorcan decisively.

"But *where*?" I look around the tables of smartly dressed beautiful people, all enjoying the band, oblivious to my agitation. "I don't know whose key is whose, and I can't find out without going to the front desk."

"Here's the plan," says Lorcan decisively. "We'll scatter them around the room like Easter eggs. Everyone's watching the band. No one'll notice."

"But how will we know whose key is whose? They're identical!"

"We'll guess. We'll use our psychic powers. I'll take half," he adds, and starts grabbing key cards out of the wallet.

Slowly, cautiously, we get to our feet. The lights are dim and the band is playing a Coldplay song, and no one turns a hair. Lorcan walks authoritatively toward the bar, leans slightly to his left, and deposits a key card on a bar table.

"Sorry," I hear him say charmingly. "Lost my balance."

Following his lead, I approach another group, pretend to look at a light fitting, and drop three cards down onto the mirrored surface of the table. The sound of them landing is covered by the band, and no one even notices.

Lorcan is planting cards on the main long bar, moving along quickly, deftly reaching between bar stools and behind backs.

"You dropped this, I think?" he says, as a girl turns a questioning face to him.

"Oh, thank you!" She takes the card from him, and my insides curdle. I am half appalled and half delighted at what feels like the most massive prank. There's no *way* that's the key to her room. There are going to be some very angry guests later on. . . .

Now Lorcan is up near the stage, leaning right over a blond lady and blatantly flipping a key card onto her table. He meets my eye and winks at me, and I want to laugh. I get rid of my remaining cards as quickly as I can and hurry back to Noah, who is now fully asleep. I summon a waiter and quickly scribble a signature on our bill, then hoist Noah into my arms and wait for Lorcan to join us.

"If I'm found out, my name will be *mud*," I murmur.

"In Bulgaria," points out Lorcan. "Population 7.5 million. That's like your name being mud in Bogotá."

"Well, I wouldn't want my name to be mud in Bogotá either."

"Why not? Maybe it is already. Have you been to Bogotá?"

"Yes, as it happens," I inform him. "And I can tell you, my name is *not* mud there."

"Maybe they were being polite."

This conversation is so ridiculous, I can't help smiling.

"Come on, then. Let's escape before we get attacked by angry key holders."

As we walk out of the bar, Lorcan holds out his arms.

"I'll carry Noah if you like. He looks heavy."

"Don't worry." I smile automatically. "I'm used to it."

"Doesn't mean he's not heavy."

"Well . . . OK."

It feels odd, handing over Noah to Lorcan. But the truth is, I do have a dodgy shoulder and it is a bit of a relief. We reach our suite and Lorcan carries Noah straight to his bed. He's so sound asleep, he doesn't stir. I remove his shoes but nothing else. He can clean his teeth and put his pajamas on tomorrow night, if he wants to.

I turn off Noah's light and head to the door, and for a moment Lorcan and I stand there together, for all the world like two parents.

"So," says Lorcan at last, and a luscious

450

anticipation starts to grow within me again. I can feel an internal limbering-up, that little dance of muscles yearning to be used. *I'm doing better than Lottie on the shag front* flashes through my mind, giving me a pinch of guilt — but only a small one. It's all for the best. She can have another honeymoon, another time.

"Drink?" I say, not because I really want one but to prolong the moment. This suite is the perfect setting for a shag-fest, what with all the smoky, sexy mirrors and soft, sensual rugs and the (fake) open fire flickering in the grate. There are also several conveniently placed pieces of furniture, which I've already eyed up.

When I've poured Lorcan a whiskey, I sit down with my own glass of wine on an amazing creation of a chair. It's made of deep-purple velvet, with wide rolltop arms and a deep seat and an erotic swoop to its back. I'm hoping that I strike quite a figure as I lean provocatively on one of the arms and allow my dress to ruck up. There's a delectable, urgent pulsing deep inside me. But, still, I'm not going to hurry anything. We can talk first. (Or just stare at each other with desperate want. Also good.)

"I wonder what Ben and Lottie are up to." Lorcan breaks the silence. "Presumably *not . . .*" He shrugs significantly.

"No."

"Poor guys. Whatever you think, it's the worst luck for them."

"I guess," I say noncommittally, and sip my wine.

"I mean, no sex on your honeymoon."

"Terrible." I nod. "Poor them."

"*And* they'd waited, hadn't they?" His face crinkles in remembrance. "Jesus. You'd think they'd shag in the loos and just have done with it."

"They tried, but they got caught."

"No way." He looks at me, startled. "You serious?"

"At Heathrow. In the business-class lounge."

Lorcan throws back his head and roars with laughter. "I'm going to rib Ben about that. So your sister fills you in on everything, does she? Even her sex life?"

"We're pretty close."

"Poor girl. Foiled even in the Heathrow loos. It's the worst luck."

I don't answer at once. The wine I'm drinking is stronger than the stuff I drank downstairs and it's going to my head. It's tipping me over the edge. My head is a bit of a maelstrom. Lorcan keeps talking about "bad luck," but he's wrong. Luck has nothing to do with it. Ben and Lottie have not consummated their marriage because of *me*. Because of my power. And suddenly I feel the urge to share this with him.

"Not so much *luck* . . ." I let the word trail in the air and, sure enough, Lorcan picks up on it at once.

"What do you mean?"

"It's not chance that Ben and Lottie haven't done it yet. It's design. *My* design. I've been in charge of the whole thing." I lean back proudly, feeling like the queen of remote-control honeymoon-fixing, all-powerful in my empress's chair.

"What?" Lorcan looks so taken aback, I feel another twinge of pride.

"I have an agent helping me on the ground," I clarify. "I issue commands, he carries them out."

"What the hell are you talking about? *Agent?*"

"A member of staff at the hotel. He's been making sure that Ben and Lottie don't get it together till I get there. We've been acting as a team. And it's worked! They haven't."

"But how — What —" He rubs his head, baffled. "I mean, how do you stop a couple from having sex?"

God, he's slow.

"Easy. Mess with their beds, spike their

drinks, stalk them everywhere they go . . .
Then there was the peanut-oil massage —"

"That was *you*?" He looks thunderstruck.

"It was *all* me! I orchestrated everything!"
I produce my phone and wave it at him.
"It's all in here. All the texts. All the instructions. I managed it all."

There's a long silence. I'm waiting for him
to say how brilliant I am, but he looks
stunned.

"You sabotaged your own sister's honeymoon?" There's something about his expression which makes me feel a little uneasy.
Also the word "sabotaged."

"It was the only way! What else was I supposed to do?" Something about this conversation is going wrong. I don't like his
expression, or mine. I know I appear defensive, which is not a good look. "You *do*
understand I had to put a stop to it? Once
they've consummated it, it'll be too late for
an annulment. So I had to do something.
And this was the only way —"

"Are you *nuts,* woman? Are you out of
your *mind*?" Lorcan's tone is so forceful, I
recoil in shock. "Of course it wasn't the only
way!"

"Well, it was the best way." I jut my chin
out.

"It was not the best way. By no stretch of

454

the imagination was it the best way. What if she finds out?"

"She won't."

"She might."

"Well . . ." I swallow. "So what? I had her interests at heart —"

"By having her massaged with peanut oil? What if she'd had an extreme reaction and died?"

"Shut up," I say uncomfortably. "She didn't."

"But you're happy for her to spend a night in pain."

"She's not in pain!"

"How do you know? *Jesus.*" He rests his head in his hands a moment, then looks up. "Again, what if she finds out? You're prepared to lose your relationship with her? Because that's what'll happen."

There's silence in the hotel suite, although words still seem to be bouncing off the smoky mirrors, sharp, accusing words. The erotic atmosphere has disintegrated. I can't find the phrases to rebut Lorcan. They're in my brain somewhere, but I'm feeling slow and a little dazed. I thought he would be impressed. I thought he'd understand. I thought —

"You talk about Unfortunate Choices?"

455

says Lorcan suddenly. "Well, what the hell is this?"

"What do you mean?" I glower at him. He's not allowed to talk about Unfortunate Choices. They're *my* thing.

"You suffer a painful divorce, so you rush out and decide to save your sister from the same fate by derailing her honeymoon. Sounds like a pretty fucking Unfortunate Choice to me."

I'm almost winded with shock. What? *What?*

"Shut up!" I manage in fury. "You don't know anything about it. I shouldn't have told you."

"It's her life." He stares back implacably. "*Hers.* And you're making a big mistake interfering with it. One you may live to regret."

"Amen," I say sarcastically. "Finished the sermon?"

Lorcan just shakes his head. He finishes his whiskey in a couple of gulps, and I know that's the end. He's going. He walks over to the door, then pauses. His back is tensed, I can tell. I think he feels as awkward as I do.

Uncomfortable thoughts are needling me. There's a painful dragging at the pit of my stomach. It feels a bit like guilt — not that I'd ever admit this to him. But there is something I must say. Something I must make clear.

"Just in case you were wondering." I wait till he turns his head. "I care about Lottie a great deal. A great deal." My voice gives a treacherous wobble. "She's not only my little sister, she's my friend. And I've done all this for *her.*"

Lorcan stares at me for a moment, his expression unreadable. "I know you think you're acting for the right reasons," he says at last. "I know you've had a lot of pain in your life that you want to protect Lottie from. But this is wrong. Deeply wrong. And you know it, Fliss. You do, really."

His eyes have softened. He feels sorry for me, I suddenly realize. *Sorry* for me. I can't stand it.

"Well, good night," I say shortly.

"Good night." He matches my tone and leaves the room without a further word.

19
LOTTIE

It was meant to be! This is my all-star, gold-plated, total dream scenario. Ben and me on a boat again. Skimming across the Aegean waves. On our way to total bliss.

Thank God we've left the Amba. I know it's luxurious and has five stars, but it's not the real Ikonos. It's not *us*. The moment we were dropped off for the day at the little bustling port, I felt something buried inside me come alive. *This* is what I remember of Ikonos. Old white houses with shutters, and shaded streets, and elderly women in black sitting on corners, and the dock for the ferry. The port was full of fishing boats and water taxis, and the overpowering smell of fish made my senses reel. I remember that smell. I remember all of it.

The sky is a bright morning blue and the sun is dazzling my eyelids, just as it always did. I'm lying back in the water taxi, the way I did when I was eighteen. My feet are in Ben's lap and he's idly fiddling with my toes and there's only one thing on both our minds.

My skin has recovered perfectly from its allergic reaction, and Ben was keen on a quick shag this morning. But I talked him out of it. How could we consummate our marriage in a boring old hotel bed when instead there's the chance to do it in the cove where we first did it, all those years ago? The romance of it makes me want to hug myself. Here we are after all these years! Going back to the guest house! Married! I wonder if Arthur will be there. I wonder if he'll recognize us. I don't think I look *that* different. I'm even wearing the same tiny tie-dye shorts I wore when I was eighteen . . . and praying desperately they don't split.

Spray splashes my face as we bump across the waves, and I lick the delicious saltiness off my lips. I'm surveying the coastline as we pass and remembering all the little villages we explored back then, with their narrow cobbled alleyways and unexpected treasures, like that half-ruined marble statue of a horse we once came across in the middle of a deserted square. I look up to share this thought with Ben, but he's engrossed in his iPad. I can hear rap coming from it and feel a flicker of irritation. Does he have to listen to that *now*?

"Do you think Arthur's still there?" I try to attract his attention. "And that old cook?"

"Can't be, surely." Ben looks up briefly. "I wonder what happened to Sarah."

Sarah again. Do I even know this girl?

The music seems to be getting louder, and now Ben's rapping along. He really can't rap. I mean, I'm being a dispassionate, loving wife here — and he's crap.

"It's lovely and peaceful out here, isn't it?" I say with a meaningful edge to my voice, but he doesn't take the hint. "Could we maybe not have the music on for a bit?"

"It's DJ Cram, babe," says Ben, and turns the volume up. *Fuck yo brudder* blares out across the beautiful sea, and I wince.

He's a selfish git.

The thought lands in my brain with no warning and makes me panic slightly. No. I didn't really mean "selfish." Or "git." It's all good. All blissful.

I don't mind rap music, anyway. And we can talk over the top of it.

"I can't *believe* I'm going back to the place where it all changed," I say, beginning a new tack. "That fire was, like, the turning point for my life."

"Will you stop going on about that bloody

460

fire?" says Ben irritably, and I stare back in hurt shock.

I shouldn't be surprised, I suppose. Ben's never been interested in the fire. He'd gone sponge-diving on the other side of the island for a couple of days when it happened, so he missed the whole thing and has always been chippy about that. Still, he doesn't have to be so snappy. He knows how important it was to me.

"Hey!" he suddenly exclaims. He's peering at his iPad and I can see he's just got a text. We're fairly near the coast, so there must be some random patch of signal.

"Who is it?"

Ben looks as though he's bursting with pride and excitement. Has he won something? "Heard of someone called Yuri Zhernakov? He only wants a private meeting with me."

"Yuri Zhernakov?" I gape at him. "How come?"

"He wants to buy the company."

"Wow! And do you want to sell?"

"Why not?"

Already my mind is whirring. This would be amazing! Ben would get a lump of cash, we could buy an old farmhouse in France. . . .

"Yuri wants to talk to *me.*" Ben seems

totally puffed up. "He asked for me personally. We're going to meet on his super-
yacht."

"That's amazing!" I squeeze his arm.

"I know. It *is* amazing. And Lorcan can
—" Ben stops himself. "Whatever," he says
moodily.

There's some weird vibe going on which I
don't understand, but I don't care. We're
going to move to France! And we're about
to have sex, finally! I've forgotten my earlier
irritation. I'm back to super-bliss. As I happily swig my Coke, I suddenly remember
something I've been meaning to say to Ben
for days.

"Hey, last year I met these scientists at
Nottingham who were researching a new
way to make paper. More eco. Something
about a special filtering process? Have you
heard of them?"

"No." Ben shrugs. "But Lorcan might
have."

"Well, you should link up with them. Do
some funding or whatever. Although I suppose if you're selling the company . . ." I
shrug too.

"Doesn't matter. That's a good idea." Ben
nudges me. "Do you have lots of good ideas
like that?"

"Millions." I grin back.

"I'm going to tell Lorcan right now." Ben starts typing at his iPad. "He's always going on about research and development. He thinks I'm not interested. Well, bollocks to that."

"Tell him about the Zhernakov meeting too," I suggest. "Maybe he'll have some good advice." Immediately, Ben's fingers freeze and his face closes up.

"Not a chance," he says at last, and shoots me a warning look. "And you're not saying a word to anyone either. Not a word."

20
FLISS

The morning after is always hell.

In Sofia, Bulgaria, after too many glasses of wine, an excruciating argument, and a night of sexual frustration, the morning after achieves fresh levels of hellishness.

From Lorcan's expression, he feels the same way. Noah ran joyfully to greet him as soon as we entered the dining room, which is why I'm sitting with him, *not* through choice. He's savagely buttering a piece of toast, and I'm crumbling a croissant. From our desultory conversation we've established that we both slept terribly, that the coffee is abysmal, that there are 2.4 Bulgarian leva to the pound and that the flight to Ikonos today hasn't been delayed, as far as we can glean from the airline website.

Areas we *haven't* touched on: Ben, Lottie, their marriage, their sexual conduct, Bulgarian politics, the state of the world economy, my attempts to sabotage my sister's honey-

464

moon and thus risk losing my relationship with her forever. Among others.

The restaurant is adjacent to the bar we were in last night, and I can see a pool attendant dabbing at the pristine water with a filtering net. I've no idea why they bother. I expect Noah is the only person to have swum in that pool all year. Although, to be fair, he might well have peed in it.

"Can I swim?" he says, as though reading my thoughts.

"No," I say shortly. "We're getting on the airplane soon."

Lorcan has his BlackBerry to his ear again. He's been speed-dialing all through breakfast but never getting through. I think I can guess who he's been calling, and this is confirmed when he says, "Ben, at *last,*" and pushes his chair back. I watch in slight resentment as he walks right away, to the side of the pool, and perches in front of the sauna entrance. How am I supposed to eavesdrop now?

I try to ignore my tension by slicing up an apple for Noah. When Lorcan returns, I force myself not to grip his lapels and demand information. Instead, I ask, with only moderate urgency:

"Well? Have they done it?"

Lorcan gives me a disbelieving look. "Is

that all you're interested in?"

"Yes," I say defiantly.

"Well, they haven't. They've just arrived at the guest house. I guess they're planning to do it there."

The *guest house*? I stare at him in horror. I can't get at them there. There's no Nico. It's out of my power zone. Shit. *Shit.* I'm going to be just too late —

"Your sister is quite something," Lorcan continues with animation. "She's come up with a great idea for the company. We're far too weak on the research-and-development side, and I've known it for a while. But she's suggested we tie up with a research project in Nottingham she knows about. It's a tiny team, which is why I hadn't heard of it, but it sounds as if it's directly relevant to us. We could get some joint funding going. It's brilliant."

"Oh yes," I say, still preoccupied. "She'd know about that. She works for a pharmaceutical company. She meets scientists all the time."

"What exactly does she do?"

"Recruitment."

"Recruitment?" I look up to see that his eyes have lit up. "We need a new head of HR! This is perfect!"

"What?"

466

"She could head up HR, keep the good ideas coming, get involved with the estate. . . ." I can see his mind working hard. "This is *just* what Ben needed! A wife who can be a business partner too. A helpmate. Someone to stand at his side and —"

"Stop right there!" I plant a hand on the table. "You're *not* poaching my sister to go and play a game of Happy Families in Staffordshire."

"Why not?" demands Lorcan. "What's your problem with it?"

"My problem is it's nonsense! It's ridiculous!"

Lorcan stares at me silently for a moment, and I feel the briefest of shivers under his gaze.

"You really take the biscuit," he says at last. "How do you know you're not ruining your sister's great love? How do you know this isn't her chance for a fantastically happy life?"

"Oh, for God's sake." I shake my head impatiently. I'm not even going to answer that question, it's so stupid.

"I think Ben and Lottie have every chance of being happy," he says firmly. "And I, for one, am going to encourage them."

"You can't switch sides!" I glare at him in fury.

"I was never on your side," retorts Lorcan. "Your side is the nutty side."

"The nutty side." Noah picks up on this and decides it's hilarious. "The nutty side!" He falls about in laughter. "Mummy's on the nutty side!"

I glare at Lorcan, stirring my coffee viciously. Traitor.

"Morning, everyone."

I look up to see Richard approaching the table. He looks about as cheery as the rest of us, i.e., suicidal.

"Morning," I say. "Did you sleep well?"

"Terribly." He scowls and pours himself some coffee, then glances at my phone. "So, have they done it yet?"

"For God's sake!" I take out some of my resentment on him. "You're obsessed!"

"You can talk," mutters Lorcan.

"Why do you keep asking if they've done it?" says Noah alertly.

"Well, aren't you obsessed too?" counters Richard.

"No, I'm not *obsessed.* And, no, they haven't done it." I put him out of his misery.

"Done what?" asks Noah.

"Put the sausage in the cupcake," says Lorcan, draining his coffee.

"Lorcan!" I snap. "*Don't* say things like that!"

468

Noah has exploded with laughter. "Put the sausage in the cupcake!" he crows. "The sausage in the cupcake!"

Great. I glare at Lorcan, who stares back, unmoved. And, anyway, *cupcake*? I've never heard it called that.

"I suppose you think it's funny." Richard turns his ire on Lorcan. "I suppose this is all a joke to you."

"Oh, give it a break, Sir Lancelot." Lorcan loses his patience. "Isn't it time to butt out? You must want to give up by now. No woman is worth this rigmarole."

"Lottie would be worth ten times this 'rigmarole,' as you put it." Richard juts his chin at Lorcan. "And I'm not giving up when I'm only six hours away from seeing her. I've worked it out exactly." He takes a piece of toast from the rack. "Six hours."

"Sorry." I put a hand on his. "But you should know. It'll be more than that. They're not at the hotel anymore. They're at the guest house."

Richard stares at me, wide-eyed with horror. *"Bugger,"* he says at last.

"I know."

"They'll shag there, for definite."

"They might not," I say, to convince myself as much as him. "And *mind your language,* please. Little pitchers." I gesture at Noah.

"They will." Richard is hunched with gloom. "That place is Lottie's fantasyland. It's her yellow brick road. Of *course* she'll —" He stops himself, just in time. "Put the sausage in the muffin."

"Cupcake," corrects Lorcan.

"Shut *up*!" I say, exasperated.

As we're all sitting there silently, a waitress approaches the table with a coloring book for Noah, and he accepts it with delight.

"You can draw your mummy or daddy," she suggests, producing a box of crayons.

"My daddy isn't here," explains Noah politely, and gestures at Lorcan and Richard. "Neither of them is my daddy."

Great. What kind of impression is he giving?

"It's a business trip," I say, smiling quickly.

"My daddy lives in London," says Noah chattily. "But he's moving to Hollywood."

"Hollywood!"

"Yes. He's going to live next to a movie star."

My stomach plunges in dismay. Oh God, he's doing it again. Even after we had the Big Talk. As soon as the waitress has moved away, I turn to Noah, trying to hide my agitation.

"Noah, sweetheart. Do you remember

what we said about telling the truth?"

"Yes," he says equably.

"So why did you say that Daddy's moving to Hollywood?" I'm losing my cool, but I can't help it. "You can't say things like that, Noah! People will believe you!"

"But it's true."

"No, it isn't! Daddy isn't moving to Hollywood!"

"Yes, he is. Look, here's his address. It says Beverly Hills. Daddy says that's the same as Hollywood. He's going to have a swimming pool and I can swim in it!" Noah reaches into his pocket and produces a slip of paper. I stare at it in disbelief. It's in Daniel's writing.

NEW ADDRESS
Daniel Phipps and Trudy Vanderveer
5406 Aubrey Road
Beverly Hills
CA 90210

I blink several times in bewilderment. Beverly Hills? What? I mean — *What?*

"Just wait there a minute, Noah," I say, in a voice which doesn't sound like mine. I'm already speed-dialing Daniel and pushing back my chair.

"Fliss," he replies in his infuriating *I've*

471

just been doing yoga, how about you? voice.

"What's all this about Beverly Hills?" My words are falling over one another. "You're moving to Beverly Hills?"

"Babe, calm down," he says.

Babe?

"How can I calm down? Is it true?"

"So, Noah told you."

My heart falls like a clanging thing. It's true. He's moving to L.A. and he didn't even tell me.

"It's Trudy's work," he's saying now. "You know she's in media law? This great opportunity arose for her, and I have dual nationality anyway. . . ."

His words carry on, but they fade to meaningless sounds. For some reason I'm remembering our wedding day. We had a very cool wedding. All ironic twists and fun details like custom-made cocktails. I was so concerned with making sure my guests would have a good time that I forgot to check the small detail of whether I was marrying the right man.

". . . fabulous realtor, and she came up with this place *under* budget —"

"But, Daniel." I cut him off in midstream. "What about Noah?"

"Noah?" He sounds surprised. "Noah can come out and visit."

"He's seven. He's at school."

"In the holidays, then." Daniel sounds unconcerned. "We'll make something work."

"When do you leave?"

"Monday."

Monday?

I close my eyes, breathing hard. The hurt I'm feeling on Noah's behalf is indescribable. It's physical pain that makes me want to curl into a ball. Daniel's moving to L.A. with barely a thought of how he'll maintain a relationship with his only child, our son. Our precious, charming, imaginative son. He's putting five thousand miles between them in the blink of an eyelid.

"Right." I try to gather myself. There's no point saying anything else. "Daniel, I have to go. I'll talk to you soon."

I switch off and swivel round, intending to join the others. But something strange is happening to me. An unfamiliar, scary sensation. Suddenly a sound escapes from my lips. A kind of yelp, like a dog might make.

"Fliss?" Lorcan has got out of his seat. "You OK?"

"Mummy?" Noah looks worried.

The two men make brief eye contact and Richard nods.

"Hey, buddy," Richard says easily to Noah. "Let's go and buy some chewing gum for the flight."

"Chewing gum!" yells Noah ecstatically, and follows Richard off.

I give another involuntary yelp, and Lorcan takes me by the elbows.

"Fliss . . . are you *crying*?"

"No!" I say at once. "I never cry in the daytime. It's my rule. I never ever cryyy-eee." The word disintegrates into a third of these strange, high-pitched yelps. Something wet is on my cheek. Is that a tear?

"What did Daniel say?" says Lorcan gently.

"He's moving to L.A. He's leaving us. . . ." I can see people looking over from other tables. "Oh God." I bury my head in my hands. "I can't . . . I have to stop. . . ."

I emit a fourth yelp, which sounds a bit more like a sob. It feels as if something is looming up inside me, something unstoppable and violent and loud. The last time I felt like this, I was giving birth.

"You need somewhere private," says Lorcan swiftly. "You're going to have a meltdown. Where shall we go?"

"I've checked out of my room," I mutter, between gasps. "They should have a crying room. Like a smoking room."

"I've got it." Lorcan grabs my arm and leads me through the tables to the swimming-pool area. "Steam room." He doesn't wait for a reply but opens the glass door and pushes me inside.

The atmosphere is so thick, I have to grope for a seat. The air is dense with vapor and there's a soft, herby scent.

"Cry," says Lorcan through the misty air. "No one's watching. No one can hear, Fliss. Cry."

"Can't." I swallow hard. Everything in me is resisting. The odd yelp still escapes, but I can't surrender.

"Then tell me. Daniel's moving to L.A.," he prompts.

"Yes. He won't see Noah anymore, and he doesn't even *care*." A shudder overcomes me. "He didn't even tell me."

"I thought you wanted him out of your life? That's what you said."

"I did," I say, momentarily confused. "I do. I think I do. But this is so final. It's such a rejection of us both." Something is rising up in me again. Something churning and powerful. I think it could be grief. "It means it's over. Our family's ooooover." And now the churning is threatening to consume me. "Our whole family is ooooover. . . ."

"Come here, Fliss," says Lorcan quietly,

and proffers a shoulder. Immediately, I re-coil.

"I can't *cry* on you," I say, my voice jerky. "Look away."

"Of course you can cry on me." He laughs. "We've had sex, remember."

"That was sex. This is *far* more embar-rassing." I gulp. "Look away. Go away."

"I'm not looking anywhere," he says steadily. "And I'm not going anywhere. Come on."

"I can't," I say desperately.

"Come *on,* you stupid woman." He holds out his suited arm, pearlescent with steam. And finally, gratefully, I descend on it in a volcano of sobs.

We're there for a while — me shuddering and sobbing and coughing, and Lorcan rub-bing my back. For some reason I keep remembering Noah's delivery. It was an emergency C-section and I was terrified, but, all the way through, Daniel was beside me in green scrubs, holding my hand. I never doubted him then. Back then I never doubted anything for a minute. And that makes me want to cry all over again.

At last I look up and push my hair back off my sweaty face. I can feel that my nose is swollen and my eyes are puffy. I haven't

476

cried like that since I was about ten, probably.

"I'm sorry —" I begin, but Lorcan holds up a hand.

"No. No apologies."

"But your suit!" I begin to become aware of exactly what we're doing here. We're sitting in a steam room, both fully dressed.

"Every divorce has casualties," says Lorcan calmly. "Think of my suit as one of the casualties of yours. Besides which," he adds, "steam is good for suits."

"At least our skin will be clean," I say.

"There you go. Loads of pluses."

A concealed mechanism in the corner is puffing fresh steam into the tiny chamber, and the air is becoming more opaque. I pull up my feet onto the mosaic-tiled bench and hug my knees tight, feeling as though the steam is a protective barrier. It's intimate in here. But it's private too.

"When I got married, I knew life wouldn't be perfect," I say into the mist. "I didn't expect a rose garden. And then, when I got divorced, I didn't expect a rose garden there either. But I hoped I might at least get . . . I don't know. A patio."

"A patio?"

"You know. A little terrace. Something small with a few plants to tend. Something with a tiny bit of optimism and love. But what I have is a post-nuclear war zone."

"That's good." Lorcan gives a little laugh. "What do you have? Not a rose garden?"

"It's kind of alien territory," he says after a pause. "Like a moonscape."

Our eyes meet through the murky atmosphere and we don't need to say any more. We get it.

The steam is still puffing and wreathing around us. It feels healing. It feels as though it's lifting troublesome thoughts up away with it, leaving behind a kind of clarity. And the longer I sit there, the clearer things are to me. There's a growing heaviness in my stomach. Lorcan was right. Not just now, but last night. He was right. This has all been a mistake.

I have to give this mission up right now. It's flashing through my brain like a TV headline. *Give up. Give up.* I can't carry on. I can't risk losing Lottie.

Yes, I want to protect my little sister from the same pain I had. But it's her life. I can't make her choices for her. If she breaks up with Ben, so be it. If she goes through a divorce, so be it. If they're married for seventy years and have twenty grand-children, so be it.

I feel as though a kind of madness has

been propelling me down a crazy path. Was it really about Lottie, or was it about Daniel and me? Is Lorcan right? Has this been my own Unfortunate Choice? Oh God, what have I been *doing*?

I'm suddenly aware that I muttered those last few words aloud. "Sorry," I add. "I just . . . I realized . . ." I raise my head, feeling abject.

"You've been doing your best to help your sister," says Lorcan, almost kindly. "In a totally deluded, fuckwit, wrong-headed way."

"What —" I clap my hand to my mouth. "Oh God. What if she found out?" The thought is so horrifying, I feel almost faint. I was so determined to succeed, I never considered the downside. I've been an absolute fool.

"She doesn't need to," says Lorcan. "Not if you turn round and go home and never say a word. I won't tell."

"Nico won't tell either. He's my guy at the hotel." I'm breathing hard, as though I've had a narrow escape. "I think I'm OK. She'll never know."

"So the honeymoon-sabotage campaign is off?"

"As of this moment." I nod. "I'll call Nico. He'll be relieved." I look at Lorcan. "I'm never going to interfere in my sister's life again," I say with emphasis. "Hold me to that. Hold me to my vow."

"It's a deal." He nods seriously. "And what are you going to do now?"

I shake my head. "I don't know. Get to the airport. Take it from there." I tug at my sweaty hair, remembering again that I'm sitting in a steam room in my clothes. "I must look a sight."

"I agree," says Lorcan seriously. "You can't get on a plane like that. You'd better go under the cold-drench shower."

"The cold-drench shower?" I stare at him disbelievingly.

"Closes up the pores. Invigorates the circulation. Gets rid of snotty tearstains."

He's teasing me. I think. Is he?

"I will if you will," I challenge him.

"Why not?" He shrugs. I feel a rising giggle. We *cannot* be planning to do this.

"OK, here goes." I push the door open and hold it politely for Lorcan. I can see the stares and nudges from hotel guests at the sight of two fully-clothed people emerging from the steam room, one in a business suit.

"After you." Lorcan gestures politely at the cold-drench shower. "I'll pull the lever, if you like."

"Go on, then." I start to laugh as I step underneath. A moment later a blast of freezing water descends on me, and I give a tiny scream.

"Mummy!" A piercing voice hails me in delight. "You had a shower with your *clothes on.*" Noah is watching from the table with Richard, his face bright with disbelief.

Lorcan takes his turn and lifts his face up to the drenching shower.

"There," he says to me when it's finished. "Isn't that refreshing? Doesn't life seem better?" He shakes out his wet suit sleeve.

I pause a moment, wanting to answer him honestly. "Yes," I say at last. "Much better. Thank you."

21
LOTTIE

I don't quite know how to react. Here we are. Back at the guest house. And it's just as it was. Kind of.

As soon as we descended from the water taxi, Ben took a call from Lorcan, which *really* annoyed me. I mean, this is our big, romantic, meaningful moment — and he takes a call. That's like Humphrey Bogart saying, "We'll always have — Sorry, love, just got to take this."

Anyway. Be positive, Lottie. Relish the moment. I've been thinking about this place for *fifteen years*. And here I am.

I'm standing on the wooden jetty, waiting for waves of nostalgia and enlightenment to engulf me. I'm waiting to cry and maybe think of something poignant to say to Ben. But the weird thing is, I don't really want to cry. I feel a bit blank.

I can just glimpse the guest house, far above, from where I'm standing. I can see the familiar dusty ochre stone and a couple of windows. It's smaller than I remember, and one of the shutters is drooping. My gaze lowers to the cliff. There are the steps cut into the rock, forking halfway down. One set leads to the jetty where we're standing and the other leads to the main beach. They've put in metal barriers, which kind of ruin the look. And a railing across the top of the cliff. And there's a safety sign. A *safety sign?* We never had a safety sign.

Anyway. Be positive.

Ben rejoins me, and I take his hand. The beach is round a jutting outcrop of rock, so I can't see yet if that's changed. But how can a beach change? A beach is a beach.

"What shall we do first?" I ask softly. "Guest house? Beach? Or secret cove?"

Ben squeezes my hand back. "Secret cove."

And now, at last, I start to feel ripples of excitement. The secret cove. The place we first undressed each other, shaking with hot, insatiable, teenage desire. The place where we did it three, four, five times in a day. The idea of revisiting it — in all senses — is so exciting that I shiver.

"We'll need to hire a boat."

He'll sail me round to the cove like he always used to, my feet up on the side of the boat. And we'll drag the boat up onto the sand and find that sheltered patch of sand, and . . .

"Let's get a boat." Ben's voice is thick, and I can tell he's as excited as I am.

"D'you think they still hire them out at the beach?"

"Only one way to find out."

With a sudden lightness of heart, I take hold of his hand and pull him toward the steps. We'll go straight to the beach, we'll get a boat; it's all going to happen.

"Come on!" I'm leaping up the rocky steps, my heart thumping with excitement. We're nearly at the fork in the steps. We'll see that familiar stretch of beautiful golden sand at any moment, waiting for us after all this time —

Oh my God.

I'm staring down onto the beach in shock. What's happened to it? Who are all these *people*?

When we were staying at the guest house, the beach seemed a massive, empty space. There were about twenty of us at the guest house, tops, and we used to spread ourselves over the sand so no one was crowded.

What I'm staring at now looks like an occupation. Or the morning after a festival. There are about seventy people filling the

484

sand in disheveled groups, some still co-cooned in sleeping bags. I can see the remains of a fire. There are a couple of tents. Most of them are students, I guess, appraising them. Or eternal students, maybe.

As we're standing there uncertainly, a young guy with a goatee comes partway up the steps and greets us in a South African accent.

"Hi. You look lost."

I feel *lost,* I want to retort, but instead I muster a smile. "Just . . . looking."

"We're visiting," says Ben easily. "We came here years ago. It's changed."

"Oh." The light in the guy's face changes. "You're one of *those.* From the golden age."

"The golden age?"

"That's what we call it." He laughs. "We get so many people your age coming back, telling us how it used to be before they built the hostel. Most of them spend the whole time whinging about how it's been ruined. You coming down?"

As we follow him, I'm prickling a little at his words. "Whinging" is a bit aggressive. And "your age"? What does that mean? I mean, obviously we're a little older than he is, but we're still, broadly speaking, *young.* I'm still in the same *category.*

"What hostel?" asks Ben as we arrive on the beach. "Don't you stay at the guest house?"

"A few do." The guy shrugs. "Not many. It's a fairly ropy outfit. I think the old guy's just sold it. No, we're at the hostel. A few hundred yards behind. It was built maybe . . . ten years ago? They had a big advertising campaign. Really worked. This place is so amazing," he adds as he walks away. "The sunsets are unbelievable. Take care now."

Ben smiles back, but I feel like exploding with fury. I can't believe they've built a hostel. I feel livid. This was our place. How dare they advertise it?

And just look at the way they treat it. There's rubbish everywhere. I can see cans and empty crisp packets and even a couple of used condoms. At the sight of them, my stomach turns. They've been having *sex* all over the place. That's so *gross*.

I mean, I know we used to have sex on the beach, but that was different. That was *romantic.*

"Where's the boat guy?" I say, looking around. There used to be a lizard-like man who hired out his two boats every day, but I can't see him anywhere. There's a tall strapping guy pushing a boat out into the water, and I hurry over the sand to the sea.

"Hi! Excuse me! Hold on a minute." He turns, his smile white in his tanned face, and I plant a hand on his dinghy.

"Could you tell me, do they still hire out boats here? Is this a hire boat?"

"Yes." He nods. "But you have to get in early. They're all gone. You could try tomorrow? The list is at the hostel."

"I see." I pause, then add plaintively, "The trouble is, we're here only today. My husband and I. It's our honeymoon. And we really did want a boat."

I'm silently willing him to be gallant and offer us his boat. But he doesn't. He just keeps pushing it out into the water and says pleasantly, "That's tough."

"The thing is, this is very special to us," I explain, splashing after him. "We really, really wanted to go sailing. We wanted to visit this tiny secret cove we used to know."

"The little cove that way?" He gestures round the headland.

"Yes!" I say. "Do you know it?"

"You don't need to sail there." He looks surprised. "You can get to it via the walkway."

"The walkway?"

"It's farther inland." He points. "A big wooden walkway. They built it a few years ago. Opened up the whole area."

I stare at him in horror. *They built a walkway to the secret cove?* This is desecration. It's a travesty. I'm going to write a furious letter to . . . someone. It was our secret. It was supposed to stay secret. How are we supposed to have sex there now?

"Everyone goes there?"

"Oh yeah. It's quite popular." He grins. "Between you and me, it's where people go to skin up."

Skin up? I stare at him in even greater horror. Our perfect, romantic, idyllic cove is now Drug Central?

I rub my face, trying to adjust to this new, grim picture.

"So . . . there'll be people there now?"

"Oh yeah. There was a party there last night. They'll all be asleep now, though. See you." He pushes off and unfurls his sail.

That's it, then. Our whole plan, ruined. I paddle back through the shallows to where Ben is standing.

"It was so perfect," I say in despair. "And now they've ruined it. I can't bear it. I mean, look." I gesture wildly. "It's hideous! It's a hellhole!"

"For God's sake, Lottie!" says Ben, a little impatiently. "You're overreacting. We used to party on the beach, remember? We used to leave rubbish around. Arthur was always complaining."

"Not used condoms."

"We probably did." He shrugs.

"No, we didn't!" I retort indignantly. "I was on the pill!"

"Oh." He shrugs again. "I forgot."

He *forgot*? How could you forget whether you used condoms or not with the love of your life?

I want to say, *If you really loved me, you'd remember we didn't use condoms,* but I bite my tongue. An argument about condom use is not what you want on your honeymoon. Instead, I hunch my shoulders and stare mournfully out to sea.

I'm so disappointed, I want to cry. This is so absolutely not what I imagined. I suppose, to be honest, I didn't imagine anyone on the beach at all. I imagined that we'd have it totally to ourselves. We would run over the deserted sand and leap through the foamy surf, landing in a perfect embrace while violins played. So maybe that was a *tad* unrealistic. But this is the opposite extreme.

"Well, what shall we do?" I say at last.

"We can still enjoy ourselves." Ben pulls me close and gives me a kiss. "It's good to be back, anyway, isn't it? Still the same sand. Still the same sea."

"Yes." I gratefully sink into his kiss.

"Still the same Lottie. Same sexy shorts." His hands cup my bum, and I feel a sudden urge to reclaim at least some of my fantasy.

"Remember this?" I give him my bag to hold. I take a deep breath, preparing myself, then give a light hop and a skip and launch into what is supposed to be a flawless series of cartwheels down the beach.

Ow. Oof.

Argh. Shit. My *head.*

I don't know what happened, except my arms buckled beneath my weight, and there were a few shouts of alarm around me, and I landed hard on my head. Now I'm sprawled in an ungainly position on the sand, my breath coming short in shock.

My arm is throbbing in pain and my mind is throbbing in humiliation. I can't do cartwheels anymore? When did *that* happen?

"Sweets." Ben approaches, looking embarrassed. "Don't do yourself an injury." His gaze shifts to my shorts. "Slight accident, I think?"

I follow his gaze and feel a fresh jolt of dismay. There's a rip in my tie-dye shorts. I've split them, in the worst possible place. I want to *die.*

Ben hauls me to my feet, and I rub my arm, wincing. I must have twisted it or something.

"You OK?" says a nearby girl in denim shorts and a bikini top, who looks about fifteen. "You need to take off with a bit more spring. Like this." She throws herself lightly over and performs a perfect cartwheel, followed by a roundoff.

Bitch.

"Thanks," I mutter. "I'll bear that in mind." I take my bag back from Ben and there's an awkward silence. "So . . . what *shall* we do?" I say at last. "Check out the cove?"

"I need some coffee," says Ben firmly. "And I want to see the guest house, don't you?"

"Of course!" I feel a last flicker of hope. Even if the beach is ruined, the guest house may not be. "Only, you go first up the steps," I add.

If my shorts are split, I'm *not* having him behind me.

I don't know if it's the cartwheel fiasco or maybe my heart monitor at the gym has been lying to me, but I'm not as fit as I thought I was. And 113 steps is a lot of steps. I find myself grabbing on to the handrail and using it to haul myself upward, and I'm glad Ben can't see me. I'm hot in the face, and my hair has escaped from its elastic, and I'm puffing in a deeply non-sexy way. The sun is starting to glare down, so I'm avoiding looking upward, but as we near the top I glance up and blink in surprise. There's a figure silhouetted against the top of the cliff. A girl.

"Hello there!" she calls down in an English accent. "Are you guests?"

She's a stunning girl, I realize as I get higher. With quite an extraordinary chest. All the clichés are springing to my mind. Her boobs look like two brown moons straining against her strappy white tank top. No, two brown lively puppies. Even *I'm* so fascinated I want to touch them. She's leaning over to greet us as we stumble upward, and I can see right into the cavernous depths of her cleavage.

Which means Ben can too.

"Well done!" she laughs as we eventually reach the top. I'm panting so hard I can't speak. Nor can Ben, but he looks as if he's trying to convey something to me — or is it to the extraordinarily shaped girl?

It's to the extraordinarily shaped girl.

"Fucking hell!" he manages at last — and he sounds absolutely stunned. "Sarah!"

22
LOTTIE

My mind is a whirl. I don't know what to focus on. I don't know where to start.

First of all, there's the guest house. How can it be so different from the way I remember? Everything is smaller and shabbier and kind of less *iconic.* We're sitting on the veranda, which is far less impressive than I remember and has been painted in a quite revolting beige color that's peeling away in strips. The olive grove is just a scrubby patch of ground with a few sparse trees. The view is good, but no different from any other Greek island view.

And Arthur. *How* could I have been impressed by him? *How* could I have sat at his feet, lapping up his pearls of wisdom? He's not wise. He's not a sage. He's a seventy-something alcoholic lech.

He's tried to grope me twice already.

"Don't come back," he's saying, waving his roll-up in the air. "I tell all you young

493

people. Don't revisit. Youth is still where you left it, and that's where it should stay. What are you returning for? Anything that was worth taking on life's journey, you'll already have taken with you."

"Dad." Sarah rolls her eyes. "Enough already. They *did* come back. And I'm glad they did." She twinkles at Ben. "You were just in time. We've sold up. We're leaving next month. More coffee?"

As she leans over to pour the coffee, I can't help staring. Up close, she isn't any less extraordinarily shaped. Everything about her is sheeny and silky, and her breasts are straining against her tank top as though they're in breast-yoga class and are showing off in front of everybody.

And this is the other reason that my mind is in a whirl. Several reasons, in fact. Number one: she's gorgeous. Number two: it's quite clear that she and Ben had some whole history here at the guest house before I even arrived. They keep alluding to it and laughing and changing the subject. Number three: there's a spark between them still. If I can see it, surely they can see it? Surely they can feel it? What does it mean?

What does any of it *mean*?

I take my coffee from Sarah with trembling hands. I thought coming back here to the

494

guest house would be the glorious finale to our honeymoon, where all the threads would come together in a big satisfying knot. Instead, it feels as though all sorts of bright new threads have appeared and nothing is tied up at all. Especially Ben. He feels like he's unraveling away from me. He won't meet my eye, and when I put my arm around him, he shrugged it off. I know Sarah saw, because she tactfully turned away.

"We get old." Arthur is still on his rant. "Life gets in the way of dreams. Dreams get in the way of life. That's the way it's always been. Anyone want a Scotch?" He brightens suddenly. "Sun's over the yardarm, Greek time."

"I'll have a Scotch," replies Ben, to my dismay. What's he doing? It's eleven in the morning. I don't want him to start sinking into glasses of Scotch. I shoot him a *Is that really a good idea, darling?* look, and he sends me back a glare, which I have a horrible feeling means, *Butt out and stop trying to run my life.*

And again Sarah is tactfully looking away from us.

Oh God, this is torture. Other women tactfully looking away while you exchange acrimonious glares with your husband is the most mortifying experience going. Tied with your tie-dye shorts splitting while you try to do a cartwheel.

"Good man! Come and choose a single malt." Arthur ushers Ben into the recesses of the guest house, and I'm left with Sarah on the veranda. The air feels prickly between us, and I don't know where to start. I desperately want to know . . . what, exactly?

"Delicious coffee." I retreat into politeness.

"Thanks." She smiles back, then sighs. "Lottie. I just want to say . . ." She spreads her hands. "I don't know if you're aware that Ben and I . . ."

"I wasn't," I say after a pause. "But I am now."

"It was the briefest of flings. I was out here seeing Dad, and we just clicked. It lasted a couple of weeks, if that. Please don't think . . ." Again she pauses. "I wouldn't want you to —"

"I wasn't thinking anything!" I cut her off brightly. "Nothing!"

"Good." She smiles again, showing perfect teeth. "It's lovely you've come back. Lots of good memories, I hope?"

"Yes, loads."

"It was an awesome summer." She sips her coffee. "That was the year Big Bill was out here. Did you know him?"

"Yes, I knew Big Bill." I unbend a little. "And Pinky."

"And the two Neds? They got arrested one night when I was here," she says, grinning. "They were thrown into jail, and Dad had to bail them out."

"I *heard* about that." I sit up, suddenly enjoying this conversation. "Did you hear about the fishing boat sinking?"

"God, yeah." She nods. "Dad told me about it. What with the fire, it was, like, the year of disasters. Even poor Ben got the flu. He was really ill."

What did she say? The flu?

"The flu?" I echo, in a strangled voice. "Ben?"

"It was awful." She draws her brown feet up onto her chair. "I got quite worried about him. He was delirious. I had to nurse him through the night. I sang him Joni Mitchell songs." She laughs.

My brain is whirring in a panic. It was *Sarah* who nursed him through the flu. *Sarah* who sang to him.

And he thinks it was me.

And that was the moment he "knew he loved me." He told a whole audience so.

"Right!" I say, trying to sound relaxed. "Wow. Well done, you." I swallow. "But no point dwelling on the past, eh? So, er . . . how many guests do you have at the moment?"

I want to get off this topic fast, before Ben comes back. But Sarah ignores me.

"He said the funniest things while he was delirious," she reminisces. "He wanted to go flying. I was like, 'Ben, you're ill! Lie down!' Then he said I was his guardian angel. He kept saying it, over and over. I was his guardian angel."

"Who's your guardian angel?" Ben's voice greets us. He appears on the veranda, holding a glass. "Your dad's taken a call, by the way. Who's your guardian angel?" he repeats.

My stomach is churning. I have to stop this conversation right now.

"Look at that olive tree!" I say shrilly, but both Ben and Sarah ignore me.

"Don't you remember, Ben?" Sarah laughs easily, throwing back her head. "When you had the flu and I nursed you through the night? You said I was your guardian angel. Nurse Sarah." She pokes him teasingly with her foot. "Remember Nurse Sarah? Remember the Joni Mitchell songs?"

Ben seems almost frozen. He glances sharply at me, then back at Sarah, then at me again. His brow is riven with confusion.

"But . . . but . . . *you* nursed me, Lottie."

My cheeks have flamed red. I don't know what to say. Why did I take the credit for nursing him, *why*?

"Lottie?" Sarah says in surprise. "But she wasn't even there! It was me, and *I'm* getting the Brownie points, thank you! I'm the one who sat up and mopped your brow till dawn. Don't tell me you've forgotten that," she adds, mock reproachfully.

"I haven't *forgotten,*" says Ben, his voice suddenly intense. "Jesus! Of course I haven't forgotten! I've remembered that night all my life. But I remembered wrong. I thought it was . . ." He looks accusingly at me.

I'm prickling all over. I have to speak. Everyone's waiting.

"Maybe I got confused." I swallow hard. "With . . . another time."

"What other time?" demands Ben. "I only had the flu once. And now it turns out you didn't nurse me, Sarah did. Which I find confusing." His voice is hard and unforgiving.

"I'm sorry." Sarah looks from face to face, as though she's picked up on the tense vibe between us. "It's not a big deal."

"It is!" Ben puts his fist to his head. "Don't you realize? *You* saved me. *You* were my guardian angel, Sarah. This changes —"

499

He stops himself.

I stare at him in indignation. This changes what? I was his guardian angel till three minutes ago. You can't just switch guardian angels because you feel like it.

"Not that again!" Sarah shakes her head, smiling. "I told you," she adds to me, as though trying to lighten the atmosphere. "He said all kinds of crazy stuff about angels and all sorts. Anyway." She clearly wants to get off the subject herself. "So. What do you guys do for a living?"

Ben glares at me, then takes a slug of whiskey. "I make paper," he begins.

As he's explaining about his paper company, I sip my tepid coffee, trembling a little. I can't believe my stupid white lie came out. But neither can I believe how seriously Ben is taking it. For God's sake. Who cares who nursed whom? I'm so distracted, I tune right out of the conversation, then wake up when I hear the words "move abroad" from Ben. Is he talking about France?

"Me too! I'll probably sail around the Caribbean for a while," Sarah is saying. "Do a bit of teaching to make money. See how it goes."

"That's what I want to do too." Ben is nodding vigorously. "Sailing's my passion.

If there's one thing I want to do in the next two years, it's spend more time on my boat."

"Have you ever sailed the Atlantic?"

"I want to." Ben's eyes light up. "I want to get a crew together. You in?"

"Definitely! And then a season sailing in the Caribbean?"

"It's a plan!"

"Settled." They high-five each other, laughing. "Do you sail?" adds Sarah politely to me.

"Not really." I'm staring at Ben, seething. He's never mentioned sailing the Atlantic to me. And how's that going to fit in with buying a French farmhouse? And what's all that matey high-fiving about? I want to address all of this straight-away, but I can't in front of Sarah.

I suddenly wish we'd never come back here. Arthur was right. Don't revisit.

"So you're selling up?" I say to Sarah.

"Yeah." Sarah nods. "It's a shame, but the party's over. The hostel took away our business. They're buying the land. They'll build more units."

"Bastards!" says Ben angrily.

"I guess." She shrugs, sanguine. "To be honest, business was never that great after the fire. I don't know how Dad has limped on for so long."

"The fire was *terrible,*" I chime in, glad to move on to a subject I can talk about. I'm hoping someone will mention the way I brilliantly took command and saved lots of lives, but all Sarah says is, "Yeah, what a drama."

"It was a faulty cooker or something, wasn't it?" says Ben.

"Oh no." Sarah shakes her head, and her earrings make little chinking noises. "That's what they thought at first. But then they worked out it was someone's candles. You know, in a bedroom. Scented candles." She glances at her watch. "I must get my casserole out. Excuse me."

As she disappears, Ben takes a sip of Scotch, then he glances at me and his expression changes.

"What's wrong?" He frowns. "Lottie? Are you OK?"

No, I'm not OK. The truth is so hideous, I can hardly contemplate it.

"It was me," I whisper at last, feeling sick.

"What do you mean, it was you?" He looks blank.

"I always had scented candles in my bedroom!" I whisper savagely. "Remember? All my candles? I must have left them alight. No one else had scented candles. The fire was my fault!"

I'm so shocked and distraught, tears are starting to my eyes. My great moment of triumph . . . It's all turned to dust. I wasn't the heroine of the hour. I was the thoughtless, stupid villain.

I'm waiting for Ben to throw his arms around me, or exclaim, or ask me more questions, or *something.* Instead, he looks uninterested.

"Well, it was a long time ago," he says at last. "It doesn't matter anymore."

"What do you mean, it doesn't matter?" I stare at him in disbelief. "Of *course* it matters! I ruined everyone's summer! I ruined this business! It's awful!"

I feel ill with guilt. And more than that — I feel as if I've been wrong, stupidly wrong, this whole time. All these years. I've been cherishing the wrong memory. Yes, I made a difference that night — but it was a disastrous difference. I could have killed someone. I could have killed lots of people. I'm not the woman I thought I was. *I'm not the woman I thought I was.*

I give a sudden little sob. It feels as though everything's fallen apart.

"Should I tell them? Should I confess everything?"

"For God's sake, Lottie," says Ben impatiently. "Of course you shouldn't. Get over

503

it. It was fifteen years ago. No one was hurt. No one cares."

"I care!" I say in shock.

"Well, you should stop. You go on and on about that *bloody* fire —"

"No, I don't!"

"Yes, you do."

Something inside me snaps.

"Well, you go on and on about sailing!" I shout, stung. "Where did all that come from?"

We glare at each other in a kind of shocked uncertainty. It's as though we're sizing each other up for a game but aren't sure of the rules. At last, Ben launches in with a fresh salvo.

"Basically, how can I trust anything you say anymore?" he says.

"What?" I recoil in utter shock.

"You didn't nurse me through the flu, but you let me think you did." His gaze is unrelenting. "Why would anyone do that?"

"I was . . . confused." I gulp. "I'm sorry, OK?"

Ben's expression doesn't alter. Sanctimonious bastard.

"Well, OK." I launch a counterattack. "Since we're doing home truths, can I ask how you're planning to sail a season in the Caribbean when we're moving to France?"

504

"We *might* move to France," he retorts impatiently. "We might not. We were only knocking a few ideas around. Jesus!"

"We weren't knocking ideas around!" I stare at him in horror. "We were making plans! I was basing my whole life on them!"

"Everything OK?" Sarah rejoins us on the veranda, and Ben instantly switches on his charming, lopsided smile.

"Great!" he says, as though nothing's happened. "We're just chilling out."

"More coffee? Or Scotch?"

I can't answer her. I'm realizing the awful truth: I'm basing my whole life on this guy sitting in front of me. This guy with his charming smile and easy manner who suddenly seems alien and unfamiliar and just *wrong,* like a guest bedroom in someone else's house. Not only do I not know him, I don't understand him, and I'm afraid I don't much *like* him.

I don't like my husband.

It's like a clanging in my ears. A death knell. I have made a monumental, humongous, terrifying mistake.

I have an instinctive, desperate longing for Fliss, but at the same time I realize I can never, *never* admit this to her. I'll have to stay married to Ben and pretend everything's OK till the end of my days. It's too embarrassing otherwise.

OK. So that's my fate. I feel quite calm about it. I married the wrong man and must simply live with it in misery forever. There's no other way.

". . . great place for a honeymoon," Sarah's saying as she sits down. "Are you having a good time?"

"Oh yeah," says Ben sarcastically. "Really great. Super." He flicks an antagonistic look at me, and I bristle.

"What's that supposed to mean?"

"Well, we've hardly been enjoying the usual 'honeymoon pleasures,' have we?"

"That's not my fault!"

"Who turned me down this morning?"

"I was waiting for the *cove*! We were supposed to be doing it at the *cove*!"

I can see that Sarah is uncomfortable, but I can't stop myself. I feel as if I'm boiling over.

"There's always some excuse," Ben snarls.

"I'm not making excuses!" I exclaim, absolutely livid. "What, you think I don't *want* to . . . you know?"

"I don't know what to think!" Ben throws back furiously. "But we haven't, and you don't seem bothered about it! You do the math!"

"I am bothered about it!" I yell. "Of

course I'm bothered!"

"Wait," says Sarah, looking warily from Ben to me. "You guys haven't . . . ?"

"There hasn't been the opportunity," says Ben tightly.

"Wow." Sarah breathes out, looking incredulous. "That's . . . unusual for a honeymoon."

"Our room was messed around," I explain succinctly, "and Ben got drunk and we were stalked by butlers and I had an allergic reaction and basically —"

"It's been a nightmare."

"Nightmare."

We're both slumped in gloom, our energy gone.

"Well," says Sarah with a twinkle. "We've got empty rooms upstairs. Beds. Condoms, even."

"Seriously?" Ben lifts his head. "There's a bed upstairs? A private double bed that we could use? You have no *idea* how we've wanted to hear that."

"Loads of them. We're half empty."

"This is great! Great!" Ben's spirits have zoomed up. "We can do it right here at the guest house! Where we first met! Come on, Mrs. Parr, let me ravish you."

"I won't listen," jokes Sarah.

"You can join in if you like!" says Ben,

then adds to me quickly, "Joke. *Joke.*"

He holds out his hands to me, his smile as endearing as it's ever been. But the magic isn't working. The sparkle has gone.

There's silence for what seems like forever. My mind is a maelstrom. What do I want? What do I *want*?

"I don't know," I say after a long pause, and hear Ben inhale sharply.

"You don't *know*?" He sounds as though he's at the end of his tether. "You don't fucking *know*?"

"I . . . I have to take a walk." Abruptly, I push back my chair and stride away before he can say anything else.

I head round the back of the guest house and up the scrubby hill behind. I can see the new hostel — a concrete-and-glass building plonked in the space where the guys used to play football. I stride straight past it and keep walking down the hillside till I can't see it anymore. I'm in a little dip in the land, surrounded by olive trees, with a derelict hut that I dimly remember from the old days. There's rubbish here too — old cans and crisp packets and the remains of some pita bread. I stare at it, feeling a swell of hatred for whoever left it here. On impulse, I go round the small clearing, picking up all the trash, working with a burst of energy. There isn't a rubbish bin, but I gather it together and put it next to a large rock. My life might be a mess, but I can clear a patch of land, at least.

When I'm done, I sit on the rock and stare ahead, not wanting to visit my thoughts. They're too confusing and scary. The sun is beating on my head and I can hear the distant bleating of goats. It makes me smile reminiscently. Some things haven't changed.

After a while, the sound of puffing makes me turn my head. A blond woman in a pink sundress is climbing up the hill. She sees me on the rock, smiles, and heads toward it gratefully.

"Hi," she says. "Can I —"

"Go ahead."

"Hot." She wipes her forehead.

"Very."

"Are you here to look at the ruins? The ancient ruins?"

"No," I say apologetically. "I'm just hanging out. I'm on my honeymoon," I add, as an excuse.

I vaguely remember people talking about the ruins in my gap year. We all intended to go and look at them, but in the end none of us ever bothered.

"We're on honeymoon too." She brightens. "We're at the Apollina, but my husband dragged me here to look at these ruins. I told him I needed a sit-down and I'd join him in a minute." She gets out a bottle of water and takes a swig. "He's like that. We went to Thailand last year; it nearly killed me. I went on strike in the end. I said, 'Not another bloody temple. I want to lie on the beach.' I mean, what's wrong with lying on the beach?"

"I agree." I nod. "We went to Italy and it was endless churches."

"Churches!" She rolls her eyes. "Tell me about it. That was us in Venice. I said to him, 'Do you ever go to churches in England? Why the sudden interest just because we're on holiday?' "

"That's exactly what I said to Richard!" I say eagerly.

"My husband's called Richard too!" the woman exclaims. "Isn't that funny? Richard what?"

She smiles at me, but I stare back, stricken. What have I been *saying*? Why did my thoughts instantly go to Richard, not Ben? What is *wrong* with me?

"Actually . . ." I rub my face, trying to calm my thoughts. "Actually, my husband's not called Richard."

"Oh." She looks taken aback. "Sorry. I

510

thought you said . . ." She peers closer in dismay. "Are you all right?"

Oh God. I don't know what's wrong with me. Tears are streaming out of my eyes. Lots of tears. I wipe them away and try to smile.

"I'm sorry." I swallow hard. "I've recently split up from my boyfriend. I haven't really got over it."

"Your *boyfriend*?" The woman stares at me, disconcerted. "I thought you said you were on your honeymoon?"

"I am," I sob. "I am on my honeymoon!" And now I'm really crying: huge, racking, childlike sobs.

"So which one is Richard?"

"Not my husband!" My voice rises to an anguished wail. "Richard's not my husband! He never asked me! He never asked meeeee!"

"I'll give you some privacy," says the woman awkwardly, and clambers down off the rock. As she disappears hastily from view, I give way to the noisiest, most abandoned crying I've ever indulged in.

I feel homesick. Homesick for Richard. I miss him so much. I feel as though when we split up he wrenched a bit of my heart out. For a while the adrenaline of the situation kept me going — but now I'm realizing just how wounded I am. My whole body's

511

throbbing with the pain, and it's nowhere near healing.

I miss him, I miss him, I miss him.

I miss his humor and his sense. I miss the feel of him in bed. I miss catching his eye at a party and knowing we're thinking the same thing. I miss the smell of him. He smells the way a man should. I miss his voice and his kisses and even his feet. I miss everything.

And I'm married to someone else.

I give a fresh, desperate sob. Why did I get married? What was I thinking? I know Ben is hot and fun and charming, but suddenly that all seems meaningless. It feels hollow.

So what do I do now? I bury my head in my hands, feeling my breathing gradually slow down. I'm twisting my wedding ring round and round on my finger. I've never felt so terrified in my life. I've made mistakes before, but never on this scale. Never with these repercussions.

I can't do anything about it, my brain is telling me. *I'm stuck. Trapped. It's my own fault.*

The sun is beating strongly on my head. I should really get down off the rock and move into the shade. But I can't bring myself to. I can't move a muscle. Not till I've sorted myself out. Not till I've made a few decisions.

■ ■ ■ ■

It's nearly an hour before I move. I jump down from the rock, dust myself off, and head swiftly toward the guest house. Ben didn't bother trying to find me to see if I was all right, I note. But I don't even care anymore.

I see them before they see me. Ben is sitting close to Sarah on the veranda, his hand curled around her shoulders and playing lightly with her strap. It's so obvious what has been going on, I feel like screaming. But, instead, I creep toward the guest house, staying silent as a cat.

Kiss, I'm willing them. *Kiss.* Confirm what I secretly believe.

I stand there, hardly breathing, my eyes fixed on them. It's like watching Ben and me when we met up in the restaurant however many days ago. They're revisiting their teenage fling. They can't help it. The hormones emanating from them are so strong, they're almost *visible.* Sarah is laughing at something Ben is saying, and he's playing with her hair now, and they've got that intense couple-y look going on and . . .

Houston, we have touchdown.

Their lips have fixed together. His hand is exploring inside her tank top. Before this can go any further, I march toward the veranda, feeling like a soap opera actress who's slightly late for her cue.

"How *could* you?" As I yell the words, I realize there's a genuine torment behind them. How *could* he bring me here, to the scene of his other teenage fling, the one which predates me and which he never mentioned? He should have known Sarah would be here. He should have known the teenage hormones would flare up again. Did he do it all on purpose? Is it a game?

At least I've rattled them. They leap apart, and Ben bangs his ankle on the bench and curses.

"Ben, we need to talk," I say shortly.

"Yes." He glowers at me as though this is *my* fault, and I bridle. Sarah tactfully disappears into the guest house, and I join Ben on the veranda.

"So. This isn't working." I stare away from him, out toward the sea, my whole body tensed miserably. "And now I see you prefer someone else, anyway."

"For fuck's sake," he says irritably. "One kiss —"

"It's our *honeymoon*!"

"Exactly!" he says furiously. "You just

turned me down! What's a guy supposed to do?"

"I didn't turn you down," I retort, immediately realizing that, yes, I did turn him down. "OK." I backtrack. "Well, I'm sorry. I just . . ."

I just didn't want to do it with you. I wanted to do it with Richard. Because he's the man I love. Richard, my beloved Richard. But I'll never see him again. And now I'm going to cry again. . . .

"It's difficult to say this," I manage at last, and blink back fresh tears. "But I think our marriage was too quick. I think we rushed. I think . . ." I exhale a shuddery breath. "I think it was . . . wrong. And I blame myself. I'd only recently come out of a relationship. It was too soon." I spread my hands. "My bad. Sorry."

"No," says Ben at once. "My bad."

There's silence as I take his words in. So we both think it was a mistake. A massive sense of failure is heaving in my chest. Combined with relief. *Fliss was right* shoots through my brain, and I flinch. That thought is too painful to deal with right now.

"I don't want to move to France," says Ben abruptly. "I hate fucking France. I shouldn't have let you think I was serious."

"Well, I shouldn't have pressed you on it,"

I say, wanting to be fair. "And I shouldn't have made you go in for Couples' Quiz."

"I shouldn't have got drunk the first night."

"I should have had sex with you in the guest house," I say remorsefully. "That was rude. Sorry."

"No worries." Ben shrugs. "Those beds squeak, anyway."

"So . . . we're done?" I can barely say the words. "Call it quits, no hard feelings?"

"We could go for quickest divorce," says Ben, deadpan. "We might get a world record."

"Shall we tell Georgios to cancel the honeymoon album, then?" I give a snort of almost painful laughter.

"What about the honeymooners' karaoke evening? Shall we still do that?"

"We won Couples' Quiz," I remind him. "Maybe we could announce our divorce at the gala prize-giving." I catch his eye, and suddenly the pair of us are in fits of uncontrollable, hysterical laughter.

You have to laugh. Because what's the alternative?

When we've both calmed down a bit, I hug my knees and look at him properly. "Was this marriage *ever* real to you?"

"Oh, I don't know." He winces as though

516

I've touched a sore spot. "Nothing's felt real to me these last few years. My dad dying, the company, giving up on comedy . . . I think I need to sort this out." He bangs his head with his fist.

"It wasn't real for me either," I say honestly. "It was like a fantasy. I was in such a bad place, and you pitched up and you looked so hot. . . ."

He still looks hot. He's lithe and tanned and taut. But to my eye he's lost something. He has a synthetic quality, like orange soda instead of freshly squeezed juice. It's orangey and bubbly and it quenches your thirst, but it leaves a bitter aftertaste. And it's not good for you.

"What shall we do?" All my laughter has abated, and all my anger too. I feel strangely detached. This is surreal. My marriage is over before it's begun.

And we haven't even had sex. I mean, how laughable is that? What kind of cruel, twisted games has fate been playing with us? Our honeymoon has been such an unbelievable disaster, it's like someone Up There didn't *want* us to stay together.

"I dunno. See out the holiday? Take it from there?" Ben looks at his phone. "I have this meeting with Yuri Zhernakov. You know he's sailed here especially to see me?"

"Wow!" I stare at him, impressed.

"I know." He puffs himself out a bit. "I want to sell. It makes sense. Lorcan thinks I shouldn't," he adds, "which makes it an even *better* reason to do it."

His face has twisted into a familiar disgruntled expression. I've already heard several rants about how Lorcan's a control freak and how Lorcan's a cynical user and once, randomly, how Lorcan's a bad Ping-Pong player. I'm not wild to hear another one, so I hastily move the conversation on.

"So you'll give up work completely?" This seems like a bad idea to me — although who cares what I think? I'm only the soon-to-be ex-wife.

"Of course I won't *give up*," says Ben, looking a little stung. "Yuri says he'll keep me on as special adviser. We'll start some new projects together. Play around with some ideas. Yuri's a great guy. Want to see his yacht?"

"Of course I do." I might as well milk the benefits of being his wife while I can. "And after that? What about you and lover-girl?" I nod sharply toward the guest house, and a look of contrition comes over Ben's face.

"I don't know what happened. I'm sorry." He shakes his head ruefully. "It was like Sarah and I were suddenly eighteen again;

all the memories came flooding back. . . ."

"It's OK," I say, relenting. "I know. It was the same for us, remember?"

I can't believe how much damage has been done, just from teenage loves meeting again. People should never come into contact with their first loves, I decide. There should be some official form of quarantine. The rule should be: you break up with your teenage lover and that's it. One of you has to emigrate.

"I don't mind what you do with her," I say. "Knock yourself out. Have your fun."

He stares at me. "*Seriously?* But . . . we're married."

If there's one thing I'm not, it's a hypocrite.

"Maybe we are on paper," I say. "Maybe we signed papers and exchanged rings. But you didn't really commit to me, and I didn't really commit to you. Not properly. Not *thoughtfully.*" I give a gusty sigh. "We never even dated properly. I don't see how I can have any hold over you."

"Wow." He looks incredulous. "Lottie, you're amazing. You're the most generous . . . broad-minded . . . you're *awesome.*"

"Whatever." I shrug.

For a while I'm silent. I might be keeping

519

it together in front of Ben, but inside I feel battered by everything. I want to fall on someone's shoulder and wail. Everything I thought is upside down. My marriage is over. I started the fire. Fail, fail, fail.

I sit there, my entire body twisted in tension. I feel like my brain is a confused, whirling cloud, with only a few tiny rays of clarity. Like little nudges pushing me in a certain direction. The thing is . . .

Here's the thing. Ben is very hot. And good in the sack. And I am absolutely desperate. And maybe it would help me briefly forget how I nearly killed twenty innocent students.

Ben is quiet too, staring out over the arid olive grove, and at last he turns to me with a new glint in his eye.

"Just had an idea," he says.

"Me too, actually," I say.

"First and final shag? For old times' sake?"

"My thoughts exactly. But not here." I wrinkle my nose. "The mattresses were always gross."

"Back at the hotel?"

"Sounds good." I nod, feeling a tingle of excitement rise through me, like a bit of comfort in this whole sorry mess. We deserve this. We need this. First, it will be closure, and, second, it will distract me from my throbbing aching heart, and, third, I've been wanting to do this for nearly three weeks and I am going to go *mad* if we don't.

If we'd simply shagged each other sense-less when we first met up, none of this would have happened. There's a lesson there, somewhere.

"I'll tell Sarah we're off and say our good-byes." Ben heads inside the guest house.

As soon as he's gone, I pull out my phone. Just then, as Ben was talking, I had a weird, psychic-type flash about Richard. It was as though I could sense him thinking about me, somewhere in the world. It was so vivid that I'm actually expecting to see Richard's name in my phone. My fingers are fumbling as I press the keys, my heart thudding with sudden hope.

But of course there's nothing. No call, no message, nothing, even after I've scrolled through twice. I'm being idiotic. Why would there be? Richard's in San Francisco, busy with his new life. I may miss him, but he doesn't miss me.

My spirits crash back down so heavily, I feel tears stinging my eyes again. Why am I even thinking about Richard? He's gone. *Gone.* He's not going to text me. He's not going to call me. Let alone fly across the world to declare his undying love and say he wants to marry me after all (my secret, stupid, never-going-to-happen fantasy).

Miserably, I scroll again through my other messages, noticing that I have loads of texts from Fliss. Just seeing her name makes me cringe. She warned me about this marriage. She was right. Why is she always *right*?

The thought of telling her the truth is too excruciating. Too humiliating. I can't — at least, not straightaway.

I start a new text, feeling a desperate, childish defiance, a determination to prove her wrong.

Hi Fliss. All wonderful here. Guess what? Ben is selling his company to Yuri Zhernakov and we're going on his yacht!!

As I stare at the words, they mock me. Happy, happy, happy. Lies, lies, lies. My fingers add a new lie:

I'm so glad I married Ben.

A tear drips onto my BlackBerry, but I ignore it and type on.

We're so happy together; it's perfect.

More tears are dripping down, and I

roughly wipe my eyes. And then my fingers start tapping again and this time I can't stop:

Imagine the best marriage in the world. Mine is better. We are so sympatico, so alive with the future. Compared with Richard, Ben is a marvel of a man. I haven't given Richard a single thought. . . .

23
FLISS

I've never felt so chastened in my life.
Finally, I can see the light. The truth. The
actuality. I was wrong. One hundred percent, totally, utterly, absolutely *wrong*. How
could my instincts have been so off? How
can I be such an *idiot*?

I don't just feel chastened: I feel crushed.
Devastated. I'm standing in Sofia airport,
reading Lottie's text, prickling all over as I
think of what I've put her through during
the last few days. Her honeymoon has been
hellish — yet she and Ben seem to be
bonded better than ever.

This whole stupid farce was about Daniel
and me. I was indulging my own needs. I
was looking at the world through skewed
glasses, and Lottie was the innocent victim.
The only saving grace is she doesn't know
what I did, and she never will know. Thank
God.

I turn back to Lottie's text, ignoring the

boarding call for Ikonos. I'm not going to Ikonos. I'm not going anywhere near my sister's honeymoon. I've done enough damage already. I'm finding a nice safe flight back to London for Noah and me. This whole ridiculous stunt is *over.*

Imagine the best marriage in the world. Mine is better. We are so sympatico, so alive with the future. Compared with Richard, Ben is a marvel of a man. I haven't given Richard a single thought, and I really can't remember what it was I ever liked about him. Ben has so many wonderful plans for the future!! He is going to work with Yuri Zhernakov on joint projects!! We are going to travel and sail in the Caribbean, then buy our French farmhouse!! Ben would like our children to be bilingual!!!

As I read, I feel a twinge of envy. This Ben sounds like Superman. Lorcan's view of him seems seriously inaccurate.

The only low point happened at the guest house. It turns out I started the fire all those years ago. It was my scented candles. So that was a shock. But otherwise it's the perfect, dreamy honeymoon.

525

Lucky me!!!!

I stare at the phone in shock. She started the fire? The fire that changed her life? I can't help exclaiming out loud, and Richard looks up sharply.

"What?"

"Nothing," I say automatically. I can't share Lottie's private text with him. Can I?

Oh, sod it. I need to tell someone who will understand.

"Lottie started the fire," I say succinctly. To my satisfaction, he understands instantly, as I knew he would.

"You're *kidding.*" His face drops.

"I know."

"But that's huge. Is she OK?"

"She says so." I gesture at the phone, but he shakes his head resolutely.

"She'll be putting on a brave face. She'll be in a real state." His expression changes to a kind of protective anger. "Does this Ben realize? Will he look after her?"

"I suppose." I shrug awkwardly. "He's doing all right so far."

"Can I see the text?"

I pause for only an instant. We've gone too far in this adventure to start being coy now.

He reads it silently, but I can see from the

hunch of his shoulders how affected he is. I can see him reading it through again, and then a third time. At last he looks up.

"She's in love with him," he says, and there's a kind of brutality to the way he speaks, as though he's punishing himself. "Isn't she? She's in love with the man, and I just didn't want to face up to it. I've been a fucking *idiot*."

"Richard —"

"I had this stupid dream that I'd arrive there, tell her how I feel, sweep her off her feet, and she'd run off with me. . . ." He shakes his head as though the very thought is painful to him. "What *planet* am I on? This has to end. Now."

I almost can't bear to see him give up, even though I'm doing the same myself.

"But what about telling her how you feel? What about the competition?" I'm trying to rekindle his fire, but he shakes his head again.

"I think I lost the competition a long time ago, Fliss," he says. "Fifteen years ago, to be exact. Don't you?"

"Maybe," I say after a pause. "Maybe you're right."

"She's happily married with the love of her life. Good for her. Now I need to get a life."

"I think we both need to get lives," I say slowly. "I'm as much to blame as you are. I encouraged you."

As I meet his eyes, I feel sadness at the realization that this is goodbye. If he and Lottie are over, then we're over too. Over as friends. Over as siblings-in-law.

There's another call for passengers on the flight to Ikonos, but I ignore it.

"Time to go," says Lorcan, looking up from his BlackBerry. He's sitting on an airport chair next to Noah, who is happily reading through a leaflet on security in Bulgarian. "What are you guys doing?" He takes in Richard's stricken face. "What's happened?"

"I've been an idiot, is what happened," says Richard with a sudden intensity. "Finally I see it. *Finally.*"

"Me too." I sigh. "That's exactly how I feel. *Finally* I see it."

"We see it."

"Both of us."

"Right." Lorcan seems to be taking in the situation. "So . . . it's just me for Ikonos?"

Richard thinks for a moment, then picks up his newly acquired City Heights Hotel tote bag.

"I might come along. I'll probably never have the chance to visit Ikonos again. I want to see the sunset. Lottie always told me the sunset was the best in the world. I'll find a quiet place to watch it and then I'll head back to San Francisco. She'll never know I was there."

"What about you and Noah?" Lorcan turns to me. I'm about to tell him that wild horses wouldn't drag me to Ikonos now when his BlackBerry bleeps.

"It's Ben. Hold on." He starts reading the text, and an odd expression comes over his face. "I don't believe it," he mutters at last.

"What?"

Lorcan raises his eyes silently. He looks genuinely poleaxed.

"Lorcan, what?" I feel a blade of worry. "Is Lottie OK?"

"I will never understand Ben," he says slowly, not answering my question. "Never."

"Is Lottie OK?" I persist. "What's happened?"

"It's not what's happened. . . ." A kind of sick expression passes over Lorcan's face. "I'm not protecting him," he says, as though to himself. "This is beyond the pale."

"Tell me!" I demand.

"OK." He exhales. "Two days into his marriage and he's already fixing up a rendezvous with some other woman."

"*What?*" Richard and I speak in unison.

"His PA is on holiday, so he wants mine to book him a weekend hotel in England. For him and some woman named Sarah. I've never even heard of her before. He's saying . . ." He passes me the phone. "Well, look at what he's saying."

I grab the phone and scan the text. I'm so stressed I can take in only about one word in three, but I get the gist.

We met up after all these years . . . amazing body . . . you have to meet her. . . .

"Bastard!" My incandescent cry echoes around Sofia airport. I feel so white-hot with fury, I may spontaneously combust. "My little sister loves this man! And this is the way he treats her!"

"Even for Ben, it's pretty low." Lorcan is shaking his head.

"She's given him her heart. She's given him her body and soul." I'm shaking with fury. "How *dare* he? Where are they now?" I consult the text again. "Still at the guest house?"

"Yes, but apparently they're leaving there after lunch and returning to the hotel."

"Right. Richard." I turn to him. "We have to rescue Lottie from this vile, odious man."

"Wait just a minute!" chimes in Lorcan.

530

"What happened to 'I'm never going to interfere in my sister's life again'? What happened to 'Hold me to my vow'?"

"That was *before*," I retort. "That's when I was *wrong.*"

"You're still wrong!"

"I'm not!"

"You are. Fliss, you've lost perspective. You had it for about five minutes, and now you've lost it again." Lorcan sounds so calm and reasonable, I flip out.

"My perspective is, I've realized what a two-timing bastard your best friend is!" I glare at him accusingly and he shakes his head.

"Don't give me that. It's not *my* fault."

"Do you want to read these texts?" I bang my BlackBerry with my hand for emphasis. "My poor trusting sister is absolutely besotted with Ben. She's planning a life in France with him. She's absolutely unaware of the fact he's hooking up with some girl from the old days with an amazing body." I'm close to tears. "It's her *honeymoon,* for God's sake. What kind of low-down worm is unfaithful on his honeymoon, before he's even consummated his marriage?"

"Now that you put it like that . . . ," allows Lorcan.

"Well, I'm not going to stand for it. I'm

531

saving my sister. Richard, are you in?"

"In?" He shakes his head adamantly. "I'm not in anything. Lottie's leading her own life. She doesn't want me. She made that perfectly plain."

"But her marriage with Ben is on the rocks!" I cry in frustration. "Don't you *see*?"

"We don't know that for sure," says Richard. "And, anyway, what are you expecting me to do, pick up the pieces? Lottie chose Ben, and that's something I have to live with." He hoists his bag on his shoulder. "You can do what you like, but I'm going my own way. I'm finding a sunset and I'm watching it and I'm going to try to find some inner peace."

I stare at him in disbelief. *Now* he goes all Dalai Lama on me?

"What about you?" I turn to Lorcan, who lifts his hands and shakes his head too.

"Not my affair. I'm strictly here for business reasons. Once the restructuring papers are signed, I'm leaving Ben alone."

"So you're both bailing out on me?" I glare at the two men. "Fine. *Fine*. I'll save the day without you." I extend a hand. "Come on, Noah. We're going to Ikonos after all."

"OK. Have they done it?" he adds chattily

as he gathers up all the Bulgarian leaflets he's collected.

"Done what?" I'm momentarily stunned.

"Lottie and Ben. Have they put the sausage in the bun?"

"Muffin," amends Richard.

"Cupcake," corrects Lorcan.

"Shut up, both of you!" I say frantically. I feel as though I'm losing control of everything. Do I have to have the facts-of-life conversation with my seven-year-old right now, in Sofia airport?

Also, more pertinent: it's a good question. *Have* they done it?

"I don't know," I say at last, and put an arm round Noah. "We don't know, darling. Nobody knows."

"Actually, I know." Lorcan looks up from his BlackBerry. "Just got a new text from Ben." His face twists a little. "Apparently the wedding night is a go. They're heading back to the hotel in order to . . ." He glances at Noah. "Put it this way. The sausage is heading toward the cupcake."

"Noooooooooo!" My agonized cry rises to the roof of the building, and a few nearby passengers turn to stare. "But she has no idea what a treacherous cheating rat he is!" I look agitatedly from face to face. "We have to stop them!"

"Fliss, calm down," says Lorcan.

"*Stop* them?" Richard looks shocked.

"She's been sabotaging their entire honeymoon," explains Lorcan succinctly. "Didn't you wonder why they were so unlucky?"

"Jesus Christ, Fliss." Richard looks shocked.

"We need to board," says Noah, tugging at my sleeve, but all three of us ignore him. Determination is coursing through my veins like molten steel. A crusader could not be any more crusading than I am right now.

"That bastard is *not* going to break my sister's heart." I'm speed-dialing Nico. "Richard, give me some more pointers. You have the inside track; you can help. What are Lottie's particular turnoffs?"

"We need to board," says Noah again, and all three of us ignore him again.

"I'm not telling you her turnoffs!" Richard sounds scandalized. "That's private information!"

"She's my *sister* —" I break off as Nico answers.

"Hello?" he says warily. "Fliss?"

"Nico!" I exclaim. "Thank God you're there! We need to take things up a level. Repeat, up a level."

"Fliss!" Nico sounds agitated. "I cannot continue with our arrangement! The staff, they are wondering what I am up to. We are arousing suspicion!"

"You have to," I say firmly. "They're heading back to the hotel, and I'll be there soon. Stop them from getting into bed meanwhile. Wrestle Ben to the ground if you have to. Whatever it takes!"

"Fliss —"

"We need to board, Mummy —"

"Whatever it takes, Nico! Whatever it takes!"

24
LOTTIE

I can hardly believe it's true. Our hotel suite is empty. No staff milling around. No butlers. No harps. As I look around the sleek, silent furniture, I can feel a buzz of anticipation in the air. It's as though the rooms are waiting for us to fill them with noise and heat and gasps and lovely, lovely sex.

We arrived back at the hotel and came straight up here. Neither of us said a word. I'm blocking everything else out right now. All thoughts about our marriage. All thoughts about Richard. All thoughts about Sarah. My shame, my sadness, my humiliation — I'm blocking it all out. The only thing I'm focusing on is that insistent pulse inside me I've been feeling ever since I clapped eyes on Ben in that restaurant. I want him. He wants me. We deserve this.

As he comes toward me, his eyes are darkening and I can tell he feels like I do:

where to start? We have the whole experience ahead of us, like a delicious box of chocolates.

"Did you put out DO NOT DISTURB?" I murmur as his lips find my neck.

"Of course."

"And lock the door?"

"Am I stupid?"

"So this is really happening." My hands run down his back and even lower, cupping his two taut buttocks, and I fleetingly wish mine were that firm. "Mmmm."

"Mmmm." He eases out of my grip and peels off his shirt. God, I fancy this man. And I know he's a flake; I know he'll be on to Sarah, or even some other girl, tomorrow. But for now — glorious now — he's all mine.

He's slowly unbuttoning my shirt. Thank God I'm wearing an expensive, froufrou bra. Richard never took any notice of my underwear, just used to peel it off in a great hurry. Then I told him I was hurt by this and he went to the other extreme, always murmuring "Great bra" or "Sexy pants." Dear Richard.

No. Stop, Lottie. No Richard thoughts. They're banned.

Ben is doing delicious things inside my ear with his tongue, and I moan urgently, reaching for his belt, unbuttoning his jeans. I thought I wanted this to be long and drawn out and epic, the stuff of memories. But now that it's happening, I realize I don't care about it being long and drawn out. I want him now. Now. *Now.* Short and epic will suit me fine.

Ben's panting and I'm panting, and I can feel he's as desperate as I am, and I have never wanted anyone so much in my whole entire life —

"Madame? A drink?"

What the fuuuck?

We both leap so high, it's as though we're Irish dancers doing a *pas de deux.*

I'm half undressed. Ben is half undressed. And Georgios is standing a meter away, holding a silver salver bearing a bottle of wine and several glasses.

"What?" Ben barely seems capable of words. "What is it?"

"A glass of wine? Or iced water?" says Georgios nervously. "Courtesy of the management."

"Fuck the management! *Fuck the fucking management!*" Ben explodes. "I put on the DO NOT DISTURB sign. Can't you *read*? Can't you see what we're *doing*? Have you heard of the concept of *privacy*?"

Georgios is speechless. He takes a step

538

forward and nervously proffers the silver salver.

"Fine!" Ben seems to reach the end of his tether. "Stay there! Watch!"

"What?" I stare at him.

"He's not going to leave us alone. Well, then, he can watch us. We're consummating our marriage," he adds over his shoulder to Georgios. "Should be fun."

He reaches to unhook my bra and I clamp my hands over my breasts. "Ben!"

"Take no notice of the butler," Ben says fiercely. "Pretend he's a pillar."

Is he serious? He expects us to have sex while the butler watches? Isn't that against the law?

Ben starts nuzzling at my cleavage, and I shoot a glance at Georgios. He's put one hand over his eyes but is still holding out the salver.

"Champagne?" he says, sounding distraught. "You would prefer champagne?"

"Why don't you just go?" I say furiously. "Leave us alone!"

"I cannot!" He sounds desperate. "Please, madame. Stop for refreshment at least."

"Why does this matter to you?" I wrench Ben's head up from my breast and turn to stare at Georgios. "You've been trying to stop us . . . you know . . . all honeymoon."

"Madame!" Another voice hails us, and I whip round incredulously. "Please! Urgent message!"

I can't cope with this. It's Hermes. He's also standing a meter away, holding out some bit of paper. I take it from him and read the words *Urgent Message.*

"What urgent message?" I snap. "I don't believe you."

"Come here, Lottie," snarls Ben, who is clearly beside himself. "Ignore them! We're doing this. We're getting it on." He rips my bra off completely and I scream.

"Ben! Stop!"

"Madame!" shouts Georgios impetuously. "I come to your rescue!" He puts down the salver and grabs Ben in a half nelson, while Hermes throws a glass of iced water over us both.

"We're not bloody *dogs*!" yells Ben. "Let go of me!"

"I didn't mean *Stop, stop*!" I say, equally livid. "I meant *Stop, don't take my bra off in front of the butlers*!"

Ben and I are both panting, but not in a good way. We're both dripping too, but, again, not in a good way. Georgios releases Ben, who rubs his neck.

"Why are you trying to stop us?" I glare at Georgios. "What's going on?"

"You're right." Ben is suddenly alert. "It can't be coincidence, all these glitches. Is someone *behind* it?"

I gasp. "Is someone telling you to do this?" My mind instantly flashes to Melissa. Maybe she wants this suite. She's the kind of person who would try all kinds of dirty tricks. "Have you been deliberately trying to ruin our wedding night all along?" I demand.

"Madame. Sir." Georgios glances uncertainly at Hermes. The pair of them look like guilty schoolkids.

"Answer us!" says Ben.

"Answer us!" I echo furiously.

"Mr. Parr." The familiar tones of Nico interrupt the conversation. He glided into the room so smoothly that I didn't even notice him arriving, but here he is, batting not an eyelid at the fact that I'm topless. He holds out an envelope to Ben. "A message from a Mr. Zhernakov."

"Zhernakov?" Ben swivels round. "What does he say?" He tears the envelope open and we all wait breathlessly, as though this will be the answer to everything.

"OK, I have to go." Ben starts looking around. "Where are my shirts?" He addresses Hermes. "Where did you put them?"

"I will find you a shirt, of course, sir.

Which color?" Hermes seems relieved to have something to do.

"You're *going*?" I stare at Ben. "You can't go!"

"Zhernakov wants to see me asap on the yacht."

"But we were in the middle of something!" I cry in frustration. "You can't just bail out!"

Ben ignores me and heads off with Hermes to the dressing area. I stare after him, quivering with rage. How can he leave? We were having *sex*. At least, we were about to. He's as bad as these butlers, interrupting all the time.

Speaking of which, where's Nico?

I spot him in the lobby of the suite and, clutching my shirt ineffectually to my chest, hasten after him. I intend to give him a piece of my mind, but to my surprise, he's standing in the corner, whispering into his phone.

"They have stopped. I assure you. They are apart."

I stiffen all over. Does "they" mean Ben and me? Who's he talking to? *Who the hell is he talking to?* My mind is working frantically. He's talking to the person behind it all. The person who's been trying to scupper us. I *know* it's Melissa.

I studied martial arts at school, and just

occasionally it comes in handy. Silently, I creep up behind Nico till my hand is poised, ready for action.

"I am in the vicinity, and I can assure you that no coupling or intercourse of any kind will take place — oof!" Nico gasps as I neatly relieve him of his phone. I clamp it to my ear without saying a word and listen as hard as I can.

"I'm nearly there, Nico. You're doing a great job. Just keep them apart, whatever it takes."

A brisk, commanding, thoroughly familiar voice greets my ear. For a moment I think I'm hallucinating. My jaw has dropped. My head is spinning. It can't be. It *can't* be.

Nico is trying to grab his phone, but I swing around, eluding him.

"Fliss?" I say, and feel a sudden, white-hot bolt of fury. *"Fliss?"*

25
FLISS

Fuck.

Oh fuck.

I feel hot and cold. I didn't see this coming. I never thought that at this late stage she would find out. We're on the island. We're nearly there. *We're so nearly there.*

We're standing outside the airport on Ikonos, our luggage assembled in a pile. Lorcan is at the taxi rank, negotiating a fare to the Amba Hotel, and I gesture to him to keep an eye on Noah.

"Hi, Lottie," I manage, but my voice has stopped working. I swallow several times, trying to regain my cool. What do I say? What can I say?

"It was you." Her voice is lacerating. "You've been trying to stop Ben and me from getting it together, haven't you? You were behind the butlers and the single beds and the peanut oil. Who else would know about peanut oil but you?"

"I . . ." I rub my face. "Listen. I . . . I just —"

"Why would you do that? Why would anyone do that? It's my honeymoon!" Her voice rises to a shriek of anguish and fury. "My *honeymoon*! And you *ruined* it!"

"Lottie. Listen." I gulp. "I thought . . . I was doing it for the best. You don't realize —"

"Doing it for the best?" she cries. *"Doing it for the best?"*

OK. This is going to be tough to explain in the thirty seconds I have before she screeches again.

"I know you'll probably never, ever forgive me," I begin rapidly. "But you were going to try for a honeymoon baby and I was so afraid it would be a mistake, and I know what it's like on the other side, postdivorce; it's absolutely miserable, and I couldn't bear that to happen to you —"

"I was about to have the hottest sex of my life!" she yells. "The hottest sex of my life!"

OK, she didn't listen to a word, did she?

"I'm sorry," I say feebly, dodging a man wheeling a huge suitcase bound with raffia.

"You always have to interfere, Fliss! Just because you think you know best. You've always been the same, my whole life, interfering, telling me what to do, bossing me

545

around. . . ."

Suddenly her words sting me. It's not as if I've done this for my own benefit.

"Look, Lottie. I'm sorry to be the one to tell you," I say, as calmly as I can manage. "But since we're discussing it, Ben isn't planning to be a faithful husband. He's two-timing you with a girl called Sarah; Lorcan told me."

There's a small, shocked silence. However, if I was expecting her to capitulate at this piece of news, I was wrong.

"So what?" she lashes back. "So bloody what? Maybe . . ." She hesitates. "Maybe we have an open marriage! You didn't think of *that,* did you?"

I'm so stunned, my mouth pops open like a fish. She's right. I didn't think of that. An open marriage? Crikey. I never thought of Lottie as the open-marriage type.

"And, anyway, what does Lorcan know about anything?" Lottie starts on a fresh tirade. "Lorcan's a twisted control freak who's been muscling in and wants to steal Ben's company from him."

"Lottie —" I'm still so confused by this view of Lorcan that I don't know what to say. "Are you sure?"

"Ben told me. That's why Ben's selling his company, because Lorcan told him not to.

546

So let's not trust the word of *Lorcan,* shall we?" She spits out "Lorcan" as though it's despicable.

There's another silence. I feel so many conflicting emotions I'm almost paralyzed. There's a lingering astonishment at Lottie's version of Lorcan. But the strongest feeling is remorse. Wave after wave of remorse. She's right: I knew nothing about the situation. I assumed far too much.

Maybe I really don't know my little sister after all.

"I'm sorry," I say at last, my voice low and abject. "I'm so sorry. I just thought that you might not be over Richard yet. And that you might find Ben wasn't the man for you. I thought you might suddenly regret marrying him. And I thought that if things had gone too far and you'd conceived a baby, then it would be the most almighty mess. But I was wrong. Obviously. Please, please forgive me. Lottie?" There's silence down the phone. "Lottie?"

26
LOTTIE

I hate her. Why is she always right? *Why is she always right?*

Tears have sprung to my eyes. I want to pour out the whole sorry story to her. I want to tell her that Ben *isn't* the man for me, and I'm *not* over Richard, and I've never felt so miserable in all my life.

But still I can't forgive her. I can't let her off the hook. She's the most controlling and bossy sister in the world, and she deserves punishment.

"Leave me alone!" I say, a catch in my throat. "Just leave me alone forever!"

I hang up. A moment later I can see her calling again, so I switch the phone off completely and hand it back to Nico.

"Here," I say shortly. "And you can stop taking calls from my sister. You can stop meddling in my life. You can bloody well leave us alone."

"Mrs. Parr," begins Nico smoothly. "On

behalf of the hotel, I would like to apologize for the slight confusion you have unfortunately experienced on your honeymoon. In recompense, I offer you a deluxe weekend for two in one of our premium suites."

"That's all you can say?" I stare at him in disbelief. "After everything we've been through?"

"The deluxe weekend for two will include all meals and one snorkeling experience," says Nico, apparently not hearing me. "In addition, may I remind you that, as winners of our Couples' Quiz, you and your husband are invited to our gala prize ceremony this evening, where you will be awarded your Happy Couple of the Week trophy." He gives a little bow. "Congratulations."

"Happy Couple of the Week trophy?" I practically scream. "Are you kidding me? And *stop* looking at my chest!" I add, suddenly realizing my shirt has slipped.

I pick up my bra and start hooking it on as Nico discreetly leaves. My mind is like a hurricane. Lots of thoughts and emotions are whizzing dangerously around, and I feel like some of them might do some damage. *My marriage to Ben is a nonstarter. He couldn't even see our consummation through. Fliss is an interfering COW. I still miss Richard. I really do miss Richard. I started the fire.*

It was me. I started it. I feel a pang of anguish and give an uncontrollable sob. That's almost the worst thing of all: I started the fire. For fifteen years I've had that memory as a comforting prop whenever life has gone wrong: at least that time, I saved the day. But now I know I didn't. I *ruined* the day.

"Hi." Ben enters the room, fully dressed, looking dapper and as if he's squeezed in a quick shower.

"Hi," I say miserably. There's no point sharing my thoughts with him. He wouldn't understand. "Just so you know, we're supposed to go to a prize ceremony tonight and get our trophy. We're Happy Couple of the Week."

"I'm going to Zhernakov's yacht," Ben says, ignoring me. "They're sending a boat for me," he adds importantly.

"I'm coming too," I say in sudden determination. "Wait for me." I'm not missing out on an oligarch's super-yacht. I'm going to go along with Ben and find the bar and drown all my sorrows, one by one, in a series of mojitos.

"You're still coming?" He stares at me.

"I'm your wife," I say pointedly. "And I want to see the yacht."

"OK," he says with bad grace. "I suppose you can come. But for God's sake put some

550

clothes on."

"I wasn't planning to come in my *bra*," I retort irritably.

We're arguing like an old married couple but we haven't even managed to have sex. Bloody marvelous.

27
FLISS

An open marriage?

I'm so thunderstruck I've sunk down onto my suitcase, right in the middle of the hot, dusty pavement, ignoring the stream of passengers who have to divert around me.

"Ready?" says Lorcan, striding up with Richard and Noah, his eyes squinting against the blazing Greek sun. "I've arranged the fare. We need to get going."

I'm too flummoxed to reply.

"Fliss?" He tries again.

"They've got an open marriage," I say. "Can you believe it?"

Lorcan raises his eyebrows and whistles. "Ben will like that."

"An *open marriage*?" Richard goggles at me. *"Lottie?"*

"Exactly!"

"I can't believe it."

"It's true. She just told me herself."

Richard is silent for a few moments,

breathing deeply. "That confirms it — I don't really know her," he says at last. "I've been an idiot. It's time to put all this to an end." He holds out his hand to Noah. "Bye, little chap. It's been good traveling with you."

"Don't go, Uncle Richard!" Noah flings his arms passionately around Richard's legs, and for a moment I wish I could do that too. I'm going to miss him.

"Best of luck." I hug him. "If I'm ever in San Francisco I'll look you up."

"Not a word to Lottie that I did this," he says with a sudden fierceness. "She must never know any of it."

"Not even *I love you, Lottie, More than a zloty*?" I say, trying to keep a straight face.

"Shut up." He kicks my case.

"Don't worry." I touch his arm. "Not a word."

"Good luck." Lorcan shakes Richard's hand. "Nice to know you."

Richard heads toward the taxi rank, and I quell a sigh. If only Lottie knew. But there's nothing I can do about it. My only priority right now is to make the hugest apology in the world. I've got my groveling kneepads on, all ready.

"Right, let's go," says Lorcan. He consults his phone. "Ben isn't replying to my texts.

553

Do you know where they are?"

"No idea. They were about to have sex when I interrupted." I wince at my own conduct. Gradually, my haze of lunacy is lifting. I can see quite how badly I've been behaving. So what if they have sex? So what if they conceive a honeymoon baby? It's *their life.*

"D'you think she'll ever forgive me?" I say as we get into the taxi. I'm hoping that Lorcan will make some reassuring reply like, *Of course she will; the bond of sisterhood is too strong to break with a mere bagatelle like this.* Instead, he wrinkles his nose and shrugs deeply.

"Is she the forgiving type?"

"No."

"Well." He shrugs again. "Unlikely."

My heart drops. I'm the most misguided big sister there ever was. Lottie will never speak to me again. And it's my own fault.

I dial her number and go straight to voice-mail.

"Lottie," I say for the zillionth time. "I'm so, so, so sorry. I have to explain. I have to see you. I'm coming to the hotel. I'll call you when I'm there, OK?" I put my phone away and drum my fingers impatiently. We've joined the main road but we're going at a modest speed, by Greek standards. I

554

lean forward to the driver. "Can we go faster? I need to see my sister, pronto. Can we go any faster?"

I'd forgotten how far the Amba Hotel is from the airport. It seems like several hours before we're arriving, climbing out of the taxi, slamming the doors, and running up the marble steps.

"Let's give our luggage to a bellman," I say breathlessly. "We can get it later."

"Fine." Lorcan summons a bellman with a trolley and swings our cases up onto it. "Let's go."

He's almost more impatient than I am. He gradually became more and more urgent and tetchy in the car, consulting his watch and trying to contact Ben.

"It's nearly close of play," he keeps saying. "I *need* these signatures scanned in and sent over."

Now, as we arrive in the familiar marble lobby, he turns to me expectantly. "Where will they be?"

"I don't know!" I riposte. "How should I know? In their suite?"

Through the glass doors at the back of the lobby, I can see the shimmering, inviting blue of the sea, and Noah has spotted it too.

"The sea! The sea!" He wrenches at my hand. "Come on! The sea!"

"I know, darling!" I rein him back. "In a minute."

"Can we have a smoothie?" he adds, spotting a waiter carrying a tray of several pink smoothie-type drinks.

"Later," I promise. "We'll have smoothies and we'll go to the buffet and you can swim in the sea. But first we need to find Aunt Lottie. Keep your eyes open."

"Ben," Lorcan is saying curtly into his phone. "I'm here. Where are you?" He rings off and turns to me. "Where's their suite?"

"Upstairs. I think I remember . . ." I'm leading him swiftly across the expanse of marble, dodging a group of tanned men in pale suits, when a voice assails my ears.

"Fliss? Felicity?"

I wheel round to see a familiar plump figure hurrying through the lobby on patent shoes. Shit.

"Nico!" I say, trying to keep my chin up. "Hi, there. And thanks for everything."

" 'Thanks for everything'?" He seems almost apoplectic. "Do you realize the damage I have done in trying to carry out your wishes? Never have I known such farce. Never have I known such shenanigans."

"Right." I gulp. "Er . . . sorry. I appreciate it."

"Your sister, she is beside herself with rage."

"I know." I wince. "Nico, I'm so sorry. But I'll be expressing my gratitude with a very big feature about you in the magazine. Very big. Very flattering. A double-page spread." I'll write it myself, I vow. Not one critical word. "There's just one more *tiny* thing you could help us with —"

"Help you?" His voice rises indignantly. "*Help you?* I have the gala ceremony to prepare for! I am late already. Fliss, I have to go. Please do not create any more chaos in my hotel."

Bristling all over, he marches away, and Lorcan raises his eyebrows at me.

"You've made a friend there."

"He'll be all right. I'll sweeten him up with a glowing review." I'm looking frantically around the lobby, trying to remember it. "OK, I think the Oyster Suite is on the top floor. And the lifts are this way. Come on!"

As we're traveling up in the lift, Lorcan tries Ben's phone yet again.

"He *knew* I was coming," he mutters ominously. "He should have been ready to sign. This is *so* unhelpful."

"We'll be there in a minute!" I retort irritably. "Stop stressing."

As we arrive at the top floor, I hare out of the lift, dragging Noah by the hand and not stopping to check any signs. I head to the door at the end of the corridor and bang on it as hard as I can.

"Lottie! It's me!" I notice a tiny doorbell and ring that too, for good measure. "Come out! Please! I want to apologize! I'm so sorry! I'M SO SORRY!" I thump on the door again, and Noah, delighted, joins in.

"Come out!" he yells, banging on the door. "Come out! Come out!"

Suddenly the door is flung open and a strange man wrapped in a towel stares at me.

"Yes?" he says bad-temperedly.

I stare back, disconcerted. This doesn't look like the photo I saw of Ben. Nothing like.

"Er . . . Ben?" I try anyway.

"No," he says flatly.

My mind is racing. She's in an open marriage. Does that mean — Oh my God. Are they having a *threesome*?

"Are you with . . . Ben and Lottie?" I say cautiously.

"No, I'm with my wife." He glowers at me. "Who are you?"

"This *is* the Oyster Suite?"

558

"No, the Pearl Suite." He points to a discreet sign by the door, which I totally missed.

"Ah. Right. Sorry." I back away.

"I thought you knew this place," says Lorcan.

"I did. I do. I was sure —" I break off as something catches my eye through a nearby window. It's a narrow window with a view of the sea, and I can just glimpse a jetty decorated with flowers. Standing in the middle of the jetty is a couple that looks very familiar —

"Oh my God, it's them! They're renewing their vows! Quick!"

I grab Noah again and all three of us hurry back along the corridor. The lift is unbearably slow but, even so, we're soon outside, running over lawns and down paths, toward the sea. The jetty is ahead, decorated with flowers and balloons, and in the center, there they are, the happy couple, holding hands.

"Swimming!" shouts Noah joyously.

"Not yet," I pant. "We need to —" I break off, peering again at the couple on the jetty. They're facing away from us, but I'm sure it's Lottie. I *think* it's Lottie. Except . . .

Hang on. I rub my eyes, trying to focus more clearly. I need my lenses checked.

"Is it them?" demands Lorcan.

"I don't know," I confess. "If they'd just turn round . . ."

"That's not Aunt Lottie!" says Noah scornfully. "That's a different lady."

"Doesn't really look like Ben," confirms Lorcan, squinting at the guy. "Too tall."

At that moment, the girl turns her head and I realize she looks nothing like Lottie.

"Oh *God.*" I sink down onto a nearby sun bed. "It's not them. I can't run around anymore. Can't we have a drink?" I turn to Lorcan. "You must have missed your deadline by now. Get it done in the morning. Have a drink. Lorcan? What's wrong?"

I blink at him in surprise. His face is suddenly like stone. He's staring at something beyond my shoulder, and I swivel to see what he's looking at. It's a normal luxury-hotel beach, with sun beds, and waves crashing onto the sand, and swimmers in the sea, and, beyond, a few sailing boats and, way beyond that, a big yacht moored in deep water. That's what he's staring at, I realize.

"That's Zhernakov's yacht," he says steadily. "What's it doing here?"

"Oh!" I gasp as I put the pieces together. "Of course. *That's* where they are. I forgot."

"You *forgot?*"

He sounds so censorious, I feel a tweak of resentment.

"Lottie told me earlier, but it slipped my mind. Ben's selling the company. He's meeting Yuri Zhernakov on his yacht."

"He's doing *what*?" Lorcan's face drains of color. "He can't be. We agreed he isn't going to sell. Not yet. And not to Zhernakov."

"Maybe he's changed his mind."

"He can't change his mind!" Lorcan seems beside himself. "Why else am I here with a refinancing agreement in my briefcase? Why else have I chased him halfway across Europe? We have plans for the company in place. Exciting plans. We've spent weeks fine-tuning them. And now he takes a meeting with *Zhernakov*?" He suddenly focuses on me. "Are you sure?"

"Here." I scroll through till I find the text and show it to Lorcan, whose face freezes as he reads it.

"He's seeing Zhernakov, alone. With no advisers. He's going to get absolutely *shafted*. The stupid *fool*."

Something about his reaction piques me. He keeps telling me to calm down about Lottie, but now he goes berserk about a company which isn't even his?

"Oh well," I say with deliberate insouciance. "His company. His money. Whatever."

"You don't understand," says Lorcan angrily. "This is a total fucking disaster."

"Don't you think you're overreacting a tad?"

"No, I do not think I'm overreacting! This is important!"

"Now who's lost perspective?" I retort.

"This is *completely* different —"

"It's not! If you ask me, you're far too wrapped up in this company and Ben feels bitter about it and it's a toxic situation which can't end well!"

There. I've said it.

"He doesn't feel bitter!" Lorcan looks absolutely incredulous. "Ben *needs* me on board. Yes, we have our fallings-out —"

"You have no idea!" I'm so frustrated, I shake my phone at him. "Lorcan, you have no idea! I know more about your relationship with Ben than you do! Lottie told me!"

"Lottie told you what?" Lorcan's voice is suddenly quiet and his face still. I stare back, nervous of what I'm about to say. But I have to. He has to know the truth.

"Ben resents you," I say at last. "He thinks you're a control freak. He thinks you've got a cushy number. He thinks you're trying to muscle in and steal his company. You once confiscated his phone in public?"

"What?" Lorcan stares at me.

"Apparently."

Lorcan's brow is creased in thought for a moment — then it clears. "Oh God, *that.* It was after his father died. Ben came up to Staffordshire and one of the older workers was making a speech. Ben took a call in the middle." Lorcan's face twists. "It was atrociously rude. I had to grab the phone and smooth things over. Jesus. He should be *grateful.*"

"Well, he's still angry about it."

There's silence. Lorcan is quivering with emotion, his eyes distant.

"Cushy number?" he bursts out at last, fixing me with accusing eyes. "*Cushy number?* Do you know how much I've done for him? For his father? For that company? I put my career on hold. I turned down offers from big City firms."

"I'm sure you did —"

"I started Papermaker, I restructured the finances, I gave it everything —"

I can't listen to this anymore.

"Why?" I interrupt bluntly. "Why did you?"

"What?" He gapes at me as though he doesn't understand the question.

"Why did you?" I repeat. "*Why* did you go up to Staffordshire in the first place? *Why*

563

did you get so close to Ben's father? *Why* did you turn down City jobs to do this? *Why* have you got so emotionally involved with a company that isn't yours?"

Lorcan looks as though he's floundering. "I . . . I had to step in," he begins. "I had to take control —"

"You didn't."

"I did! The whole thing was in a complete mess —"

"You *didn't*!" I take a deep breath, marshaling my words. "You didn't have to do any of it. You *chose* to. You were in a horrible place after a relationship broke down. You were sad. You were angry." This is hard to say, but I'm going to. "You were just trying to do the same as Lottie. And the same as me. Fix your broken heart. And you chose to do it by trying to save Ben's company for him. But it wasn't the right way to go." I meet his eyes and add gently, "It was your Unfortunate Choice."

Lorcan is breathing hard. His hands are clenched into fists, as though he's bracing himself against something. I can see pain rising in his face, and I'm sorry I caused it. But at the same time — I'm not.

"I'll see you later," he says abruptly, and strides away before I can reply. I have no idea if he'll ever talk to me again. Still, I'm glad I said what I said.

I look affectionately down at Noah, who has been waiting patiently for us to finish talking.

"*Now* can I go swimming?" he says. "*Now* can I?"

I think of his swimming trunks, all the way back in his case in the lobby. I think of what a hassle it will be to go and get them. I think of how there's only a few hours left of sunshine.

"Swimming in your underpants?" I raise my eyebrows at him. *"Again?"*

"Underpants!" he cries joyously. "Underpants! Yay!"

"Fliss!" I look up to see Nico making his way across the beach, his white shirt as starched as ever and his shoes shiny against the sand. "Where is your sister? I need to talk through the arrangements for the gala ceremony. She and her husband are our Happy Couple of the Week."

"Well, good luck with that. She's there." I gesture at the yacht.

"Can you contact her?" Nico looks harassed. "Can you phone her? We should have had a rehearsal for the ceremony; everything has been thrown off course —"

"Swimming?" begs Noah, who has already ripped all his clothes off and thrown them on the sand. "Swimming, Mummy?"

As I stare down at his eager little face, something seems to pierce my heart. And suddenly I know what's important in life. It's not gala ceremonies. It's not wedding nights. It's not saving my sister. And it's certainly not Daniel. It's right here in front of me.

My underwear is plain and black. It would just about pass as a bikini.

"Excuse me," I say cheerfully to Nico, and start stripping down to my bra and knickers. "I can't stop. I'm going swimming with my son."

After half an hour of splashing with Noah in the turquoise Aegean waves, all's right with the world. The late-afternoon sun is baking my shoulders, my mouth is salty from the surf, and my ribs hurt from laughing.

"I'm a shark!" Noah is advancing on me through the shallows. "Mummy, I'm a splashing shark!" He splashes me furiously and I give as good back, and then we both tumble down onto the soft sandy floor of the sea.

He'll be OK, I find myself thinking, cradling his lithe little body. We'll both be OK. Daniel can go and live in Los Angeles if he likes. Good place for him, in fact. They like plastic people out there.

I beam at Noah bobbing alongside me.

"Isn't this fun?"

"Where's Aunt Lottie?" he demands in return. "You said we'd see Aunt Lottie."

"She's busy," I say soothingly. "But I'm sure we'll see her."

Every time I glance up at the yacht looming huge in the bay, I vaguely wonder what's happening on board. The bizarre thing is that, when I was still in England, Lottie's affairs all felt so close and important and immediate. But now that I'm here, they feel distant.

Not my life. *Not* my life.

Suddenly I hear something that sounds like my name. I turn instinctively and see Lorcan standing at the water's edge, incongruous in his business suit.

"I have something to say to you!" he shouts indistinctly.

"Can't hear!" I yell back without moving.

I'm not rushing around anymore. Even if he wants to tell me that Lottie has had twins by Ben, who has turned out to be a Nazi warlord, I can hear it later.

"Fliss!" he calls again.

I make a hand gesture which is supposed to mean, *I'm busy with Noah; let's catch up*

567

later, but I'm not sure he gets it.

"Fliss!"

"I'm *swimming!*"

Some emotion seems to be gathering in Lorcan's face. With an abrupt movement, he dumps his briefcase on the sand and marches into the shallows, still in his shoes and suit. He strides briskly through the waves until he reaches Noah and me, then stops. He's up to his thighs in water. I'm so gobsmacked I don't know what to say. Noah, who started gasping as Lorcan approached, now collapses in paroxysms of laughter.

"You really haven't heard of swimming trunks, have you?" I say, trying to stay deadpan.

"I have something to say to you." He glowers at me as though this is all my fault.

"Go on, then."

There's a long, long silence, apart from the noise of waves and beach chatter and the cry of a gull. Lorcan's eyes have an extra charge of intensity, and his hand is constantly raking through his hair as though trying to order his thoughts. He takes a deep breath, and then another, but doesn't speak.

A rubber dinghy full of children pulls near us, then bobs away again. And *still* Lorcan doesn't speak. I think I'm going to have to do this for him.

"Let me guess," I say gently. "In no particular order: You realize I was right. You find this difficult. You'd like to talk about it sometime. You're wondering what you're doing here, chasing after Ben, when he's betraying everything you hold dear. You're suddenly looking at your life in a different way and thinking that things need to change." I pause. "And you wish you'd brought your swimming trunks."

There's another long silence. A tiny muscle is working in Lorcan's cheek, and I feel apprehensive. Did I go too far?

"Close," he says at last. "But you missed out a couple." He takes a step through the sea, the water washing around his legs. "No one's ever understood things like you. No one's ever *challenged* me like you. You were right about Ben. You were right about my website photo. I went to have another look, and you know what I saw?" He pauses. *"Who the hell are you? What are you looking at? I haven't got time for this."*

I can't help smiling.

"And you're right: Dupree Sanders is not my company," he continues, his jaw tightening. "Maybe I wish it was, but it's not. If Ben really wants to sell, he should sell. Zhernakov will close the whole operation

569

down within six months, but so be it. Nothing lasts forever."

"Won't you feel bitter if that happens?" I can't help pushing him. "You put so much into it."

"Maybe." He nods seriously. "For a while. But even bitterness fades away eventually. We both have to believe that. Don't we?" He meets my eyes, and I feel a wave of empathy for him. Emotional investment — it's the hardest game of the lot.

"You were wrong on one thing, though," Lorcan adds with sudden energy. "Completely wrong. I'm *glad* I didn't bring my swimming trunks."

With that, he peels off his jacket and tosses it toward the shore. It lands on the waves, and Noah dives for it joyously.

"Here!" He holds it aloft. "I got it!" He giggles in delight as Lorcan takes off one shoe, then the other, tossing them toward the shore too. "They've *sunk*! Your shoes have sunk!"

"Noah, can you dive down for Lorcan's shoes," I say, giggling, "and put them on the beach? I think he's going to swim in his underpants."

"Underpants!" yells Noah. "Underpants!"

"Underpants." Lorcan grins at him. "It's the only way."

28
LOTTIE

I can see the tiny figures of swimmers bobbing around in the sea as I gaze back to
shore. The late-afternoon sun is casting long
shadows on the beach. Children are screaming and couples are embracing and families
are playing together. And I suddenly wish
with all my heart I was one of them. People
on simple holidays, without complicated
lives, without flaky, self-centered husbands,
without disastrous decisions they have to
unpick.

I hated the yacht the minute we got on
board. Yachts are *awful.* Everything is clad
in white leather and I'm terrified of making
a mark, and Yuri Zhernakov just ran a
glance over me as though to say, *No, you
won't make the cut as my fifth wife.* I was
instantly banished to the company of two
Russian women with plumped-up lips and
boobs. They're so puffed up with silicone
they make me think of balloon animals, and

they have made no conversation except "Which limited-edition designer compact are *you* examining your reflection in?"

Mine's Body Shop, so that didn't go very far.

I sip my mojito and wait for my worries to drown in it. But instead of sputtering and fading, they're circling my brain, bigger and bigger. Everything's a catastrophe. Everything's terrible. I want to cry, I realize. But I can't cry. I'm on a superyacht. I've got to be sparkling and bright and somehow increase my cleavage.

I lean over the rail of the deck I'm standing on and wonder how far it is down to the sea. Could I jump?

No. I might hurt myself.

God knows where Ben is. He's been unbearable ever since we arrived here, showing off and preening and telling Yuri Zhernakov about fifteen times how he's planning to buy a yacht himself.

My hand steals into my pocket. There's a thought that's been sitting in my brain like a very patient person who isn't going to give up. The same, simple thought. It's been there for hours now. *I could call Richard. I could call Richard.* I've been ignoring it and ignoring it, but now I can't remember all the reasons why it's a bad idea. It seems like an exciting idea. A joyful idea. I could just call him. Now.

I know Fliss would tell me not to, but it's not her life, is it?

I don't exactly know what I want to say to him. In fact, I think I don't want to say anything. I only want to make a connection. Like when you reach for someone's hand and squeeze it. That's it: I want to squeeze his hand over the ether. And if he pulls his hand away, well, then I'll know.

I can see the two Russian women coming on deck, and I hurry round the corner so they won't see me. I pull out my phone, stare at it for an instant, then plunge my finger down onto the keypad. As his number rings, my heart starts to thud, and I feel sick.

"Hello, it's Richard Finch here."

It's gone to voicemail. My stomach corkscrews in panic and I press *stop.* I can't leave a voicemail. A voicemail isn't a squeezed hand. It's an envelope pressed into the palm. And I don't know what I want to put in the envelope. Not exactly.

I try to visualize what he might be doing right now. I have no concept of his life in San Francisco. Getting up, maybe? Having a shower? I don't even know what his apartment looks like. He's drifted right away from me. Tears sting my eyes and I look miserably at my phone. Could I try again? Would that count as stalking?

"Lottie! There you are!" It's Ben, along with Yuri. I shove my phone back in my pocket and turn to face them. Ben is pink-faced from booze, and my heart sinks. He looks manic, like a small child who's stayed up too late. "We're going to seal the deal over some champagne," he says excitedly. "Yuri's got some vintage Krug. Care to join us?"

29
ARTHUR

Young people! With their hurrying and their worrying and their wanting all the answers *now*. They wear me out, the poor, harried things.

Don't come back, I always tell them. *Don't come back.*

Youth is still where you left it, and that's where it should stay. Anything that was worth taking on life's journey, you'll already have taken with you.

Twenty years I've been saying this, but do they listen? Do they, hell. Here comes another of them now. Panting and puffing as he reaches the top of the cliff. Late thirties, I'd guess. Attractive enough, against the blue sky. Looks a bit like a politician. Do I mean that? Maybe a movie star.

I don't remember his face from the old days. Not that that means anything. These days I barely even recall my own face when I glimpse it in the mirror. I can see this chap's gaze raking the surroundings, taking in me sitting in my chair under my favorite olive tree.

"Are you Arthur?" he says abruptly.

"Guilty."

I scan him adroitly. Looks well off. Wearing one of those expensive-logo polo shirts. Probably good for a few double Scotches.

"You must want a drink," I say pleasantly. Always useful to steer the conversation in the direction of the bar early on.

"I don't want a drink," he says. "I want to know what happened."

I can't help stifling a yawn. So predictable. He wants to know what happened. Another merchant banker having a midlife crisis, returning to the scene of his youth. The scene of the crime. Leave it where it *was*, I want to answer. Turn round. Return to your adult, problematic life, because you won't solve it here.

But he wouldn't believe me. They never do.

"Dear boy," I say gently. "You grew up. That's what happened."

"No," he says impatiently, and rubs his sweaty brow. "You don't understand. I'm here for a reason. Listen to me." He comes forward a few paces, an impressive height and figure against the sun, intentness of purpose on his handsome face. "I'm here for a reason," he repeats. "I wasn't going to get involved — but I can't help it. I have to do this. I want to know *what exactly happened the night of the fire?*"

30
LOTTIE

When I give my Making Your Job Work for You! seminar to staff members at Blay Pharmaceuticals, one of my themes is: *You can learn from everything.* I take a sample workplace situation and we brainstorm and then list as bullet points *What You Learned from This.*

After two hours on Yuri Zhernakov's yacht, my bullet points would go as follows:

- I am never having my lips done.
- Actually, I wouldn't mind a yacht.
- Krug is ambrosia from heaven.
- Yuri Zhernakov is so rich, it makes my eyes water.
- Ben's tongue was practically hanging out. And what about all those embarrassing sycophantic jokes?
- Whatever Ben may think, Yuri is *not* interested in "joint projects." The only

578

thing he wanted to talk about was the house.

- If you ask me, Yuri will get rid of the paper company altogether. Ben doesn't seem to realize this.
- I think Ben may be quite thick.
- We should never, ever have come back via the beach.

This was our big mistake. We should have got the boat to drop us a mile up the coast. Because, the moment we landed, we were seized by Nico.

"Mr. and Mrs. Parr! Just in time for the gala ceremony!"

"What?" Ben stared at him quite rudely. "What are you talking about?"

"You know." I nudged him. "Happy Couple of the Week."

There was nothing we could do to escape. Now we're milling around with about twenty other guests from the hotel, drinking cocktails and listening to a band play "Some Enchanted Evening." Everyone is gossiping about Yuri Zhernakov's yacht being moored in the bay. I've heard Ben tell at least five sets of people that we were there earlier on, drinking Krug. Every time, it makes me flinch. And any minute we're going to have to go up onto the platform and receive the

579

Happy Couple of the Week trophy. Which is insane.

"Do you think we could get out of it?" I murmur to Ben as conversation lulls. "Let's face it, we're hardly Happy Couple of the Week."

Ben looks at me blankly. "Why not?"

Why *not*? Is he for real? "Because we're already discussing divorce!" I hiss.

"But we're still happy." He shrugs.

Happy? How can he possibly be happy? I glare at him, suddenly wanting to hit him. He was never into this marriage. Never. It was just a diversion. A craze. Like the time I got into Scandinavian knitwear and bought a knitting machine.

But a marriage isn't a knitting machine! I almost want to yell this at him. This whole thing is a joke. I want to leave.

"Ah, Mrs. Parr." It's Nico again, swooping down as though suspecting I was about to escape. "We are nearly ready for the trophy presentation."

"Great." My sarcasm is so pointed that he winces.

"Madame, may I apologize yet again for the inconvenience you have suffered on this holiday. As I said, I am pleased to offer you, in recompense, a deluxe weekend for two in one of our premium suites, to include all meals and one snorkeling experience."

"I hardly think that's appropriate." I glare at him. "You've ruined our honeymoon. Ruined our marriage."

Nico drops his eyes to the sand. "Madame, I am desolate. But I must tell you, this was not my own idea, this was not my own will. It was a huge mistake on my part and one that I will always regret, but the original idea, it came from —"

"I know." I cut him off. "My sister."

Nico nods his head. He looks so abject that I feel a pang of sympathy for him. I know what Fliss is like. When she gets into crusading mood, no one can refuse her.

"Look, Nico," I say at last. "It's OK. I don't blame you. I know what my sister's like. I know she's been sitting there in London like a puppet mistress pulling the strings."

"She was very determined." He bows his head again.

"I forgive you." I hold out my hand. "I don't forgive *her,*" I add quickly. "But I forgive you."

"Madame, I am not worthy." Nico takes my hand to his lips. "I wish you a thousand happinesses."

As he walks away, I wonder what Fliss is doing now. She said in her voicemail she was coming to the hotel. Maybe she'll arrive tomorrow. Well, maybe I'll refuse to see her.

I take a few more sips of cocktail and have a conversation with a woman in blue about which spa treatment is the best value, while trying to avoid Melissa. She keeps trying to quiz me on what *exactly* Ben and I do for a living, and isn't it a bit dangerous, keeping a gun in my handbag? And then, all of a sudden the band comes to a halt and Nico has mounted the stage. He taps the microphone a few times and beams down on the gathered throng.

"Welcome!" he says. "We are delighted to see you all at our cocktail and presentation event. Just as Aphrodite is the goddess of love, so the Amba is the home of love. And tonight we celebrate a very special couple. They are here on their honeymoon and have won our Happy Couple of the Week award: Ben and Lottie Parr!"

Applause breaks out around us, and Ben gives me a nudge. "Go on."

"I'm going!" I say bad-temperedly. I make my way over the sand to the platform and step up, squinting a little as a spotlight hits my eyes.

"Congratulations, dear lady!" exclaims Nico, as he hands me a large silver trophy in the shape of a heart. "Let me give you both your crowns. . . ."

Crowns?

Before I can protest, Nico places silvered plastic crowns on our heads. He deftly fastens a satin sash over my shoulder, then steps back. "The winning couple!"

The audience claps again and I give a rictus smile into the lights. This is hideous. A trophy, a crown, and a sash? I feel like a beauty queen without the beauty.

"And now a few words from our happy couple!" Nico passes the microphone to Ben, who promptly passes it to me.

"Hello, everybody." My voice booms out, and I wince at the sound. "Thank you so much for this . . . honor. Well, obviously we're a very happy couple. We're so, so happy."

"Very happy," adds Ben into the microphone.

"Blissful."

"It's been the ideal honeymoon."

"When Ben first proposed, I had no idea that I would end up so . . . so happy. So very *happy.*"

Suddenly, with no warning, a tear snakes down my face. I can't help it. When I look back to myself in that restaurant, elatedly agreeing to marry Ben, it's like looking at a different person. A mad, deluded, crazy person. What was I *thinking* of? Marrying Ben was like drinking four double shots of vodka. For a bit, it masked the pain and I felt fabulous. But this is the hangover, and it's not pretty.

I smile harder and lean into the microphone. "We're just so happy," I repeat for emphasis. "Everything's gone so smoothly and brilliantly, and there hasn't been a tense moment between us. Has there, darling?"

Two more tears are rolling down my face. I'm hoping they'll play as tears of joy.

"What a delightful, heavenly time we've had," I add, wiping my face. "What a wonderful, idyllic time. It's been perfect in every way, and we couldn't be happier —" I break off mid-flow as my eye is caught by a trio of silhouetted figures making their way up the beach from the sea. They're all wrapped in towels, but even so . . .

Is that . . .

No. It can't be.

Beside me, Ben is looking the same way, his mouth falling open in astonishment.

"Lorcan?" He grabs the microphone from me and calls into it loudly. "Lorcan! What the fuck? How long have you been here?"

"Aunt Lottie!" cries the smallest toweled figure, suddenly spotting me. "Aunt Lottie, you've got a crown on!"

But it's the third figure that I'm staring at, my jaw sagging.

"Fliss?"

31
FLISS

I'm frozen. All I can do is stare mutely back. This was *not* how I was planning to let Lottie know that I'd arrived on Ikonos.

"Fliss?" she says again, and now there's a sharp edge to her voice which makes me flinch. What do I say? What can I say? Where do I even begin?

"Fliss!" Nico speaks before I can marshal my thoughts, and snatches the microphone from Ben. "And here we have the sister of the happy couple!" He addresses the audience. "May I introduce Felicity Graveney, editor of *Pincher Travel Review*. She is here to give the hotel a special five-star review!" He beams delightedly. "As you can see, she has been sampling the delights of the Aegean Sea."

The audience gives a polite laugh. I have to hand it to Nico. No marketing opportunity left unexploited.

"Now let us have the whole family on-

586

stage!" He's bustling Lorcan, Noah, and me onto the platform. "A family shot for your special honeymoon album. Stand together!"

"What the *hell* are you doing here?" Lottie's eyes are dark with anger as she turns to face me.

"I'm sorry," I say feebly. "I'm so, so sorry. I thought — I wanted —"

My mouth feels dry. Words have deserted me. It's as though they can sense my guilt and have scampered away to the other side.

"Hello, Aunt Lottie!" Noah is greeting her enthusiastically. "We came to see you on your holiday!"

"You enlisted Noah too, I see," Lottie spits out. "Nice."

"Smile, everybody!" calls out the photographer. "Face this way!"

I have to get myself together. I have to apologize. Somehow.

"OK, listen," I begin rapidly as the flash almost blinds me. "I'm so, so, so, so sorry. Lottie, I didn't mean to ruin your honeymoon. I only wanted to . . . I don't know. Look after you. But I realize I've got to stop. You're an adult and you have your own life and I made a huge, huge mistake, and I just hope you can forgive me. And you make a brilliant couple." I turn to Ben. "Hello, Ben, nice to meet you. I'm Fliss, your sister-in-

587

law." I lift a hand awkwardly. "I expect we'll be meeting at lots of family Christmases or whatever. . . ."

"This way!" shouts the photographer, and we all obediently swing back.

"So you were behind *everything*? Does that include the lounge at Heathrow?" Lottie turns her head to see my guilty look. "How *could* you? And the peanut oil! I was in agony!"

"I know, I know," I gulp, almost crying. "I don't know what got into me. I'm so sorry. I just wanted to protect you."

"You always try to protect me! You're not my *mother*!"

"I know I'm not." There's a sudden shake to my voice. "I know that."

I meet eyes with Lottie, and suddenly it's as though a silent, sisters-only set of memories is transmitting between us. Our mother. Our life. Why we are who we are. Then something shuts down in Lottie's eyes and it's over. Her face is closed up and unforgiving again.

"And big smiles, everyone." The photographer waves his arms. "Look this way!"

"Lotts, will you ever forgive me?" I wait breathlessly for her answer. "Please?"

There's a long, agonizing silence. I don't know which way this will swing. Lottie's eyes are unfocused, and I know better than to rush her.

"Smile! Nice wide smiles, everyone!" the photographer keeps exhorting us. But I can't smile and neither can she. I'm clenching my fingers, I realize. And my toes.

At long last Lottie turns her head to face me. Her expression is disdainful, but the hatred has lessened a tad. My towel is slipping and I take the opportunity to wrap it around me again. "So," she says, her eyes flicking over me. "Did you actually go swimming in your *underwear*?"

I give a little inward cheer. I want to hug her. In our code, that's forgiveness. I know I'm not completely off the hook yet — but at least there's hope.

"Bikinis are so over." I match her detached tone. "Didn't you know that?"

"Nice panties." She gives a reluctant shrug.

"Thanks."

"Underpants!" shouts Noah. "Underpants! Hey, Aunt Lottie, I have a question," he adds chattily. "Have you put the sausage in the cupcake?"

"What?" Lottie says, as though stung. "Does he mean —" She stares at me incredulously.

"Have you put the sausage in the cupcake yet?"

"Noah! That's . . . that's none of your business! Why shouldn't I have? Anyway, why are you asking me?" She seems so flustered that I look at her, suddenly alert. The way she's behaving, it's almost as though — *almost* as though . . .

"Lotts?" I say, raising my eyebrows.

"Shut up!" she says frantically.

Oh my God. She's totally giving herself away.

"You *haven't*?" My mind is working overtime. They haven't had sex yet? Why not? Whyever not?

"Stop talking about it!" She seems near tears. "Just butt out of my marriage! Butt out of my honeymoon! Butt out of everything!"

"Lottie?" I look at her more closely. Her eyes are wet and her lips are quivering. "Are you OK?"

"Of course I'm OK!" She suddenly flips out. "Why wouldn't I be OK? I've got the happiest marriage in the world! I'm the luckiest girl in the world, and I'm totally utterly, ecstatically —" She breaks off and rubs her eyes as though she can't believe her own vision.

I squint past her, trying to focus, and suddenly I see what she's staring at. It's a figure. A man. Coming over the beach toward us, with an unmistakable, heavy, sure-footed gait. Lottie has turned so pale, I'm worried she's going to faint — and no wonder. I stare incredulously at the familiar figure, my mind scurrying with possibilities. He vowed he was going to stay away. So what on earth is he doing here?

32
LOTTIE

I think I'm going to have a heart attack. Or a panic attack. Or some other kind of attack. The blood is zooming from my head to my feet and back to my head as though it doesn't know what to do with itself. I can't breathe. I can't move. I can't . . . *anything.*

It's Richard. Here.

Not zillions of miles away, leading a completely new life in which he's forgotten I exist. But here, on Ikonos. Walking toward me over the beach. I blink at him rapidly, my eyelids almost in spasm; I'm unable to speak. It makes no sense. He's in San Francisco. He's supposed to be in *San Francisco.*

Now he's making his way steadily through the audience. I'm shaking all over as he draws near. The last time I saw him was in that restaurant, telling him I didn't accept his nonexistent proposal. That seems like a million years ago. How did he even know where I was?

I glance sharply at Fliss, but she looks as flabbergasted as I do.

And now he's in front of the stage and he's looking up at me with those dark eyes that I love, and I think I'm going to lose it. I was just about holding it together, but now he goes and turns up —

"Lottie," he says, and his voice is as deep and comforting as ever. "I know you're . . . m—" He seems to have difficulty saying the word. "*Married.* I know you're married. And I wish you every happiness with that." He pauses, breathing heavily. Around him, all the chatter has died away. The audience is watching us, riveted. "Congratulations." His eyes flick to Ben, then away again, as though Ben is some loathsome creature he can't bear to look at.

"Thanks," I manage at last.

"So I won't keep you. But I thought you should know something. You didn't start the fire."

"What?" I peer at him, unable to process his words.

"You didn't start the fire," he repeats. "It was another girl."

"But what — How —" I swallow hard. "How did you even —"

"Fliss told me that you thought you'd

593

started the fire. I knew you'd be devastated and I couldn't believe it was true. So I went to find out the truth."

"You went to the guest house?" I say disbelievingly.

"I talked to your friend Arthur." Richard nods. "I made him get out the original police reports. He let me spread them over his table and read through all of them. And it was quite clear. The fire didn't start in your room. It was above the kitchen."

For a moment, my thoughts are so jumbled I can't reply. No one's even whispering. The only sound is that of the bunting flapping in the sea breeze.

"You went to the guest house?" I repeat at last, falteringly. "You did all that? For *me*?"

"Of course," says Richard, as though it's obvious.

"Even though I'm married to someone else?"

"Of course," says Richard again.

"Why?"

Richard shoots me a disbelieving look as though to say, *Do you really have to ask?*

"Because I love you," he says matter-of-factly. "Sorry," he adds to Ben.

33
FLISS

Of all the moments I've experienced in life, this is the one I will remember forever. I'm holding my breath. The whole place is silent. Lottie's staring at Richard, transfixed, her eyes huge. Her Happy Couple of the Week sash is glimmering in the lights, and her crown has slipped.

"Well . . . well . . ." She doesn't seem able to get the words out. "Well, I still love you!" She tears off her crown. "I love you!"

Richard visibly jolts with shock. "But —" He gestures at Ben.

"It was a mistake!" She's almost sobbing now. "It was all a mistake! And I was thinking about you all the time, but you'd gone to San Francisco, but now here you are —" She suddenly turns to me, her face tearstained. "Fliss? Did you bring Richard here?"

"Er . . . kind of," I say cautiously.

"Then I love you too." She flings her arms

around me. "Fliss, I love you."

"Oh, Lotts." Tears are welling up in my eyes now. "I love you. I just want you to have the happiest, happiest life."

"I know." She squeezes me tight, then turns and leaps off the stage, straight into Richard's arms and the tightest embrace I've ever seen. "I thought you were gone forever!" she says into his shoulder. "I thought you were gone forever. I couldn't bear it! I couldn't *bear* it."

"I couldn't bear it either." He's looking warily at Ben. "The only thing is, you're married —"

"I know," she says miserably. "I know. But I don't *want* to be."

My antennae are on full alert. This is my moment! I leap down off the stage and tap Lottie, hard.

"Lotts! Tell me. This is important." As she turns, I grip her by both shoulders. "Have you —" I glance at Noah. "Have you put the sausage in the muffin? Have you done it? Tell the truth! This is important!"

34
LOTTIE

What's the point in lying anymore?

"No!" I say, almost defiantly. "We haven't done it! We're complete frauds. We're not a happy couple; in fact, we're not even a couple! Here." I turn to Melissa, who has been watching avidly with all the others. "Have my crown. Have the sash." I rip it off and grab the trophy from Ben. "Have everything! We were telling lies the whole time." I press them all onto her, and she gazes back at me, her eyes narrowed.

"So the first date in the mortuary?"

"Lie." I nod.

"Sex on the district attorney's desk?"

"Total lie."

"I knew it!" She turns to her husband triumphantly. "Didn't I tell you?" She puts the silver crown on her head and holds the trophy aloft. "This belongs to *us*, I think. We're the Happy Couple of the Week; thank you, everybody —"

"For Christ's *sake,* Melissa," snaps Matt. "No, we're bloody not."

Richard, meanwhile, is gazing at me tensely. "So you really haven't . . . ?"

"Not once."

"Yesss!" Richard's air punch is the most ecstatic I've ever seen. "In your *face.* Result! Yesssss!" He looks more aggressive than I've ever seen him. God, I love him.

"You flew halfway across the world for me." I nestle into his shoulder again.

"Of course."

"And then you flew to Greece."

"Of course."

I don't know why I ever thought Richard wasn't romantic. I don't know why we ever split up. My ear is pressed against his chest, and I can hear the familiar, soothing thump of his heartbeat. This is where I want to be forever. I've tuned out the rest of the world, although I'm dimly aware of the others' voices.

"You can get an annulment," Fliss keeps saying. "Do you see, Lottie? This is brilliant! You can get an *annulment.*"

"It's put the sausage in the cupcake," Lorcan keeps saying. *"Cupcake."*

35
FLISS

Well, she was right about the sunsets. I've never seen anything as spectacular as this in my life. The sun is slowly glowing down the sky, and it's not just sinking, it's shooting rays of pink and orange with such dramatic force, I'm put in mind of one of Noah's superheroes. "Sunset" sounds quite passive, quite nothing-y. This is more like *sun-pow! Sun-take-that!*

I look down at Noah's face, all rosy in the light, and I think again, *He'll be OK.* For the first time in ages, I don't feel angst or stress or anger. He'll be OK. He'll sort himself out. I'll sort myself out. It's all good.

We've had an odd time. Kind of cathartic and uncomfortable, embarrassing and joyful, awkward and wonderful, all at the same time. Nico rustled us up a table at the beachside restaurant, and all five of us sat around eating meze to make your taste buds sing with joy and slow-cooked lamb to make your insides whimper with ecstasy.

The food here really *is* good. Must make sure I big it up in my piece.

There were a lot of questions. There were a lot of stories. There was a lot of kissing.

Lottie and I are . . . OK. I think. There are still sore spots and rough patches between us, but there's also been a kind of revelation. We're on the way to a gradual understanding about who we are to each other, which maybe we'll look at properly later. (Or not bother and just charge on with life, probably more likely.)

Lorcan was the quiet star. He steered the conversation whenever it was threatening to become awkward, and he ordered fantastic wine, and he kept a kind of humorous knee-nudging thing going on with me, which I liked. I like him. I don't just fancy him, I like him.

As for Ben, he's disappeared. Which is understandable. Once it became plain that he'd been publicly rejected for another man by his brand-new wife, he skedaddled. Can't blame him. I expect he's found solace at a bar somewhere.

Richard and Lottie have gone for a walk down the beach, and Noah is skimming stones at the water's edge, so it's just Lorcan and me, sitting on a low wall with our bare feet in the sand. The smell of cooking from the restaurant is mingled with the salty sea air and the faint aroma of his aftershave, which is bringing back all sorts of memories.

I don't just like him, I fancy him. Really quite a lot.

"Oh, wait. I got you something," he says suddenly.

"You *got* me something?" I stare at him.

"It's not much. I put it aside . . . Hold on." He heads toward the restaurant and I watch him, intrigued. A few moments later he comes back, holding a plant in a pot. A little olive tree in a pot, to be precise.

"For your patio," he says, and I stare at him in disbelief.

"You bought that for me?" I'm so touched, tears spring to my eyes. I can't remember the last time someone bought something for me.

"You need something," he says gravely. "You need . . . a start."

He couldn't have put it better. I need a start. As I look up again, his eyes are so warm I feel something stumble inside me.

"I don't have anything for you."

"You already gave me something. Clarity." He pauses. "I thought I'd give you peace." He fingers the olive leaves. "What's done is done."

What's done is done. The words resonate in my brain, round and round. And then I get to my feet. There's something I have to do, right now. I detach my memory stick from the chain around my neck and look at it. All my pain and anger toward Daniel seems to be contained in this one tiny piece of metal. It feels toxic. It's contaminating me. It has to go.

I head briskly to the shallows and put a hand on Noah's shoulder. As he looks up, I smile.

"Hi, darling. I've got something for you to skim." I hand him the memory stick.

"Mummy!" He looks up at me, his eyes wide with shock. "This is a computer thing!"

"I know." I nod. "But it's a computer thing I don't need anymore. Just throw it in the sea, Noah. As far as you can."

I watch as he takes aim and skims it. Three bounces and it's gone, into the Aegean Sea. Gone, gone, gone, *really* gone.

I walk slowly back up the beach to Lorcan, relishing the feel of my bare feet on the sand.

"So." He reaches out and entwines his fingers in mine.

"So." I'm about to suggest a walk along the beach, when Ben's voice hits the back of my head.

"Lorcan. There you are. At bloody *last.*"

I don't even need to look to know that he's drunk, and I feel a squirm of sympathy. It can't be easy for him.

"Hi, Ben," says Lorcan, getting to his feet. "You OK?"

"I met with Zhernakov today. On his yacht." Ben eyes both of us expectantly, as though waiting for a reaction. "I met him on his yacht," he repeats. "Drank some Krug, shot the breeze, you know. . . ."

"Great." Lorcan nods politely. "So you're selling after all."

"Maybe. Yes." Ben sounds aggressive. "Why not?"

"Shame you couldn't have let me know that before I spent weeks on those refinancing and restructuring agreements. They're all a bit irrelevant now, aren't they?"

"No. I mean . . . yes." Ben seems confused. "Thing is . . ." His swagger dips a little. "Yuri and I made an agreement. A gentleman's agreement. But now . . ." He wipes his face. "He's already sent me an email I don't understand. . . ." He holds out his BlackBerry to Lorcan, who ignores it and gazes at Ben, his expression unreadable.

"You really want to sell," he says quietly. "The company that your father built up

603

over years and years. You're just letting it go."

"It's not like that." Ben glares at him. "Yuri says nothing will change for the company."

"Nothing will change?" Lorcan bursts into laughter. "And you bought that?"

"He's interested in developing new projects!" says Ben hotly. "He thinks it's a great little company!"

"You think Yuri Zhernakov is interested in creating a new aspirational paper range for the middle-class consumer?" Lorcan shakes his head. "If you believe that you're even more naïve than I thought. He wants the house, Ben. Nothing else. I hope you got a good price out of him."

"Well, I'm not sure exactly . . . I'm not sure what we . . ." Ben wipes his face again, clearly beleaguered. "You need to look at it." He holds out his BlackBerry again, but Lorcan lifts his hands.

"I don't need to do anything at this moment," he says calmly. "My office day is done."

"But I don't know what I've agreed to." All hint of bravado disappears from Ben's demeanor. "Have a look, OK, Lorcan? Sort it out."

There's a long silence, and just for a moment I wonder whether Lorcan is going to capitulate. But at last he shakes his head.

"Ben, I've sorted out enough for you." He sounds weary and a little sad. "I have to stop."

"What?"

"I'm resigning."

What?" Ben looks absolutely staggered. "But . . . you can't do that!"

"Consider this my notice. I've been with you far too long already. Your father's gone and . . . well, it's time for me to go too."

"But . . . but you can't! You're really into the company!" Ben's eyes are wide with panic. "You're into it more than me! You love it!"

"Yes. And that's the problem." There's a wryness to Lorcan's voice, and I reach out to squeeze his hand. "I'll help you till my notice period is served out, then I'm going. And it'll be for the best."

"But what will *I* do?" Ben sounds genuinely freaked.

"You'll take charge of the situation." Lorcan takes a step toward him. "Ben, you've got a choice. You can sell the company to Yuri if you want to. Pocket the cash and have fun. But you know what else you could do? Take the reins. Take control. It's your company. It's your heritage. Make a go of it."

Ben seems poleaxed.

"You can do it," adds Lorcan. "But it'll be a pretty big challenge. You'll need to *want* to do it."

"I made a gentleman's agreement with Yuri." Ben's eyes dart wildly about. "Oh Jesus. I don't know. What do I do?"

"Yuri Zhernakov is no gentleman," says Lorcan sardonically. "So I think you're safe there." He sighs, ruffles his fingers through his hair, his face unreadable. "Look, Ben. I have the restructuring agreements in my briefcase, and I'll take you through them tomorrow. I'll explain what all your options are, as I see it." He pauses. "But I'm not telling you what to do. Sell, not sell, it's your choice. *Yours.*"

Ben's eyes are fixed on Lorcan. He opens and closes his mouth a few times, apparently unable to speak. Then at last he turns on his heel and walks away, pocketing his BlackBerry as he goes.

"Well done." I squeeze Lorcan's hand again as we sit back down on the wall. "That was courageous." Lorcan says nothing, just tilts his head.

"Will he make a go of it?" I ask tentatively.

"He might." Lorcan exhales. "But if he

doesn't do it now, it's never."

"And what will you do when you leave?"

"Don't know." He shrugs. "Maybe I'll take up that job offer I had in London."

"London?" I say, brightening in spite of myself.

"Or Paris," he says teasingly. "I'm fluent in French."

"Paris is crap," I say. "Everyone knows that."

"Quebec, then."

"Funny." I hit him.

"I'm a lawyer." Lorcan's teasing tone disappears; he looks thoughtful. "That was my training. That was my career. And maybe I was knocked off course for a while. Maybe I *did* make the wrong choice." His eyes flicker toward mine, and I nod in acknowledgment. "But now it's time to get back on course."

"Rev up the engine."

"Full steam ahead," he counters.

"You see life as a boat trip?" I say, in mock incredulity. "It's a *road trip*. Everyone knows that."

"It's a boat trip."

"It's *so* a road trip."

We sit there for a while, watching as the sunset turns from orange and pink to mauve and indigo and streaks of vivid crimson. It really is a corker.

Presently, Lottie and Richard come sauntering along the beach, and they perch on the wall beside us. *They look good together,* I can't help thinking yet again. They just fit.

"So, I'm out of a job," says Lorcan conversationally to Lottie, "and it's all your sister's fault."

"It's not my fault!" I exclaim at once. "How is it my fault?"

"If you hadn't made me look at my life with a fresh pair of eyes, I never would have resigned." His mouth twitches. "You have a lot to answer for."

"I did you a favor," I retort.

"Still your fault." His eyes twinkle.

"Well . . ." I cast around. "No. I dispute that. It's actually Lottie's fault. If she hadn't run off and got married, I would never have met you and we never would have discussed the matter."

"Ah." Lorcan nods. "Good point. I blame you." He swivels to Lottie.

"It's not my fault!" she retorts. "It's Ben's fault! That stupid marriage was all his idea. If he hadn't proposed, I would never have come out here, and you would never have met Fliss."

"So Ben's the villain of the piece?" Lorcan raises a quizzical eyebrow.

"Yes," Lottie and I say in unison.

"Yes," agrees Richard firmly.

The sky is a deep purple by now, mottled with midnight blue. The sun is a sliver of orange brightness at the horizon. I imagine it sliding down to another bit of the world, another bit of the sky, shining on other sets of Lotties and Flisses, with all their troubles and joys.

"Wait," I say, and sit bolt upright at the realization. "The villain of the piece isn't Ben, it's Richard. If he'd proposed to Lottie in the first place, none of this would have happened."

"Oh," says Richard, and rubs his nose. "Ah."

There's a weird, silent little beat, in which I wonder wildly whether Richard will hurl himself onto one knee on the sand and do the business, but it passes, and no one says anything. Yet there's a strangeness in the air now; this is pretty awkward; I should never have mentioned it. . . .

"Well, I can do something about that." Lottie has a strange fire in her eyes. "Wait there. I need my bag."

We all watch in puzzlement as she hurries back to the restaurant, heads straight to our table, and starts scrabbling in her handbag. What on earth is she up to?

And then suddenly I gasp. Oh God. I know. I want to hug myself with glee, with nerves, with anticipation. This could be amazing, this could be brilliant. . . .

Do *not* fuck it up, Richard.

And now she's coming back toward us and her chin is up but trembling, and I can see exactly what she's going to do, and I am so, so, *so* glad I am here to see this.

I can't breathe. Lottie is walking slowly and deliberately up to Richard. She kneels down in front of him and holds out a ring.

It's quite a nice ring, I see, to my relief. Quite manly.

"Richard," she says, and blows out sharply, as though with nerves. "Richard . . ."

36
LOTTIE

Tears are in my eyes. I can't believe I'm doing this. It's what I should have done in the first place.

"Richard," I say for a third time. "Even though I'm currently married to someone else — will you marry me?"

There's a taut, still silence. The last sliver of light from the sun slips away into the sea, and, above us, tiny stars start to glimmer in the deep-blue sky.

"Of course. Of course. Of *course.*" Richard envelops me in a bear hug.

"You will?"

"Of course! It's what I want. Marriage. To you. Nothing else. I was an idiot before." He hits his own head. "I was a fool. I was a —"

"It's OK," I say gently. "I know. So . . . it's a yes?"

"Of course it's a yes! Oh God." He shakes his head. "Of course it's a yes. I'm not letting you get away again." He's holding my hand so tightly, I think he may break a bone.

"Congratulations!" Fliss throws her arms around me, while Lorcan pumps Richard's hand energetically. "You're engaged! For real this time! We need champagne!"

"And an annulment," puts in Lorcan drily.

I'm engaged! To Richard! I feel light-headed with euphoria and shock at myself. I proposed? *I* proposed? Why didn't I do this before? It was easy!

"Good work!" says Lorcan, kissing me. "Congratulations!"

"I'm so happy." Fliss is hugging herself. "So, so, *so* happy. It's exactly what I hoped for." She shakes her head disbelievingly. "After all that." She reaches out and squeezes my hand.

"After all that." I squeeze it back. A waiter is passing, and Fliss summons him over.

"Champagne, please! We have an engagement to celebrate!"

And now, as we all finally draw breath, there's a pause. Everyone's looking at the ring lying in my palm. Richard still hasn't taken it from me. Should I slide it onto his finger? Or just hand it over? Or . . . what? What are you supposed to *do* with men's engagement rings?

"Sweetheart, about the ring," says Richard at last. I can tell he's trying to contort his face from "dubious" to "enthusiastic," but it's not working.

"Nice ring," observes Lorcan.

"It's lovely," says Fliss encouragingly.

"Absolutely," says Richard quickly. "Very . . . shiny. Very smart. It's just that —"

"You don't have to *wear* it," I say hastily. "It's not for *wearing.* You can keep it on your nightstand or whatever . . . maybe keep it in a drawer . . . or in a safe. . . ."

The look of relief on Richard's face is so palpable, I can't help laughing. As he hugs me tight again, I slip the ring into my pocket. We'll just quietly forget it.

I knew that ring was a mistake.

ACKNOWLEDGMENTS

To everyone who helped: thank you.

ABOUT THE AUTHOR

Sophie Kinsella is the author of the best-selling Shopaholic series, as well as *I've Got Your Number, Twenties Girl, Remember Me?, The Undomestic Goddess,* and *Can You Keep a Secret?* She lives in England.